THE NAZI HOUSEWIFE OF QUEENS, NEW YORK

THE
NAZI HOUSEWIFE
OF
QUEENS, NEW YORK

A NOVEL

STACY KEAN

First published by Level Best Books/Historia 2024

Copyright © 2024 by Stacy Kean

All rights reserved. No part of this publication may be reproduced, stored or transmitted in any form or by any means, electronic, mechanical, photocopying, recording, scanning, or otherwise without written permission from the publisher. It is illegal to copy this book, post it to a website, or distribute it by any other means without permission.

This novel is entirely a work of fiction. The names, characters and incidents portrayed in it are the work of the author's imagination. Any resemblance to actual persons, living or dead, events or localities is entirely coincidental.

Stacy Kean asserts the moral right to be identified as the author of this work.

Author Photo Credit: Kelly Mooney Photography

First edition

ISBN: 978-1-68512-812-8

Cover art by Level Best Designs

This book was professionally typeset on Reedsy.
Find out more at reedsy.com

Dedicated to Grandma Jeanne, Justin, and Allie

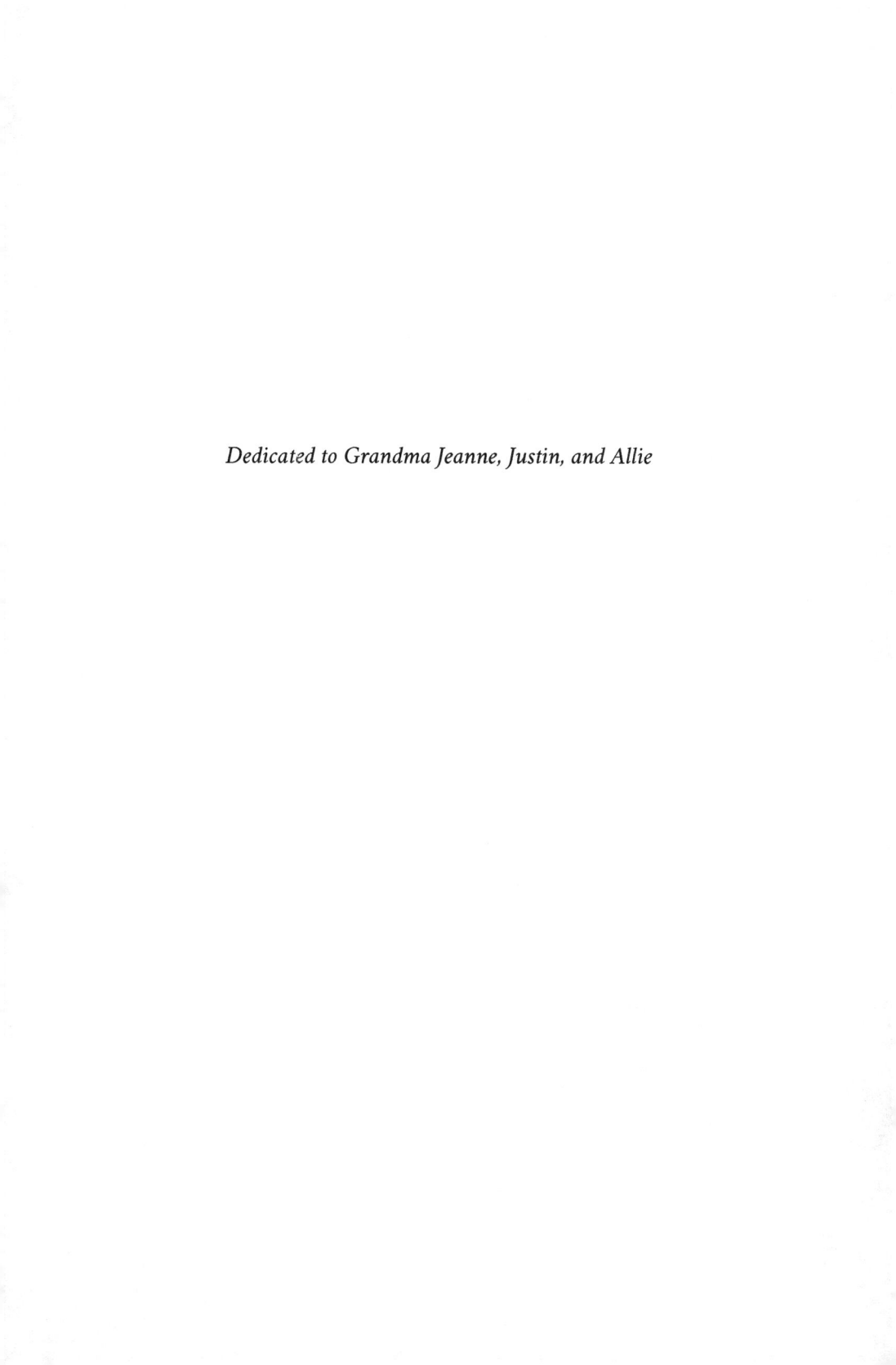

Chapter One: Hannah's Discovery

Hannah stared at the table in the breakfast nook. There it was, the daily paper, spread open on the table. She looked at it cautiously, as if the paper might burn her hand. Hannah thought maybe she had imagined the headline. It could be she had experienced an unexpected, horrible flashback. As she glanced at the paper, the headline took her breath away again: "Queens Housewife Alleged to be Notorious Nazi Concentration Camp Guard."

Hannah scrutinized the grainy black and grey picture. The woman in the photo had a long nose and a strong jawline. She looked thinner, and she was wearing a feminine Jackie Kennedy-style white pillbox hat. It had been twenty years since Hannah last saw her menacing face. Seeing her, and knowing she was not only in America but living a few miles away made her mind swim and her body shake. This was an impossible turn of events.

She abruptly abandoned the kitchen, leaving the paper sprawled on the table. Upstairs, she filled the bathtub with scalding hot water and threw off her nightgown and robe, leaving them in a heap on the floor. The hot water soothed her, and her mind traveled back to memories she had never allowed herself to revisit.

The first time she saw the guard was on that horrifying and confusing night. Hannah struggled to cling to her sister Rebecca's arm on that night long ago, trying desperately to hold on as they were shoved out of a cattle car. Her mother, father, and sister Esther were separated from Rebecca and Hannah so quickly that she had no time to react. Esther was so weak and ill their father had carried her off the train. The bright lights, barking dogs, and menacing soldiers blurred much of the memory of their surroundings. Her father was pulled away from her mother and her sisters and thrust into a long line of other men. Esther, barely able to stand in her blood-stained dress, was held up by her mother, who was always so elegant, but on this night, looked like a brutalized vagrant in her dirty dress with her forehead horribly wounded and her left eye blackened and swollen shut.

Her mother and Esther were propelled to the right, and Rebecca and Hannah were pushed to the left. When Rebecca began shouting, "We are together! We are together!" she was forcibly moved into place by a soldier's truncheon. Another soldier with a barking dog drove the two lines further apart. The exhausted, filthy, confused, and petrified women coalesced into some sort of line, driven into formation by the soldier and his dog pacing back and forth in front of them.

Hannah stood in line as close as possible to her older sister. Rebecca leaned over and hissed loudly in Hannah's ear, "If anyone asks you, you are eighteen years old!"

As the women huddled tightly in the line, Hannah saw the guard's face for the first time. Taller than average, and much thicker than the woman Hannah saw in the photograph in this morning's newspaper, she had moved through the prisoners in a snugly tailored uniform and tall black jackboots. She had a riding crop in her hand.

She walked the line brusquely, giving each woman a cursory up-and-down glance. Suddenly, she stopped and angrily yanked a small woman out of the line. Hannah could see her victim was much older than the other women in the line, her mostly white hair was tucked back in a surprisingly tidy bun at the nape of her neck. Hannah figured she was in her seventies.

The woman cowered as the guard pulled her further away from the line, her arm in a vise-like grip. The woman with the crop began screaming at the woman so closely that the guard's spittle hit the old woman's face, causing her to startle back from the guard.

"Why are you in this line?" she shouted. "Why are you in this line?" she shouted again.

The old woman looked as though her knees were about to give out.

CHAPTER ONE: HANNAH'S DISCOVERY

Somehow, she spoke in a small voice, "I wanted to stay with my daughters," she offered.

"You are in the wrong line!" the guard shouted, "You are in the wrong line. You do not choose your line! You do not choose!" She was still shouting as she threw the old woman to the ground and began kicking her in the abdomen.

The old woman folded her body into a protective ball. The guard stomped on her side as she walked around the quivering body. She stopped and positioned herself before slamming the bottom of her boot on the old woman's head. Again, and Hannah heard a sickening cracking sound. Again, and the old woman stopped moving. The guard paced around her. Satisfied that her work was complete, the guard joined the soldier with the dog in restraining two screaming women that Hannah assumed were the old woman's daughters. The female guard hit the screaming, weeping women with her riding crop. She and the soldier and the dog managed to get the line of women moving forward with similar blows.

Rebecca walked behind Hannah and leaned close to whisper through her teeth, "Don't look at the old woman's body when we pass it by."

Hannah couldn't help but look and let out a strangled gasp. It was the third murder she had witnessed in the past two weeks. When she walked by, she stared at the old woman's broken and distorted skull. The tidy white bun was now disheveled, and her hair was steeped with blood.

They marched through a gate. Hannah became aware of a bizarre burning stench in the air. They were then marched into a room with benches and pegs on the wall. The guard shouted, "Listen carefully. You are to remove all of your clothing, stockings, shoes, everything. Hang your clothing on the peg. Leave your shoes and any belongings you carried with you on the bench. You are dirty. You need to be cleaned."

As they undressed, Hannah leaned closer to Rebecca, "What is this place?"

"I don't know. Just do as they say. Stick close to me."

Like many of the other women, when Hannah had disrobed down to her underwear and slip, she paused in her undressing. The guard scanned the room and shouted, "Everything! You are to completely disrobe! You are dirty!" Hannah and the others hurriedly removed the last of their clothing. Hannah's arm instinctively covered her breasts, and her other hand covered her pubic area. She was startled to see Rebecca nude with her arms at her sides.

She was scrutinizing all the women in the room, "Everyone here is younger and healthier, I think we will be made to work. This is possibly a work camp," she murmured to Hannah.

The women lined up again and walked through the next set of doors. Skinny bald women in rough, gray prison dresses with shears in their hands began shaving the heads of the women who had arrived in the train car. Before Hannah could fully comprehend this bizarre scene, one of the skeletal women grabbed her arm and began to shave her head. Hannah began to shiver, and the woman pushed her head down. Hannah felt the scrape of the shears over her skull and watched in amazement as her hair gently sailed to the ground. She looked at the woman who was shaving her head, and her dead-eyed gaze made Hannah's heart drop. Once the woman had finished shaving her head, she knelt down and began to shave Hannah's pubic hair. Horrified, Hannah shook even harder, causing the woman to cut her. Now Hannah was weeping loudly. She caught a glimpse of the angry guard approaching her, and the woman with the shears froze and knelt closer to the ground.

That was the moment Hannah first saw her up close. Her most arresting features were her strong jawline and long, narrow nose. Her eyes were small and deeply set. Hannah was staring at her when the blow from the riding crop landed on her cheek. The woman with the shears tightly gripped Hannah's hands to prevent her from falling to the ground. Hannah leaned in on the woman's strength to stand perfectly still. The guard moved on. So did the woman with the shears. Hannah tried to look her in the eyes again, but her silent helper had simply moved to the next prisoner.

After the women were shaved, they were covered in delousing powder. Hannah desperately looked around through the puffy, white clouds for her sister. All the women looked the same, with their bald heads covered in fine, white delousing powder. The women surged to the back of the room, and

CHAPTER ONE: HANNAH'S DISCOVERY

Hannah was pulled along with them. She felt someone grab her hand and give her a rough, gray prison dress and wooden shoes. Hannah put on the large potato sack dress and slipped on the wooden clogs. The woman took Hannah's hand again. Hannah looked at her with a mix of gratitude and suspicion. The woman stared back.

"Hannah, it's me."

Hannah believed the voice but couldn't believe what she saw. Rebecca, without her wild, untamed curls, was not Rebecca. Hannah felt her heart sink even lower. Her formidable older sister was reduced, like the rest of the women, into a pitiable, grotesque creature. Rebecca silently turned away from Hannah but held her hand even tighter. The women were herded out of the building to rows of wooden barracks.

Hannah and Rebecca stumbled into one of the barracks along with an ungainly flock of other new women. Wooden pallets stacked three levels high were packed with bodies. Few stirred to look at the new inmates.

Hannah's cheek throbbed, and as she ran her tongue along the corner of her lip, she tasted blood. A woman emerged from the corner of the barracks. "Hello. I'm Stella. There is space here, on the second level."

She pointed to an empty level on the wooden pallet. Rebecca went to her and extended her hand. "Thank you. I'm Rebecca, and this is my sister Hannah."

Stella smiled, "It was a rough night, no? What happened to your sister's face?"

"This very crazy guard who attacked an old woman and killed her when we got off the train. She smacked Hannah in the face with her riding crop."

"Ah! You have faced the Stomping Mare! That is what we call her. You're right. She is crazy. You should steer clear of her. She is unpredictable. Some days, she is by the book, and other days, you may see her in an uncontrolled rage. Beating people, stomping on people, blowing people's heads off," said Stella casually.

Hannah quietly spoke up, "My mother and another sister were segregated into another line off the train. Is there a way to see what barracks they might be in? Do you know where we might find them?"

Stella smiled sweetly, "Why, of course, dear, I can show you exactly where your mama and sister are."

Stella put her arm around Hannah and gently walked her out the door. She pointed to a tall chimney with billowy smoke and ash pouring out of it. Stella still had her arm around Hannah's shoulder and said in a sing-song voice, "Look up at that sky! Floating away! It's sweet Mama! It's dear sister!"

"I don't understand," Hannah said.

Rebecca roughly shoved Stella away from Hannah. Stella looked at Rebecca, "You girls better figure this place out if you want to survive."

Rebecca and Hannah climbed into their bunk, which was utterly barren and just wooden slats. Hannah leaned close to Rebecca over the wooden slats, "I don't understand what is happening. Where are we? What is happening to us?"

Rebecca gave no answer. She just gently touched Hannah's cheek.

Hannah was startled out of her horrible reverie by the ringing of the telephone. As the ringing stopped, she realized the bathwater was now freezing cold. She stumbled out of the tub and put on her bra and panties. She paused to look in the mirror. She combed and teased her chocolate brown hair into a shoulder-length bouffant. It astonished her to remember that she had a shaved head at age fourteen. She put on a silk floral blouse and navy blue Capri pants. Such a far cry from the scratchy gray prison dress.

Hannah froze as she stared in the mirror; she held the coral pink lipstick in her hand. Her life in Kew Gardens, Queens, New York, in America was real. Her lovely home was real. Her husband was real. Her children were real. That hellscape of her youth was unreal. Her life twenty years ago was a nightmare. How could it be back?

She walked downstairs to the kitchen. Her untouched scrambled eggs and toast sat on the table next to the paper. She threw away the uneaten breakfast. She drew an ashtray close and took a cigarette from her leather cigarette case. She lit it and drew the smoke in deeply. Then, she allowed herself to look at the article again. The words "Queens Housewife" leaped off the page. How could she, the "Stomping Mare," the infamous Helma

CHAPTER ONE: HANNAH'S DISCOVERY

Braun, be a "Queens Housewife?"

According to the article, she only lived a few miles away. Hannah became mesmerized by the grainy photo. The Stomping Mare looked so much softer now, more feminine. Hannah drew some satisfaction from the fact that the woman in the picture looked startled, unsafe, and hunted.

She tried to read the article, but it was impossible. It was like swimming in syrup. Hannah smoked another cigarette. She got up and got a pair of scissors out of the drawer next to the phone to carefully clip the article out of the paper. She slid the newspaper clipping into her wallet and dropped it into her purse, folded the rest of the paper, and left it on the kitchen table. Hannah shakily lit another cigarette and stared out the window.

Chapter Two: Hannah Before the War

Nine-year-old Hannah crept into the living room adjacent to her father Max's study. He spent many hours in the oversized leather chair, and Hannah liked to climb up on a small coffee table to watch her father. Climbing on the table was strictly forbidden by her mother, so Hannah had to be watchful when she took up her perch. Hannah loved watching her father with his well-groomed goatee, engrossed in thought. Hannah enjoyed coming up with schemes to make her serious father laugh. She liked climbing on furniture and climbing trees. She had even, on occasion, scrambled out on the roof of their home from her bedroom window. Her older sister nicknamed her "monkey girl."

Hannah's other favorite was her eldest half-sister, Rebecca. Eleven years older than Hannah, she was tall with wild, dark hair. Rebecca studied music and played the piano. Rebecca often picked up Hannah from school, took her swimming, and was even Hannah's accomplice in a variety of rule-breaking activities.

The rules were made and enforced by Anna Goldberg, Hannah's mother. Anna had been a great beauty in her youth and still a very vain woman, clinging to her looks as she aged. Anna was French and traveled each year to Paris to buy her clothing. Her other obsession was Esther, her oldest daughter, and Hannah's other older sister. Esther had very severe asthma and was quite frail. At age fourteen, she had the same interest in fashion as her mother. Esther was a great beauty like Anna. Esther only occasionally attended school and often had to take breaks from school to be tutored at home.

CHAPTER TWO: HANNAH BEFORE THE WAR

Anna tolerated Rebecca, who was Max's daughter from his first marriage. Rebecca was not beautiful or refined enough for Anna, and Rebecca was strong and opinionated.

"Hannah! You will get off that table this instant. You have been told repeatedly not to be on that table!" screamed her mother.

Hannah scrambled off the table as her father calmly emerged from his study. "Anna, you are quite loud."

Hannah saw her mother's eyes light up with anger, "She is disobedient, and you do nothing about it! Esther is resting, and now we have this disturbance!"

"Hannah sitting on the table is not disturbing Esther's rest. It is your shouting that is disturbing her rest and disturbing my work."

Anna stomped away with a scowl on her face. Max knelt next to Hannah, "My darling one, you cannot sit on this table. You have been told many times. It upsets your mother. If you wish to keep spying on me, I suggest you get a pillow and strategically place it so that you can see what I am up to."

Just as Hannah and her father made their way to the dining room, Rebecca burst into the house. She shed her raincoat on the polished coat rack. Esther, with her chestnut brown hair and flawless skin, came down the stairs dressed in a light blue dress, with a beautiful bow at the neckline. Hannah's father tenderly took Esther's hand and guided her to her seat at the dinner table. Rebecca flew into the room, pinched Hannah's nose, and kissed her father on the cheek. She leaned over to Esther and patted her cheek, "Hello, beautiful. You look as if you are feeling better!"

Hannah noticed as Rebecca looked toward Anna that she became serious, and the joyful twinkle in her eye disappeared, "Good evening, Mother," she said as she dutifully kissed their mother's cheek.

As the family sat at the large mahogany table with the cut glass rose bowl at the center of the table, their plump, unhappy maid, Marta Dorn, brought the first of the dinner trays. Rebecca's game was to see if she could make Marta smile. "Hello, Mademoiselle Marta Dorn!"

"Rebecca! Please leave Marta alone. Marta is married and, therefore, would be Madame Marta Dorn. If you had paid the slightest bit of attention to the many years of French lessons, you would have known that. Your father speaks French as well; it is not just me. It is only you and Hannah in this family who do not know French. Esther's French skills are developing so nicely."

"Yes, developing so nicely when I'm not hacking and coughing my way through verb conjugations." Rebecca and their father chuckled at Esther's self-deprecating remark.

Anna sighed in exasperation, "So, Rebecca, how was University today?"

"About the same. Much talk about our future overlord, Herr Hitler. The usual knuckleheads think this will be a splendid change for Austria. I don't speak up much, because it should be evident to anyone that Hitler will be a disaster for a Jewess such as myself."

"Ugh, Rebecca, do not refer to yourself as a 'Jewess.' It sounds like the low-class Jews from the East. Besides, we aren't religious."

"Well, Mother, we are Jews. I don't think Hitler discriminates between the Eastern observant kind, or the less devout kind, or the high-class kind or the low-class kind. We're in for it."

At this point, Hannah looked to her father. He winked at her, "Let's enjoy our dinner without further thought to Hitler. That illiterate, nasty little corporal upsets my digestion. A change of topic. I believe you girls should take a trip to see your grandmother in France. It will give you all an opportunity to brush up on your French-speaking skills. I will make arrangements for you to go next week."

"Max, why on earth would we go to visit my mother? It's the beginning of February. France is just as dreary as it is here this time of year."

"Anna, normally, I would agree with you. Rebecca is right. Hitler is coming. I need some time to figure out what we might do if the worst happens. I don't want you to worry. I want you and the girls to have a little break."

Hannah noticed that her mother still looked annoyed, but Rebecca's face became ashen and severe. The awkward silence at dinner was broken by Marta's re-entry into the dining room.

"Herr Goldberg, your student, David Schneider, is here to see you."

CHAPTER TWO: HANNAH BEFORE THE WAR

Hannah's mother stood up and threw her linen napkin in the chair, "Well, Max, it appears you need to return to work, and I need to apparently start preparing to take the girls to France." With that, she stomped out of the room.

Max stood up, smiled, and asked Marta for coffee for Rebecca, David, and himself.

David entered the room sheepishly, "Was I early? I'm so sorry if I have interrupted your family dinner," he said.

Max put his arm around David's shoulder, "No, no, our dinner started late, and then the topic of Corporal Hitler came up and upset everyone's digestion. Let's take a break and listen to Rebecca play a little for us before we delve back into our work."

David smiled with relief. Hannah noticed how he smiled and looked at Rebecca and how Rebecca's cheeks would turn pink whenever David appeared. Hannah looked at David and thought he wasn't too bad-looking. He was tall and muscular; his face was a little rounded, but he had a strong jaw underneath his beard. Most young men his age didn't have a beard, but Hannah thought David was copying her father. She knew how much he wanted to be like him.

He had thick dark brown hair that he frequently ran his fingers through and looked down, especially when he was conversing with Rebecca. Hannah looked at her father as they walked to the parlor to listen to Rebecca play; he was smiling and chatting with David. Hannah wondered if he was trying to make a match between Rebecca and David. Her father beckoned Hannah to sit by him on the velvet loveseat. He put his arm around her as they listened to Rebecca play. David leaned back in his chair and smiled as Rebecca became absorbed in the music.

Hannah rested her head against her father's chest, closed her eyes, and listened to Rebecca's playing. She thought back to the summer when Rebecca was teaching her how to dive into the pool. She felt herself drift to sleep in her father's arms.

Hannah would remember this as one of the last happy, safe, and peaceful days in her family home in Austria.

A few days later, Hannah came home from school and was shocked to find Rebecca and her father in her room. Her father had her mother's jewelry box open on Hannah's bed; Rebecca was carefully tearing open the hems on one of Hannah's dresses. She then laid the jewels in the hem of the dress.

"What are you doing?!"

Hannah's father grabbed her shoulder and pulled her into the room, closing the door behind her. He knelt down and pulled her close.

"Hannah darling, I need you to listen to me very closely now. Tomorrow, you, Mama, Esther, and Rebecca are going to France to visit your grandmother. You have heard us talk about Hitler and the Germans. They may come to Austria. It will become dreadful for us if that happens. I want to do everything I can to make sure you girls and your mother are safe. We will need to bring some of Mother's jewelry to Grandmother's house for safekeeping. It is best if we keep this hidden, even from mother."

Hannah felt her eyes begin to burn with tears, "But Papa, what about you? When will you come?"

"Shhh…Hannah, did you know I was in the Great War? I was just a young doctor, but I kept my head about me in many dangerous situations. No matter what happens, I will find my way to my girls."

Hannah felt her father's arms tighten around her. For the first time in her short life, Hannah's whole body tingled with fear. Her throat tightened, and she felt slightly dizzy. Her father stood up and put his hand on Hannah's shoulder.

"Darling, I need you to promise that you will listen to Rebecca. I am putting her in charge. Your mama is very nervous and must use her energy to take care of your sister, Esther. I need you and Rebecca to be strong and to be careful. Do you understand?"

Hannah looked up at her father and nodded. Rebecca glanced up from her sewing and gave their father a worried look.

**

The next morning, Hannah awoke to find her bags packed. Rebecca was at

CHAPTER TWO: HANNAH BEFORE THE WAR

the foot of her bed, laying out her clothes.

"Hey, darling monkey, it is time to wake up! Papa is taking Mama and Esther to the train station with a few trunks that he wants to ship to grandmother's house as well. So, David will come to get us and take you and me to the train. Get up and get dressed quickly."

Hannah scooted to the foot of her bed. Rebecca left the door open, and Hannah heard her father and mother arguing. Hannah quickly dressed and headed downstairs. She crept quietly around the corner, making herself as small and invisible as possible to silently observe her mother and father.

"Max, I truly don't understand! Why have you packed so many of our things in these trunks to ship to my mother's? If this is just 'a little visit,' why are you doing this? I don't really care if the Germans come and Hitler is in charge. This whole thing is overblown. Politics and games! It has nothing to do with us!"

Hannah sucked in her breath as she saw her father's face redden, and he grabbed her mother's shoulders. "It has everything to do with us! You don't know who these people are. What they are capable of. I'm not going to gamble and wait to find out. We need to protect ourselves. The best-case scenario is that I lose my job as a professor and I am not allowed to practice medicine. We need to prepare for that financially. It is potentially worse than that. These people are thugs. It could get violent. Do you think for one second that I would let something happen to you and the girls?"

Her mother began to weep. Her father held her close. Hannah didn't notice Rebecca standing silently behind her. She softly touched her shoulder, "Come on, darling monkey, let's get a little breakfast."

David arrived to give Rebecca and Hannah a ride to the train station. He looked a little sad, yet handsome in his beige trench coat. When they arrived at the station, David took the suitcases out of the trunk. He knelt down to talk to Hannah.

"Hannah, I'm going to miss you, my little spy. I would be talking with your father and catch you out of the corner of my eye, sitting atop that side table. I'd like you to make me a promise that I will be invited to cheer you on at the 1948 Olympics when you are a famous lady swimmer. Is it a deal?"

"It's a deal," Hannah said as she gave David an unexpected hug.

David stood and faced Rebecca. Hannah saw Rebecca's cheeks turn pink as David drew closer to her. "I'm sorry to see you all go, Rebecca, but your father is doing the right thing. I do think it will get pretty bad. I haven't told your father this, but I think you should know that Marta's husband is part of the Nazi movement in Austria. If the Germans do come, they will know about your father and his opposition to them."

"I had no idea about Marta's husband. Things have become so surreal. Thank you, David, thank you for everything," Rebecca began to softly cry. David held her for a few moments and stroked her cheek. "You will make it. You're strong. Your father is an amazing man."

Rebecca turned away, grabbed Hannah's hand, and they ran for the train. Hannah looked back and saw David turn and walk back out into the rain; his shoulders hunched as if he carried a great weight.

Hannah stared out the window of the train. She was glad she and Rebecca were not traveling with her mother and Esther. Rebecca was trying to read a book, but Hannah wasn't fooled. She wasn't reading. She never turned a page. Her jaw was tight. She saw Hannah staring at her.

"Are you making a study of me, little monkey girl?" Rebecca asked, and Hannah laughed in relief.

"Ha! Yes! I'm like Father, and I study all sorts of things. Everyone is so upset, and I don't understand. I also don't like grandmother's house."

Rebecca sighed, put down her book, and wrapped her arm around Hannah. "Oh, monkey, I know. The thing is, we are probably going to have to stay with Grandmother for a while. You know this Hitler character, well he is going to take over Austria, and he hates Jewish people, we are Jewish, and our lives could be awful if we stayed home. So, I need your help to keep Mother calm and to help Esther with her health."

Hannah slumped in her seat. She scooted closer to the reassuring side of her sister as the train chugged through the rain.

Max joined the family in France after the Nazis annexed Austria in March 1938. Rebecca and Hannah met him at the train station, and he arrived looking defeated. Rebecca rushed into his arms.

CHAPTER TWO: HANNAH BEFORE THE WAR

Hortense Blauer stared out the window of her large country home. The furnishings were threadbare, and the home was slightly dilapidated. Time had frozen at the house, and nothing had been updated since the early years of the century. Hortense had become a widow in 1910 and lost both of her sons in the Great War in 1915. Anna was her only surviving child.

Hortense saw the car pull into the drive with Rebecca, Hannah, and Max. She had been corresponding with Max for many months to prepare to take in the family. She walked out the door to greet him. "Max, at last, you are here, and the whole family is together," she said as she extended her hand for him to kiss. Hortense had not updated her Edwardian-era hairstyle, high lace collars, and formal manners.

Hannah struggled in her new life. Once they arrived in France, speaking German was forbidden by her grandmother, who employed a tutor to teach Hannah and Esther French and to tutor them in other academic subjects. Every morning after breakfast, Hortense administered one tablespoon of cod liver oil to Esther and Hannah and inspected their clothing before they could leave the dining room for their lessons.

A year quickly flew by. Hannah had become so proficient in French, she struggled to remember how to speak German. She had grown fond of Grandmother Hortense's ways. At the end of summer in 1939, she sat with her grandmother in the garden. Hannah's father had transformed from a scholarly university professor to a worker in the garden with his shirt sleeves rolled up. He had repaired much of the Blauer home and was turning the garden into a harvest of vegetables and an organized array of beautiful plants and flowers. Hortense Blauer had pulled her silvery gray hair into an elaborate bun. She held up an ancient parasol to block the sun as she sat drinking tea with Hannah.

"You know Hannah, your grandfather bought me this parasol. Oh, it must have been in the late 1880s, right before we were married. I didn't have money growing up, but I was very well educated. Even then, I spoke several languages. I was working as a governess when I met your grandfather. He was ambitious and making money. We bought this house, and your uncles and mother were born here. I wish you could have seen it then. It was amazing. It all changed so quickly." She put her hand on her throat and paused. "Your grandfather died so suddenly and unexpectedly. Then, your uncles were swept up in the patriotism of the Great War. They were killed within a few months of each other. After the war, I sent your mother to stay with the Blauer cousins in Austria. It was so depressing here. I wanted her to have some fun with cousins her age. Then she married your father. The house was empty for many years. Now you and your sisters and mother and father are here, and there is life."

Hannah watched her grandmother lower her parasol and lift her face with her eyes closed to the sun. It was the first time she saw joy cross her strict grandmother's face. Her grandmother usually looked stern or serene or a combination of both, but when she glanced at the framed photo of her sons in their French army uniforms, a very real sadness shone on her face. Often, she would run her index finger over the top of the frame before carrying on with the rest of her day. Hannah liked to stare at the picture of her unknown uncles. They had matching outsized black mustaches and friendly faces. Hannah allowed herself to daydream about what it would be like if the uncles had lived and occupied this large home with her family. She imagined them to be full of high spirits and willing to play games with her in the garden or sing loudly while Rebecca played the piano.

Max joined them at the table. He was admiring the trellis he had built, which was now covered by a climbing wisteria. He wore a faded cotton Henley shirt and had grown suntanned and muscular.

"Madame Blauer, I do believe I missed my calling. I should have been your gardener and handyman all along and not a doctor or a professor."

"Ah, then I wouldn't have let you marry my daughter! She would have never been happy with a handyman gardener!" Hannah was a bit shocked at how hard they both laughed at this notion.

Rebecca biked up the gravel driveway in the distance. She had taken a job in town teaching piano. She was pedaling hard and sweating. She dropped her bike at the garden gate. Her face was red and tear-stained. She ran to the arms of their father, who stood to catch her.

"It has begun…the war. The Germans have invaded Poland, and…it is

CHAPTER TWO: HANNAH BEFORE THE WAR

war."

Chapter Three: Helma Before the War

Helma Braun's earliest memory as a child was her mother's empty eyes. Every morning, Helma remembered her mother putting on a gray apron to prepare breakfast for her father, brothers, and Helma. While her mother was physically present, her spiritual and emotional self was elsewhere. Her mother routinely cooked, cleaned and absently withstood the wrath of Helma's father. She was a pale imitation of the other mothers in town. She went to Mass every Sunday and, in her detached way, followed the service and took communion. She nodded politely to the other ladies, as her broken body and spirit were in stark contrast to the other animated women, who regarded her with pity.

Helma's father's eyes blazed with intensity. An obese man with a red face, he felt that he had been wronged, cheated, and his intelligence and leadership ability had been overlooked time and time again. His only dinner table talk was of the many villains at his workplace repressing him, jealous of his superior intelligence and ability. He taught Helma and his sons to be wary of people. People were out to take something from you, exploit you, and keep you down. He taught them not only to watch out but not to be shy about using strength and anger to defend themselves.

Helma's father despised her mother. Her passive and pitiable state would occasionally incite anger. "No wonder I can't make any progress! I have a worn-out dishrag for a wife!!" he would rage in her face, turning red and covering her ashen white face in his vitriol. Occasionally, he would jerk her up by the arm and slam her body into a wall. She would merely slide down the wall and protectively draw her knees up to her body in anticipation of

CHAPTER THREE: HELMA BEFORE THE WAR

more blows. If they didn't come, she would slink along the wall back into the kitchen.

Helma hated her. She was so weak. Many times, Helma fantasized about joining her father and beating her mother about the head with her fists and kicking her sides. During these fantasies, Helma thought about the time she and her brothers took a cat in a bag into an open field and lit it on fire. The clueless skinny cat was so quickly scooped up in the bag, and the fitful spasms as it burned to death.

It was left to Helma to shore up her mother's housekeeping. Her mother inattentively cleaned with little regard for the outcome. Helma's father insisted that Helma thoroughly clean the entire house. She enjoyed the task and appreciated even more the praise from her father on her work. She rigorously scrubbed the floors on her hands and knees, even burrowing into corners with a scrub brush.

When Helma was fourteen, her father began to listen to Hitler's speeches on the radio, and he would devour every bit of news about the new German chancellor.

"You boys should listen to him. He's right about those nasty Jews," he would tell his sons as the radio blared one of Hitler's speeches.

At age fourteen, Helma was growing into a young woman. She had her father's red, ruddy complexion. Her hair was a frizzy strawberry blond. Her body was square and stocky, and she had large, strong hands. Her eyes were unusually small and made her face asymmetrical. She did not connect well with other girls her age. She looked at them quizzically, as if they were another species. She wanted to try to be like them but didn't have the smallest clue where to begin.

The girls ignored her or mocked her unfortunate appearance behind her back. The angry, dirty boys who had been her childhood playmates were beginning to change. They were starting to take an interest in the prettier girls. They began to ignore Helma. The boys called her "horsey Helma" and laughingly asked if she could plow a field.

Helma was a dutiful student. Though she lacked imagination, she was diligent in following the instructions of her teachers. If she struggled to master a subject, she would stay after hours in the library to work harder.

On a cold, damp November evening, Helma was walking back from the library at dusk. She had on her brown wool coat and new brown shoes that she was especially proud of. She began to study the styles of the more popular girls and tried to improve her wardrobe. She had saved to purchase these shoes and would glance down at them once in a while, and a feeling of satisfaction bloomed inside her.

Her pace was slowing when she heard a boy's voice say, "There is horsey Helma!" and another boy laughed and said, "Will you come to us for some hay or an apple?"

Helma recognized the boys from her school. They were a year older than her. They were tough boys, always fighting. She was one minute bewildered and looking up from her shoes, and then she was overpowered and dragged into a muddy side lot by a dilapidated building. She felt her body being pressed down into the mud as she lay on her back as the boys eagerly unbuttoned her sweater and her blouse. They squeezed and bit her breasts. She felt the mud seeping into her hair. She struggled, but when she felt one of the boy's hands go up her skirt and his fingers stabbing inside her, she began to rage. Her screams alerted one of the elderly residents of the building.

An elderly woman armed with a broom chased the boys away. She turned and looked at Helma as she lay in the mud. "Whore! Get up, you nasty thing! Cover yourself! Go ply your trade elsewhere!"

Helma's head rang. She pulled down her skirt and wrapped her sweater tightly around her. She scrambled away. She couldn't shake the ringing in her head from her own screams. She felt dizzy as if she might faint but kept briskly walking toward home. She felt the mud caking in her hair. She felt the trickle of blood down the inside of her thigh.

When she came to her house, she crept quietly through the back door. She left her mud-soaked coat and shoes by the back door as she scrambled to the bathroom. She took off her clothes and briefly examined the welts on her breasts as the bathtub filled with scalding hot water. She braced herself and lowered herself in the bath. Everything burned. She scrubbed

CHAPTER THREE: HELMA BEFORE THE WAR

and scrubbed.

As she got out of the tub, she could hear her mother opening the linen closet. "Mother, I slipped and fell in the mud. My coat is by the back door. Can you clean it for me?" She heard her mother shuffle through the hallway. Helma quickly dressed for dinner.

In the dining room, her father looked at her quizzically. "Why is your hair wet?"

"I slipped and fell in the mud."

Her father and brothers started to laugh. "Good God, you're a clumsy ox!" Her father loudly exclaimed.

After dinner, her mother asked Helma to come to help her with the dishes. There was a stunned silence in the dining room. The shock of Helma's mother speaking and giving a direct order to Helma no less left them all astonished.

Helma followed her mother into the kitchen. After a few minutes of silently washing the dishes, her mother turned to Helma and asked, "What really happened to you? You can tell me."

Helma froze in place. There was life in her mother's eyes, which she had never seen before. Her look was gentle and imploring. "I slipped in the mud, Mother. I told you this."

"Was there something else, Helma?"

"No. Is slipping in the mud too difficult for you to understand? Did you clean my coat?" Helma's mother looked away. She stared down at her hands. She drifted away, and the blankness returned to her eyes. She didn't answer but silently folded a dish towel. Helma fled the kitchen.

The next morning, Helma found her cleaned coat and her new brown shoes were meticulously clean. She put them on and headed to school. When she saw the boys, she kept her head down and tried to blend into the crowded school hallway.

On Sunday, her mother stayed in the church after the service. Helma was leaving with her father and brothers, and her father sent her back to get her mother. The church was empty, but her mother was kneeling in a pew toward the front, her shoulders hunched and rounded under the black fabric of her tattered and threadbare coat. Her head was covered by an incongruently cheerful scarf. Helma stared at her for a moment as her mother was lost in prayer.

"Mother, we need to go," Helma's mother looked at her with gentle eyes and extended her hand. "Helma, pray with me."

"No, we have to go. Father is waiting for us. Church is over. We must go to prepare dinner now."

"Helma, no matter what happened to you on the day you fell in the mud, you can pray to be healed, if you are carrying a burden of guilt, and it can be lifted."

Helma felt the anger rising in her, "You don't know what you are talking about; you are a silly, stupid fool!" Helma hissed at her mother.

Helma's mother reached out her hand again. Helma angrily grabbed her wrist and twisted it as she knelt next to her. "I could break this wrist, you know. I could snap it and leave you in excruciating pain. You are so stupid and weak. Nothing has happened to me, and nothing will happen to me. I'm not like you. Get up, you stupid woman!" Helma growled.

The light, the gentleness, and energy drained from her mother's eyes as she jerked her hand away from Helma.

Helma no longer stayed late in the library. She began to detach from school. She barely finished high school. She got a job as a housekeeper in a hotel. Both of her brothers worked there, one as a handyman and one as a waiter. The hotel had beautiful, crisp white sheets. Helma loved making the beds. Making tight corners and smoothing the sheets gave her great satisfaction. Scrubbing everything clean allowed her mind to clear.

Helma thought it ironic that her job as hotel housekeeper put her on the bottom rung and that the guests were the superior ones. It made her laugh inside. She was the superior one. She saw their messes. They walked into the hotel with their fashionable clothes and their money. Helma could see what they did in the dark. Getting drunk, the traces of their sexual activity, and the stains of menstrual blood on the sheets, she took out their trash; she saw everything that no one spoke of in polite company. The evident traces of the messy, sexual, physical body were on display in every room.

CHAPTER THREE: HELMA BEFORE THE WAR

The job made Helma feel as if she knew all the secrets. The wealthy in their beautiful clothes were not any different. She felt mildly repulsed and angry about it at times, especially if the guests were rude. She felt annoyed by the polite guests as well. She would rather be invisible.

Sometimes, she would stealthily break or ruin some item that belonged to a guest. It didn't matter to her who the guest was, they could be tidy, messy, polite, or rude. The game for Helma was to find the thing that would hurt the guest most keenly. Many times, it was taking a small photo out of a frame and burning the picture. Sometimes, it was a photo of a child, or a family, or maybe a long since dead relative. After burning the image, she would return the frame or locket to the location where she found it. Sometimes, she created minor chaos by breaking off the stem of a pair of glasses or carefully cutting the zipper out of a guest's prettiest and fanciest dress. Very often, she never saw the reaction of the guests, but every once in a while, sometimes she would get a satisfying glimpse of a confused and dejected guest staring at an empty picture frame or a frantic woman asking for a seamstress to repair her dress.

When she wasn't working at the hotel, she liked to knit. She had become quite good at it. She knit blankets, scarves, gloves, baby booties. She always kept her hands busy.

She continued to accompany her parents to church every Sunday. It was the only time she saw any life in her mother. Helma liked the routine of the Mass. She liked going and hearing their neighbors talk about what a good daughter she was. Many of the things she knit were given to the church for sale in the Christmas Bazaar or given to needy families. Helma continued to live at home with her parents. Her brothers had moved out. Her eldest brother, Klaus, had become the head waiter at the hotel. When he wasn't working, he would drink until he passed out. Her brother Hans recently married. He was as full of rage as his father. He frequently beat his wife, a meek girl named Klara. They came to dinner, and Helma thought how foolish Klara was to believe she could hide her bruised eye with loads of cheap makeup.

Helma's mother became more of a ghost as she aged. She didn't cry or protect herself when the blows came. She just lay on the floor and let his fists and feet pound her into unconsciousness.

As Hitler increased in power and fame, the beatings became less frequent. Helma's father was consumed with joy. Hitler was his new Jesus. His round, red face was alight with enthusiasm at dinner as he talked about Hitler. "He is a great man. A man of the common people. He wasn't even an officer during the Great War. A regular soldier. Not a snobby, over-educated donkey's ass. He is bold in speaking the truth. The Jews did stab the Germans in the back. Not just the Germans, but all the Nordic people, the clean people. These dirty Jews have been at it for years and years. They get control of money; they use all their fake 'education' when they really know nothing to act superior. Hitler's calling it all out. It makes me laugh to see them howling like helpless toddlers! Crying like babies, Jews, and their stupid friends. Yes! They are getting beaten in the street! As it should be! If I were a younger man, I would be joining in!"

Hans smiled and laughed along with their father. Klara just silently pushed the food around her plate. Helma chimed into the conversation.

"I've been working at the hotel a long time now, and I agree they are dirty and spoiled people. These Jews. They are slobs. They are different from us. I wonder, how did they get their money? It doesn't seem right to me."

Helma's father laughed. "Oh, daughter, now I'm a bit sorry for calling you the stupid cow for all these years! It seems even a thick-headed, stupid female can see these Jews for what they are. Now, we have the power and freedom to tell the truth. A truth so evident that even someone as simple as Helma can see it! Hitler is going to join Austria, his homeland with Germany, and the common, good people are going to be in charge. Decent and pure Germans and Austrians will be in charge, not the money-grubbing Jews and their elite friends. Finally!"

Helma's father slapped the table and laughed. As it turned out, he was right. Helma would never forget that fantastic day. Anschluss, March 12, 1938. The hotel was abuzz with excitement. Soldiers and German officials checked into the hotel, and there was high energy and enthusiasm.

After her shift, Helma joined her work friends and brothers at the pub,

CHAPTER THREE: HELMA BEFORE THE WAR

singing songs and drinking beer. She pushed through the crowd and saw her brother Hans. "Hey, sister! It's finally happening! Did you look around at all the upper-class assholes that lectured everyone about how stupid Hitler was, how unrefined and bombastic Hitler was? How Hitler would never amount to anything? Look at them now! They're stunned. We don't have to bow and scrape to the upper classes, the Jews, the pushy sluts. We'll put them in their place! It's our time! Father was right." Hans excitedly kissed her cheek.

It was the most exciting thing that had ever happened to her. Later that year, her brothers joined the army. They were proud that they had been among the first to join the Nazi movement in Austria. They left for training in Germany. Helma looked forward to their letters. It made her feel as if she was some small part of an amazing thing that was happening.

Klaus was the most encouraging. He reminded her that Hitler was looking out for them. He was making the world right for the good, decent people. The corrupt people, the scam artist Jews, the sex perverts, the weak, and the imbeciles would finally be gone. It would be a better world. Helma was feeling better about herself and her family. They were the good people all along, even though, all those years, they had been looked down upon. Helma received a couple of letters from Hans, too, and wanted to share them with Klara. When she arrived at Klara's house, she was disappointed to see her sister-in-law show very little interest in the letters.

"Klara, I don't think you understand what is happening. Hans and Klaus are part of something huge. They are going to be part of cleaning things up. Getting rid of the sex perverts, the deformed and imbeciles. They are a huge burden; they contribute nothing. And the Jews, they are backstabbing criminals. We have put up with it for years, and now it is going to stop."

Klara stared blankly at her, "I'm happy for you. Hitler and his cause have given you purpose, but it doesn't mean the same to me. A Jew never beat me." Helma threw the letters on the table and stormed out. How could Klara be so blind?

In the summer of 1939, Helma was considering a big move herself. Klaus had written that the greater Reich needed women like Helma to help in so many roles. They wanted sturdy, clean-living, and simple young women who were true believers in the cause. He told her these girls were coming from small towns all over greater Germany. They were farmer's daughters, common girls like herself. Hitler was giving them a chance. All the excitement wasn't left to lazy, immoral city girls with too much education. Now, good and hardworking girls dedicated to the Reich were having a chance. Helma lay awake at night, thinking about enlisting in the women's services, finally experiencing something different. She would be able to be part of the exciting movement to clean up society.

On September 1, 1939, Helma's heart raced with excitement as she listened to the tiny radio in the basement of the hotel. The war had begun.

Chapter Four: Hannah's Family
1939–1943

On the day the war started, Max stood in the garden, arms embracing Rebecca next to her bike. He wasn't surprised, but his mind raced to think of what it might mean for his family.

Hannah sat with her grandmother, unable to move. It was always unsettling to see her father or Rebecca distressed or sad. She looked to her grandmother and noticed her face had become ashen. She folded her parasol and stood up and walked over to the door to the house from the garden. She turned toward Hannah, "Hannah dear, come with me. We need to prepare for dinner."

Hannah dutifully followed her grandmother into the house. She walked into the kitchen with her grandmother, and Caroline, her grandmother's maid and cook, stood up quickly and smoothed her apron.

"Caroline, I think we should change the planned dinner menu. Let's roast that chicken instead of soup tonight. There are apples in the pantry; let's make a nice crisp with cream for dessert and bring out one of the nicer wines from the cellar."

Caroline looked puzzled but said, "Yes, ma'am." And quickly set off to prepare the special dinner and dessert.

Hannah was puzzled, too. The mood had become so tense, it hardly seemed the time to celebrate. Hannah looked out the window to see her father and Rebecca slowly walking through the garden arm and arm. Her father joined Hannah in the sitting room, and he was adjusting her grandmother's antique wireless radio.

High-pitched squeaks and static fuzz sounds filled the room until Max barely captured a station that solemnly recapped the day's events. Anna came downstairs and sat stiffly still and listened to the news of the German invasion of Poland. Max walked over to Anna and rested his hands on her shoulders. Hannah scanned their faces and felt a cold shudder run through her body. She felt as if she was intruding on an intimate moment between her parents. She ran out of the room in search of Rebecca.

She found her upstairs, emerging from the bathroom, having just washed her face. "Hey, it's my monkey, Hannah," she was trying to make her voice sound light and carefree.

Hannah didn't know how to put into words what she was thinking. The past year for Hannah had been fun. She loved having her father around all the time. Esther was healthier. Despite the strict lessons and old-fashioned manners, Hannah had grown to admire her grandmother Hortense. Life had developed a happy rhythm in the French countryside. Of course, she had heard the tense, whispered conversations between her parents. Her father's careful tracking of events back in Austria left him distracted, but he threw himself into the repair of the house and the cultivation of the garden. It had all been background noise to ten-year-old Hannah. Now, in just a single day, everything had changed, and Hannah could feel the fear seeping into the once-safe refuge of their new home.

She took Rebecca's hand. Rebecca squeezed back. Rebecca sensed what was on Hannah's mind.

"Look, monkey, today, the war we had been anticipating has started. Poland has been invaded by the Germans, and the war is on now. I don't know what's going to happen." Rebecca's voice broke slightly, and she turned to Hannah. "Whatever happens, we are going to stick together and ride it out. You and me. Okay?" Rebecca squeezed Hannah's shoulders. Hannah grabbed her sister in an embrace.

Downstairs, Hortense was overseeing the preparation of the dining room for the special dinner. She smoothed out the lace tablecloth and then lit the candles in the ornate silver candelabra at the center of the table. She turned

CHAPTER FOUR: HANNAH'S FAMILY 1939–1943

to Rebecca and Hannah, "Ah, girls, we will have a lovely dinner tonight. I think even Hannah should have a glass of wine tonight." Smiling, their grandmother swept out of the room.

Later, as they all assembled in the dining room, Hortense had the table laid with the most delicate china, cut glass dishes, wine glasses, and hand-embroidered linen napkins. Max looked a little puzzled at the elaborate display, "I don't want to appear ungrateful for your efforts Hortense, but it hardly feels like a day for a celebratory meal," his voice trailed off as he surveyed the elaborate table.

Hortense walked over to Anna and took her hand, "You remember, dear you were a little girl like Hannah is now, 1914, the start of the Great War. Your brothers were so excited to fight for France. Before your brothers left, we had a special dinner. Like tonight, the table was set. It was much grander then, and it was a wonderful night. I still remember my handsome sons and their excitement to go to war, their fear that it would be all over before they could be a part of it. That night lingers in my mind. Wonderful food, candles, and wine. It remains in my mind because it was the very last meal we had as a family." Hortense paused and encouraged everyone to sit down, and she continued, "We don't know what the war will bring. I hope and pray we will stay together unharmed until the war's end. Whatever happens, let's make tonight a good night. Let's enjoy the food, the wine, the beautiful table together."

Max wrapped his arm around Anna as tears welled in her eyes. Rebecca squeezed Hannah's hand under the table. Esther had tears in her eyes as Hortense opened the bottle of fine wine. The night was wonderful.

The dramatic day the war began was followed by months of uncomfortable waiting. In Britain, they called it the "phony war."

Fall faded into winter. Max managed to have some colleagues in Austria sell many of their items and send a little money. The items were sold at bargain prices. Anna had written to Marta to ship her some of her personal things, despite Max's warning of divulging too much information to Marta.

"Anna, you shouldn't let Marta know too much information about us. David warned us that Ernst is involved with the Nazi party."

"I'm not too worried. Ernst isn't that well-educated, and I'm sure his involvement is at a low level. Marta has been with us for a long time, and we've been very good to her."

"Do you think the Nazis are picking the well-educated to beat up Jews? I don't think so. Who knows what Ernst is involved in? I think you're wrong about Marta."

Max had received letters from David about the increasingly repressive measures against Jews in Austria. David was reaching out to relatives in America, despite his mother's objections.

In June 1940, what they feared most had come to pass. The Germans invaded France. The French Army fell quickly, more rapidly than anyone anticipated. Hortense Blauer couldn't believe the news when Paris fell into the hands of the Germans just a few weeks after the invasion. She was equally heartbroken when the Great War's "Old Marshal," Marshal Petain, became the leader of a collaborator puppet government of France under the Germans.

To Hannah, her grandmother seemed to age ten years in a few weeks that June. Sitting in the garden, her grandmother wearily said, "I never thought a hero of France, The Old Marshal, would betray us. I never thought anyone who lived during the Great War would roll over for the Germans like that."

Though her grandmother was in despair, her father seemed to be agitated and restless. He dismissed Hannah's and Esther's tutor and did not allow Rebecca to go into town to teach piano. He tore out the seams of the clothing and was counting the jewels.

As the Germans established themselves over the next few months, predictably, repressive measures against Jews were put into practice. Grandmother Blauer's home became almost claustrophobic for Hannah. Her father insisted that no one could leave the house or garden. The family was dependent on Hortense Blauer's maid, Caroline, for anything they needed from town.

Rebecca played games with Hannah in the garden, and they continued to play endless games of cards. After experiencing a rebound in her health, Esther was now again in decline, experiencing shortness of breath and what

CHAPTER FOUR: HANNAH'S FAMILY 1939-1943

Hannah thought of as just profound sadness that caused Esther to spend many days in bed.

One day, Caroline brought a letter to Rebecca from David. They had regularly been corresponding over the past few years. Rebecca summoned her father to the garden, and she read part of David's letter aloud.

> *"...My attempts to leave Austria for America have been unsuccessful. I haven't been able to work for almost two years now, and Mother and I have sold everything to survive. Jews are being rounded up and sent east. To Poland, to ghettos or work camps. My mother and I will certainly be going soon. I've heard many rumors about the ghettos and camps, and none of them are good. I don't know what will happen in France. I think of your family often and hope for all of us to be safely reunited someday. This will probably be the last letter for a time. My connection to get correspondence through without censorship will no longer be able to help me. I would beg you to ask your mother to discontinue her correspondence with your former maid, Marta. Her husband is a leader among Austrian Nazis. I'm sure he knows exactly where you are in France, and that is not safe. There are no words to express what your family means to me. Please be cautious, and I am looking forward to the day when this horrible war is over, and we are together again..."*

Rebecca's voice wavered as she read the last sentence, and tears rolled down her cheeks. Hannah looked at her father, who sat stone-faced in the beautiful garden. He stood up and walked to the house.

For several months, Hannah watched as her father, grandmother, and her grandmother's maid would huddle in whispered conversations. At night, strange men would come to the door with Caroline and meet with her father and grandmother in the basement.

The stash of jewels the family had brought from Austria was quite depleted, but in a repeat of the scene of their last days in Vienna, Hannah walked in on Rebecca sewing loose jewels in the hem of one of her dresses.

Hannah slammed the door behind her, "What is going on now?! Where are we going?"

Rebecca quickly hushed her and said, "Shhh! Mother doesn't know. It's happening tonight. There has been a round-up of Jews at the Velodrome in Paris. That has pushed up the schedule a bit. Father has been working on a hiding place for us. Caroline's family are farmers west of here. On their property is an abandoned barn. That's where we will stay."

Hannah stared at Rebecca. She looked frazzled and scared. Hannah asked, "Do you really think it is that bad? We've been hiding out here for years, and nothing has really happened."

"Hannah! Don't you understand what is happening? Do you remember David's letter? People are getting rounded up and put on trains and sent to God knows what! Thanks to Mother, they know exactly where we are. We could be pulled out of here and sent on a train at any time."

Hannah felt her stomach tighten. She had become so comfortable at her grandmother's house. She was bored and heard talk of the war but had been shielded from the realities of it. She was thirteen now, and it was hard to live such an isolated life. Relying only on Rebecca for companionship while her father and grandmother intentionally kept Hannah, Esther, and their mother shielded from the realities of the war.

Hannah tried to get in a few hours of fitful sleep. Then Rebecca tapped her shoulder, and Hannah slipped the dress with the jewels in the hems on and, despite it being a warm summer evening, pulled on her coat.

When they came downstairs, Hannah heard her mother say, "Max, where are we going in the middle of the night like this?"

"Anna, we are going somewhere safe. Jews are being rounded up now, and we need to go into hiding."

As Hannah reached the bottom of the stairs, she saw her grandmother with a shawl wrapped around her shoulders, but she was in her nightdress and had no suitcase. Hannah's father walked over to her and took her arm. "Where are your things? We're leaving in about ten minutes."

"I'm not going with you. I'm staying here. I'm a harmless old woman; they won't bother me, and I can be of help to others."

"Hortense, that is a bad idea. If you think those animals care that you are

CHAPTER FOUR: HANNAH'S FAMILY 1939–1943

an old woman, you're wrong. Pack your things; you're coming with us."

Hortense didn't move. "Max, I appreciate what you're doing, but I'm not leaving. I'm not leaving my home. You're doing the right thing; you're keeping everyone safe, but I'm not coming." Hannah rushed over to her grandmother. "You need to come with us, Grandmother. It isn't safe to stay."

Her grandmother patted her cheek. "Darling, I'm an old woman now, more than seventy years old, so it's hard for me to change. I'm going to spend my last years, whatever they may be, in my house."

As soon as she said those words, two men whom Hannah had seen in the clandestine basement meetings entered the door. They led Hannah and her family to a car. They all squeezed in. Hannah sat in front, between the two men. She could feel that the man driving the car had a gun in his coat pocket. They didn't talk during the two-hour ride. The sun was just rising when they came to the small farmhouse.

Pierre and Henrietta Dufour were a stout older couple in simple clothing. Henrietta had an easy laugh and pink cheeks. Hannah noticed her rough, wide hands. So different from her mother's soft, white hands and varnished fingernails. They welcomed the family with coffee. Pierre Dufour was very tall and strong. Almost comically too tall for his short, plump wife, who was barely five feet tall. He didn't talk much. After chatting for a short time, they were led behind the house to a dilapidated old barn with berry brambles growing in front of the barn doors. The barn looked like it hadn't been used in many years.

Mr. Dufour led them to the back of the barn. There, he popped open a hidden door. It opened to a small room that looked recently refurbished. It had the smell of freshly cut wood. The room had several beds, a table, and five chairs. There was a closet-like space that was the latrine. There were a few kerosene lamps for light. There was a ladder to a small loft, which had the only window that could open. There was no stove, no sink, no running water.

Max turned to Mr. Dufour. "Thank you so much to you and your wife for helping us." He just smiled and left. Max turned and said, "I know this isn't much, but the Dufours are risking their lives by hiding us here. It's remote, and he has done a good job disguising the entrance. We should be safe here."

What hiding meant was never leaving the barn. Hannah would sometimes sit in the loft and look outside to the Dufour's farm. In the distance, she could see the Dufour's sheep and sometimes Mr. Dufour, walking with a stick and accompanied by a black and white dog. Once a day, Mrs. Dufour would bring a bucket of fresh water and whatever food she had. Sometimes, it was sausages, cheese, and apples. Other times, she just brought some bread. She often brought wine, which was a treat. The best days were the days she would bring out books, which Max read aloud in the evening. For Rebecca, she fulfilled a special request and brought a long piece of butcher paper and a pencil. Rebecca drew piano keys and would occasionally "play" songs that the rest of the family sang along to.

Sometimes, Mr. Dufour would check on them and bring some lye for the latrine. Unlike Mrs. Dufour, he didn't talk much. When it got colder, he gave them extra blankets, as there was no heat source in the barn.

Rebecca and Hannah practiced songs on the butcher paper keyboard together. They read and re-read books. Occasionally, they would crack the door open to let the barn cat, who they named Siggi, into the room. They spoiled Siggi with bites of sausage and loving pets. Siggi returned the favor by occasionally bringing them a dead rat. Siggi, the cat, was the only thing that seemed to cheer Esther. She was still very ill and had a mattress in the loft so she could get a little fresh air. Sometimes, the three girls would sleep in the loft together. This was Hannah's favorite time. Singing a few songs and laughing and falling asleep together.

The isolation was hardest on Anna. For the first time in her life, she was without a lovely home to live in, without servants, without beautiful clothing, and she had, at long last, lost her breezy assurance that things would, in her words, "blow over." Hannah noticed that she still would pull out her make-up compact, apply a little lipstick, and tidy her hair every morning.

Max looked serious and drained. The energy he had at Grandmother Hortense's home had been sucked out of him. It was all about survival now.

CHAPTER FOUR: HANNAH'S FAMILY 1939–1943

It was early spring, and Hannah would prop open the upstairs loft window and smell the March rain.

Rebecca, Hannah, and Max were in the downstairs room, and Anna and Esther were resting upstairs in the loft bedroom when they heard a truck. There was no road near the barn, so the truck had driven through the field. Max yelled to Anna and Esther to stay upstairs and stay quiet. They listened and heard the truck stop and then German voices. The door burst open.

Hannah screamed, and her father threw his arms around her to protect her. One soldier was already dragging Rebecca out of the door. The other soldier drew a gun, and Max threw his hands up. The soldier marched him out the door while roughly dragging Hannah out by one arm. When they got outside, an officer was standing by a pick-up truck. The Dufours, hands tied behind their back, were standing next to the truck. Mrs. Dufour looked as if she had been crying. An officer wearing black leather gloves walked over and inspected the three of them and turned to the soldiers. "Where are the other two? According to the information from Vienna, it is the doctor, his wife, and three daughters. Where is the wife and other daughter?" Max quickly spoke up, "They left. My wife and other daughter are not here."

The officer ignored him and instructed the two other soldiers to go back into the barn. She heard her mother screaming. Her mother screamed, "No!" Louder and louder. Then she heard Esther screaming, "Stop!" They were both screaming, and then she heard a thud. Max was pleading with the officer to just bring them out here.

Moments later, one soldier emerged, dragging Hannah's mother out of the house. She was stumbling and had taken a rifle butt blow to her head above her eyebrow. She fell into her Max's arms. The officer turned to the soldier. "Where's Paul?"

"You know him. The other sister is very pretty. He's having a little fun." Max angrily stepped forward to the officer. "This is outrageous. I was in the army. This is not done. Get my daughter out here!"

The officer slammed his rifle butt against Max's head. Hannah began shaking. Rebecca took her arm and steadied her. Max struggled up to his feet, barely able to stand. After about twenty minutes, the other soldier dragged Esther out. She had been punched in the face. Her lip was bleeding. Her dress was twisted awkwardly around her body and the top two buttons on the dress had been torn away. She had welts on her neck that looked like thumbprints, and Hannah noticed blood running down her leg. She had trouble standing. Max and Anna wrapped their arms around her. The officer shook his head. "We can't have shenanigans like this. We need to get going."

He then turned to the Dufours. He shouted, "You know the penalty for helping Jews is death." Before the information could even register, the officer turned to the soldier named Paul, and Paul drew his pistol. He shot Mrs. Dufour and then Mr. Dufour in the head. Their bodies collapsed next to the truck. The officer turned to the soldier, "Jesus, Paul, do you ever think? Look at the mess on the hood of the truck?"

Hannah looked and saw blood and chunks of white brain matter on the hood of the truck. She felt herself begin to urinate, and she could feel the urine go down her leg and soak one of her socks.

They were all thrown into the bed of the truck. Hannah looked at her father. She had never seen him cry before. Tears were streaming down his cheeks. She couldn't bear to see her father cry, so she looked out to the field as they pulled away, leaving the Dufours lying dead and perfectly still. As the barn disappeared from view, she saw the black and white dog running toward the Dufours' lifeless bodies.

They rode in the truck until nightfall, and they were thrown on a crowded train first for the camp called Drancy. At Drancy, they were shoved out of the cattle car. On the train, Max had stopped talking. He just stared ahead in shock. Esther would start a crying jag and wheeze, and then Rebecca and Anna would comfort her. Drancy had low-slung, drab buildings on all sides. Train loads of people came and went. People were dazed and too numb to do anything but scramble out of packed cattle cars and wait to be shoved tightly into another cattle car, always headed east.

Hannah and her family were in Drancy for only a few hours. Despite the filth and the stench, at least they were outside for a time. Esther could breathe a little better. Hannah noticed that blood had pooled and left a stain on the back of her dress, and the blood on her leg had dried and flaked off. When she didn't cough and gasp, she cried. Hannah looked down at her yellow-stained sock. She knew she reeked of urine, but it didn't matter now; in the crowded field where hundreds were waiting, her stench was just a tiny contribution to the horrible smell. Rebecca and her father went in search of food and water. They returned with a gray metal flask. Everyone in the family greedily took a drink. Hannah thought water had never tasted or felt so good as that one big gulp from the flask.

Yells, whistles, and barking dogs hustled the crowd back to the train just as the sun was rising. Terrified families clung together as they were packed yet again into another cattle car. Hannah felt Rebecca's hand grip hers as they were shoved along. Hannah wrestled her hand away from Rebecca when she noticed a small chunk of wood had been broken out of one slat in the railcar. She wondered what desperate person who had ridden this train before her had smashed away the wooden slat for this tiny opening.

Hannah slumped down to bring her face near the small hole and tried to inhale fresh air. She didn't let herself cry.

Chapter Five: Helma's New Start
1939–1941

Letters from Klaus in Berlin were the highlight of Helma's days. He brought news of the exciting life he had in the German army and the thrill of the many victories throughout 1939 and 1940. Helma lived on the fringes of the excitement through his letters and the sharp-looking German officers who now frequented the hotel.

Austria itself was changing, too. The bright red flags emblazoned with swastikas fluttered from many windows. There was an energy and excitement about the future and becoming a part of the greater German Reich. The veneration of the old way of life, of country living, Germanic tradition, old-fashioned motherhood, and classical art forms were forming the vision for the future. The depressed haze of the last few decades following the catastrophic destruction of the Great War had lifted.

Then there was what Helma referred to as "the clean-up," in which Jews and their anti-German allies were forced out of jobs and positions of power and were publicly humiliated. Helma thought of this as a cleaning because it was making everything orderly and simple. A return to her grandparents' day. It was a cleaning of people who didn't belong here. Specifically, Jews, but also others who didn't respect authority, sexual perverts, and people who didn't contribute, or didn't follow orders. It was pleasing to see her own personal views melding with what was happening to society.

If Helma was pleased about the new direction under Hitler, it paled in comparison to her father's delirious joy at Hitler's leadership and continued

CHAPTER FIVE: HELMA'S NEW START 1939–1941

success. He eagerly consumed news about the war. He took the unusual step of having pictures of Helma's brothers in uniform framed and placed on the mantel. He had never shown his children any tiny scrap of fatherly tenderness or pride, but basking in his son's service to his idol, he finally mustered some respect for his sons, Klaus and Hans.

Helma's mother remained unchanged. If she had any thoughts or opinions about Hitler, she never expressed them, nor did anyone inquire or care. She grew alarmingly thin and even more remote than even Helma dreamed possible.

In 1940, shortly after the invasion of France, Hans had leave and came home for a short visit. He would soon be headed to Poland and wanted to see Klara before what he believed would be a long deployment.

It was a rare, happy family time. Klara and Helma made several special desserts, and the family sat around the table laughing and enjoying a wonderful meal. Even Helma's mother showed a small spark of life seeing her son at home.

Helma's father beamed with pride. At dinner, he gobbled up not only the food but also any of the details about life in Germany under Hitler.

Helma's father grilled Hans for details about his upcoming deployment. Hans smiled and said, "Well, I can't say much, but it's going to be important to do what we need to do in Poland to grow greater Germany. There are a lot of Jews there that need to be taken care of. The SS is starting to work on that, and I assume the army will get involved, too. Then, it's also a matter of bringing the Poles in line. The resistance, the intellectuals, and bringing them into general obedience. They need to conform to their subservient role in the new Reich. So, that involves getting rid of the radical element, closing down their universities and schools. It's all a lot of work."

Helma's father nodded in agreement. She couldn't help but notice the look of pride and admiration on her father's face. None of them had ever received this sort of affirmation growing up. It made Helma feel good that not only was Hitler's Germany bringing order to the world, it was also bringing harmony to her family.

Helma and Hans managed to arrange a time to get a beer together at the hotel. Hans wanted to say hello to his old co-workers, and Helma wanted a chance to talk with him alone.

Helma beamed with pride to be out and about with her older brother in uniform. They settled down with their beers, and Helma was finally able to ask about life in Germany. "You know, I keep getting letters from our brother Klaus about how there are opportunities for war work for young women. I keep thinking about it, but you know Klaus always makes things seem brighter than they really are, and I would hate to get there and find myself out of work. Also, mother and father are not getting any younger."

Hans nodded thoughtfully, "For once, I don't think Klaus is overstating. I know that there is a tremendous need for workers. Naturally, women should be at home and raising the next generation, but in this critical time, there is an understanding that women are needed to support the war effort. I think it would be wonderful if you were to get war work in Germany. You're a hard worker, and you, unlike most women, are able to understand the big-picture changes that need to happen."

Helma smiled at Hans' compliment. She was still a bit unsure if it was the right move, but Hans reassured her. "Look, Klara is actually more suited to take care of mother and father. Unlike you, she can't understand these big-picture ideas, and she is very easily made upset by things. I would not let your obligation there hold you back. Also, this war is going to be over in a couple of years. It's a short-term role for you. Eventually, a smart man is going to see your attributes and marry you. Then, you can fulfill a rightful role as a mother to Aryan children. That's ultimately your role to serve the Fatherland. I've been thinking a lot about the future. It will be exciting in the next thirty years for our children to remember us as the vanguard of this whole new world. They will be telling stories about our generation! Heroes! Just picture yourself as a grandmother in the 1970s! You can say you served the Fatherland during the war."

Helma laughed to think of herself as a grandmother or even picture the remote world of the 1970s. Now she was just a twenty-one-year-old young woman, trying to figure out her next move.

It was a difficult day when Hans left. Klara was weeping at the train

CHAPTER FIVE: HELMA'S NEW START 1939–1941

station, and Helma was feeling a bit choked up herself, although she had too much pride to let herself be seen crying in public.

Over the next few months, Helma kept in correspondence with Klaus in Berlin and had him update her on potential work opportunities. Hans' dreams about future fatherhood would soon become a reality. Two months after his visit, Klara announced she was pregnant. The following February, Klara had a baby girl, Greta. Helma was excited for her brother, but sad that he wasn't home to greet his new daughter. She saved a little extra money to pay for Klara and Greta to get a studio portrait done and had it sent to her brother in Poland.

Shortly after Greta's birth, the letter Helma had been hoping for from Klaus finally arrived.

Dear Sister –

I think I may have a line on a job for you in an airplane factory just outside of Berlin. Not only that, but I also think I have a place for you to live. That's a big piece of the puzzle as it is crazy here and so hard to find living quarters. I met a young woman who works at the factory named Letty. Her roommate left, and she can't afford her place on her own. The factory is ramping up. Something big is in the works, but I don't know what it is! Anyway, I think it's the right opportunity. Letty is nice, but a little high-strung, and a little man crazy. I wanted to warn you of that upfront, but I think you would be a stabilizing influence for her. Underneath it all, she's okay and really wants to serve the Reich. Hope I will be seeing you soon, Sister!

Your Loving Brother,
Klaus

Helma was shaking with excitement as she put down the letter. At dinner, she told her father about the opportunity. For the first time in her life, her father reached over and affectionately squeezed her shoulder and smiled broadly at her. "I think that is a wonderful plan. I think it is amazing that Hitler has even found a way for women to be useful in this great struggle. I give my permission."

Not normally giving a lot of thought to her wardrobe, Helma found herself indulging in a little shopping for a couple of fashionable dresses, a new coat, and a hat for her trip to Berlin. She brought a book to read on the train, but she was so excited she couldn't concentrate on it. Klaus was waiting for her at the station. "Hey, Sister! Look at you! Nice looking hat," he said as he embraced her. Klaus was unlike the rest of their family. He was more emotional. He could be affectionate and funny. He was tall, like their father, and big, except he was muscular rather than fat. Helma felt proud to be on his arm. She was thrilled to be in Berlin on this beautiful April day. That evening, they went to the restaurant in the hotel where Helma had arranged to spend the night. Klaus peppered her with questions about Greta, his new niece. Helma thought how sweet her brother was to be so interested. She looked around the restaurant. Most of the men were in sharp uniforms, and the women looked very glamorous. She was so glad she thought to get a few new dresses for the new life she was starting in Berlin.

The next morning, Helma saw a nervous, bird-like woman with dark hair in the lobby. She scampered up to Helma. "Oh, you must be Helma. So tall! Just like your brother. He's such a nice fellow, your brother. Oh, I'm such a scatterbrain! I'm Letty! I have a friend with a car to drive us outside of Berlin to the new apartment. Is your dress new? It's so fashionable. Come this way."

Helma followed Letty as she quickly fluttered her way out of the hotel lobby. In a complete reversal of his normal habit of overstating things, Klaus had very much understated his assessment of Letty as simply "high-strung."

It was non-stop chatter on the car ride during the near-one hour drive to the apartment. Letty pointed out the airplane factory on their way. Once inside, the apartment was drab and small. Letty had put crochet doilies and plastic flowers around the place, but that only served to make it more drab rather than less.

Helma started work at the factory the next day. It was a big and impressive facility. Helma felt excited to finally be a direct contributor to the war effort. The work was repetitive and hard, and the hours were long, but Helma

CHAPTER FIVE: HELMA'S NEW START 1939-1941

didn't mind. Letty was forever asking Helma to come to supper clubs or out dancing to meet soldiers, but Helma always declined; she preferred the silence of the apartment in Letty's absence.

In late May, Klaus was being shipped out to serve in the east. Helma was a little sad as they ate one last dinner together before his departure. "I don't know what it is, and I've been wondering about it all spring, but something big is coming up, Helma. There is just a ton of men headed east. I don't know what. I hope you keep writing and keep me posted on what's happening in Germany."

As it turned out, Klaus was right. Something big was coming up. The invasion of the Soviet Union. Although most people were low-key about it, Helma heard critical opinions of Hitler's choice to start a second front in the war at this time, but the criticism soon died down as the army conquered more and more territory in rapid succession.

As the months passed, Helma and Letty were growing tired of the long hours and repetitive work at the factory. Because Letty spent all her spare time around military men, she heard a rumor that they were looking for female prison guards. Letty was considering the opportunity. "I think it pays nearly twice what we're making at the factory, Helma. And consider that they pay for your living quarters, that's a bonus. And I don't think it would be that hard. I think these people are criminals, but not violent ones, just Jews, people who are shirking work, and boy, after our long hours at the factory, I would not mind seeing those lazybones locked up."

Helma eagerly agreed to pursue this opportunity. They were accepted for duty and underwent a short training course. Helma was particularly proud of her uniform. The black jackboots weren't fashionable, but she knew if she got a violent woman on the ground, these heavy boots could subdue them. The physical training was demanding, but even though she was heavy, Helma was strong. She was very interested in the classroom training they received about the enemies of the Reich, the Jews, the handicapped, the imbeciles, collaborators, the dissidents who wanted to drag Germany back to the Weimar days, and the work-shy, who were lazy and apathetic. These people were a severe threat to Germany. Not only that, but their offspring also just carried on their destructive traits. A lot of soft-hearted and soft-minded people, in Helma's view, were upset and critical of imprisoning women and children. They clearly didn't understand that these women and their children were like poison to the future of Germany. She eagerly consumed the educational films and manuals about race hygiene during her training.

After their training concluded, they received their assignments. Letty ran over to Helma's bedside, waving her letter as she sat down. "Oh Helma, I'm going to Poland! I don't even know anything about Poland. I just hope it all goes well, and I don't have a lot of trouble with the Jewish women, I mean I know they won't work hard, but I just don't know."

"Calm down, Letty, it will be fine. Just keep in mind that you're in charge. You don't have to listen to their complaints; you whip them into shape. These Jews haven't had to work an honest day's labor, so it's our job to teach them. These people are a threat to our way of life. A threat. We have to treat them that way."

"Helma, you're so strong, and so smart about these things. You're so lucky to be staying in Germany and going to Ravensbruck. I hear it is nice. I'm going to miss you." Helma stiffened as Letty hugged her. She wouldn't be so cruel as to say so, but she was so relieved not to be serving in the same camp as Letty.

When Helma arrived at Ravensbruck, she was surprised by the size of the camp. She was greeted by a pretty, young blond woman named Irma. She was one of the leaders of the female camp guards. It was a well-run camp. It was a little unsettling at first to see the condition of the women, but Helma thought to herself that these women were criminals and enemies of Germany. Irma trained Helma to take a firm hand with the prisoners. Irma carried a braided whip around the camp. Any prisoners found slacking, making trouble, or any other infraction were shown no mercy. Helma also learned about the need to eliminate prisoners unable to work, including the sick and elderly. There were always new transports of incoming prisoners, and room needed to be made. Helma admired the efficient system of eliminating prisoners. She knew such measures were necessary for Germany to win the war, this effort to eliminate the enemy within.

Helma felt she was just getting settled into a routine when orders arrived for her to move on to a new camp in Poland. She reviewed her orders again as she sat on her bed. Her new assignment was a camp in Lublin, Poland.

Chapter Six: Helma in Poland 1941–1943

Helma got off the train in Lublin and was greeted by Bridget, a guard at the camp. Bridget was young and had beautiful skin, which was set off by her dark hair. Not a strand was out of place. She helped Helma with her bags.

"Welcome! I'm glad you're here. We really need the help. Before we head to the camp, let's make a stop in town. There is a little coffee shop in town where we all gather. A friend of yours is there." Helma looked at her quizzically. Bridget smiled, "I think you worked with her at the aircraft factory. Her name is Letty. A high-strung chatterbox, that's our Letty."

Helma exhaled and gave a little laugh, "Well, it seems to be my destiny to be connected with poor Letty. We were roommates in Berlin when we both worked at the aircraft factory, and we were in training together before I went to Ravensbruck. I have to give her credit, though; I wouldn't have the opportunity to be a guard without her." When they arrived at the cafe and walked in, Helma saw Letty, who scurried up to her as she walked through the door.

"Oh, Helma! I'm so glad to see you. We could sure use you at the camp. More people arriving every day! We have fun, though. This cafe is a nice gathering place, and there is a farm not too far from the camp where we can go horseback riding." Letty chatted on as she walked with Helma and Bridget to the back of the cafe. They came to a little table where an overweight, older man in his late fifties and a young man with thick black hair and arresting blue eyes who looked like he was in his early twenties were seated. As they sat down, the young man stood up, shook Helma's hand, and casually

CHAPTER SIX: HELMA IN POLAND 1941–1943

said, "Hi, I'm Werner," he sat down and lit a cigarette. The older man bowed slightly as he stood and introduced himself as Otto. Letty was still chattering away, "Hey, you know, Otto, that Helma is from Austria too! How exciting that we all work together from all corners of the German Reich!"

Helma and Otto chatted politely about Vienna, but Helma was watching Werner and Bridget. He lit her cigarette and leaned in closely. They seemed to have an intimacy. Helma's thoughts were interrupted by Letty, "I hate to say it, but we probably need to get back to the camp. New arrivals are coming every evening! Such a mess. I can help get you settled, and I think it's then straight to work. So many coming every day, Helma, you wouldn't believe!"

Helma arrived at a spare but nice barracks. The camp was large and housed a diverse group of prisoners. Soviet army prisoners, Jews from everywhere in Europe, and the usual group of criminals and sex perverts. Helma learned she would be in the women's block of the camp and would be helping Bridget and Werner with selections of incoming prisoners. Bridget and Helma would be the lead guards for the women's block, responsible for roll calls twice per day and getting the women to their work assignments. There were a variety of work assignments. Letty oversaw the sorting warehouse, as well as the adjoining warehouse which produced uniforms for the army. Otto, the older Austrian guard, oversaw the garden.

Bridget was clearly the leader. She had a little makeshift office near the women's barracks. A couple of desks and chairs, and just outside the little structure was a sawhorse with a little padding and ropes.

That night, Bridget, Werner, and Helma were in the rail yard for the latest shipment of Jewish prisoners. It was much more chaotic than Helma was expecting, and she had to adjust to the stench. Werner let Helma know that the prisoners were transported in cattle cars for several days. When they disembarked, they were stunned and stumbled out of the rail cars with their bags and clinging together. They needed to be pushed and pulled along for the walk into the main camp.

Helma was in charge of the selection of the women. It was pretty easy: just pull out the single, young, healthy women and shove the rest over. She became annoyed with the cries and protests of these women. It didn't take long for her to get physical and administer a few beatings to get the women on their way to the barracks.

There was an especially unruly young woman protesting being separated from her mother. She made the mistake of yelling at Bridget. Later in the evening, after the new arrivals were settled in the barracks, the unruly young woman, now with a shaved head and in her prison dress, was dragged to Bridget's office by Werner. Bridget tied the woman to the sawhorse, pulled away the back of her dress, and beat her with a horse whip. Helma watched as red stripes rose on the woman's back and flecks of flesh flew off as Bridget's zeal increased and her face grew red and sweaty.

When she stopped, Bridget was breathing heavily and pacing around the woman. When she had calmed herself, she tenderly pulled the dress up on the woman's bloodied back and untied the woman. She helped the woman stand, gently cupped the woman's face in her hands, and said, "Now we are going to have no more problems, right, love? You will be at roll call, at your job and not argue. Are we alright?" She smiled as she handed the woman to Werner to drag back to the barracks.

Bridget exhaled and smiled at Helma. "Well, that's how I keep order around here. They call me 'Bloody Bridget' for this type of discipline, but I find that it settles things. We want to get the most work out of them as we can until we need to make room for the new ones." She offered Helma a cigarette, and they sat in the office. Helma had seen similar discipline administered at Ravensbruck, so it wasn't surprising.

As the weeks went by, Helma found herself settling into a routine. She was able to do the selections easily and took her cues from Bridget. She wasn't reluctant to use the whip and her own preferred method of control, getting the woman on the ground and kicking her. Much of the time, she was able to carry out her duties professionally, but sometimes, the noise, the tears, and the disarray of the prisoners pushed her to the edge. The women were typically most hysterical when they needed to be separated from their young children. The screaming, clinging, and begging often became too much. A severe beating of one of the mothers often caused the

CHAPTER SIX: HELMA IN POLAND 1941–1943

other mothers to comply.

On an afternoon horse ride with Bridget, Helma was able to vent her frustration. "I realize this separation and elimination of the children sounds harsh, but what would we do with the children of criminals who carry those genes or Jewish children who will just perpetuate the problem we are trying to solve? We have to think of the future of the Reich. These women's children will contribute nothing, are inferior, and it is part of that larger plan, you know?"

Bridget raised her eyebrows, "Wow. You're a true believer, huh? That's all a little above me. I think that these people come to this camp because they're lazy scum! It's also a good place to get a little ahead. Have you been to the warehouse to go through and get a few items? Some nice things to send home?"

Helma hadn't taken advantage of going through the warehouse where the prisoners' items were sorted. She didn't judge Bridget though, they worked such long hours and had to put up with so much hardship, that little extras to send home or to help get ahead financially seemed like it was an earned perk. Nice breaks at the nearby farm to ride horses or to go into town to the cafe were pleasant, but not enough to make up for having to spend every day with the lowest of the low in the Reich and to do the unpleasant work necessary to rid the world of Jews.

She had gotten to know Werner a little bit. She was surprised that Werner and Bridget had not been romantically involved. Theirs was more a brother and sister relationship and Bridget was very much the older sister. Werner was only twenty and very immature and lazy in Helma's estimation. Bridget was always prodding Werner to keep better order in the camp. Like Bridget, he was eager to maximize ways to get ahead. The camp commander had even reprimanded Werner for his frequent visits to the warehouse and his shakedowns of prisoners seeking favors. Werner's other claim to fame was his good looks. The female prisoners had even taken to calling him 'the angel of death,'—'angel' because of his looks, was the rumor that Helma had heard. The other striking thing about Werner was how unbothered he was by it all. He never lost his temper, or excessively abused prisoners, except to have fun at their expense, nor did he ever seem upset to escort prisoners to the gas chambers or to oversee the transport of the bodies to the crematorium. It was almost as if he was working the assembly line at a cannery.

For as much as Werner was unbothered, Otto was the polar opposite. Obese, looking much older than his fifty-five years, Otto was painfully slow and plodding. He interacted very little with the prisoners and paced around the garden, frequently smoking and stopping to sit on a bench. He seemed to have a soft spot for fellow Austrians and was greatly bothered when those young girls were imprisoned. He often contrasted the camp with the more heroic effort, in his mind, of the Great War. Helma sniffed at this assertion. If the Great War had been successful, we wouldn't be involved in this difficult effort now.

The camp was increasingly busy. Almost non-stop transports arrived, and the effort was exhausting, thought Helma. One warm spring night, a trainload of French prisoners arrived. Helma was already on edge. As the selection of the women was underway, she saw an old woman blatantly step out of her line. Helma just wanted to get through the night. She grabbed the old woman by the arm. The woman just stood there shaking and stuttering some nonsense about wanting to stay with her daughters. This stupid woman! Didn't they know that they didn't get to choose their line? That there wasn't time to baby them and listen to how they needed to stay with this family member or that? Didn't they know how many of them needed to be processed efficiently every day and night? Of course, they didn't, and that was why they were here because they thought of nothing but themselves and were an absolute drain on the Reich.

The old woman just stood there shaking and babbling about her daughters. Helma felt herself fill with a white, hot rage. She grabbed the woman and threw her to the ground. She kicked her several times, and as the woman lay quivering in a ball, Helma stomped on her head. The woman still spasmed, and Helma delivered the final blow with her boot.

This wasn't the first time Helma had administered justice in this way. She was becoming known around the camp for this practice. Like Bridget and

Werner, she had even earned a nickname among the prisoners; they called her the 'Stomping Mare.'

Chapter Seven: Hannah in the Camp
1943–1945

The first night in the camp, Hannah leaned in close to Rebecca and tried to snatch at least a couple of hours of sleep. The next morning, she saw Rebecca talking to other women in the barracks. When they had to assemble for roll call, Hannah didn't see the "Stomping Mare" that morning. She was pulled aside and assigned to the sorting area. Fortunately, it was indoors. She was to assist in sorting through the belongings of the transports. There were piles of suitcases, some with names written in chalk on the sides. A carefully managed and guarded group of prisoners went through them first. Hannah noticed how quickly the guards scooped up anything clearly of value and took it to a separate warehouse.

The guard at the sorting station was a dark-haired, nervous woman named Letty. On Hannah's first day, Letty scurried up to her.

"So, you're new today? A Jew? I will have you know in this section we work! I know that's against your nature, but you'll have to overcome it. If you work hard and don't cause any trouble, you won't have problems. But if you're lazy, or mouthy, or worst of all try to steal anything out of here, it will be big trouble. These items are property of the Reich, and if you pinch something hoping to trade it for food or whatnot, you will be turned over to Bridget for a serious beating, and then you will be put to death. I know a lot of you Jews have sticky fingers and love to trade, but you better fight that impulse. Do you understand?"

Hannah nodded, "Yes, I understand. I will be a hard worker."

CHAPTER SEVEN: HANNAH IN THE CAMP 1943–1945

Letty shook her head, "Well, good. I hope you can keep your word. We'll see. Come over here. See this pile of picture frames? You will be pulling pictures out of the frame and reassembling the frame. Separate the wood, metal, and silver frames. The photos go in the burn pile. And the frames are to be stacked here for transport to the warehouse."

Hannah nodded. She looked at the huge stack of framed photos. They were of varying sizes, but there were many small frames. There were photos of old people, families, newlywed couples, babies, and all kinds of people. Some in cultural dress, some in bathing suits by the shore. Hannah imagined the people hurriedly packing their suitcases and grabbing that one photo off the mantle or piano as they hustled out the door to some future they didn't know. She remembered how her father had sent trunks ahead to her grandmother's house and how they contained photos of her parents on their wedding day, of her father during the Great War, looking so young and so serious in his Austro-Hungarian Imperial uniform. Grandmother Hortense had taken them out and placed them in the room Hannah's parents had stayed in. Hannah was lost in these memories as she pulled photos out of frames and separated the frames by type into a large pile. She didn't notice Letty looming over her shoulder.

"Hey, lazy new Jew girl! You need to pick up the pace! You don't have to stare at the picture; just get it out of the frame!" Hannah's hand burned as Letty's thin leather stick hit her hand with a stinging *thwack*.

Hannah knew enough not to make a sound. She quit looking at the photos and quickly removed them from the frames and hurriedly sorted them.

After work, Hannah stood in line with the others for a tin cup of something that was supposedly soup. Rebecca pulled Hannah to the back of the soup line.

"Get back here. You will get better soup in the back of the line. Not the thin stuff off the top," Rebecca said as she pulled her to the back of the line. The "better soup" had what looked like potato peels and a few chunks of a turnip. Regardless, Hannah consumed it greedily.

Laying in the bunk together, Rebecca listened as Hannah talked about Letty and the many pictures that Hannah discarded and the big sorting room. Rebecca shared that her assignment was tending the garden, and she was hoping that she would be able to glean a little bit of extra food for them to eat or trade.

"I think it was a good first day. The guard at the garden is a disinterested old man named Otto. He warmed up to me when I said I was from Vienna and that I was a musician. He's an old duffer who likes traditional songs. I'm working out how much I can get away with, and I'm seeing how I can make a connection to the men's barracks and see if Father is there. He looked good for a man his age, and he had medical knowledge. Hopefully, he made it. I'm determined to find out."

Hannah laid back and marveled at Rebecca. She seemed not to let the nightmare of the camp depress her too much. She was already figuring out ways to ensure their survival. Hannah didn't know what Rebecca had said to Stella, the snake-like unofficial leader of their barracks, to earn them a coveted top bunk together not too far from the latrines.

As the days wore on, spring turned to summer. Hannah felt herself growing thinner and thinner. Her cheeks were sunken, and her menstrual cycle had stopped. In the first few weeks of camp life, Hannah hated not being able to clean herself, but now it made little difference. She was in a permanent state of filth, and it didn't matter to her. Rebecca did all she could to buoy Hannah's spirits, but it was hard given that all of Rebecca's ingenious efforts and food bribes turned up nothing on their father. No one by his name or description could be found in the men's barracks. Rebecca was careful and strategic in how she managed to get a little extra food from the garden to help gain information and to stay in Stella's good graces.

As the cold weather came that fall, Rebecca was able to get a little extra burlap fabric to sew on the insides of their clothing for at least a little extra warmth. She found extra strips of cloth to wrap around their feet.

One cold night, Rebecca wrapped her arms around Hannah in their bunk.

"You know monkey girl; we need to survive. These little things, small extra amounts of food, and the little bit of extra fabric will give us the advantage. It's a game of inches here."

Hannah rested her head on her sister's shoulder.

CHAPTER SEVEN: HANNAH IN THE CAMP 1943-1945

"Rebecca, where I work, I have access to so much valuable stuff. Maybe I could try to get something?"

"No, no, you stay safe. Leave it to me; I'm in a much better situation. Otto is much easier to get by than Letty. They aren't watching us in the garden as they are in the sorting warehouse. Also, the guards are looting that. They are protective of it. They call it 'shopping' they pick good articles of clothing or other things for themselves or ship them off to their families. These guards aren't educated, and they don't come from well-off families. They are poor or working-class people who believe the 'stab in the back' propaganda from Hitler. They are filled with resentment; that's why they can do what they are doing."

Hannah looked at Rebecca and wondered how she could stay so determined. The camp was such a miserable and grotesque place. There was a girl named Mina in the barracks who was very beautiful. Even with her shaved head, she was still striking. Bloody Bridget started coming at night and taking her out and then bringing her back in the early morning hours. The rumor was that Bloody Bridget was "selling" her to male camp guards. Even though she got extra rations and got to bathe a bit more, she was pitied by the other women in the barracks.

Rebecca just shook her head, "There is no bottom to this, Hannah. No end to the depravity."

Hannah kept her head down at the warehouse with Letty. She moved on from sorting small valuables to sorting through clothing that needed mending. Like Hannah's family, many people sewed jewels into their clothing. Those who did the initial sorting were on to this and tore open hems and seams. Some of the clothing pulled apart for hidden jewels was worthy of repair. Hannah proved adept at sewing seams and hems back in fur coats or expensive suits. Hannah lost herself in the task of sewing a ripped bright orange liner in a luxurious fur coat perfectly. The repaired coats and suits were then taken off to the warehouse. It boggled Hannah's mind to think that the Nazis were profiting handsomely on their mass murder scheme.

Rebecca continued to hope to find some news of their father. Hannah knew in the pit of her stomach that there wasn't much hope. At night, as they lay together in the barracks, they tried to have a little bit of an escape from camp life. When they were home, no one was allowed to speak of Rebecca's mother, their father's first wife. Hannah had only learned of it through eavesdropping and snatches of conversation she pieced together. Now that it was just the two of them in the camp, Rebecca opened up.

"I don't remember her really at all. I was two when she died. I have a vague memory of her. Father had a picture hidden in his desk he let me see. When I was about eighteen, we went to an off the beaten path gallery in Vienna. They had a couple of her paintings. They were abstract, vibrant, and joyful. Father said that was what she was like. A true rebel. He said they lived in an apartment with huge windows. He said that his only happiness during the war years was with her. She died rather suddenly of the flu during the Spanish Flu outbreak right after the war. I often think about those paintings Father showed me. When this is all over, I'm going back to Vienna to buy them. When the war is over, you and I will find a house or apartment with huge windows and bake cakes every Saturday."

Hannah laughed. It was the beginning of one of their favorite distractions, dreaming up different food scenarios. At least these diversions brought a little bit of peace to Hannah and helped her drift off to sleep, and that was the only other escape she had from the camp.

One evening in late October, Rebecca pulled Hannah aside in the barracks. "Something's up. I don't think it's good. There are more soldiers and guards around, and everyone is tense. I just saw some more trucks with more men, and they were unloading tons of shovels. I tried to get something out of Otto, but he doesn't seem to know anything. I have a little bit of extra food that I'm hiding that we can eat or trade. Hannah, just stick with me, follow what I do. I have a really bad feeling."

That night, Hannah couldn't sleep very well. The next day at the sorting warehouse, Letty seemed on edge, and they were suddenly hit with a ton of items flooding into the warehouse for secondary sorting. They worked fast and hard. It was late at night when Hannah made it back to the barracks where Rebecca was waiting.

CHAPTER SEVEN: HANNAH IN THE CAMP 1943-1945

"It's bad, Hannah. The men spent the whole day digging these zig-zag trenches all around the camp. They were screaming at the men and beating them."

"What do you think it means?'

Rebecca tightened her jaw and said, "Honestly, I think they are digging their own graves. I heard rumors of uprisings at another camp during the summer, and I've heard rumors that they are clearing Lublin of all the Jews there."

Hannah froze in place. The gassed bodies of transports were dragged to the ovens every day, and now they were going to do more killing?

Rebecca and Hannah climbed into their bunk. Rebecca pulled Hannah close, stroked her shaved head, and hummed a song until Hannah fell asleep.

* * *

Before dawn, guards and dogs were in the barracks. Terrified, they assembled for an early roll call. Hannah was shivering in place when she glanced over and saw the Stomping Mare. She was looking especially angry as she paced through the line of women. She stopped by Rebecca. She pointed the handle of her whip in Rebecca's face.

"You think you're really smart. I know you are the planner and the schemer of this barracks. But your time is up! It all ends today. Time to clean up the Jew vermin. I will start with you."

The Stomping Mare jerked Rebecca's arm. Before she could stop to think, Hannah heard herself yelling, "No! Stop!"

Hannah lunged towards Rebecca and the Stomping Mare. The Stomping Mare landed a punch squarely in Hannah's face. She felt her ears ringing and felt like she did when she stayed too long underwater at the pool. She felt herself stagger and hit the ground. She could see Rebecca's feet as she fought with the Stomping Mare. Rebecca then hit the ground. In her mind, Hannah was willing herself to get up, but she couldn't move. She saw the Stomping Mare's boots walk in front of her face.

Then she saw it. The boot blow on Rebecca's head. She saw Rebecca's face convulse, and Hannah started to crawl over to her. She inched through the mud as The Stomping Mare paced around again as Hannah slowly dragged herself across the mud. She was inching closer to Rebecca when the next blow landed, cracking open Rebecca's skull and spattering Hannah with her blood. Hannah crawled closer. She thought if she could only stop the bleeding, and then she felt herself being jerked up from the ground.

Her head bobbing, she expected to turn to see the Stomping Mare, but instead, it was Letty.

"Oh, Helma, I need this one! We are overwhelmed at the warehouse, and I can't wait for the Polish workers and then to train them! It's too much work!"

Hannah heard the Stomping Mare answer, "She's a Jew, and we're getting rid of all of them today."

"I know, I know, but I need the help now. I can't wait until they sort out the Polish women for workers. I need someone today!"

The Stomping Mare exhaled and looked annoyed.

"Okay, Letty. We have so much to do today I can't stand here and argue with you. Take her. Get out of our way!"

Blood was still running out of her nose and down her chest as Letty angrily dragged Hannah into the warehouse. She threw a cold glass of water into Hannah's face.

"Get to work! You have no idea the trouble you have caused me! Look at all we need to do!"

Hannah knew her survival now depended on working, so she set about sorting through knickknacks like candlesticks, frames, and figurines quickly sorting them. As she sorted, she even entertained a fantasy that Rebecca would still be alive at the end of the day.

As the morning wore on, the camp loudspeakers blared marching band music. It was intended to drown out the screams and gunfire that lasted all day and well into the evening. Hannah's head throbbed as she felt her nose swell and the blood cake and dry on her face and clothes. As it grew dark, the blaring music, screams, and gunfire did not subside. She saw Letty approaching, dragging alongside her what looked like a new prisoner. A

CHAPTER SEVEN: HANNAH IN THE CAMP 1943–1945

small girl, probably Hannah's age. Newly shaved and in new prison garb.

"I've got you a helper. Another Jew. We're keeping this one around because she can speak German and Polish. She can help us understand what the stupid Poles are saying since this place is going to be filled with Polish criminals. Tonight, she's helping you."

The girl looked angrily at Letty as Letty shoved a pile of knickknacks for sorting in front of her.

They worked silently side by side, deep into the night. Finally, Letty sent them back to the barracks. Hannah hurried as fast as she could to see if Rebecca was there. She ran into the barracks, and it was full of new unfamiliar women. She saw no one except for Bloody Bridget's girl, Mina, sitting and staring at the ground. Hannah ran to her.

"Where is everyone? Have you seen my sister?"

She slowly looked up. Her eyes were glistening with tears.

"Everyone's gone. They took them all out to the trenches and shot them all. Everyone in our barracks. They left your sister's body in the mud, and then the Stomping Mare had two prisoners drag her to a trench and throw her in. They had them all strip naked and then shot them and let them drop into the trenches." Tears flowed down Mina's beautiful cheeks as she clutched her arms around her waist in a protective hug.

Hannah nodded and walked away. The barracks was full of women speaking Polish. Out of the corner of her eye, she saw the girl from the sorting warehouse.

"What do you know about today?" Hannah implored, hoping the story wasn't true.

"What she says is right. It was a mass killing day. I was in Lublin for the round-up. They kept me because I spoke German and Polish, so I translated. They're getting rid of all the Jews and the Poles they think are trouble."

The girl gently took Hannah's arm and sat her on a nearby bunk. She sat silently with her for a while. She was small, and Hannah thought she was maybe fourteen or fifteen years old, yet she seemed strong and almost defiant.

"My name is Miriam. I lost my family, too. I'm very sorry about your sister. I know about that woman, the Stomping Mare. I've been translating at the camp for a few days. I was at a selection of young mothers and their children. All the children were toddlers. The Stomping Mare was trying to get the mothers to load their babies on a truck. It started off fine at first, but then the mothers were clinging to their babies and not letting them go. They were in a panic. Then, the Stomping Mare became enraged. One woman was crying and holding her baby, and the Stomping Mare pulled the baby away from the mother, and the baby started toddling away, could barely walk, but was wobbly and walking away quickly, and the Stomping Mare pulled her pistol out, and…" she paused and steadied herself to continue.

"She shot the baby in the head. It was the most horrific thing. There was a split second of silence as what happened just registered in our minds, and then the mothers were crying. The babies were crying as they put those babies in that truck. And that woman, the Stomping Mare, just looked angry, and then they did the selection with these weeping mothers. Most of them went to the gas chamber or the trench to be shot. So many people died today." Miriam gripped her hands in her lap and started to shake.

Hannah looked at Miriam and watched her stare into space, her face devoid of emotion.

Most of the women were settling into sleep. Hannah looked for Rebecca's hiding place. There were a few pieces of bread and an apple. She shared it with Miriam, and they fell fast asleep just before dawn.

Miriam was put to work alongside Hannah in the sorting warehouse along with a few new Polish prisoners. Hannah couldn't bring herself to cry about Rebecca. In her mind, she developed a fantasy where Rebecca was still alive and had somehow escaped, so Hannah tricked herself into doing all she could do to survive to be reunited with Rebecca after the war. She pushed aside the reality of the final blow of the Stomping Mare's boot to Rebecca's skull, which was most certainly deadly. It was too much to accept.

Every day at the warehouse, Hannah made sure to work quickly and efficiently. Miriam worked alongside her except those times she was pulled out to translate. Miriam had a fierceness about her that not even the camp could break. Small and intense, she radiated energy. Over time, Hannah

CHAPTER SEVEN: HANNAH IN THE CAMP 1943-1945

found herself growing closer to Miriam.

The cold in the barracks in December was excruciating. All the women were so thin that their prison dresses hung off them, so they had plenty of room to wrap their blankets around their bodies for extra warmth during the day while they worked. This was apparently how Mina was able to disguise a pregnancy.

She started moaning late one night. Several of the prisoners gathered around her. Miriam translated Mina's German to Polish to a Polish prisoner who was a nurse. With their meager resources, the prisoners tried to comfort and help her.

Her screams of pain were loud enough to draw the attention of the guard they called the "Angel of Death." Wearing an expression of consistent boredom, the Angel of Death was a truly handsome young man in his early twenties. He had sensuous lips, thick black hair, and light blue eyes. That was the "angel" part. The "of death" part was his dispassionate role in selections and his complete nonchalance in the daily atmosphere of the camp.

As he came closer to the bunk and saw the Polish nurse cutting the umbilical cord, he said, "Jesus Christ! What the hell is going on here!"

Miriam was explaining to him in German. Hannah leaned in to hear snatches of the conversation. Miriam was clearly angry.

"Do you know what your friend Bloody Bridget had her up to? What the hell would you expect would be the consequence? She gets extra rations, so she still gets her period. You need to find out which guard is paying Bloody Bridget to fuck her and let him know he has a baby."

Hannah felt her chest tighten as she waited for the Angel of Death to strike her, or worse, shoot her on the spot.

He then did something completely unexpected. He gently scooped up the infant while making cooing sounds and wrapped the baby in his coat. As everyone stood staring in silence, he took the baby out of the barracks.

Mina was pale and unconscious. Blood was everywhere. The Polish nurse looked frantic. Hannah knew it was almost time for roll call. The Polish nurse held the wrist of the girl, and then slowly placed her hand on the girl's chest. She whispered a prayer and crossed herself.

Miriam worked her magic to get out of work at the warehouse that morning and was on a mission to find out what happened to the baby. That afternoon, Hannah watched as Miriam slumped dejectedly into place beside Hannah. She exhaled and then told Hannah the story.

"The Angel of Death took him, it was a baby boy, to the camp commandant. He asked what he should do with this baby. And the camp commandant said to take the baby to the crematorium. And even the Angel of Death asked for clarification on this, and the commandant made it clear he was to throw that living baby into the fire, and the Angel of Death did it. He went ahead and did it."

Hannah felt a wave of nausea overcome her. "Miriam, no, just don't tell me anymore. I'm going to be sick. I can't think about this stuff, or I'm not going to make it."

Miriam nodded and got to work helping to sort the mountain of items at the warehouse.

The days of winter dragged on. Without Rebecca's extra rations, Hannah grew thinner than she ever dreamed a person could be. She watched as Miriam grew thinner, but nothing seemed to dim her intensity. It frightened Hannah to think Miriam could meet the same fate as Rebecca. It was a wonderful distraction to hear Miriam's sometimes profanity-laced descriptions of the guards, especially her mockery of Letty.

"They all have these scary nicknames here, the guards, except Letty. She's such a fucking idiot. What would her name be? 'The headless chicken?' Or the 'inbred nervous poodle?'"

When spring came, the sorting warehouse gained a new guard, Otto, the old man that Rebecca had worked under in the garden. He came over to Hannah and Miriam in their sorting area.

"Hello, I hear you girls are from Austria? I am also."

Hannah nervously looked down and kept sorting. She actually preferred the blatant hostility of Letty and the Stomping Mare to this friendliness. She didn't know if she would make a misstep and end up being beaten on Bloody Bridget's sawhorse. At least with the others, she knew where she stood. Miriam, though, turned and started chatting with Otto.

CHAPTER SEVEN: HANNAH IN THE CAMP 1943-1945

"Yes, I'm originally from Poland, but moved to Vienna when I was a little girl."

Otto laughed and said, "Well, you're a little girl now. I understand you are doing a great service for us by using your Polish and German language skills; what a clever girl you are."

"Yes, well, whatever it takes not to get gassed to death and burned up in an oven. I'm pretty lucky to be clever, or I would be a pile of ash right now."

Hannah felt herself stiffen as she readied for a potential outburst from Otto. All the gossip aside of him as a doddering old fool, he was one of them and potentially capable of shooting them on the spot.

Instead, Otto sighed and drew close to the girls and said in a whispered conspiratorial tone, "Yes, it's an ugly business. I'm not in favor of it. As much as I agree with the Fuhrer's dream of a strong united Germanic peoples, he has taken things a bit too far. Obviously, there are a number of bad Jews out there, but they can be taken care of or allowed to immigrate to America—they seem to like them there, but this wholesale killing, it's a bad business."

Hannah listened to Otto talk about his beloved Austria with Miriam. Then he turned his attention to Hannah.

"You've been quiet. Tell me where you are from?"

"I'm from Vienna."

"Ah, wonderful. I loved it there. Visited many times. You know one of our guards, she is also from Vienna. She is very strict, but a true believer in the Reich."

Hannah felt herself stiffen. She knew he was referring to the Stomping Mare. In addition to being known for her cruelty, she was also known in the camp for not 'shopping' the warehouse for items for herself or to ship home, and for her unalloyed adoration for Hitler and his policies. It made Hannah sick to think that the Stomping Mare was from her hometown. As she was lost in these thoughts, Otto pressed her for more information.

"So, tell me, young lady, where about in Vienna? Tell me about your family."

Hannah didn't stop her work at the sorting table, before clearing her throat to answer, "I lived in the city of Vienna, in Dobling, my father was a doctor and professor. He served as a doctor in the Great War."

Otto's face brightened, "Oh! I served in the Great War, too. It was a difficult time, but different than this. I can't tell you how nice it is to chat with you both. Keep up your good work."

With that, he lumbered away across the warehouse. Hannah looked over to Miriam, who rolled her eyes in disgust, "Oh, he's not for the 'wholesale' murdering, just a few murders! How noble!"

Hannah shot back, "At least that's something. I mean, at least he might be of some help. Like you said, whatever it takes not to be gassed or shot in this hell hole."

Miriam shook her head, "Yes, Hannah, you're right. Look at you, a doctor and professor's daughter from Dobling, fancy! You probably would have hated my family, poor, uneducated Polish Jews."

Hannah didn't say it, but Miriam would be exactly the type of person her mother would have discouraged her from associating with and the 'type' of Jew her mother would have looked down upon. None of that mattered now, of course, and Hannah found herself growing attached to Miriam.

As the spring turned to summer, Hannah again sensed something was up. Nervous Letty was even more nervous. Transports and the volume of items at the warehouse began slowing down.

Then, the rumors started flying through the camp. The Soviet army was getting closer. At the warehouse, Hannah and a few other prisoners were sewing seams back into expensive fur coats. Letty came over to the group and started chatting about how they were all "working together." She then handed one of the prisoners, known for her sewing skills, a plain linen handkerchief and asked her to embroider it as a "memento of their time working together." The puzzled woman took the handkerchief and later returned it with some floral embroidery.

On a bright July day after roll call, the guards and the dogs were hurrying the prisoners back on cattle cars. They were being evacuated to the west. It was true, the Soviet army was coming, even faster than the guards had imagined. Miriam and Hannah sat in a cramped, open cattle car for several

CHAPTER SEVEN: HANNAH IN THE CAMP 1943–1945

days with no food or water. When they arrived at the new camp in Germany, there was another selection. Fortunately, Hannah and Miriam were chosen to work in the camp kitchen. A few days later, they saw Otto.

"Ah, it is good to see you girls made it. It is so distressing that the Russians have somehow made their way into Poland. Shocking, but our army will soon push them back."

Over the months, there was less and less food, and the pace of murder and death in the camp became more frantic. Typhus tore through the camp, and as fall turned to winter, Hannah and Miriam fell ill. The "infirmary" didn't offer much in the way of medical care for the inmates, but that is where Hannah and Miriam lay side by side in delirious, fevered states. Otto came by and gave them a little water and a little stale bread. One day, Otto appeared to them in civilian clothes.

"My dear Austrian girls, it looks like the end. I'm leaving the camp. Praise be to the Lord; it's the British and Americans who are coming, not the demonic Russians."

He gave them a little bread and clean water before leaving. Miriam looked to be getting stronger, but Hannah felt herself unable to move. Miriam held her head and made her sip a little water. A few days later, the remaining guards walked into the infirmary and began shooting every patient in their bed. Miriam quickly rolled out of her bed and pulled Hannah off her bed. They squeezed behind a green metal medicine chest. When the gunshots ceased and they heard footsteps leaving the building, Miriam helped Hannah into an empty bed and wrapped her in a blanket.

"Hannah, I'm going to see what's going on. I will be back for you."

Hannah tried to speak to tell her not to go, but she couldn't. The energy it took to hide took all of Hannah's strength. She felt herself losing consciousness as Miriam left the room.

Chapter Eight: Helma 1943–1947

It was a perfect early fall evening at the camp. Helma thought it might be a good time to see if Bridget wanted to go for a horseback ride at the farm or take a walk around town to the guards' favorite cafe. But first was the rather unusual all-camp meeting called by the commandant and the unfamiliar SS soldiers who had appeared at the camp. The SS stood at the back of the room. Helma sat with the other women as the meeting came to order.

Helma was shocked to learn about inmate rebellions at nearby camps and uprisings in Jewish ghettos. She glanced over at Letty, who was shaking her head. It was explained that the effort to eliminate the undesirable elements from society needed to be accelerated. It wouldn't be pleasant, but a massive effort needed to be undertaken. The operation was called "Harvest Festival," and the burden of the hard work would fall on their camp to take on even a higher volume of Jews and other undesirables.

After the meeting, Letty clutched Helma's arm.

"I can't believe it! How are we expected to do this work! I hardly have any assistance at the warehouse and more and more items will be coming in. This is so unfair. We are so overburdened here to get rid of all of those Jews and criminals from all over! We work non-stop."

"Listen, it is our service to the Fatherland. This is a crisis. We need to eliminate the vermin even faster. It is, no doubt, hard work. If we don't do our work to eliminate this element, then who knows what they will do. We're cleaning up a mess hundreds of years in the making with the Jews, defective people, cripples, imbeciles, perverted people just running loose in

CHAPTER EIGHT: HELMA 1943-1947

society."

In late October, roundups began, and more and more transports arrived. Finally, at the beginning of November, the work would begin in earnest. Prisoners were digging deep trenches in zig-zag formations around the camp. Helma and the other guards put in exceptionally long days as the transports came in, and the priority shifted to eliminating the Jews.

Helma had her eye on a couple of prisoners she was looking forward to finally getting rid of, and in Helma's mind, things had become a bit lax, with Bridget's tolerance of bribes and her own money-making schemes, and Werner was no better. As for Otto, he was far too sentimental about these Jews, especially the younger girls. One barracks, in particular, had two prisoners who had drawn her ire. One was an Austrian Jew named Rebecca. Helma knew that this prisoner had somehow snuck gemstones into the camp and managed to bribe Bridget into getting Rebecca's little sister a cushy job in the warehouse with Letty. Helma suspected the little sister was up to no good as well, but Letty seemed to think she was fine. Otto was also too dense to see through this prisoner's manipulations. Helma was pretty sure that this prisoner was stealing from the garden and passing her stolen food on to another scheming Jew prisoner, Stella, who was smart, ruthless, and manipulative, as Helma thought so many of that race were.

It was decided they would play dance music from the loudspeakers in the camp that day, to deter any issues or curious onlookers from the nearby town. It was an early morning, and they had roll call as usual. Helma couldn't help but take the opportunity to let Rebecca know her time was up. It was something Helma looked forward to, letting this sneaky Jew know that she wasn't going to get away with it. Helma felt the same sense of exhilaration that day as she had back in 1938, when the Nazis took over Austria. This day was going to be a historic day.

Helma shoved the handle of her whip into the prisoner Rebecca's face. Helma felt rage boiling in her as that prisoner stared ahead stony-faced. Then, the little sister was screaming and lunging at Helma. A solid punch knocked her down, and Helma focused her energy on Rebecca. No prisoner had put up such a fight, but finally, Helma got her on the ground and delivered a blow to her head with her jackboots. The prisoner shuddered and convulsed. As had become her habit, and in keeping with her nickname as the Stomping Mare, Helma paced around the shuddering body. She was always fascinated to watch a body respond to head trauma. She was taking one final turn around the body when she saw the little sister pathetically inching toward Rebecca in the mud. She waited until the little sister got a bit closer and then thrust her boot down with all the energy she could muster. Helma felt a rush of ecstatic joy overcome her when the skull cracked, and blood and brain matter sprayed out from the prisoner's head. She was just catching her breath and marveling at her own strength when Letty appeared and hauled up the shaking body of the little sister.

She didn't have time to listen to Letty's complaints on this day; she just let her take the little sister away to the warehouse. She had to get busy getting the rest of the prisoners to the trenches or gas chamber for elimination. The realization of what was happening dawned on them. Some of them were quiet and resigned, some cried and begged, and some lashed out screaming. Helma used her whip often that day and even had to pull out her sidearm to shoot a few, especially unruly prisoners. The loud dance music was no match for the screams and non-stop gunfire over sixteen hours. The majority of prisoners were eliminated that day, and a few new ones were brought in from town to continue to work.

At the end of the day, Helma had a prisoner clean her boots, which were completely caked with blood, flesh, and mud. Her uniform was also spattered after her days' work. Late that night, the guards were getting drunk, passing out, and generally out of control. Helma felt mild contempt for them. Why were they so weak? Why did they need to do this after a hard day's work for the Fatherland?

A few days later, they received the grateful congratulations of not only the officers but the leaders of the Reich. Operation Harvest Festival was a great leap forward in the Final Solution. Estimates were that over 18,000 Jews and prisoners were eliminated on that day at their camp.

Helma felt pride at being a part of something so historic. Though the work was difficult, it was worth it. Bridget and Werner just laughed at this

CHAPTER EIGHT: HELMA 1943–1947

patriotic notion, and Otto was visibly upset. His old-fashioned ideas seemed ridiculous to Helma.

Helma's joy was short-lived. She received a telegram from her father in Vienna, which delivered a double blow. Her beloved brother Hans was killed in action, and her mother succumbed to pneumonia. She was headed back to Vienna for a very sad Christmas.

When she arrived, she was shocked to see how much her father had aged. Her brother's death had been a huge blow. Helma was utterly astonished when he teared up talking about her mother. Never in her life had she witnessed a tender moment between them. Klara had pulled out her parents' wedding photo. Helma looked at it in amazement. Her father looked exactly like Klaus. Her mother looked young, beautiful, and vibrant. There was life in her eyes. Klara placed the photo on the mantel next to the photo of Hans in uniform, which had a black ribbon tied around the corner of the frame.

Little Greta was too small to understand what was happening. It pained Helma that Hans wouldn't be here for the little girl.

After family and friends had dispersed, Helma and her father sat alone at the dining table. He stared into a cup of cold tea.

"You know, Helma, I'm glad that Hans gave his life for this cause. It is so sad for Klara and Greta, but he was doing something great. I'm almost jealous, wishing that I were a younger man and could take part."

He looked up and gave Helma a weak smile, "You don't have to worry about me. Klara and Greta are moving in here, and they will take care of me, and I will take care of them. You keep doing your important work. I know it must be hard, but the vision of the Fuhrer is the right one. Even though it is difficult, these enemies within must be eliminated. In a way, they are more dangerous than the Soviet Army."

He got up and took his teacup into the kitchen. To Helma he looked decades older than he did just three short years ago.

Helma stayed with her family through the New Year. 1944 gave Helma pause, but she quickly pushed aside any negative thoughts. Setbacks would happen, but the Fuhrer had an inspired vision that had brought them so much glory in such a short time that, surely, he would lead them through these dark moments. She knew her father was right and that she had important work to do.

Klara and Greta had softened Helma's heart. Watching them together made her think of her hope of having her own family someday, and having a life of domesticity, when she could cook meals, keep a house clean, return to her knitting and a quiet life.

At the end of January, she was ready to get back to work. Helma felt herself stiffen at Klara's public display of affection, giving Helma a warm and extended hug before she boarded a train. She said her goodbyes to her father, Klara and little Greta.

Back at work, the unsettling news kept coming. The Soviet army was on the move, pushing back the German army and steadily heading west. That spring, Helma received notice that she was being re-assigned to Ravensbruck. She said her goodbyes, and Letty was especially shook up by her departure.

"Oh Helma, I don't know what we will do without you. You're so levelheaded. You're lucky to be headed back to Germany. I'm getting a little worried here. What if the Army isn't able to hold off the Reds? That would be horrible!"

"Letty, don't think that way. Their army is full of sub-human brutes and peasants. And the other element is a bunch of Jew Communists. They might have some temporary success, but they are really no match for our army."

Letty gave Helma a few items from the warehouse that Helma reluctantly accepted. One was a nice diamond bracelet, and a few sweaters that Helma knew would be very flattering on her. Helma felt a little drained and tired on the train to Ravensbruck. Once she arrived, she was reunited with Irma and the other guards she knew from her training a few years earlier. One evening a few weeks after her arrival Helma and Irma were at dinner, Irma said, "Helma, you don't look very good. You should go to the infirmary and get checked out. Don't report for work tomorrow."

Irma was right. Helma was very sick. She was hospitalized immediately. She had pneumonia. Her condition became worse and worse over the weeks. She was in and out of consciousness. It became so bad that her father and

CHAPTER EIGHT: HELMA 1943-1947

Klara came from Vienna. Through the fog, she could hear her father's voice.

"It's so unfair, this illness took her mother, and now is taking her. I'm so shocked, she was so strong. It was probably being around those dirty, disease-ridden prisoners that brought her to this!"

She heard Klara's voice gently chastising, "Father, please be quiet. We just have to pray and hope she gets better. She's in a good hospital now."

Helma lost track of time. She couldn't remember when her father and Klara came and went. She was given last rites by an elderly priest.

Miraculously, she didn't die. She started to recover. The doctors and nurses marveled at the turn her health took. She was moved to a different wing of the hospital for a slow recovery. It was mid-August when Letty arrived for a visit.

"Helma! You're so thin! You don't look like yourself at all, but, silly me, that doesn't matter! All that matters is that you're getting well. I'm so thankful to see you. We had to flee from our camp in Poland in July. Unbelievably, the Red Army was getting so close we had to just abandon the camp. We didn't have time to dismantle it, and we had to send some of the prisoners west. It was so crazy. I'm really concerned that prisoners might be saying things, about you know, how things were in the camp. I'm just very concerned."

Helma tightened her jaw. It made her so angry how many Germans were wavering now that the going was getting tough. How dare they! Fair weather patriots!

"Letty, there is no need for concern. Things will turn around soon. I cannot believe the disloyalty, the attempt on the Fuhrer's life, which was horrible. Now that the traitorous element is gone, things will improve. You'll see."

Letty shook her head, "I hope you're right. I just don't know. The British and Americans are making progress in the west, and the Reds in the east, I can't help the feeling that we are caught in a tightening vise grip! I'm worried!"

Helma just shook her head and feigned tiredness to get Letty to leave. Helma would spend a few more months in the hospital, but never regained the strength or weight she had before her illness. She was reassigned to desk work connected with Belsen camp due to her compromised health. To make matters even worse, Helma found out her brother Klaus was now "Missing in Action" in the east. Helma tried not to let her failing health, the bad news about her brother, and the war wear her down as she worked her desk job.

Letty had somehow been relieved of her duties and was engaged to an injured soldier who had served on the Eastern Front. Helma attended their sad engagement party that January. An unspoken feeling of doom hung over all of Germany. Winter victories against the Allies in the West only gave them an anemic boost of the old patriotism of just a few years before. Letty and her pale, one-legged fiancé offered a meager assortment of hors d'oeuvres and just one bottle of cheap wine as everyone pretended to be joyous.

Typhus was killing prisoners, and the advance of the Soviet Army made it clear that they would need to eliminate those prisoners who weren't killed by disease and decide what their "exit plan" should be. Prisoners were sent on deadly forced marches. Helma knew the Soviet Army was getting closer and closer. Rumors were rampant about the Red Army cutting a path of terror through Germany, hanging camp guards, and regularly raping women.

Helma felt fear for the first time since she was assaulted as a teen by the boys in the alley. She would rather face the Allies than the Soviets. She decided to abandon her post and head home to Vienna. She gathered her civilian clothes and managed to trade the diamond bracelet from Letty to get on a train bound for Vienna. She got off the train late at night. The city had just fallen to the Allies days before her arrival. She walked several miles to her family home. She banged on the locked door.

Klara opened the door.

"Thank God you have come! I'm sorry you are late for the funeral. It wasn't much because of the war, and you know, how he died. But it was all we could do given the circumstances. I'm so glad word reached you, and you were able to come home, Helma."

"What are you talking about? What funeral?"

CHAPTER EIGHT: HELMA 1943–1947

"I thought you came home because I sent the telegram, but communication is so unreliable, and I thought you got it, and that's why you're home."

"Klara, quit being a babbling idiot and tell me who died? What funeral? What are you on about?"

"I'm so sorry, Helma, it was your father. He, um, died. Well, it was suicide. He heard about Hitler's suicide, and he killed himself. Shot himself in the head in the bathroom. I found him. It was unbelievably awful. I'm glad I was able to keep Greta away from the bathroom."

Maybe because she hadn't eaten anything for a while, or maybe out of shock, Helma felt her head swirling as she stared down at Klara. Then it happened. Her knees gave out, and she felt herself crumple to the floor and black out.

She awoke to Klara applying a damp cloth to her head as she lay on the sofa. Greta, now four years old, stared at Helma blankly. Her cheeks were sunken, and her legs were skinny in her short nightdress. Helma noticed she was very clean though, and Klara had taken care to braid her hair.

"Helma, I know it's a shock. The British are occupying here. They seem decent enough, but food is very scarce. I've had to sell some things."

Klara gestured around the room. Leather chairs and a prized antique family clock were gone. Helma sighed. She was disappointed in her father. She was disappointed in Hitler. Both, at one time, were her great heroes, her hope, and now it was so disappointing. It was supposed to be a new world, but now what?

Helma spent a few weeks resting. Going into the bathroom was unsettling. The white tiles beside the bathtub were broken from the bullet from her father's gun, and as much as Klara tried, she couldn't get the blood out of the grout around the hexagonal floor tiles.

Klara had learned a little bit of English and now was working at a restaurant serving the new occupying army of British soldiers. Klara had English language records she would play on the gramophone to continue to practice. Helma kept an eye on Greta while Klara worked. She became fond of her little niece, even though the child was very quiet and timid. Klara found some children's books and Helma started to teach Greta to read.

Helma also regularly checked with the Red Cross to try to determine the fate of her brother Klaus, who had been taken prisoner by the Russian Army in late 1943.

Over the course of the next year, the food Klara was able to sneak out of the restaurant kept them alive. Food was scarce, and the future seemed uncertain. Helma was content to help Klara with Greta and take care of the house. Klara occasionally brought home a British soldier late at night. They typically didn't stay long, but they usually had food, chocolate, or something of value that they gave Klara in exchange for her affections.

In a different time, and not too long ago, Helma would have been outraged at such behavior from her brother's widow. But now, she knew it was about survival for them all, and she took care to protect Greta from exposure to her mother's late-night visitors.

Shockingly, a Jewish woman returned to their neighborhood. She had a tattoo on her forearm, so Helma knew she had been through the camps. Her whole immediate family and extended family had perished. She stubbornly took up her residence in her old neighborhood, living in a shabby apartment not too far from what used to be her family home, which was now occupied by Austrians who had been loyal to the Nazis.

"The nerve of that woman! Isn't it clear that she is not wanted here? They're like cockroaches, these Jews, so hard to kill them all. It's disgusting!"

Klara rolled her eyes and looked up from her newspaper.

"Calm down, you're all red-faced and in a rage just like your father. It's over. None of that racial purity stuff matters anymore. Quit pacing and yelling, you'll frighten Greta."

"I thought all of the remaining scum was on a boat to Palestine to build their Jew country! They should get the hell out of Austria!"

It wasn't too long after her tirade that she found herself in line behind her Jewish neighbor at the post office. Helma felt the rage building inside of her. She shifted on her feet and folded her arms. It made her itch for her old uniform, whip and jackboots.

As the woman finished her business at the window, she turned and was walking past Helma. Without thinking Helma grabbed the woman's arm.

CHAPTER EIGHT: HELMA 1943–1947

"It's a shame we didn't have time to get rid of you all!" Helma hissed at the woman under her breath.

The woman jerked her arm away and narrowed her eyes and glared at Helma.

"You're one of the Braun family. Drunken wife-beater father and a bunch of Nazis! He used to brag about his Nazi sons and even his ugly Nazi daughter. I know who you are!"

It was only a few weeks after the post office incident when two British officers were at the door of Helma's house. One of them spoke in broken German, "Are you Helma Braun? Were you a guard at Ravensbruck?"

Helma whispered, "Yes, I'm Helma Braun."

She felt the other officer grab her arm and place her in handcuffs. Greta was cowering behind the sofa weeping, and Klara was yelling, "What should I do? What should I do?"

The officers marched her out to a truck and lifted her into it. She stared out of the back of the truck as Klara stood in the street in front of her house.

Chapter Nine: Hannah 1945–1947

Hannah could sense the silence. She was in the corner in a cot of what used to be the infirmary. Every day, Miriam would come to see if she was still alive. She gave her a sip or two of water.

Miriam was shaking her. "Hannah, Hannah, can you hear me?"

She couldn't answer. Two other women were with Miriam, and they had a cart.

"Forget it Miriam, she's practically dead."

"No, she's not. Let's put her in the cart."

Hannah felt Miriam and the other women lift her into the cart. They wrapped her in the dirty blanket she had been laying on.

Miriam pushed the cart in the dark. She was part of a long stream of refugees from the camp. They were all headed to the displaced persons' camp.

The cart shook and rattled over the road. Hannah awoke one night when they had stopped. She opened her eyes to see the clear sky above her. She managed to lean over the side of the cart and saw Miriam sleeping along the side of the road with dozens of others. She didn't know how long they had been on the road.

As she looked up to the sky, she realized the war was over. They had left the camp. She felt dizzy again after turning on her side and leaning against the rough sacks on the cart with her.

Hannah drifted in and out of consciousness for several days. Occasionally, her eyes would open as Miriam lifted her head and gave her a few sips of water. On one of the days, Miriam held up a little square of chocolate to

CHAPTER NINE: HANNAH 1945-1947

her mouth. Hannah could hardly believe it. The last time she had chocolate was at her grandmother's house in France.

Hannah heard unfamiliar voices around her. Finally, she heard Miriam's familiar voice, "Hannah Goldberg. She's from France by way of Austria. I think her family is dead."

She heard a woman's voice, and she was speaking accented German. She pressed her thumb against Hannah's eyelid and lifted it. All Hannah saw was a blurry face.

The woman sighed heavily, "Ugh, I don't know. We will get her cleaned up and hydrated, but I have to say your friend doesn't look good."

Miriam's voice was pleading, "Please help her. She has survived all this time. We walked to this camp with her, and she lived through that, only with a little water and just a square of chocolate when we arrived."

The woman replied, "We will do all we can. This is a good displaced persons camp we have medicines and supplies."

Hannah felt herself breathe a sigh of relief. She struggled to open her eyes and sat up slightly. The woman in the white nurse's uniform came closer, "Well, well, you may have a little life in you yet. I'm going to get you cleaned up and deloused. That will make you feel better, huh?"

Hannah struggled to nod her head in affirmation.

The nurse gently took her arm. "I'm Helen, by the way. I speak great German, but I'm Canadian. My parents came from Germany to Canada way back after the last big war. I'm here taking care of many of the people from the camps. Never have I seen anything like this."

Hannah wanted to speak and thank this Canadian nurse. These were the first gentle and caring words she had heard in such a long time.

Two men came with a stretcher as Helen and Miriam lifted Hannah out of the cart. One of the men said, "Jesus Christ! Is she still alive?"

Miriam nearly shouted, "Yes! Why don't you shut your trap and help?"

"Okay, sorry, I've seen a lot of the camp people. She's by far the thinnest and the sickest." Helen chimed in, "She's got a bit of life in her yet, right, Hannah?"

Hannah managed a smile and a nod.

While she was being washed, Hannah looked at her body. She hadn't thought about how she looked in so long. It didn't seem to matter. But, with the stretcher barer's comment, she looked down her torso and saw her ribs and hip bones protruding. Her skin was a waxy white. She felt her head. She was nearly bald except for a few scraggly patches of hair. The severe malnutrition caused her hair to fall out. When she was finally cleaned, put in a cotton hospital gown, she was amazed. It was the first time she had felt so clean since she was in hiding with her family.

She lived for the times that Helen would come by and check on her. Carefully measured nutrition, hydration and rest were starting to improve her condition.

"There she is!" Helen would cheerfully declare, as she came beside the bed to rest her hand on Hannah's forehead. Hannah was well enough to take in a little porridge. Helen patiently sat next to her, and spoon fed her a few bites.

Miriam occasionally came by to check on her. Recently, she brought along a wiry haired young man she introduced as Benny.

Benny came next to the bed and shook his head, "Hey kid, I saw you come in and I was sure you weren't going to make it. You're looking better. I work for the transportation department at this DP camp, and I'm hooked up. I can get you just about anything. Just say the word. Any friend of Miriam's is a friend of mine."

Benny playfully kissed Miriam's cheek before leaving. Hannah managed to sit up and eyed Miriam suspiciously.

"So, Benny?" Hannah said.

"I can't wait for you to get well and get out of here so you can come meet some of the people here. There's a lot going on. Benny's a good guy, and he is smart, and he is connected here. He can get you anything! It's crazy."

Miriam's face grew dark and serious. She sat on Hannah's bed.

"So, Hannah…I…um…The Red Cross has information for survivors. Information from the camps. Some of this you know. Your sister and mother were gassed on arrival, as you thought. I'm sorry to say, so was your father. Benny was able to find out that your grandmother Hortense, she

CHAPTER NINE: HANNAH 1945–1947

didn't make it either. She wasn't shipped to the camps, but she died in 1944."

Hannah had felt in her heart that her father was gone. She knew that being unable to protect them had broken him. She suspected he wasn't fit for work and was killed. To hear about her grandmother was sad. Some part of her wished or hoped that her grandmother imperiously outlasted the Nazis.

"Thank you for finding out, Miriam. It's what I suspected might have happened, but to know the truth is good. No false hopes."

Miriam squeezed her hand, "You need to get better. There can be a future for us. This camp isn't a bad place. There are lots of young people like us on our own. You know, Benny isn't the only smart single guy around and they are planning dances here! People are getting married, planning to go to America or Palestine."

Hannah settled back into the bed and continued to hold Miriam's hand. She couldn't bring herself to cry.

The weather had grown colder. It was fall, and Hannah's recovery was slow and steady. Her hair was growing back. Her beloved nurse, Helen, would take her for walks and was helping her build her strength.

One day, nurse Helen came to see Hannah in a state of excitement.

"I found a family friend of yours, Hannah! Miriam told me that you were from Vienna and that your father was a doctor and professor. I had met a fellow survivor who is working here in the infirmary from Austria! Turns out he knew your family. He's just finishing up his work. I'll be right back."

Hannah sat up eagerly, as nurse Helen ushered a gaunt, middle-aged man with silver-streaked hair into the room. The man looked to be in his fifties. Hannah searched her memory to recall associates of her father.

The man sat on the edge of the bed.

"Oh, Hannah, I'm so glad to see you. So glad," his voice trailed off, and his eyes welled with tears.

Hannah looked at him quizzically. Something was familiar, but she couldn't place him.

"I'm sorry, it's been a long time, and so much has happened. You were an associate of my father?"

"Don't you know me? It's me, David."

"I'm sorry, I don't know you, I don't remember."

"Hannah, I worked with your father right before your family went to France, I spent many days with your family, I, um, informally courted your sister Rebecca. I took you both to the train station when you left for France."

Hannah stared at him in confusion.

David smiled and looked down at his slim frame, "I admit I look very different. When I was a student in Austria, I ate well! I had an unfashionable beard back then, too."

Hannah stammered, "…but David, well, you, would be in your twenties, but you…"

He playfully tousled his short hair and laughed softly.

"These past years have not been a friend to me. I was in the camps too. I was there for three years. My mother, my friends, all dead. The things I saw there and the things I did to survive…"

He stroked the number tattooed on his forearm.

Hannah felt embarrassed and felt her face flush.

"I'm so sorry. I didn't mean, I'm sorry, but is it really you?"

David looked up and smiled.

"Yes, it's me, Hannah."

She leaned forward and hugged him tightly as tears rolled down her cheeks, and she laughed simultaneously.

David squeezed back.

He sat on the edge of her bed and held her hands.

"I've been hearing about you, even though I didn't know it was you! You are one of Helen's favorites. She talks about you and your progress. She was afraid you weren't going to make it, but she marveled at your will to get well. You are going to be able to leave the infirmary soon."

Hannah smiled. She was glad to know she was one of Helen's favorite patients. She was so happy David was here. As he talked, the memory of him came back. It was a comfort that at least someone who had known her family had survived.

David stood up, "Well, I have work to do. I'm employed here at the

CHAPTER NINE: HANNAH 1945–1947

infirmary, and I'm working with the Red Cross to get in touch with my cousin Sam in America. But I plan to visit you often, Hannah. I can't begin to tell you how happy I am to find you."

David bent at the waist and kissed Hannah's hand.

As the weeks went by Hannah was feeling stronger and gaining weight. She hadn't looked at herself in the mirror for so long. One day after her bath, she examined herself in the mirror. She was still very thin, but not skeletal. Her hair had grown back, but it was still short and sort of odd looking. She stroked her face. Her large hazel eyes stood out. Her hand went down her neck and chest. Her periods had come back for the first time in two years. She thought about Miriam and Benny. Miriam hinted at the single men in the camp. Hannah wondered if they would look at her and just be reminded of the starvation and sickness? Or would she have a chance at finding someone? She shook her head at such a thought. Finding someone? What would that even mean?

In early December, the nurse Helen came to see her. "Hey, Hannah! I've got good news. You will be out of the infirmary soon! But before you go, we're going to have a little birthday party for you. I came to ask if there is something special you would like."

Hannah smiled, thinking this would be the first birthday she had celebrated in years. Then she felt her heart sink; she was so confused after the camps, the trauma, and being so sick for so long.

Helen looked a bit more closely at her. "Hannah, what's wrong?"

Hannah looked up, "How old am I going to be?"

Helen sat on the edge of the bed, leaned closer to Hannah, and softly said, "You will be 17 years old. You were born in 1928. Is there something else? Are you okay?"

Hannah stared out the window. "I feel crazy for not remembering what birthday this is! Everything is all scrambled, and Miriam found out for me that my family is all dead. I'm getting well, and I'm in this displaced persons' camp, and I don't know what to do."

Helen leaned in and gently held both of Hannah's hands. "I don't know what to say. What you've been through, what happened with the concentration camps, it defies comprehension. Many of the young people here are like you. Their families are gone. They are looking to the future. Maybe going to Palestine like your friends Miriam and Benny, or America like David. All I know is that you've beat the odds by surviving. I'm not a religious person, but I do believe things happen for a reason. You survived to tell the story, to go on and live a life that will reveal what your purpose is. I've watched you get better. There's a spark in you."

Hannah leaned back in bed. "You know what I would like for my birthday? A nice dress and some fashionable shoes. I know those things are hard to come by, but I think that's what I would really like."

Helen stood up and smiled. "I will do my best!"

On her birthday, Helen, Miriam, Benny and David came into her room singing with a small cake and a candle. Hannah sat up and laughed at their little parade.

Helen had managed to get Hannah a nice bottle green dress in a fashionable cut. The shoes weren't as fashionable, but rather sensible t-strap black leather shoes with a low block heel. Benny managed to find her a black wool coat. Miriam gave her a knit hat and scarf. David's gift was a whole bar of chocolate. Before the war such gifts would have been unremarkable, but for this birthday, Hannah felt overwhelmed with all the gifts. It felt like she had opened a treasure box.

Hannah moved out of the infirmary into a room with Miriam. She started taking a sewing class at the camp. David made time to visit her almost every day. They never talked about the past, not the time before the war, not the camps or anything that had happened to them. David talked about his work in the infirmary, his cousin Sam in America and how hard it was to learn English. Hannah mostly just listened.

Miriam and Benny grew closer and closer. Sometimes Benny would spend the night and Hannah would roll over and pretend not to hear. As spring came around, Benny made arrangements to get a jeep and to leave the confines of the DP camp for a picnic together by a nearby lake. Benny, Miriam, Hannah and David swam in the lake in their underwear, ate sandwiches, cheese and fruit. It was a perfect day.

CHAPTER NINE: HANNAH 1945–1947

As they lay on the blanket, Benny had a sly smile on his face. "Hey, this picnic isn't just a normal picnic—it's an engagement picnic! Miriam and I are getting married!"

David stood up and shook Benny's hand and Hannah rushed over to embrace Miriam.

As they drove back to the DP camp, Hannah felt David gently take her hand as they sat in the back of the jeep.

Marriage ceremonies were a common occurrence at the DP camp. Young people were eager to put the past behind them, and like Hannah, their entire families were gone. They were anxious to build new families. Most of the weddings were improvised and simple affairs, but Benny's connections and ingenuity made his and Miriam's wedding a cut above the usual. Benny was able to secure Miriam a beautiful cream-colored suit with a stylish hat and short net veil. When Hannah saw her in the suit, she drew her breath in. "Ohhh! You look like an American movie star!"

Miriam spun around. For the first time since Hannah had met her, she saw the girlish side of Miriam. It gave Hannah hope. For all they had been through, maybe there was still a chance to be young and happy as if nothing had happened.

Benny and Miriam's wedding was one of the best at the DP camp. There were many guests, music, dancing, and amazing black-market food. Hannah wore her green dress and David managed to find a suit and colorful tie.

There was a rumor that Benny had a connection that supplied some alcohol. Good Irish whiskey. Benny, David, and other men were huddled in a corner, sharing shots of whiskey. Miriam, looking flushed, came over and took Hannah's arm. "So, how are you and David getting along? People are saying you're an official couple now and lots of broken hearts because you look so good in that green dress. Many of the men would like a chance." Miriam laughed at Hannah's shocked expression.

"Really, Miriam, that's ridiculous. David is like a brother. I grew up with him and he liked my sister. Plus, no one is looking at me, a scarecrow with this short hair."

Miriam looked shocked. "Do you even look in a mirror? Yes, your hair is a little short, but it's beautiful! And you are filling out that dress okay—more than okay! I don't think David is having 'sisterly' thoughts about you."

Hannah just laughed but realized that Miriam was right. She hadn't looked in a mirror. She knew she had gained weight back, and she felt the stares of the men in the DP camp. She didn't know what to think of this. She saw Miriam and the other young women focused on finding a boyfriend, thinking about the future. Hannah, in some way, felt as numb inside as she did when she arrived.

David was flushed and a little drunk when Hannah saw him again. They danced a little longer and stayed at the party late. As he always did after he walked Hannah to her room, David bent slightly at the waist and kissed her hand. This time, he paused, looked at her, and gently kissed her on the forehead before leaving.

Miriam moved in with Benny, and Hannah's new roommate was a stout Hungarian girl, who only spoke Hungarian, so they didn't really connect. Hannah was spending most of her time advancing her sewing skills, thinking it would be a marketable trade when she could make a plan to leave the DP camp. Like so many others, she was looking for a way out and making a little money altering dresses, collecting fabric scraps, and making them into a small purse or stuffing them to make a little toy for all the newborns who followed in the wake of all the weddings.

One day, David was able to get the use of a jeep with Benny's help, and they went out to the lake again to have a picnic. This time, just the two of them. Hannah's eyes widened when David took out a whole bottle of wine with cheese, bread, and little petit fours. He smiled and took something else out of his pocket. A simple gold band.

He cleared his throat and took her hand in his. "Hannah, I want to know if you will marry me? I want to take care of you. I think only you and I can really understand each other. I know it might not be a romantic connection right now, but it is a connection on which to build a good life. I can't go to America and leave you here alone."

He looked up at her with a pleading look in his eyes. Hannah felt herself start to get dizzy and sweat.

CHAPTER NINE: HANNAH 1945–1947

"I…I…don't know what to say. You're like a brother, and I keep thinking about you and Rebecca. I know that's ridiculous now that she's gone. It still feels strange. I can't even picture my future. I wander around most days in a haze. I'm so sorry. You are so wonderful to me, and you were so wonderful to my family before the war. I just don't know."

David smiled. "Listen, you should think about it. There is a movie night in two days. Give me your answer at the movie. I will either be the happiest man or the saddest man in the theater. I know you are one of the prettiest girls at the DP camp. You have options if you want them."

He winked at her. Hannah laughed, and they lay down on the picnic blanket together.

When they got back, Hannah went to talk to Miriam, who listened intently as Hannah laid out her feelings.

Miriam asked, "Do you love him? How is the sex?"

Hannah practically choked. "What are you talking about? We don't have sex! He's never even kissed me on the lips! I suppose I do love him; what's not to love? He is so kind. He's smart, and he has a plan for the future, and that's something I don't have. I think he loves me."

Miriam leaned back. "Well, you two are a couple of Victorians! He just kisses your hand! At least he's a gentleman. I actually think you should do it. He's such a good guy. Plus, with his cousin in America, odds are he will move there. Think of it! You will live in America. That's incredible. That's my advice, but you have to follow your heart."

Hannah thought about it more. Following her heart sounded good, but she didn't even know how to listen to her heart. She thought more about David and his kindness, and how the future in America was some sort of future she could look forward to.

David was pacing nervously outside the DP camp's makeshift theater. Hannah wore her special green dress. She didn't make him wait. She boldly kissed him on the lips and said, "My answer is yes."

He looked astonished, and then just embraced her. "I'm so happy. I will take care of you. I will be a good husband." His voice broke a bit as he talked, and Hannah was moved by his genuine emotion.

They watched the movie on a stretched sheet that served as the movie screen and held hands throughout the movie.

He walked her back to her room. Her stout Hungarian roommate was out. For the first time, David came into the room. He pressed her against the wall and kissed her deeply. Hannah tried to relax, but nervous thoughts were racing through her mind. His hand went up her dress and between her thighs. Hannah felt herself stiffen, and David quickly withdrew his hand.

"I'm sorry...I thought...the girls I know who went through the concentration camps were...experienced. They did what they needed to do to survive. I don't judge about that."

Hannah just stared at him. His face softened. "I'm glad that you didn't have to do that, or it wasn't forced on you, and we can wait and take our time. I just saw so many things."

For reasons that weren't even clear to her, Hannah blurted out a story from her time in the camp. "I know. One of the guards was trying to earn some extra money by making sort of a mini brothel with some of the girls. She would arrange for some of the girls to go with the male guards. There was one girl, who was very pretty. She was the main girl that would go at night. She had extra food for doing it but Bridget, the guard, kept the money. The girl was pregnant. It was winter and we all wrapped our blankets under our prison dresses to stay warm, so she was able to hide it. But she went into labor at night on the bunks. The others tried to help her. The commotion caught the attention of a male guard we called 'the angel of death' because he made selections and he sort of had a soft, angelic face. He came in and took the baby and wrapped it up and asked the camp commandant what to do and he said to put it in the crematorium. We heard the baby was just thrown in the oven. The girl bled to death in her bunk, which seemed like an act of mercy."

David exhaled and shook his head. "There were so many horrific things like that. Let's make a promise right now. Let us never speak of that time ever again. Let's leave it all behind us. Do you promise?"

Hannah looked up at him and wondered if leaving it all behind was possible, but she said, "I promise."

CHAPTER NINE: HANNAH 1945–1947

Hannah and David moved up their wedding date so Benny and Miriam could attend before they left for Palestine. Hannah was fretting about what to wear. The fabrics she was able to get weren't right. Miriam came to her room with the cream-colored suit. "Here. This is yours—you can alter it for the wedding and keep it."

Hannah declined. "I couldn't take it. It's so nice; you can wear it again for special occasions."

Miriam laughed. "With any luck, I will be in Palestine on a farm in a few months! I won't need a suit like that."

Hannah altered the suit, which was a bit short for her, but looked beautiful otherwise. The wedding, like most at the DP camp, was short and sweet, and there was a fun party afterward.

That night, they awkwardly lay down on the bed together. Hannah tried to stay still and not shake from nervousness. It was uncomfortable and quick. David patted her hand and said, "It will be better with time."

David and Hannah said goodbye to Miriam and Benny. Hannah felt tears well up as she hugged her friend.

A few months later, David burst into their room, out of breath, holding a letter. "It's here. It's official. We can go to America! We can get on the ship in two weeks!"

Hannah jumped up and hugged David. It was happening. The future that Hannah struggled to picture was taking shape.

Chapter Ten: David and Hannah in America 1947–1949

Hannah couldn't believe she was traveling to America. She packed her few belongings from the displaced persons camp, including a framed photo of her, Miriam, David, and Benny. That simple photo was the only memento she had of her past.

David was abuzz with excitement as they boarded the ship. He straightened and smoothed his tie over and over and checked their tickets and paperwork a half dozen times. Hannah was more apprehensive. She was worried that she had not learned enough English to get along in America, and she was unsure about how things would go with David's cousin Sam and his wife, Sylvie. She occasionally went on a walk on deck to get fresh air. During those moments, Hannah allowed herself to daydream about her future in America. She remembered seeing American movies in Vienna as a child. She remembered some of the movie star magazines that her sister Rebecca had in her room and how she had swooned over pictures of Clark Gable. For many people in the DP camp, America was the dream.

The opportunity to come to America was the result of many years of effort by David. He had tried to arrange to come to America with his mother in 1939, but the new Nazi regime in Austria made that nearly impossible, and David's mother did not want to leave Austria. She did not understand the gravity of the threat to their lives.

Sam was the only child of David's uncle Isaac, who had immigrated to America before the First World War. They had not been in close contact

CHAPTER TEN: DAVID AND HANNAH IN AMERICA 1947-1949

over the years, but as the threat of Hitler loomed over Austria, David got in touch with Isaac and Sam. Both did their best to try to get David and his mother out of Austria, but it never happened.

When the war ended, David made contact with Sam through the Red Cross. They began exchanging letters, and David was very grateful for Sam's diligence to get both David and Hannah to America. Sam's wife Sylvie was a mystery to David. Sam had mentioned her a few times. David knew that they were both in their mid-thirties and had no children. He knew they lived in a section of New York called "Queens."

As the ship sailed into New York, David and Hannah were awestruck by the cityscape before them. They disembarked with other refugees to wind their way through a warehouse maze of immigration officials and paperwork. As they came through the final checkpoint, David scanned the crowds for his cousin, who said they would have a sign with his name on it. Finally, his eyes locked on a man of average height, slightly overweight, wearing a light gray suit and holding a sign that read "David and Hannah Schneider." Next to him stood a short, plump woman with rosy cheeks and black hair who seemed to be anxiously scanning the crowd. She was wearing a dark pink suit and a hat with a black ribbon.

Gripping Hannah's hand tightly, David quickly walked over to his cousin. Hannah scurried alongside him; he could tell that she was anxious. Hannah took a deep breath, and David pulled her closer to him as they made their way through the crowd.

A broad smile broke out on Sam's face as he vigorously shook David's hand.

"Welcome, Welcome David!" As he shook his hand, Hannah saw tears well in his eyes, and he reached up and embraced David. Hannah was relieved at this warm welcome, and as she watched the moving scene, she felt Sylvie touch her arm.

"You must be Hannah. Welcome to America! We're so glad you're here. Sam has worked for years to get David here, and he was so thrilled that David found you and that you both came."

Hannah nodded and smiled gratefully at Sylvie. She was struggling to find the correct English words when Sam and David turned to her. She managed to stammer the words "thank you."

"So, David, this is your beautiful bride? Welcome, Hannah!" Sam gave her a hug.

Hannah felt herself exhale a sigh of relief that this new family in America seemed so welcoming and kindhearted. She and David followed Sam and Sylvie out to their car. They only had two suitcases to load in what Hannah thought looked like an enormous automobile. As they drove to Sam and Sylvie's house, Hannah stared out the window at the wide streets, the pedestrians, and many cars.

Sam and Sylvie's house was a mid-sized Tudor style, similar to other houses on the street in a neighborhood called Kew Gardens. On the drive, Sam said many people in the neighborhood were Jewish and came to this neighborhood before the war and many refugees afterward. He said people had come from all over Europe to this neighborhood. He was proudly explaining that America was a "melting pot" of many different people, religions, and races, and that was what made America such a wonderful country. David was nodding, and Hannah thought that Sam really didn't need to do a sales job for America.

In the DP camp and among refugees, the American soldiers were like gods and saviors. Everyone loved everything American—the movies, the music, and the country itself. On the ship, Hannah was trying to learn as much as she could about America by looking at magazines. She liked the look of the president, Harry Truman. He looked like a friendly shopkeeper. Sam laughed when Hannah said this. "You know, he was a shopkeeper! Not a very successful one. His hat shop went bankrupt. That's the great thing about this country. You can start from a very humble beginning and go far. I know you and David will have such a wonderful future here."

Hannah was feeling more relaxed and even a little excited about being in America. Sam and Sylvie had an extra room with two small twin beds and a dresser. Sylvie told Hannah that some relatives from Sam's extended family would be arriving for a welcome dinner. She told Hannah she had time to "freshen up." Hannah didn't know what that meant, but she decided

CHAPTER TEN: DAVID AND HANNAH IN AMERICA 1947-1949

she should change into her cream-colored suit she wore at her wedding and tidy up her hair, which had finally grown back and was thick and a dark chocolate color. David kissed her cheek and said approvingly, "You look so beautiful, Hannah. This is a wonderful day. We can leave everything that happened in the past behind us now."

Sam and David's various cousins and family friends descended on the house, bringing more food than Hannah had seen since her childhood in Vienna. She felt a little like she and David were exotic animals on display at the zoo. The gawking looks, and the measured and simplistic way people spoke to them unnerved her. One older, overweight aunt took Hannah's hand and blurted out, "You're so young! So much younger than David."

For the most part, everyone was kind and solicitous and the men seemed anxious to help David find employment. The women remarked on Hannah's youth and seemed moved by the fact that she was wearing her wedding suit and that she and David had wed in a displaced persons' camp. There were few questions about the past, other than references to how horrible the war was and reassurances about how much Hannah and David will love America. When everyone left, Hannah was exhausted. It was hard to keep up with the conversations and the constant feeling that she was being stared at and evaluated.

She was lying down in one of the twin beds when David crouched down beside her. "I'm going to have a drink with Sam and stay up a bit longer. Hope you sleep well." He kissed her cheek and left the door open a crack so Hannah could see the hallway light.

She drifted to sleep but woke up to hear Sam and David talking.

"I have to say, David, I was surprised when I met Hannah. A real child bride there. I thought you two had dated before the war?"

"No, that was Hannah's older sister Rebecca. She was the girl I was seeing before the war. Sadly, Rebecca and the whole family were wiped out. It's a miracle that Hannah is alive and that we met again. You should have seen her. Rail thin, sick, shaved head and all alone. I couldn't just leave her there in that DP camp. We spent some time together, and she's a real sweet kid. I decided that marrying her was best for both of us. I knew I wanted to marry someone who would understand what I went through at the camps. I didn't want to have to explain it. There is no explaining it. I also knew that she needed me. So, here we are."

Hannah heard the clinking of ice in a glass, and she heard Sam ask cautiously, "Do you think it will work? Do you love her?"

Hannah scooted to the edge of the bed and pushed the door open further. She heard David sigh, "I think so. I don't know that I love her in the conventional way a husband loves a wife. She's a good kid, a sweet gal. I think we can build something together. I want to protect her and help her have something good with me here in America. I know that."

"Well, David, that's more than some couples have. She does seem real sweet. Maybe Sylvie can help her."

"That would be great. She didn't really get much of a chance to grow up in a normal way a young woman would. She's nineteen and spent most of her teen years in that horrific camp. I want her to put all that behind her and have a good life here."

Hannah gently pushed the door shut. She felt numb as she lay down on the bed. Thoughts raced through her mind. Did her husband love her or just pity her? What did romantic love even look like? Like something in the movies? Should she like sex more, rather than just concentrating on relaxing and staying still until it was over? There was no one to ask about these things. But, she thought, it was too late. She was married to David, and, like he said, their goal now was trying to make it a good life here in America.

The first few weeks in America passed by. Hannah was constantly amazed at how large everything was. Sylvie took Hannah to a department store to buy some new outfits. The selection of clothes and the crowds were unbelievable. Hannah bought two new dresses and a couple of pairs of shoes. It felt awkward to rely on Sam and Sylvie's charity, but they were gracious about it. David was working on getting a job in a hospital. Eventually, he got the administrative job at the hospital he was hoping for, and they went out to celebrate. David wanted to try out a typical American diner. Sam and Sylvie took them to a local diner with Formica tabletops and a

CHAPTER TEN: DAVID AND HANNAH IN AMERICA 1947–1949

coin-operated jukebox. They ordered burgers and cokes. It had been so long since Hannah had a Coca-Cola. The carbonation caused her to wrinkle her nose. The burgers had too much ketchup. As she was trying out the French fries, Hannah saw two tall men out of the corner of her eye. They wore black uniforms like Nazi SS uniforms. She saw the guns on their hips. She felt herself start to shake and sweat. Sylvie reached over and steadied her hand. "Are you okay, Hannah?'

Hannah whispered, "Who are they? Is it safe here?"

Sylvie swiveled around and looked. She smiled at Hannah, "Oh, those are police officers. Nothing to worry about."

Hannah felt like she would be sick. She jumped up and ran to the ladies' room with Sylvie not far behind. Hannah slammed through the stall door and threw up. She sat hyperventilating on the floor. Sylvie cautiously tapped on the stall door. Sylvie helped her back to the table. Sam and David were standing with worried looks on their faces.

"Hannah's not feeling well. I don't think the hamburger agreed with her."

Over the following weeks, Hannah was unable to leave their little room with the twin beds at Sam and Sylvie's house. David went to work each day and checked on her in the evening. She could hear the three of them talk about her in hushed tones in the hallway. She had stopped eating. Sylvie thoughtfully brought in tea and toast, but Hannah could only manage a few bites of toast.

Sam came to the room with a prescription bottle and a glass of milk. "Hey, sweetheart, I understand you're feeling really low. I know it's a big adjustment coming here, and you went through a lot during the war. I talked with a doctor friend of mine, and I have something to calm your nerves and help you."

Hannah took the pills and went to sleep. She took the pills every day and felt numb. Eventually, she was able to leave the bedroom, but not the house. She contented herself by helping Sylvie do household chores. Hannah didn't understand why she needed the pills not to feel terrified, and when she was helping Sylvie in the kitchen, she felt as lifeless and detached as she had in the camp, and she couldn't understand it because she was safe now. Sylvie kept up the chatter as they cooked and did the dishes, or they listened to radio programs. It was a world away from the camps.

She listened to the conversations about her when they thought she was asleep. David's voice drifted down the hall, and Hannah tipped the door open a little further.

"Well, if she's not spending the day in bed and if she's up and functioning, that is progress. If she doesn't feel up to leaving the house, then that's okay. We will just have to give her time."

Weeks bled into months. To Hannah, every day simply blurred into the next. She tried to help Sylvie as much as she could. Sylvie offered trips out shopping or to the beauty parlor, but Hannah couldn't bring herself to leave the house. The thought of stepping outside caused her to hyperventilate. She felt guilty because David was working hard at the hospital. He was patient and kind. He tried to buoy her spirits.

"Hey, Hannah! I have great news. With Sam's help we're able to put some money down on a house not far from here. Do you want to come look at it? We can walk from here."

Hannah took an extra sedative pill and walked out the front door for the first time in nearly a year. The breeze felt good as she walked on the sidewalk, with David's arm around her. She looked up at him and realized how much he had changed since moving to America. He had gained weight and was smiling more, and his hair had grown in a bit thicker. Just a few blocks away, they stopped at a modest red brick house with a carport. It was done in a quasi-Tudor style similar to Sam and Sylvie's house, only a bit larger.

Hannah rested her head on David's shoulder. She wanted to believe everything was finally going to be alright.

Chapter Eleven: Helma 1947–1955

Helma had sat in a jail cell for six months. It was explained to her that an Allied tribunal would be judging her role in Nazi crimes. She had heard about other captured female guards, like the beautiful, but brutal guard Irma, who was so young, even younger than Helma, who was hanged by the Allies.

She was losing weight again and was very tired. Her contact with Klara was sporadic. One day, she was allowed to not only meet with Klara, but also to receive a care package. Her trial was just days away. A British soldier led Helma into the visitors' room, a spartan room with a table, a few chairs, and two stony-faced military police guards by the door.

"Klara, thank you so much for coming," Helma said as Klara reached out and touched Helma's hand. Klara looked wide-eyed at how thin Helma had become. She handed her a few items. A tin with shortbread cookies, new socks, and a drawing from Greta. Uncharacteristically, Helma was moved by the small care package.

"My trial is in a few days. It's a show trial for the Allies. They won, so they can make us look worse. I was just serving my country and following orders, just like they did," Helma said as she gestured over to the soldiers at the door.

"Helma, I wanted to ask you about the camps where you were a guard because there are pictures and newsreels of some of those places. Old people, women, children, babies were killed by gassing them and burning them in ovens and the most horrible conditions. People starved and looked like walking skeletons. You weren't a part of that sort of camp, right?"

"Klara! It's a bunch of phony newsreels and propaganda! Doctored photos, a bunch of whiny Jew criminals acting like they are the victims when they have been betraying Germany for years! They have American movie makers, who are Jews, come in and make all these dramatic newsreels. I did my job. I served the Fatherland. I did what had to be done. I did nothing wrong."

Klara nodded her head cautiously, paused, and finally said, "I'm glad you weren't part of something really bad like that and that you were at a camp legitimately serving the Fatherland. I hope everything goes well for you in the trial. Greta misses you, and I do too."

"Thank you. You are a true sister. I don't think it will go well. It's not a court of Austrians; it's the Allies looking for revenge. I'm not hopeful."

As Helma predicted, her trial did not go well. She was charged with crimes against humanity for her role at Ravensbruck and was sentenced to three years. Prison conditions were difficult, though not completely unbearable. She felt her anger and resentment against the Allies grow. How dare they imprison people for just doing their duty?

She was released early after serving two years, and the Austrian government granted her amnesty from further charges. She was gratified that the Austrian authorities recognized that she was being unjustly persecuted.

Klara and Greta were there to greet her as she left prison. Greta had grown, but was still a thin, shy child. Klara looked happy and less worried than she had in the time immediately following the war.

When Helma returned home with Klara and Greta, she was happy to sense that a new mood had come over Austria. The world was starting to put the war behind them. She was particularly happy that the anger had shifted from the Nazi regime to where it really belonged—to the communist menace. It was heartbreaking to hear that Eastern Germany and most of Eastern Europe were under a brutal communist regime. It caused her to reflect on Hitler's wisdom about the threat of communists, and finally, the veil was lifted from the Allied nations' eyes. The British, French, and Americans had awakened to the communist threat. It helped temper her rage against the Allies. The police force in Austria even had some former Nazi soldiers that Helma had known, and it indicated to her that the British and Americans

CHAPTER ELEVEN: HELMA 1947–1955

finally knew that the real enemy was the communists.

Klara had secured Helma a job at the restaurant where she had been working. The restaurant catered to British and American soldiers and now tourists were coming back to Austria. Helma brushed up on the little bit of English she had learned. It surprised her how fluent Klara had become. She could easily chat with British and American patrons and make jokes and small talk with them.

Helma quickly learned more English as she picked up more shifts waiting tables. Over time, she really came to like the British and American guests. Shockingly, even the soldiers. Some of the American men had very nice manners, and they were handsome. Helma thought that they had so much in America. Good food, good schools, and good dentists! That is why they had such broad smiles and were so tall and healthy. To her, the Americans were more Germanic in character than British, which surprised her.

Helma never regained the health, weight, or strength she had before the war. She tried to take daily walks, but she never completely regained her vitality. Other than that, it was a happy, and peaceful, few years in her life. She was helping Klara raise Greta and teaching her how to knit. She started going back to church and attending Mass. It seemed the turmoil of the war years and her imprisonment were finally behind her. Helma had friendly interactions with a few men at the restaurant, but she didn't get a lot of male attention. She often wondered if she would ever marry, and now that she was in her thirties, she felt her prospects were even dimmer.

In 1955, the Allied occupation of Austria was finally ending. As the end of the occupation was negotiated, the final group of German prisoners were released from the Soviet Union. A telegram came from Berlin, and Helma was shocked to learn Klaus was among the 10,000 final prisoners to come back to Germany. Klara and Helma boarded a train headed to Berlin. They were informed that Klaus was very ill and in the hospital.

Nothing prepared them for what they saw in the hospital room. Klaus, the large, hearty brother who was quick with a smile, was no longer there. A starved husk of a man in a hospital gown lay in bed with an IV in his arm. He stared blankly at Helma and Klara. His teeth had rotted out, and he had a large scar on his forehead. He seemed confused when they tried to talk to him and responded to them with Russian phrases. A doctor came in and patted Klaus's arm and explained that his sister and sister-in-law were there to visit him. He squinted and managed to say their names and speak in broken German. The doctor told him to rest and gestured for Klara and Helma to leave the room with him.

"Your brother was in a hard labor camp for over a decade. He was in the copper mines and was subjected to starvation, beatings, and he was nearly dead when he was put on a train back to Germany. His mental fitness has also obviously suffered. We will do our best, but I don't think your brother can make a journey home to Vienna."

Helma felt the rage burning inside of her. First, her unjust conviction and jail time, and now she discovered what they had done to Klaus. She was grateful to be in the Allied sector. God knows what may have happened to her if she had been captured by the Soviets!

Helma and Klara stayed in Berlin for a few days. They agreed with the doctor's prognosis. It was hard to tell Klaus that Hans, Mother, and Father were all gone. He seemed to understand the news, but Helma felt it further drained his will to go on.

A few months later, Klaus died. Helma spent the money she had saved to have her brother brought back to Austria. The least she could do for her poor brother was to bury him next to their parents.

That summer, she noticed an American serviceman who usually ate dinner alone in the restaurant. She had become familiar enough with American military uniforms to know he was in the Air Force. He was very polite and clean-looking. One night she looked at his name tag, it said "O'Neal."

"Good evening, Mr. O'Neal. So nice to have you back for dinner tonight." He smiled in that big, friendly American way that Helma so admired.

"Thank you! I don't know your name, though, and that hardly seems fair. Miss?" Helma just laughed and said, "I'm Miss Braun, but no need to be so formal with me; you may call me Helma."

"Well then, you may call me Charles. I'm so glad to meet you, I think you're the first Austrian that I'm on a first name basis with and I love Austria. What

CHAPTER ELEVEN: HELMA 1947–1955

a beautiful country and wonderful people."

Charles O'Neal came in every evening for dinner for a couple of weeks. Helma enjoyed chatting with him. He had good manners, and he seemed like an intelligent man. He had served in the Air Force performing maintenance on planes for many years, he said, but would soon be discharged.

On Sunday, when she was leaving Mass, she saw Charles O'Neal. Apparently, he was Catholic. She walked up behind him and tapped his shoulder.

"I don't know if you recognize me out of my waitress uniform, but…"

"You recognized me out of my Air Force uniform! You have a sharp eye, Helma." He laughed as he said this, and so did she.

He asked if she would join him for a coffee. They walked to the coffee shop together. As they sat down, Charles smiled his broad smile again.

"I have a confession to make. I asked one of your co-workers where you went to church. I remember you talking about knitting for your church Christmas sale, so I thought I would see if I could arrange a 'chance' meeting. I wanted to get to know you outside of work."

"I'm so glad you did! That's the best luck, right? The luck you make yourself?"

Charles laughed and said, "As an Irish American, I am an authority on luck, and it has very little to do with four-leaf clovers."

Helma could not believe what was happening. Here was a charming man who was interested in her. She thought she was too old to ever find someone, yet here he was.

Over the next few weeks, he continued to visit the restaurant and when she was off work, they went for long walks and went to the coffee shop after church.

"Helma, I'm going back to America and I'm going to be discharged from the Air Force. I have an opportunity to move back to Queens and work as an electrician for one of my buddies. It pays good and I'm ready to settle down. When I think about my future, I think of a lady like you in it, someone with the same traditional, old-fashioned values, who would be content with a quiet life. Taking walks, having a little house with a garden, you know, peaceful."

Helma stared attentively at him. She was replaying his words in her mind. Could it be possible that he was serious? Was this an opportunity for a marriage and life in America?

"It sounds like a beautiful and ideal life you have in mind, Charles. I am a lady of old-fashioned values and would be more than content with the life you describe. But there are a few things you should know about me."

Helma stared at Charles anxiously. He didn't seem shocked, just curious.

"Well, Charles, I'm not a young woman. I'm thirty-six. I don't know if I could give you children. Despite my age, I haven't had any serious relationships with men. I had to do my part during the war, and after the war, I was focused on helping my widowed sister-in-law and niece. What I'm trying to say, is that, unlike many women my age in these days, I haven't had sexual relationships."

Charles blushed and gently took Helma's hand across the table.

"I'm not surprised you are a virtuous lady. I'm not disappointed at all. I could tell your faith meant a lot to you, and I admire what you have done to honor your brother's memory by looking out for his wife and child. As for age, I'm thirty-six too! I don't mind at all, and if we are blessed with children, that's fine, but if not, I really want that simple, quiet life I described. I don't know about you, but after all of these years of the war and craziness in the world, it would be enough of a blessing to have peaceful years together."

Helma felt herself breathe a sigh of relief. Since this hurdle had been overcome, she felt confident about sharing a little bit more.

"Oh Charles, I'm so happy. But I worry about the lingering shadow of the war. We were on opposite sides, so to speak, during the war years. I had to do my part to serve. I served the Fatherland for just a few years, as I was compelled to do. I didn't serve very long. I was sick for much of the end of the war, and I did clerical work. But, in the days immediately following the war, the Allies were looking to punish people. The Jews fueled this absurd theory that they were victimized in these camps, and the camps were for criminal elements, but anyway, I was punished for my service. I spent a short time in jail before I was completely exonerated by the Austrian government. I wanted you to know that, so that there are no surprises or

CHAPTER ELEVEN: HELMA 1947-1955

secrets between us."

Helma's heart raced as she saw a concerned and contemplative look cross Charles' face. He thought for a bit before he spoke, and for Helma, the silence was excruciating.

"Gosh. I hadn't thought about that. You know, now the Americans and Austrians are on the same side. The communists are the real problem now, and a lot of them are Jews. People don't want to make the connection, but it's there. Where I live in America, there are tons of Jews, but we all get along okay, and that's what makes America great. We have to be on guard with the Jews, though. They're sneaky, and a person has got to watch themselves when dealing with them. We even have a phrase: 'Jew 'em down' when we're negotiating a price. I mean, that's how they are! In my neighborhood, we keep to our own, and they keep to their people, and we try to make it work because we have to be tolerant."

Helma nodded her head. She knew this was how Americans were. Despite their reputation as being so candid and upfront about everything, they had this illusion about tolerance. Helma was no fool. She knew it was mostly for show. She knew enough about America to know that they treated their negroes as the Fatherland used to treat the Jews. Restricting them from jobs, schools, transportation. Even now, their negroes were protesting and trying to get the right to ride in the front of their buses in the American South. She was gratified to know that she and Charles had the same outlook about the Jews. It made her uneasy to know if she went to America, she might be living among them.

"I admire America very much for this. In Austria and Germany during the war, we had been so betrayed by the Jews in the first war that we couldn't practice the tolerance the Americans were able to. I so admire the generosity of spirit the Americans have for Jews. The Jews are very lucky to have Americans to be advocates for them. I hope you understand how it was different for us. An American couldn't imagine how horribly we were betrayed and how the international Jewry made our lives miserable. I don't concern myself with politics or international affairs, and the war is long over now. I just hope our pasts don't stop us from having a future. That's why I wanted to be honest with you."

She saw Charles' face soften. He was reaching in his pocket. He pulled out a velvet box. Helma's heart was racing.

"Let's put all of the war talk behind us. We are allies now, both as countries and as you and me. I don't meet sensible women like you back in America. I know I'm lucky to have met you. I think we are more alike than you know. I want to have a future with you if you will have me. This ring has my mother's wedding diamonds re-set in a new setting. I had a jeweler here in Austria who designed for me. This isn't an impulsive decision. That time I first saw you at the church, I knew you were the woman for me. That night I cabled my cousin to send my mother's old ring to me here for this purpose. So, what do you say?"

Helma felt her cheeks burning. Was this really happening? She felt her throat dry up, but she managed to speak.

"I say yes! I can't believe my good fortune. I can't believe a wonderful man such as you would be my husband!"

Chapter Twelve: Hannah 1949–1953

It was Hannah's first day alone in the new house. They didn't have any furniture, except for a bed that had been delivered and a card table with folding chairs that Sam and Sylvie had lent them. David had left for work, and Hannah had put on some dungarees and a checked blouse and pulled her hair back with a kerchief. She stood in the middle of the living room. It was a nice-sized house, with three bedrooms and a good-sized bathroom. It wasn't as nice or as large as her childhood home in Vienna, or her grandmother's elegant old home in France, but it was more than the Dufour's barn in France, the concentration camp, the displaced persons camp, and Sam and Sylvie's guest bedroom, which were Hannah's most recent addresses.

She was mentally measuring the large living room picture window when Sylvie knocked on the door. She was going to give Hannah a ride to the store for cleaning supplies and some groceries.

Sylvie broke into a big smile when she entered the house, "Wow! This is a great place. Such a spacious living room and the hardwoods are in nice shape! Are you ready to head to the store? We should probably stop at several places to get everything you need to get this place cleaned up."

Hannah smiled to cover the dread that was starting to overtake her. The thought of leaving the house and encountering crowds still rattled her. She told Sylvie that she had to go to the bathroom, and she would be right back. She opened her medicine cabinets and realized she was out of the pills she took to calm her nerves, the pills that David explained were called "barbiturates."

As they were headed out the door, Hannah confessed to Sylvie how nervous she was. Sylvie knitted her brow, but then dug into her purse as they stood on the doorstep. She pulled out a pack of cigarettes.

"Have you ever had one?" Sylvie asked, "I know it helps me if I have a quick smoke if I'm feeling a bit rattled." Sylvie lit the cigarette in her mouth and handed it to Hannah. She instructed her to draw in the smoke.

Hannah choked a little but took a few more drags on the cigarette. She was starting to feel a little lightheaded as she climbed into the car. They stopped at the hardware store to get a broom, mop, bucket, and a few small tools. Then they stopped in to get groceries. Hannah was always overwhelmed by the amount of food at American grocery stores. It was unbelievable. Sylvie asked Hannah what she wanted to cook David for dinner.

"Gee. I don't know. The only things I know how to cook are the things you've shown me, Sylvie. I don't even know what to get." Sylvie picked out a "Ladies Home Journal" magazine and said that there were interesting articles and recipes in the magazine. Hannah decided to keep it simple with soup and sandwiches. She also purchased a pack of cigarettes.

When David arrived home, Hannah had polished the hardwoods and had tomato soup and chicken salad sandwiches ready when he walked in the door, "Wow! Hannah! The floors look amazing. They are shining."

Hannah watched David eating the sandwich and the soup and could tell how pleased he was. She thought buying the house and having a good job had done so much for him, and she was hoping whatever lay in store for her could be at least as satisfying. After dinner she lit a cigarette, and David's eyes grew wide with surprise, "Hey, when did you start smoking?"

"I started today. I ran out of pills, so I bought some cigarettes today. They are helping calm my nerves a bit and it gives me something to do with my hands," she laughed as she said this. She didn't want David to worry too much about her nerves and her strange fears. He smiled and laughed a little, "Well, I think it's okay. Maybe this will help you not be as reliant on the pills, and there is nothing wrong with a smoke once in a while."

Over the next few months, they went shopping on weekends, picking out furniture for the living room and dining room, and a dresser and side

CHAPTER TWELVE: HANNAH 1949-1953

tables for the bedroom. Sylvie bought Hannah a cookbook called *The Joy of Cooking*, and Hannah tried a new recipe each week. For her 21st birthday, David bought her a sewing machine, and Hannah picked out a deep green floral print for the curtains in their bedroom. For the living room they decided to have custom draperies installed in a dove gray velvet. It felt very luxurious to Hannah to have the special drapes made and the nice sofa and matching chairs and area rug in the living room. It made her feel like an adult.

Things with David were starting to feel comfortable for Hannah. She no longer worried about being in love and if the sex was what it was supposed to be. They were comfortable together. David was caring and looked out for her and tried to make their home as nice as it could be. She baked a special chiffon cake for New Year's Eve and purchased a new dress. She had been reading magazines to find out how an American housewife should live and what she should wear. She felt like she was succeeding when David came home and lavishly complimented her on the chiffon cake and her lovely dress.

They sat on the sofa together with a couple of glasses of wine, and David took her hand, "Cheers! Cheers to 1950! Goodbye to the 1940s!" They enthusiastically clinked their glasses together. Hannah took a sip and thought for a moment of New Year's Eve in 1939. How scared they all were at Grandmother Hortense's house, but the war wasn't quite real yet for Hannah, she had her mother, father, and her sisters. Her thoughts must have registered on her face as David gently chucked her under the chin, "Hey, Hannah, what is the matter? Why the sad face?"

"Oh, I was just thinking of New Year's Eve in 1939. We were at my grandmother's house. Nothing really horrible had yet happened, but we all felt it was out there, this sense of dread, but we were all together, Mother, Father, me and Rebecca, and Esther. I miss them, you know."

David exhaled heavily, "I thought we agreed not to talk about all that? We can't let ourselves get mired in sad thoughts about the past. Besides, look at our lovely house. I can't wait to have a piece of that chiffon cake!" He held her chin in his hand and whispered, "Let's never speak of the past again."

A few months into the new year, Hannah found herself trying to steady her nerves by staring at a water stain on the ceiling and pressing the arches of her feet into the cold metal stirrups as the doctor was examining her. He patted her leg, stood up, and said, "You can get dressed now, and we can talk in my office." She quickly dressed and fixed her hair and lipstick in the mirror, and she put her white gloves back on.

The doctor was smoking a cigarette and making notes in a manila file folder as he motioned her to sit down. He looked up at her and smiled, "Well, I see nothing that would hinder you from having a child. You are young and healthy. Is there any reason you might suspect you and your husband have not yet conceived?"

"During the war I was in Europe, and we didn't get enough to eat, I had typhus toward the end of the war, and it took quite a long time to recover. I was in a camp, you see, and it was difficult."

The doctor took on a serious expression and lit another cigarette. "I have examined several ladies who have come to the States after having endured the concentration camps. There are a number of families here who have experienced that. May I ask if you were part of some of the medical experiments that took place? Some women were injected with substances and subjected to gynecological experiments in the camps. Did that happen to you?"

Hannah stared at the doctor in astonishment. She knew there were other families in her neighborhood who had survived the camps. She thought she knew the full horror, but she had no idea about gynecological medical experiments; she shook her head, "No, no, I wasn't part of any medical experiments. I just didn't have enough food for a number of years, and I was terribly sick at the end of the war. I didn't have my period for about three years when I was a teenager, but I have them regularly now."

"That's good news. You appear healthy. Sometimes, nervousness can hinder the process. I will restart your prescription for Valium. That will help you relax and let nature take its course. Sometimes I see housewives who have worked themselves up in anxiety and near hysteria and that is not the right frame of mind for conceiving a child."

CHAPTER TWELVE: HANNAH 1949-1953

Over the next few months, Hannah kept to a routine of fixing breakfast, cleaning the house, working on a project or grocery shopping, and then cooking dinner for her and David. She typically waited until after dinner to take a pill and sit in the living room on one of the side chairs with the small table and lamp next to her, with an ornate ashtray that she flicked her ashes into as she smoked and flipped through a magazine. Sometimes, she had a glass of wine or a cocktail with her evening cigarette. David would often join her in the living room and read a book or have the radio on. He would put Sinatra on the Hi-Fi. During that time, Hannah could feel herself drifting into numbness, and it was easy enough to fall asleep and wake the next morning to start the routine all over again.

One morning, the fried eggs seemed to smell incredibly strong. As usual, David didn't eat much, but as he was headed out the door, he cocked his head at her, "Man, you look positively green! Are you coming down with something? You should go lie down." Hannah nodded and walked back to the kitchen, planning to do the dishes, but the smell was so overwhelming she couldn't do it. She stepped outside for a cigarette. Over the next few days, she couldn't eat much, and she started upping the number of pills she took to calm her nerves. She went back to the doctor.

"Congratulations," he said, standing at his desk and smiling. "I would say you are just a couple of months along. You can expect your baby to arrive in about seven months." Hannah felt herself stiffen. This was terrifying news, and the doctor went on about eating, resting, and letting her know she could continue smoking to calm her nerves and to ensure she didn't gain too much weight during her pregnancy.

David, Sam, and Sylvie were thrilled. They insisted on a night out on the town to celebrate. Hannah took several pills and chain-smoked throughout the evening. The crowd, the loud talking, everything jangled her nerves, but on the outside, she smiled and agreed with how thrilling it all was. Secretly, she hoped it was all a mistake, but her belly kept getting larger. She distracted herself by decorating the nursery. This made David extremely happy. Every night when he came home from work, the first thing he did was go to the nursery to see the day's progress on the curtains or the clown print wallpaper or the new yellow paint. Hannah decided to write to Miriam, who was happily living in Israel and had mailed Hannah and David a letter with a picture of their new baby boy last year.

Dear Miriam,

I hope this letter finds you well. I have some exciting news to share. David and I are having a baby. Since you sent that sweet picture of your son Daniel, I was wanting to ask your advice. I don't have many friends to ask here so I wanted to know how it was giving birth and how that works (I can see you rolling your eyes now, but I really need to know how they are going to get this baby out of me) and what it is like being a mother.

America is very nice. We have so much of everything, but I miss you and Benny and the friendship we had years ago.

Write back soon.

Your Friend,

Hannah

Thankfully, she didn't have to wait too long until a letter came from Israel from Miriam. The letter was thick, and Hannah waited until the evening to read it with her glass of wine. When she opened it there were a couple of pictures enclosed with the letter. One of the baby Daniel, who was almost two, in a studio portrait. He was chubby and had the mischievous smile of his father. The other was a casual photo of Benny and Miriam on the porch of their home. They looked relaxed and happy.

Dear Hannah,

I'm so happy for you and David. I was amused to find you are unchanged and not a very sophisticated American (haha!) Bad news kid—you will need to push that baby out the way the little seed got in, and it is going to hurt! It's going to wreck your cute figure, and your boobs are going to hurt. You will be exhausted. But you will have an adorable baby to love, and you will make it through. I know David is a

CHAPTER TWELVE: HANNAH 1949-1953

good husband, and you will have everything you need. You'll make it, I promise.

Kick your feet up now and get some sleep, as those luxuries will be a thing of the past. I know you will do well.

It is funny, but I miss our friendship too. I have nothing like it here, but we are keeping busy.

Much love to you, David, and your bundle of joy,
Miriam

How Hannah missed Miriam. How she wished Miriam and Benny had chosen America too and they could have been neighbors. It would have been so much easier. Then she would have a friend to confide in, and she felt bad for not feeling that way with Sylvie, but because Sylvie and Sam couldn't have children, it was not a subject they could talk about.

It went differently than Hannah thought. A nurse injected her arm, and she went into a "twilight sleep," and she didn't remember much, other than the horror of being out of control and having her pubic area shaved, which reminded her so much of the camps she started shaking uncontrollably, and then the nurse grabbed her arm and gave her the injection. After that she didn't know what was real and what she imagined. She awoke very sore with David lightly snoring in a chair next to the bed. After David woke up the nurse brought the baby in, and David smiled at Hannah, "We should name him Max, after your father." So, it was a boy. Hannah nodded.

She knew how she was supposed to feel, but she couldn't seem to muster those feelings. For the most part, she just felt inadequate. She didn't breastfeed, and Max was always hungry, so she was forever washing, sterilizing, and refilling the bottle. If she couldn't feel like the perfect mother, she could at least do all the things the perfect mother was supposed to do. She was highly attentive to the baby's needs and she tried to keep the home clean and continue to prepare meals for David. It was exhausting. When the baby slept, she would slip out to the patio for a little peace and to smoke. Every night, she relied on a glass of wine and a pill.

Little Max kept growing and was a content little baby. Hannah sometimes felt sad that she didn't have those feelings of delirious love she was supposed to have. It was several months before Hannah felt secure enough to leave Max with Sylvie so that she could go grocery shopping. David had done all the shopping for months with lists from Hannah. Sylvie came over and Hannah showed her the prepared bottle and went through his care routine.

"Oh Hannah! You are such a wonderful mother. So worried! It will be okay," Sylvie said as she squeezed Hannah's shoulder.

Hannah took in the fresh air as she walked to the A & P market. It felt good to leave the house and the mind-numbing daily routine that had become all-consuming. She took her time walking through the aisles at the store and actually felt a little refreshed as she carried her two bags of groceries through the front door.

She found Sylvie in the rocking chair with Max asleep on her shoulder. Sylvie was softly humming. She turned her head and kissed Max on top of his head. She gently laid him in the crib and then rubbed his back as he stirred and then fell back asleep. Hannah froze in place as she scanned her memory to try to find a time when she kissed her baby or hummed a tune as she held him. She felt crestfallen when she realized all she had been doing was taking care of him in a machine-like way. Giving him a bottle, burping him, rocking him to sleep, changing his diaper, and changing his clothes. She felt tears start to well in her eyes. Sylvie rushed over to embrace her.

"Oh Hannah, he is fine! I know it must have been so hard for you to leave that sweet little fellow because he is so adorable. We didn't have a moment of trouble. I'm so glad you asked me to help. Sam and I have missed you but know it's a busy time with the new baby."

Sylvie stayed that afternoon, and David and Sam came to the house. They had dinner together. Sam made funny sounds and faces with Max as he sat in his highchair. Max flapped his tiny arms and laughed as Sam made faces.

Later that evening, Hannah brought Max to his room, changed his diaper, and put him in his pajamas. As she laid him in the crib, she made sure to lean in and kiss his forehead. She walked back to the living room sipped her glass of wine lit her cigarette, and was happy that she and David had some sort of family with Sam and Sylvie and that they had the chance to

CHAPTER TWELVE: HANNAH 1949-1953

make life good for baby Max.

Max was growing into a sturdy little toddler. Hannah still felt like she wasn't feeling all the things she was expected to feel, so she doubled down on all the tasks that she seemed to think a perfect mother should perform. She tried to remember her own mother but could only conjure an image of the old house in Vienna with her mother exquisitely dressed and Marta, their grumpy maid, doing all of the housework and cooking. Max was too little for Hannah to do the motherly things she remembered her mother doing: monitoring for correct behavior, fussing over the proper clothes, employing tutors, and presiding over a formal dinner table while correcting the children's manners. Hannah knew she was living a different life, so she threw herself into keeping the house clean, continuing to learn to cook, and making outfits for Max at her sewing machine in the small home office where she had a table next to David's desk.

David was thrilled with their home life. Hannah envied his ability to so joyfully embrace this new life. He was even more thrilled when Hannah shared that she was pregnant again.

"Wow! I'm so excited. We are so lucky!" he jumped up from his seat at the dining table and kissed Hannah's cheek. Max dropped his fork and started clapping, although, at just over a year old, he didn't understand what was happening or that he was soon to be a big brother. Hannah felt herself smiling, while feeling utterly terrified on the inside. She already felt awful about her lack of natural feeling and emotion for little Max. What would happen with this next baby? She literally needed a pill or two, a glass of wine, and three or four cigarettes at the end of the day to be calm enough to get into bed. How would she manage as a mother of two?

Several months later, Hannah was about six months along in her pregnancy when she, David, Sam, and Sylvie went to see the new Marilyn Monroe picture, "Gentlemen Prefer Blondes." It was turning out to be a muggy summer, so going to the movie was as much about the air conditioning as it was about seeing the movie. Hannah remembered David talking about Marilyn Monroe being romantically involved with some baseball player he liked.

Part of David's thorough embrace of American life was a new-found enthusiasm for baseball. He had purchased a little radio to enable him to listen to games on the back patio, very often with Sam. Hannah settled into her seat just as the newsreel before the movie started. It featured Senator McCarthy, who Hannah had heard on the radio, and a re-cap of the execution of the Rosenbergs, which showed footage of their young sons outside the facility where their parents were jailed before their execution. Something about hearing about the execution, the orphaned children, and McCarthy's hectoring demagoguery caused Hannah's anxiety to rise. Her hands were shaking, and she felt herself feeling dizzy and sick.

She excused herself and rushed out of the theater. She stood outside smoking, thinking about how what she experienced as a child could happen here. She knew some Americans conflated Jews with communism, and she had to turn off the radio when they replayed McCarthy during the hearings. She must have been lost in those thoughts for a while, as Sylvie came out to check on her. When she sat back down, the newsreel had been replaced by the bright and beautiful Marilyn Monroe and Jane Russell.

The next morning, Hannah asked David for extra money for groceries. He shrugged and gave her extra money, "Well, I guess I should get ready for a bigger grocery bill, as we will be a family of four soon!" He gave Hannah a quick kiss on the cheek on the way out the door.

Hannah took Max to the store and looked for food that would keep well and an extra can of coffee. She took the extra canned goods to the basement and put them on a shelf next to the washing machine. She took an empty tea tin, put in some of the cash, and pushed it to the back of the shelf. She played out different scenarios in her mind. If Jews like David lost their jobs, it would be wise to have some money set aside. If David was accused of being a communist, she wanted to create a plan for her and the children. She thought on her next trip, she might buy more canned coffee to sell or trade, as she remembered how precious coffee supplies became during the war. Her mind swirled with McCarthy's hectoring voice, and his sweaty square face from the newsreel filled her imagination, and she realized her hands were shaking again. She raced upstairs and had a cigarette, hoping to

CHAPTER TWELVE: HANNAH 1949–1953

appear calm and cheerful when David came home from work.

Over the next couple of months, Hannah continued to add to her basement supplies. One day, David came up from the basement and asked, "Hey, what's with all the extra coffee cans in the basement?"

Hannah tried to sound casual about it, "Oh, you know I won't want to shop after the baby comes, and it's always wise to have extra."

David leaned in and kissed her cheek, "I guess we can indulge these little oddities that pregnant ladies have."

The second labor and birth were a bit less terrifying. She was thankful to be in a state of semi-consciousness. When she awoke, she saw David looking adoringly at their baby girl. She asked him if it was okay if they named her after Rebecca. He looked very solemn but agreed to the name.

Rebecca proved to be a more difficult baby than Max. She was fussier and not as good an eater or sleeper. Hannah was disappointed that she didn't experience the magical emotional transformation she had hoped for. She soon found her days an exhausting round of baby bottles, diapers, cleaning, and meals.

Right before Thanksgiving, David came home in a state of excitement. He asked Hannah to bundle up the children and bring them outside. In the driveway, there was a large, gleaming green car.

"It's the 1953 Chrysler Imperial coupe! I just bought it today. Hop in!" David exclaimed. Hannah held baby Rebecca in her lap as Max clambered around in the back seat and David backed out of the driveway. Hannah couldn't help but feel excited about the new car. They drove to Sam and Sylvie's house to show it off.

That night, as David lay next to her sleeping soundly, Hannah allowed herself to hope and believe that life in America truly was different and she and her little family were safe.

Chapter Thirteen: Helma 1956–1964

Charles O'Neal left Austria for America. He wanted to get his affairs in order in America before coming back to marry Helma. For Helma, the six months they were apart felt like an eternity. She couldn't stop looking at her engagement ring. She felt a little silly, a woman of her age, acting like a schoolgirl with a crush. She continued her work at the restaurant. Things at home were difficult. Klara was clearly jealous. Helma's fate had been the one Klara had been angling forever since taking on the job at the restaurant and making a point of getting to know British and American men in uniform.

Helma didn't say anything, but she thought that perhaps the men, on some level, could discern that Klara had loose morals. She thought of the phrase, 'You reap what you sew,' and Klara had developed a character undesirable for men looking for a wife. Plus, she had baggage; what man wants to raise another man's child?

Helma felt she had to be the bigger person, and not only did she overlook Klara's obvious jealousy, but she was also willing to deed the family house to Klara. After all, Greta was to have the rightful inheritance of the family home, and Klara stood by Helma during her two years of unjust imprisonment in Austria. Plus, Helma still had a soft spot for her meek niece. Especially since it seemed unlikely Klara would marry, and Greta needed the stability.

Helma checked the mail every day, her heart racing to see if she would receive a letter or a postcard from Charles. When he arrived back in America, he had sent her a postcard with the Statue of Liberty and the New York skyline in the background. Helma couldn't wait to see it for herself. Now,

CHAPTER THIRTEEN: HELMA 1956-1964

he had been away for over five months. The postcard was propped up on the lampstand on Helma's bedside table. She stared at it, willing herself to have pleasant dreams about her new life in America.

One day, she received an especially exciting letter.

Dear Helma,

I'm making my travel plans to come back to Austria and to you. I have big news! After a few months of hard work and getting in some overtime, I was able to buy us a little house in Queens. It's not big, but it has a nice little yard in the front and the back. I have been staying with my cousin and saving every penny to put the down payment on this little place. I went to the bank and got my veteran's loan and bought it!

I hope you aren't mad about me choosing a place before you get here, but I want everything settled before we're married. I want you to come to America and settle right in, give this house a woman's touch and make it something special.

The other bit of big news (and I hope you're not too mad about this either) is that I've booked our honeymoon. A wonderful fishing trip to Nova Scotia. That's in Canada, if you didn't know. I've been dreaming of going there for a fishing trip for many years, and it's beautiful country there. We can go there straight from Austria, right after we're married. We can come to the United States from Canada. I think this will resolve any of your concerns about being questioned about your past. I want it all to be hassle-free so we can get started on our new life together.

Thinking of you always,
Charles

Helma clutched the letter to her chest. He truly was thinking of her always. The only little dark cloud that hung over her was the potential difficulty of entry into America and if she would face any trouble due to her past. She only wished he had enclosed a photo of the house, but it didn't matter, she would be excited no matter how it looked. She could put her 'woman's touches' into the home, as he said. She was so proud. Her fiancé was so smart, so industrious.

Finally, the day came. Helma met him at the train station in Vienna. He bounded off the train, with that big smile she so loved. He kissed her cheek. They went back to the house. Graciously, Charles had brought presents for Klara and Greta. A beautiful brooch for Klara and a sweet silver necklace for Greta engraved with her initials in a fancy script.

The wedding was a simple affair. Only two friends from the restaurant and Klara and Greta at the church. Helma felt excited and a little giddy during the ceremony. Afterward, they headed back to the house for cake and punch.

Helma wore a robin's egg blue suit and a stylish hat with netting in the front. She had her pumps dyed to match. She felt very attractive in her suit, and Charles looked handsome and more than a little nervous when they stood and exchanged their vows. After the cake and punch, they immediately departed for the train station. They had a sleeper car, and that evening, Helma didn't know what to expect, but as usual, Charles was the perfect gentleman, preferring to wait until they made it to their honeymoon destination before they had relations. They departed for Canada from Calais. Helma was a little sorry they didn't see more of France.

Helma stood on the deck of the ship and breathed in the fresh air. She could hardly believe it was all happening. She had been so hurt and disappointed that the war was lost, and the great destiny of the German Reich wasn't fulfilled, and that she was made out to be so bad by the other side after the war, with that unfair judgment and her time in prison. She had been sad about losing her brother and her father to the war and, finally, poor Klaus and all that he suffered in that horrible communist camp.

Now, she thought, she could put all those disappointments away and throw all of her energy into her marriage and a new life in America.

The honeymoon in Nova Scotia was perfect in Helma's mind. The cabin where they stayed was cozy with a river stone fireplace and wood paneling. She accompanied Charles on a few of the fishing excursions, and they had some long walks together. As for the more intimate times, Charles was respectful, and Helma was relieved that, like her, he was not overly physically

CHAPTER THIRTEEN: HELMA 1956–1964

or emotionally demonstrative. She understood that men had needs and was willing to fulfill her duties as a wife. She was pleased that in this arena, as in others, she and Charles were well-matched.

After an extended honeymoon, they came to the United States from Canada. It was smooth sailing as they crossed the border, and she had no difficulties obtaining her new identification as Helma O'Neal.

She was excited that Charles insisted that they go to their new house right away. Charles opened the door of his 1954 blue Dodge Coupe for Helma. She didn't know he had such a nice car, but it seemed like everyone in America had nice cars! They pulled up to the modest grey house in a tidy middle-class neighborhood. The front yard was small, but Helma saw ways she could improve it. Inside, it was a two-bedroom house with a cozy kitchen and charming breakfast nook. Although the house was only 900 or so square feet, to Helma, it was perfect.

Charles had held off on getting much furniture other than the bare necessities, so that Helma could have more of a hand in the household decor.

"I'm so glad you like it, Helma! Sorry it's not all put together, and I will have to save up some money before we can really fix it up, but I think we could be happy here."

Helma smiled at Charles as he gestured to the living room. He only had a simple sofa in the room, and on the other side of the door was a small dining room and the kitchen. He led Helma down the short hallway where there was one larger bedroom with a queen bed, a bathroom, and a small bedroom that Charles referred to as the "spare room." He led her past a little utility space with an old-fashioned washing machine to the door to the backyard. She stepped down two steps into the yard and looked around.

"This is good, Charles. We can plant a little vegetable garden here and maybe some flowers or even a trellis here to make a shaded area, and look, you already have a clothesline up!"

Charles smiled, "I knew you would know how to make this place a home," as he squeezed her shoulder.

Helma loved her new life. She would get up every morning, make Charles breakfast, and pack his lunch in his black metal lunch pail. As soon as Charles worked a little more overtime, he gave Helma some money to start picking out furniture and decorations for the house. She found two comfortable matching chairs with matching ottomans for the living room. There, she and Charles would sit at night watching some television, or he would read, and she would knit.

She set to work in the back yard, planting a vegetable garden, some rose bushes in the side yard. One weekend, Charles erected a trellis. Helma planted climbing wisteria and found small metal outdoor chairs with a small matching table. In the summer, Helma and Charles would sit outside after dinner, drinking lemonade or iced tea.

The first few years in America, Helma focused on making their house a home, making sure Charles was well looked after, and perfecting her English. She learned about American culture and liked most of the people in her neighborhood. Even though she wasn't overly social, she knew a few people from her church. Most of her neighbors were blue-collar Irish or Italian Americans; there were some Jewish people in her neighborhood, but she didn't socialize with them. She and Charles were both reticent and liked being home more than anything else. They attended church regularly but weren't involved much beyond that. Helma knitted blankets and baby items for Christmas bazaars occasionally.

Helma's fortieth birthday was on the horizon. She visited her doctor, and he confirmed what she knew in her heart already. She wouldn't be having any children.

That evening, she told Charles that she believed that there was no longer a chance for them to have children. He reached across the dining table and took her hand.

"That's okay, Helma. I'm happy, and I hope you are too. I think we will be fine. We should take advantage of our freedom. Let's plan a fun vacation."

She smiled gratefully at him. Truthfully, even though she felt it was her duty as a woman to have children for her husband, she was secretly relieved that she wouldn't be having any. Motherhood seemed messy and unappealing to her.

CHAPTER THIRTEEN: HELMA 1956–1964

Helma decided that she would become an American citizen. It was an exciting day when she took her oath of citizenship, and she and Charles went out to a fancy restaurant for dinner. It was something they rarely did, which made it seem even more like a treat. As a newly minted citizen she decided to volunteer with some of her church friends to help elect Kennedy for President. Helma hadn't concerned herself with politics since the war ended and the dream of the Reich was over, but she thought she should take part in this new chapter of her life. While she didn't agree with Kennedy on everything, he was an Irish American like her husband and a Catholic. Once a week, she would fold flyers and stamp mailers for the Kennedy campaign. Her husband was proud.

"You are a real American now, Helma! You're not thinking of running for office yourself now, are you?" He asked in a kidding way.

Helma was thrilled at Kennedy's narrow victory and the optimistic and futuristic attitude that had overtaken the country. She noted, as Kennedy promoted the goal of reaching the moon, that German scientists, notably Wernher Von Braun, a former Nazi, were part of the American effort. This reassured her that the dark days just after the war were behind her and that the Americans were moving on. too.

One day, Charles brought home an adorable Airedale Terrier puppy. Taking care of the puppy, training him, and walking him was Helma's new joy. A few weeks later, Charles brought home the puppy's litter mate. Her first puppy was named Laddie, after President Harding's famous Airedale Terrier, and the littermate they named Macaroni, after Caroline Kennedy's pony. Charles took out the Brownie camera and captured several rolls of film of Helma in the backyard with Laddie and Macaroni. She dropped several copies in the mail to Klara and Greta back in Austria. She and Charles were planning a vacation to Switzerland in about a year, and Helma was excited to see Klara, but especially Greta.

Helma was organizing her knitting in the spare room after taking the dogs out for their daily walk when she heard a crash and glass shatter in the living room. She ran out to see a baseball rolling around on the living room floor amid shattered glass. Helma, full of anger, jerked the front door open.

Standing sheepishly in her yard were two neighbor boys. She knew that they were brothers and attended her church.

"So, what happened here?" She stared down at them as she folded her arms. The older brother stood up a little straighter and cleared his throat.

"I'm very, very sorry, Mrs. O'Neal. We were playing catch here on the sidewalk, and the ball we accidentally threw through your window. We're awfully sorry, ma'am."

Helma felt herself relax. She knew it was an accident, and it flashed in her mind that this was something that Charles would expect her to be forgiving and generous about.

"Okay, boys, I accept your apology. Mr. O'Neal and I will take care of the window. You can go on home now, but in the future, you must be careful when playing your games."

The boys thanked her and scurried down the street to their home. Helma boarded up the window. Charles noticed when he came home.

"Oh, Charles, the boys were truly sorry, and we can take care of the window. They are the brothers that live down the street. They go to our church."

"You're sure a soft touch for kids, Helma. That's pretty nice of you to let them off the hook like that."

Helma smiled. She knew that he appreciated her kindness to the boys. It was important to her to try to live up to the ideal of a good wife, even if that meant being more of a soft touch than she naturally was.

They had saved enough money for a nice hotel near a lake in Switzerland. They spent their days relaxing, hiking, and seeing the sights. One day, the resort was offering the opportunity for guests to be photographed by the lake with two lion cubs. Helma had her photo taken and had an extra print made for Greta.

Returning to her home on the outskirts of Vienna near the woods was a little depressing. It looked old and dilapidated, especially seen through the lens of living years in America, where everything seemed new and vibrant.

Greta had grown into a tall, blond, and still shy young lady. She had finished a few years of study at university and was working at the same

CHAPTER THIRTEEN: HELMA 1956–1964

restaurant where Helma and Klara had worked for her summer job.

"You look so good, auntie!" Greta gave Helma a warm hug. Helma gave Greta the framed photo of herself with the two lion cubs. While it was delightful to catch up with Greta, it was hard to see how old and haggard Klara had become. She no longer worked at the restaurant and just did occasional catering jobs to sustain herself. Helma suspected that Klara had started drinking heavily. Helma thought it was a pity that Klara was so weak and how disappointed Hans would have been had he lived to see her giving up in this way.

A darkness overtook Charles and Helma that fall when President Kennedy was assassinated. Like millions of Americans, they watched the television for days in horror and sadness at what had happened. In the following months, Helma was increasingly irritated and concerned about the civil rights movement. She sympathized with those in the South who wanted to keep the races separate. It seemed like a sensible policy, but it seemed to her that those who were sensible and knew what was right were losing ground.

During the spring of 1964, Helma decided to re-decorate the house. She spent time sewing new curtains and hours at the hardware store picking out new paints. As spring turned to summer, Helma found herself more content and less bothered by the negative developments in the news. The routine of walking the dogs and working on refreshing a new room in the house gave her a lot of satisfaction. One morning in July, Helma put on her new pink blouse, pairing it with pinstriped pink shorts, and prepared to paint an accent wall in the living room. The doorbell rang, and when she answered, there was a young man in a blue button-down shirt and khaki pants holding a notebook. Helma felt herself stiffen when she suspected he was a Jew. Was he here to try to sell her something?

"Hello, I'm Joe Lerman. I'm looking for Mrs. O'Neal, a Helma Braun O'Neal. Is that you?"

"Yes, I'm Mrs. Charles O'Neal. How can I help you?"

"Was your maiden name Braun? Are you from Vienna, Austria?"

"Yes. Is there something I can do for you?"

"Ah, yes, well, I'm a reporter for *The New York Times*. Simon Wiesenthal is working with the United States Justice Department, tracking down a Nazi prison guard named Helma Braun O'Neal living in Queens. Did you work as a prison guard at Ravensbruck and Majdanek concentration camps?"

Helma felt herself step back. The young reporter looked concerned. A thousand thoughts flooded Helma's mind. She knew that her life with Charles in America was too good to be true. She looked at the reporter and finally found the will to speak.

"I knew this day would come."

Chapter Fourteen: Hannah 1953–1964

Taking care of two small children consumed Hannah's days. She tried to make sure she was providing them with what they needed. Max was the easy one. He was growing into a calm, kind, and curious little boy. Rebecca, who David called "Becky" or "Becks," was a different story. She could be fussy and unreceptive to attention, even arching her back as a baby when Hannah tried to rock her to sleep. This was a contrast to Max, who would snuggle right in until he fell asleep.

Hannah remembered someone told her that when you name your child after someone, you are hoping they will take on the characteristics of that person. Hannah thought with Max, it had come to pass and that her little son had many of her father's attributes he was affectionate, thoughtful, and easy to be around. As for her daughter, Hannah felt she had no attributes of her sister Rebecca, but should have been named Anna, after her mother. Becky was a little high-strung, particular about her clothes and food, and could be a little greedy. Nevertheless, she was the apple of David's eye, and he indulged her.

Hannah never liked the name Becky, and when David started using the name, Hannah found it hard to conceal her annoyance, "I really don't like the name Becky. It sounds like a silly, unserious person and not one of our family names. We never called Rebecca 'Becky.'"

David sighed heavily, "We are in America, and that is a common diminutive for Rebecca. It's more American sounding. Don't you want our children to fit in? It's a sweet name for a girl. I know we never referred to your sister by that name, but that was in Austria a long, long time ago."

Hannah stood up from the table and headed to her living room chair. She lit a cigarette and picked up a magazine. She saw David's shoulders slump as he sat at the table. This had become Hannah's way of dealing with David when she felt like she wasn't being listened to, and she simply just shut down. They kept a certain peace this way, and it never interfered with the day-to-day routine. Hannah got up early and fixed breakfast for David and the children. Then David headed off to work.

As time passed, David thrived at his job and received several promotions. He bought Hannah her own car, a station wagon. They bought a black and white T.V. so they didn't have to go to Sam and Sylvie's house to watch "*I Love Lucy*" and other shows. They also started taking annual summer trips to upstate New York with Sam and Sylvie to stay at "The Pines" resort. The resort was well known for its pools—one indoor and one outdoor. Hannah loved to swim, and Sylvie called her "Esther Williams" after the famous swimmer in the movies.

"Hannah, if I looked like you in a swimsuit, I would want to swim all the time, too. You are such a good swimmer and diver," Sylvie told Hannah the first summer they went to The Pines together in 1955. Sylvie was wearing a wide-brimmed hat, sunglasses, and a matronly swimsuit with a skirt. Sylvie liked to dangle her feet in the water but never went swimming herself. Hannah was thankful, as Sylvie looked after the children when she wanted a stretch of time to swim by herself. Hannah and Sylvie would pack up the children and luggage in the station wagon at the end of July and head out for The Pines. David and Sam typically came up on Friday nights for the weekends. They would have drinks and sometimes play cards in the evenings. They would head back after a few weeks, and the regular routine of Hannah's life resumed.

After fixing breakfast, David would leave for work, and Hannah would clean and take the children out to the park, maybe stop by the store, and put the kids down for a nap. Hannah would do a little more cleaning and then start on dinner. David would come home and play with the kids for a bit. After dinner, Hannah cleaned up and got the kids in the bathtub and ready for bed. After they were asleep, Hannah would join David in the living

CHAPTER FOURTEEN: HANNAH 1953–1964

room to watch T.V. or read a magazine. She always had a pill in her hand and would wash it down with a glass of wine or a cocktail. It sometimes worried her how much she needed a drink and a pill at the end of the day, but as long as the house was in good order and the children were taken care of, she felt it was fine to end the day this way.

Finally, it was time for Max to head to school. Hannah made sure to go to the hairstylist the day before the first day of school and wore her sharpest navy dress with matching heels, pearl earrings, and pearl necklace to escort Max to school at Kew Garden's P.S. 99. Max was such an obedient boy, there was no fuss. Driving home, Hannah took several deep breaths; she hoped that she had been as good as the other mothers and that Max would do well at school. Sylvie was waiting at her house with Rebecca. Sylvie had braided Rebecca's hair, and Hannah marveled at how sweet Rebecca was with Sylvie and how she could be such a pill for her.

Hannah put the coffee on, sat down with Sylvie, and had a long drag on a cigarette. "Sylvie, I just don't understand why Rebecca is so sweet for you and such a stubborn little girl for me."

"You know girls and their mothers. There is always a conflict. Becky is willful, but she's a bright girl. You and David are blessed. Maybe you need a break. Now that the children are a little older, you and David could join our regular bridge game."

Hannah nodded. It would be another routine to add to the other routines, such as the weekly "wash and set" at the Beauty Bar with Sylvie, the occasional Saturday night out or movie night, and then, every summer, the annual trip to The Pines.

Max was very excited when Hannah picked him up from school. His teacher let him take a little book home. Rebecca was pedaling her tricycle out on the patio when they got home. Max opened the patio door and ran outside to a large, scraggly cat in the yard. He and Rebecca were petting him when Hannah came out to the yard.

"Mom, can we keep him?" Max implored. Rebecca squealed, "Yes, yes! Let's keep him."

"Well, I'd have to check with your father. I've seen this kitty hanging out in our yard quite a bit. I don't think he has a home. It might be nice to have a pet. My sisters and I had a pet cat when I was a girl."

"What was your kitty's name?" Rebecca asked.

"We called him Siggi. He was a good hunter."

Hannah could feel Max staring at her. He had a serious look on his face. "Where are your sisters? When can we meet them?"

Hannah was startled. She hadn't considered how she would talk to her children about her family. She rested her hand on Max's arm. "Max, a long time ago, there was a very bad war where Daddy and I used to live. It's sad, but my family died during the war."

Max's little face became somber, and he wrapped his hands around Hannah's neck. "I'm sorry, mom. You don't have to be sad anymore about your family. I love you." Hannah squeezed him tightly and swallowed the lump in her throat.

Rebecca said, "We can name this kitty Siggi Two!" Hannah laughed and said, "Yes, we can call him Siggi Two."

That evening, after the children were in bed, David put a Frank Sinatra album on the Hi-Fi. Hannah asked him about the cat. "The kids want to adopt that scraggly cat that has been hanging out in our backyard the last few weeks. They want to name him Siggi Two after a cat I used to have."

David smiled, "I can't really object, as I have been feeding that cat some leftover chicken at night a few times now."

"Ha! You big softie. You've been feeding him chicken? No wonder he is hanging around!" David wrapped his arm around Hannah's waist, and they started dancing to the music. Hannah wasn't sure how to broach the other subject of how to talk to their children about their families and their past. She waited until they were lying in the dark in bed.

"David, there was one other thing today. I mentioned my sisters when I was talking about my old cat. Max asked about my sisters, and I just said that my family died in the war."

David sighed heavily and said, "Yes, I think if they ask, we just need to say that our families died in the war. Nothing more. We don't need to bring any of that ugliness into our home about the camps."

CHAPTER FOURTEEN: HANNAH 1953–1964

Hannah agreed. It didn't seem fair to burden the children with all of that. Even though she didn't want the children to be burdened with the knowledge of what had happened, she still kept a store of extra food and her tea tin of money in the basement. She even kept a cedar chest with extra coats and extra copies of the children's birth certificates. She thought even if something happened to her and David, maybe the fact that the children were natural-born U.S. citizens might help them. David was very exasperated by her basement cache of supplies.

"Hannah, this is ridiculous. This is not Austria or Germany. We are going to be safe. I wish you would quit obsessing over this. It isn't good for you."

As time went by, and as the children grew, their family was like so many other families in their neighborhood who were living in the prosperity of 1950s America. It had been a couple of years since Hannah had heard from Miriam. It was the end of May 1960, and Hannah was scrambling to set up summer activities for the children. And was sorting through the mail, and saw a letter from Miriam.

Dear Hannah,

I hope you, David, and the children are well. Thanks for your postcards from The Pines Resort over the past two summers. It's so nice to hear from you, and I'm sorry I've been such a lazy correspondent. As you may remember about Benny, he's always got something new going, but we are doing well. Daniel is doing well and growing so big!

I don't know if it is receiving news coverage in America, but the capture of Eichmann is big news in Israel right now. There is a man in Austria, Simon Wiesenthal, who is tracking down some of the Nazi criminals. He was involved in tracking down Eichmann.

It has left me wondering whatever happened to all of those monstrous people at Majdanek, especially the Stomping Mare. I know you (and especially David) don't want to talk about those times, but I wonder about that. Anyway, thankful they got Eichmann, and some people are being held to account.

Keep sending those postcards and updates. Much love to you, David,

and the children.
Sincerely,
Miriam

Hannah re-read the letter in the evening. She hadn't thought about the Stomping Mare in years. It never occurred to her to wonder what happened to her after the war. Hannah thought David's influence must be rubbing off on her, as her desire to look back had waned over the years.

Dear Miriam,
   It was wonderful to hear from you. I forgive you for being lazy! Yes, the news of Eichmann is pretty big news here as well. I was somewhat surprised that people are still in pursuit of the Nazis. It seemed like the world had moved on, but now there is a renewed interest in what happened. I don't know how I feel about it.
   To say, "David doesn't like to talk about it," is a radical understatement. It's pretty much forbidden in our house. I never mention the Stomping Mare.
   I will be curious to see how things go with Eichmann. I'm glad you wrote to fill me in a little more about it. You are the only person in the world I could ever talk about it with, and I'm glad we are still pen pal friends, despite your laziness!
   My love to you, Benny, and Daniel.
   Sincerely,
   Hannah

Hannah watched with interest as the Eichmann trial unfolded over the next couple of years. She read about it in the newspaper after David was at work, as she knew it wasn't a topic that he would want her dwelling on. When Eichmann was finally executed by hanging for his crimes in 1962, it gave Hannah the chills.

On New Year's Day, 1963, David surprised Hannah with the news of a trip for just the two of them to Boca Raton, Florida. He brought home flowers

CHAPTER FOURTEEN: HANNAH 1953–1964

and a big envelope. Inside the envelope, there were two plane tickets and a color brochure of a fancy Florida resort.

"Well, Hannah we never had a honeymoon, and we've been working so hard at building this new life in America, and raising the kids, I thought it was time for us to celebrate together."

Hannah's eyes grew wide. She wasn't expecting this at all. She had never really been anywhere except the upstate resort they went to in the summer, a few excursions to the theater and a fancy dinner in Manhattan, and a trip to the shore in New Jersey, but that was it; she hadn't been anywhere else in America. She looked over the brochure, there were pools, the cabana club and nightly entertainment. She started counting the months until November 1963.

Thankfully, Sam and Sylvie agreed to stay at their house to take care of Max and Rebecca. This was the first time that Hannah would be away from her children overnight, and even though Max was now twelve and Rebecca was ten, it filled her with anxiety to be away from them.

It was Hannah's first time ever on a plane, and it was hard to contain her excitement. She had splurged a bit on a few new outfits and swimsuits. For her plane trip, she wore a sunny yellow suit with matching hat and gloves. The resort was like a dream. She could swim and enjoy the cabana while David relaxed and read. The hotel staff brought them endless cocktails. In the evening, they enjoyed an elegant meal, live music, and drinks. Hannah felt like a queen in her cream and pink strapless evening dress with opera-length gloves. She had her hair done in an elegant French twist. David looked handsome and distinguished in a tuxedo.

The next morning, Hannah went swimming and then relaxed in the cabana next to David. He looked over his sunglasses appreciatively at her, "You are such a wonderful swimmer. I remember when you were a little girl back in Austria, you loved to swim. Your father loved going to your swimming competitions. He was so proud."

It made Hannah happy that at least there was some part of their past that they could talk about. She was just dozing off on a lounge chair next to David when she heard people talking in alarmed tones and leaving the pool, and David put down his book, as a staff member brought him a drink, David asked, "What is all the commotion?"

"Sir, there are news reports that President Kennedy has been injured in a shooting."

Hannah bolted up from her lounge chair and collected her things, and David stood up too. They went to their room and turned on the news. Hannah curled up in her robe with David's arm around her. Walter Cronkite's voice broke as he confirmed the news that President Kennedy was dead. Hannah felt the tears sting her eyes, and David held his head in his hands before looking up at Hannah, "We should call Sam and Sylvie and check on the kids."

David spoke with them. Hannah couldn't stop crying. They ordered room service, and it took a long time. The hotel staff member explained there were many calls for room service as nobody wanted to go out for dinner tonight. David encouraged her to come to bed, but Hannah stayed up to watch T.V. She watched Mrs. Kennedy as she was helped off the plane in Washington, D.C. She looked so composed in her blood-spattered suit. Hannah always scooped up any magazine featuring Mrs. Kennedy. She loved her style, her hair, her clothes. Hannah and Mrs. Kennedy were about the same age and were both young mothers. Hannah felt so deflated. A sick feeling in her stomach did not subside, even when they were back home in Queens.

Nothing was the same after that in Hannah's mind. Everything in the atmosphere felt disconcerting. The news was full of dissension about civil rights and the growing conflict in Vietnam. Regardless, the routine of school for the children, work for David, card games with neighbors, and the weekly trip to the beauty parlor continued.

Hannah found herself unexpectedly alone on a bright sunny morning in July 1964. The house was unusually quiet as David had left for work, Max got up early for a stickball game with his friends, and Rebecca had a special Camp Fire Girls meeting. Hannah whipped up some scrambled eggs and thought she would spend part of the morning with her coffee and *The New York Times*. She was scanning the pages when a headline stopped her cold,

CHAPTER FOURTEEN: HANNAH 1953-1964

"Queens Housewife Alleged to be Notorious Nazi Concentration Camp Guard."

Chapter Fifteen: Hannah Summer 1964

"Mom is upstairs. She's sick." Becky said to David when he came in the door. Becky was still in her Camp Fire Girls uniform. Max was watching TV.

David went to the kitchen and got a glass of water from the tap. He gently knocked on their bedroom door before pushing it open. Hannah was curled in the fetal position on the bed with the curtains drawn. David sat next to her and spoke to her in a hushed tone. "I have water and a couple of aspirin."

Hannah sat up. Her eyes were puffy. There was a newspaper clipping on the nightstand next to the bed. She drank the water, took the aspirin, and then took a deep breath and handed David the newspaper clipping.

"That woman in the article. She was my camp guard. She killed Rebecca. She killed lots of people."

David scanned the article. His face grew pale. "Hannah, it is so many years ago. You can't be sure if this is the same woman. Besides, it has nothing to do with us."

"David, what do you mean? It has everything to do with us. She lives here in Queens. Practically our neighborhood! Near our family, our children. She is a murderer, and she is living a free life here. I have to do something!"

"Hannah, slow down. You can't be sure, and it is not up to you to do something. If she is a criminal, then I'm sure the proper authorities will take care of it. You're clearly upset. Now, lay back down. I will take the kids out for hamburgers and milkshakes while you rest. Put this out of your mind. It's not your business. Get a good night's sleep. We must get ready for Max's Bar Mitzvah. We are taking him to the tailor tomorrow, and as

CHAPTER FIFTEEN: HANNAH SUMMER 1964

you said, there are lots of things to plan yet. Focus your mind on that."

Hannah lay in the dark until she heard the door slam. She went to the bathroom and opened her bottle of Valium. She shook two pills into her hand. She thought about taking the whole bottle. This wasn't the first time she thought about doing this, but a wave of guilt would overcome her when she pictured her children. She shook out one more pill. This should knock her out for the night.

The next morning, she felt groggy. Rather unusually, David made coffee before Hannah came downstairs. He was acting extra cheerful and solicitous. After breakfast, David, Max, and Hannah headed to the tailor's shop. Max was being fitted for a custom-made suit for his Bar Mitzvah. Hannah sat on a cushioned bench and fumbled around for her leather cigarette case while David and Max were back in a fitting room. She closed her eyes and took a deep drag on her cigarette. She could feel her anger at David boiling up in her. A few minutes later, David stepped out of the fitting room. "Max is changing. I think the suit is going to look great on him." Hannah realized she must have been glaring at David. When he asked what was wrong, she found herself blurting out exactly what was on her mind. "What's wrong? The murderer of my sister lives in this community; that's what's wrong. What's wrong? I tell you this, and you treat me like a stupid child. That's what's wrong!"

David's face grew red. "Let's step outside," he growled under his breath. He roughly grabbed Hannah's arm and marched her out to the side of the building in the alleyway. He grabbed both of her arms tight. Hannah was shocked. David had never acted this way. He shook her and said, "You are forbidden to get involved in that case with that prison guard. You are never, ever to bring this up in our home!" Hannah felt the tears come to her eyes. David released her arms, and they throbbed with pain. David exhaled heavily, "You should go to the ladies' room and wash your face. I don't want Max to see you like this."

They drove home in silence.

* * *

The next morning, Hannah woke up early. She made herself a sandwich and put some coffee in a thermos. David emerged from the bedroom in his pajamas and his bathrobe just as Hannah was pulling on her sweater and heading out the door.

"Hannah, where are you going at this hour?"

Hannah just glared at David, "I will be home around dinner time. You can look after the kids today," and then slammed the door. She hopped in her station wagon. She had the address in Queens where the Stomping Mare now lived. It was only a few miles away. It was in a blue-collar neighborhood where the houses were a bit more modest. Hannah pulled up across the street from the O'Neal house. It was a small house painted gray with white trim. The yard was well-kept. Hannah poured herself a cup of coffee from the thermos. She wanted to make sure it was the Stomping Mare, not only to confirm it for herself, but to make a stronger stand with David. After about an hour, a man emerged with two dogs. Hannah thought this must be the husband. She wondered if he had any idea of the things his wife had done. He was of medium build and had sandy blond hair. In about fifteen minutes, he had returned home. He seemed like a normal, nondescript middle-aged man.

As she sat in her station wagon for a few hours, Hannah had time to reflect on the confrontation at the tailor's shop with David. This was the first time she ever saw David react in this way and the only time he had ever been so angry and so out of control. She realized this was the only time she had been so defiant or had ever expressed that she felt as if she was treated like a child. She was lost in these thoughts when finally, it happened. A woman emerged from the house in white capri pants, canvas tennis shoes, and a pink button-down sleeveless blouse. Hannah knew immediately it was the Stomping Mare. She was much thinner now, and her hair was short, curly, and blond, but the deeply set eyes and strong jaw were the same. She had the same determined, brusque way of walking. She was carrying her purse and a mesh bag. Hannah hopped out of the car and started following her on foot. Hannah's heart was racing, not only from scurrying to try to catch up with her, but also with sheer terror. It was one thing to have the knowledge

CHAPTER FIFTEEN: HANNAH SUMMER 1964

that the Stomping Mare was alive and living in Queens, it was quite another to see her in the flesh.

Hannah followed at a distance for quite a while; she thought they may have walked close to two miles when the Stomping Mare stepped into Conte's Meat Market. Hannah opened the door to the market and watched the Stomping Mare out of the corner of her eye as she pretended to peruse the cuts of meat in the store. The Stomping Mare stepped up to the counter, and a balding, middle-aged man in a white apron greeted her.

"Good afternoon, Mrs. O'Neal. Would you like your usual Sunday pot roast?"

Hannah was stupefied to hear the Stomping Mare speaking in heavily accented English, "Yes, Mr. Conte, the pot roast, and I would like some sliced Black Forest Ham as well." Hannah saw that she smiled pleasantly at the butcher as he prepared her order and handed him the mesh bag in which he placed the butcher paper-wrapped pot roast and sliced ham. The Stomping Mare nodded and thanked the butcher. She turned around. She must have seen Hannah staring at her.

Hannah felt her face flush and terror overwhelm her as the Stomping Mare narrowed her eyes, clenched her jaw, and stepped forward to Hannah. In an angry voice that had filled her with terror years before, the Stomping Mare confronted her, "What are you staring at?" The same angry face and voice, but this time speaking English.

Hannah was too terrified to say anything. After a few seconds, the Stomping Mare brushed past her and out the door. Hannah's whole body was shaking. She knew her knees were giving out. She tried to steady herself on the curved glass of the meat display case, but she felt herself going down. A young man with dark hair rushed out from behind the counter with a stool in his hand. He grabbed Hannah's arm and prevented her from hitting the ground. He helped her settle on the stool. "Are you okay, Miss? Would you like a glass of water?"

Hannah looked up to him gratefully. "Yes, a glass of water would be nice." He nodded, went back behind the counter, and came back with a glass of water. Hannah had a few sips and was starting to feel better. The handsome young man looked at her with concern. "Are you feeling better? Is there someone we should call for you?" By this time, the butcher had come out from behind the counter as well. Hannah smiled at them both and was able to stand up. "Thank you for your kindness. I'm feeling much better. I just had a spell, and I haven't eaten anything today."

The butcher turned to the young man, "Son, go get that roast beef sandwich from the back." The butcher took Hannah's hand in his and patted it, "Miss, we have a sandwich for you, and you know the roast beef is fresh," he said as he chuckled. Hannah protested, but they insisted she take the sandwich.

Hannah walked out of the butcher shop, and the streets were full of people going about their day. Hannah felt so strange as if she had fallen through a hole in time. She couldn't reconcile the Stomping Mare living in Queens and buying pot roast and ham at the nice butcher's shop and living in that tidy little home with her normal husband. Hannah ate the sandwich as she slowly walked back to her car. As she turned the key to start the car, she wondered what on earth she was doing.

That night, she made a cold salad, but she couldn't eat. David stared at her wearily, and the children were oblivious to the tension. Later, Hannah contemplated the Valium bottle in the bathroom. How many would it take to sleep tonight?

A week had passed since David and Hannah's confrontation at the tailor's shop. Hannah's stomach had been hurting vaguely all week. She had to concentrate to listen to Sylvie's chatter about the upcoming hospital benefit gala as they drove to the beauty parlor. As she sat under the dryer, Hannah's mind was a scramble. She still didn't know how she could make it through the evening with David.

When she got home and slipped into the bright blue brocade dress she had selected weeks ago, it occurred to her that she didn't even remember the woman who had purchased the dress with such great delight and excitement. Hannah looked at herself in the mirror. The bruise on her arm was beginning to fade. She couldn't believe that David had grabbed her arm so roughly as to leave a mark. Her dress was tight fitting, low cut, blue and floor length.

CHAPTER FIFTEEN: HANNAH SUMMER 1964

It was by far the most risqué dress that Hannah had ever worn. She picked up the sheer shoulder wrap and met David waiting at the door.

He glanced down at her breasts and looked at her dress. "It's a wonderful color, but I don't know that it is entirely appropriate," he said as he opened the door to let her pass. They drove to the event in silence.

The ballroom was very bright. She saw Sam and Sylvie. Sam kissed her cheek, "Vavoom! Hannah, you look like Sophia Loren's sister," as he led her to their table. Hannah tried to smile as Sam introduced them to the couples already seated around the table. Many she already knew from the hospital. Then Sam introduced her to Weston and Susan Bradley. He was very tall with bright blue eyes and thinning dark blond hair. He stood to shake David's hand, and Hannah knew Weston Bradley appreciated her dress much more than David did. Mrs. Weston Bradley looked bored.

Hannah was lost in a fog throughout dinner. She drank much more wine than she ever allowed herself. David was in a deep conversation with a colleague. Hannah excused herself to the lobby of the hotel. She found herself staring out the window watching the young men smoke at the valet parking stand.

"There you are, Mrs. Schneider! I was hoping you would do me the honor of at least one dance." It was Weston Bradley, with a cigarette in hand.

"I'm very sorry to disappoint you, Mr. Bradley. I don't know how to dance, and I've had a bit too much to drink."

"Having a 'bit' too much to drink actually helps, even without any formal dance training. However, having too much isn't good. You have to find that sweet spot. Do you feel like giving it a try? I am a very strong lead."

"I thank you, but I will have to pass. But, if I could trouble you to accompany me outside and if you had an extra cigarette, that would be a great help to me. So much more so than trying to dance."

Weston Bradley smiled, stepped close to Hannah, and extended his arm. "I would be happy to," and as he stood next to her, Hannah realized how bright his frosty blue eyes were. She felt herself relax and lean against his arm as they walked outside. They stood next to a large cement planter. Hannah really knew she had too much to drink. She felt wobbly. She put her hand on the planter to steady herself. Weston reached over to steady her. He chuckled and handed her a cigarette.

Hannah was shaky, and Weston leaned in closely to light her cigarette. Being close to him again, she felt herself wanting to collapse into his arms and have him guide her somewhere safe and quiet. She wanted to listen to his confident and reassuring voice. He seemed so at ease. There was something Hannah liked very much about how he openly appreciated her body; it made her feel sexy and alive.

"Are you alright, Mrs. Schneider?"

"Since you have saved me from falling into a cement planter and given me a cigarette, you may call me Hannah."

"Well, thank you, Hannah. It's very nice to be on a first-name basis with a beautiful, if unsteady, woman like you. But I do want an answer to my question. Are you okay?"

Hannah stared out into the distance. She wasn't sure if it was the alcohol, the events of the past few weeks, or if she had truly lost any control of her emotions, but she began to weep, "Nothing is okay, nothing is right. My world is upside down. Buried demons are quite literally coming back from the past. I don't know what I will do. I could just stand here and scream."

Weston's face became serious. He put his hands on her shoulders, "I don't know what to say," and he pulled her close to his chest. Hannah began to take deeper breaths. Weston pulled back from her and kissed her wet cheeks. He kissed her neck. Hannah did not want him to stop, but he did.

He pulled back from her and spoke very softly, "I really want to know you better, Hannah. I'm not going to lie to a smart gal like you and say that my interest is only platonic, because it's not. Especially since you are wearing that dress. But I do want to know you. I'm giving you my card, and I want you to call me. We can have lunch and talk. You seem like you need someone to talk to about things."

He reached into his jacket pocket and pulled out a business card. He took Hannah's little blue purse and put his card in it, "Now I'm going to escort you back to the ladies' room, where you will freshen up, and we will go back to the table and be good little guests."

CHAPTER FIFTEEN: HANNAH SUMMER 1964

As they walked back into the ballroom, Hannah saw David stand up. He walked over to Hannah and Weston.

"I was worried about you, Hannah."

"No need to worry. I escorted your lovely wife outside for a bit of fresh air and a quick smoke. She is right as rain now," Weston Bradley offered.

Hannah was thankful for Weston's confident manner and for running interference for her with David. She felt David's hand touch her elbow gently as they walked back to the table. Sam stood up to greet her and kissed her cheek, "Good night, Hannah. David said you are heading home."

Hannah looked toward David as he was saying his goodbyes. Susan Bradley still looked terribly bored but managed a slight polite smile. Just as they were turning to leave, Weston Bradley stood up and shook David's hand, "It was a pleasure to meet you, Mr. Schneider, and you too, Mrs. Schneider," and he took Hannah's hand and kissed it. Just like something out of the movies, she thought, like William Holden kissing her hand. She felt herself float out of the hotel ballroom. She felt relieved, but completely untethered. The car ride home was silent.

As they were undressing in the bedroom, David walked over to Hannah and he helpfully unzipped her dress, "Hannah, I know this has been hard. Probably one of the hardest times since we have been here in America. But look around us. Look at our house. Look at the lovely evening we had tonight. Look at our children. They are safe, healthy, receiving an education; they are American citizens. Max will have his Bar Mitzvah in just a few days. Why you would give a moment's thought to what happened back there is confounding to me."

"David, I'm grateful. You know that. I don't know how to explain it to you. I don't understand how you can't remember our home, my family, and my sister Rebecca. You were there. You knew us. It was as real as what we have here. I'm not crazy. I was there. I know that woman. I saw her kill people. She beat me. She killed Rebecca."

"Stop Hannah. You're getting upset. You've had a bit too much to drink. Come, let's go to bed."

Hannah just shook her head and went to the bathroom. When she came out, David was already in bed, and the lights were out. She slid into bed next to him. He put his hand on her shoulder, "Get some sleep, and things will look different in the morning."

The morning came, and it wasn't different. It was the same as it had been for many years. Hannah got up and made breakfast for her family. David ate only a few bites, drank his coffee, and kissed Hannah's cheek. The children ran out the door to see their friends. She washed the dishes, cleaned the table, and did the dusting. She went upstairs and soaked in the tub. She put on a dress and styled her hair.

She found the little blue purse and took out Weston Bradley's card. She sat at the table with her cigarette and coffee and traced the edges of the card. She thought awhile about where she could hide the card. She put it in her vanity drawer with her make-up and perfume.

She made a roast chicken and vegetables for dinner. She set the table in the formal dining room, not at the kitchen table. When David came home, he looked so pleased at this. He gave Hannah effusive compliments on the meal. He leaned over and patted her hand. Their children looked surprised. Hannah surmised that they had sensed the tension between their parents.

When they went to bed. Hannah felt David's hand rubbing her arm. This was the signal for what had become the twice-monthly ritual. David would remove Hannah's nightgown and underwear. She concentrated on lying perfectly still. She mentally tried to detach from her body. She could hear him in her left ear, breathing rhythmically like a metronome. The pace of the breathing quickened, and she heard a breathy grunt. A few seconds later, he was off her. He patted her shoulder. This was the signal that she could go to the bathroom and tidy up and put her nightgown back on.

The next morning, Hannah made breakfast. David had a piece of toast and coffee. He came over to her before leaving for work and said, "It is good to see you coming back to yourself."

The kids were out. Hannah cleaned the house, took a couple of pills, and soaked in the tub. She met friends for lunch, and they talked about the Bar Mitzvah. It was a small affair compared to some others. Just Sam, Sylvie, and then a few friends from Little League and neighbors at the banquet

CHAPTER FIFTEEN: HANNAH SUMMER 1964

room at Arrowbrook Country Club for a buffet-style dinner to celebrate.

Hannah still didn't know if she believed in God. She knew it was important to David to at least attend Temple on holy days and for Max to have his Bar Mitzvah. Hannah went along with this as she did so many other things. It was easy to live this way in Kew Gardens. In fact, the Schneiders were quite lax in their observance compared to some other neighbors. Max had been very dutiful in his studies. At Temple, Hannah found herself tearing up at the ceremony. Even if she didn't know what she believed, she knew that it was a miracle that she, David, Max, and Rebecca were here. They had survived. She was so glad to see the joy on David's face. Max was truly a gift to David. He loved his son, who was so much like him. Someone in which he could see a bit of himself.

It was a wonderful celebration. Hannah had not experienced anything like it. She enjoyed the dances and the food. Max received some wonderful gifts, and this usually reserved boy seemed to genuinely enjoy himself.

When they were lying in bed, David squeezed Hannah's hand, "You see how good our lives are? We have everything."

Chapter Sixteen: Helma Summer 1964

Helma felt frozen in place. The young reporter had a notebook in his hand and was looking at her expectantly. He asked again, "So, Mrs. O'Neal, you were Helma Braun, and you served as a camp guard at both Majdanek and Ravensbruck concentration camps?"

Helma felt herself start to cry. The young man had a look of concern pass over his face. She tried to compose herself and said, "Oh my God. This could be the end of everything for me."

Helma looked to the reporter again, "Yes, I was a camp guard. I had no authority. I was no different than a guard at a jail today. Besides, I was very sick for a long time during the war."

The young man was rapidly making notes in his notebook. Helma turned away, pulled a handkerchief out of her pocket, and tried to compose herself. She turned back to the young man and said, "Besides, I spent nearly three years in jail. Can you imagine that? Three years for just doing my job, as I was told. America is supposed to be about freedom and peace. Why are you bothering me?"

Helma felt her anger rising. The young man must have sensed this. "Mrs. O'Neal, I'm just doing some follow-up work on information supplied by Mr. Simon Wiesenthal. I believe he is referring your case to the United States Immigration and Naturalization Service."

By now, Helma was angry. She knew she had to control herself and not let it show. She was a simple American housewife now, and she should give this reporter no reason to think otherwise. When he looked up from his notes, she cleared her throat. "I don't think I should say anything further. I

CHAPTER SIXTEEN: HELMA SUMMER 1964

think you should speak to my husband about this matter."

He nodded and pulled a business card from his pocket. "Thank you, Mrs. O'Neal. I hope you have a good evening." He turned and walked down the front walkway.

Helma closed the door, sat down on the couch, and put her hands on her throbbing head. She wondered how she would explain all of this to Charles. She was so glad that she had explained everything to him before they were married. It was so unfair. She had already gone to jail for years even though she had never in her life done anything illegal. She cleaned up the paint cans and paint brushes, started dinner, and rehearsed what she would say to Charles when he came home.

Charles walked into the kitchen. He placed his black metal lunch pail on the counter. He started washing his hands. "So, Helma, what are we having for dinner?"

Helma couldn't answer. He turned to her with a perplexed look on his face. She held out the business card, and he took it from her hand. "Joe Lerman, reporter, *New York Times*? What is this, Helma?"

"Sit down, Charles, let's eat."

Over dinner, Helma told him the story of how that meddling Jew Wiesenthal was coming after simple camp guards like her, how this reporter just showed up at the door asking a bunch of questions, and how she answered a few before she realized she should not be the one speaking, and she should leave it up to him to handle the questions. Charles dropped his fork on the plate.

"Unbelievable. I don't understand why this Wiesenthal character would be bothering someone like you. Okay, the masterminds, like Eichmann, well, you can see that. They were high-level decision makers, but you didn't do anything except what you were asked to do."

Charles exhaled, got up from the table, picked up the phone, and dialed it. "Yes, I would like to speak to Mr. Joe Lerman, please. I'm Mr. Charles O'Neal. You spoke with my wife earlier, and she told me about the circumstances around the reason for your inquiry. let me tell you this—she was doing what she was required to do; she was just a guard, and she's a woman. She had no authority, and she wasn't making any decisions. There is no more decent person in the whole world than my wife. She wouldn't hurt a fly," Charles paused and appeared to be listening. "Mr. Lerman, these people are just swinging axes at random. It's been nearly twenty years. Haven't you people ever heard the phrase 'let the dead rest'?" Charles paused again. "What people? I think you know exactly what people, Mr. Lerman," and with that, Charles hung up the phone.

Charles came back to the table. He reached for Helma's hand. "Darling, we will figure this out together. I don't know why they are coming after you, but I will find a good attorney, and we will work it out. I don't want you to worry too much." He smiled at her, "Did you make us some dessert?"

Helma stood up, she had forgotten she had put a pineapple upside down cake in the refrigerator this morning. It seemed like such a long time ago when she was happy and carefree, but it was just this morning. Now, there was this cloud. Thank God her husband was so supportive.

Two days later, the article was published on page ten of *The New York Times*. She was thankful that it was a short story buried in the paper. The newspaper lay open on the dining room table, and Charles shook his head as he read it. Helma felt her stomach tighten. What would happen now?

That Sunday, Helma and Charles decided not to go to church. Charles got up early and walked the dogs. Helma had planned to stay in for the day and just relax, but she was restless and decided that they should have their regular Sunday pot roast, and she would get some air and walk to Conte's Meat Market, even though she usually drove, she decided a walk would be better, and she could shake off some nervous energy.

As she stepped out of the house, she noticed a station wagon across the street she hadn't seen before. She took a deep breath and tried to enjoy her walk to Conte's. Mr. Conte, the butcher, greeted her as usual. She decided to get some sliced ham for Charles' lunches. Everything felt like a normal day until she noticed a strange young woman staring at her. Helma had never seen her before. She was very pretty. She had dark brown hair styled in a bouffant and very large hazel eyes. Helma turned after the butcher completed her order. The young woman continued to stare at her. Helma

CHAPTER SIXTEEN: HELMA SUMMER 1964

wondered if she had seen the newspaper article. It made her angry to think people would be gawking at her at the market. She stepped toward the woman and confronted her. The woman looked terrified and said nothing. Helma rushed out the door and started to walk home. It troubled her that this revelation would cause people to stare at her if she was out doing the marketing or walking the dogs.

Helma felt the joy draining out of her life. She cooked the pot roast, and Charles tried very hard to be cheerful and supportive. She cleaned up the kitchen and wondered what might happen next.

The next day protesters came to the neighborhood, some Jewish group that protested in front of their neighbors' house. Some militant, angry Jews who had the wrong address. Thankfully, the police came and cleared them away. The protesters yelled and had signs that said, "Nazis Out!" Instead of Helma's house they were in front of the Gleasons' house. The Gleasons were the family who had the two boys who broke their window playing baseball. They told the protesters how kind Helma was and that they were sure that the authorities were accusing the wrong person. Charles went over to apologize for the troubles, but they extended their support to Helma. At least, that was something.

Charles tried to reassure her and cheer her up. "Helma, this is some scheme dreamed up by Jewish groups to gin up sympathy. The war was a long time ago and people are forgetting things, and they want to bring it back up for their manipulative purposes, that is why they are picking on you."

Helma was so grateful to have a husband who understood. He was looking into finding a lawyer for her. She was so sad about the drain on their finances. There would be no vacations now, as their resources must go to defending her from this unfair attack.

A few weeks later, Helma put on her nicest suit, white gloves, and a nice hat with a ribbon and flowers. Charles looked equally dressed up in his Sunday suit and his hair styled with Brylcreem, and he wore the cufflinks that Helma had purchased for him on their trip to Switzerland. He had a folder with all of their important papers and the newspaper clipping of the article from *The New York Times*. Helma had done a little research, and the reporter was a Jew. That is probably why he was ready to do the bidding of that Jew Wiesenthal.

Their lawyer, Mr. Perry, was an older man who inelegantly tried to disguise his bald spot with a thin combover. He silently perused the contents of the manila folder Charles brought with them. He read *The New York Times* article, exhaled heavily, and shook his head. "You both should not have given the reporter all this information. This puts you in a bad spot. If there are any other reporters asking you questions, keep your mouths shut."

Helma could feel Charles bristle at the criticism. Mr. Perry then closed the folder. He then turned to Helma. "This is not a good situation. Mr. Wiesenthal has had quite a good reputation since the Eichmann case. Additionally, the West German government has started ferreting out Nazis since 1958. There is a renewed energy to pursue these types of things. And, with what you've essentially confessed to in that *New York Times* article, I have to say this does not look promising."

Charles reached over to hold Helma's hand. "I appreciate your honest assessment, Mr. Perry, but what we want to know is if you are willing to take on this case and help us. Yes, Helma was a guard in these camps, but she was just a guard, and she is a woman, so naturally she wasn't making any decisions, she was doing as she was told. Everything she did was legal at the time. It was only after the war that everything changed. She was arrested and tried by the Allies in Austria, and she served her time and received amnesty from the Austrian government. Surely, that means something?"

Mr. Perry got up and sat on the edge of his desk and rubbed his chin. "Yes, that is very important and will be useful to us. I will help you, but I want you both to know it won't be easy. No offense, Mrs. O'Neal, but you are not a very sympathetic figure."

Helma felt the anger building inside her. How dare this lawyer judge her or criticize her husband. "Mr. Perry, I'm glad you are willing to help us. But I want to be able to share my side. These Jews and their supporters are upset about losing family in the camps. Let me tell you something: we sacrificed, we lost our family. My brother died fighting the communists;

CHAPTER SIXTEEN: HELMA SUMMER 1964

my other brother was in a communist slave labor camp for more than ten years. Ten years! That's longer than any Jew was in a camp. These Jews and communists want to distract us by bringing up things from twenty years ago, acting like they are the only ones who suffered. I suffered!"

Mr. Perry stood up and put a hand on Helma's shoulder. "Mrs. O'Neal, if this is going to work at all, you need some self-awareness. You are not the victim here. Do yourself a favor and keep quiet. I will start talking with the State Department and Immigration and Naturalization Service and see where we are at and exactly what your risk of losing your citizenship might be, and in the meantime, please no more talking to reporters. Keep your story to yourself."

Helma felt her cheeks burning. How dare this lawyer speak to her this way. She felt Charles squeeze her hand. "Thank you, Mr. Perry. We will heed your advice about talking to reporters, and we will help you with any documentation you need. We are here to cooperate and help you guide us through this, aren't we, Helma?"

Chapter Seventeen: Hannah Fall 1964

Hannah met Sylvie at the "Beauty Bar," the salon where they met every week for the "wash and set."

The Beauty Bar was full of housewives like Hannah and Sylvie, smoking cigarettes as they sat under domed hair dryers and read magazines. It was the first time Hannah had seen Sylvie alone since the Bar Mitzvah and hospital benefit where Hannah had worn the controversial low-cut dress.

"Hey, how have you been? I'm so excited that we have a chance to catch up," said Sylvie with excitement.

Hannah knew that Sylvie could sense something was amiss between Hannah and David.

Hannah pretended to be engrossed in a magazine article, but she was really lost in thoughts about the past sixteen years in America. They all seemed to pass in a blur when her only purpose in life was to try to become an American housewife and mother. All these things were supposed to make her happy, fulfilled, and grateful. Her husband was a "good provider," and she had a son and a daughter. But she so often felt nothing. What even mattered? She wasn't sure anymore.

Hannah was staring at the pink and mint green chairs at the Beauty Bar when she and Sylvie were summoned by the stylists.

Sylvie was trying to be casual, but was failing miserably, "I really thought the hospital benefit was a fun night! I noticed you disappeared for a while and then came back with that lawyer, what was his name? Was it Weston?"

Nice touch, pretending to struggle to remember the name. Hannah knew that Sylvie was keenly aware of who Weston Bradley was and that, in fact,

CHAPTER SEVENTEEN: HANNAH FALL 1964

they had disappeared from the banquet for almost an hour. All eyes were trained on them as they made their way back to their table, with Hannah a little unsteady on her feet. Hannah and David left shortly after, but not before Hannah noticed Sylvie whispering furiously to Sam at their table.

"Yes, Weston Bradley. I wasn't feeling well. I had a little too much to drink, so I stepped outside for a cigarette. He was nice enough to check on me, and we ended up having a long chat. He is an attorney, and I guess he was a big war hero, a B-17 pilot," she said. She left out the tearful breakdown that she had in the parking lot, Weston's kiss and proposition, and the business card he gave her.

"Oh, well, that was nice of him. Did you meet his wife? She looked very bored and was very unfriendly. Are you feeling better? You don't seem like yourself lately."

The stylists were teasing their hair into ever higher bouffant styles. Hannah didn't respond; she just lit another cigarette. Sylvie's mouth turned down in disappointment. It was clear that she was not getting any more information out of Hannah.

As they walked out, Sylvie mustered a smile and shrugged her shoulders, "Well, I guess I'm off," hoping for and expecting a response. None came.

Hannah simply said, "Have a good afternoon."

* * *

Hannah slammed the door to the station wagon, and her hands shook as she stamped out the cigarette and rushed home. She had maybe an hour before the kids came back from swimming lessons and two hours until her husband came home. She took the business card out of her purse. Over the past days she had looked at it numerous times. It was funny that having her hair styled made her feel more confident about calling him on the phone.

His secretary put her through. "Hello, Mrs. Schneider. How may I help you?"

"Well, I need some legal advice, and, uh," her voice trailed off.

"That's really disappointing because I was hoping this was a personal call and not a professional one."

Her mind raced. She hoped the legal advice she needed would give her another chance to interact with him and see if she wanted to kiss him again.

"It is professional and personal. You offered to buy me lunch. We can have lunch, and you can advise me on my legal issues. I can advise you on things of a personal nature."

He laughed and said, "What about Wednesday? We could have lunch and a few drinks at P.J. Clarke's. How does that sound?"

"Yes, I will meet you at P.J. Clarke's on Wednesday at 1:00."

Wednesday morning came, and she tried on three different outfits. She decided on a Chanel style suit with matching gloves, it was a professional meeting after all.

The restaurant was nicer and more intimate than Hannah expected; she was excited to see the tavern, as she remembered that a scene with Ray Milland in the movie "The Lost Weekend" was filmed at P.J. Clarke's. Weston stood up and smoothed his tie. He was taller than she remembered and older-looking. He pulled out her chair. His smile was broad and almost boyish, and he said, "I would like it if we got the legal, professional side of the meeting out of the way first."

Hannah reached into her purse. The newspaper clipping was folded into an envelope. Her hand shook a little as she unfolded it.

Weston looked confused as she pushed the newspaper clipping across the table. He scanned the headline, "Queens Housewife Alleged to be Notorious Nazi Concentration Camp Guard."

He looked up at Hannah as color drained from his face. He scanned the article quickly. A look of relief when he saw the picture that accompanied the article was not Hannah.

"I'm confused. What does this have to do with you?"

Hannah felt her face getting increasingly warm. She never, ever spoke of the camps. She drew in her breath.

"I knew her. I was in the camp. I saw her beat people, kill people, tear children from their mothers, and throw them on trucks to be…" her voice trailed off. Weston stared at her in stunned silence.

CHAPTER SEVENTEEN: HANNAH FALL 1964

"She killed my sister. I want to testify against her. My husband doesn't want me to. He wants to keep the past in the past, and not draw attention to ourselves. But when I saw this article and she is here, free in America. In Queens, she's practically my neighbor. I don't know what to do."

All the breezy confidence that Weston had moments ago was gone. He smoothed the edges of the newspaper clipping with his fingers.

"Um, I don't know what to tell you. I have some buddies from the service who work at the State Department, I could talk to them and get back with you."

Hannah leaned back. She felt him shifting away from her. She was no longer the woman in the sexy dress at the hospital benefit that he stole a kiss from in the parking lot. Now, she was one of those sad, skeletal victims of a horrific war. Everyone who lived it, wanted to forget it. To drown it out in martinis, new cars, evenings out in your best clothes, to live in a nice house and to provide your children with everything.

He averted her gaze. The lunch came. What Hannah had disclosed was so disorienting that they both silently agreed to revert to small talk.

At the end of the lunch, Weston walked her outside.

Hannah smiled weakly, "We never got to the personal agenda. I was working out whether or not I wanted another kiss from you."

He put his hand on her forearm, as one might do to reassure an elderly relative. He looked somber.

"It seems like you have a lot happening in your life right now. I don't want to be a complication."

Hannah was filled with regret and shame. Maybe she should keep quiet and pretend it never happened. She turned quickly away.

She felt him grab her arm. "Wait, wait! I want to help you. I didn't know this happened to you. I'm so sorry you had to endure all of that. I didn't know that some of the people responsible for all that happened over there, that they are living normal lives here. It's not right. I promise you I will investigate it. I will see what is involved."

This was the first time she felt like anyone acknowledged what had happened to her. The first time anyone said to her personally that what had happened to her was wrong. For this she was deeply grateful.

All she could manage to do was nod.

On her drive home, she felt a sense of relief and of hope. Maybe there was something she could do to bring the Stomping Mare to justice. The other feelings were a bit more complicated. She had never felt the way she felt around Weston before in her life. It wasn't as if he was the first to flirt with her. On occasion when she was swimming at The Pines, a man would chat her up, but she just ignored it. She knew that she loved David, but it was a comfortable kind of love, nothing that made her feel a jolt of energy.

When she arrived home, she changed out of her suit and started dinner preparations before the children and David got home. The mail arrived late, and in the stack of mail, she saw a letter from Miriam.

She opened it, and after the first line, she had to sit down and have a cigarette and pour herself a glass of wine.

> *Dear Hannah,*
>
> *I don't know if you saw it in* The New York Times, *but the Stomping Mare is living in Queens. I don't know if she lives close to you or if you even know about this, but I wanted to write and let you know that I am involved in the effort to bring her to justice.*
>
> *I had met a woman who survived Majdanek as well. She was in a different block than you and me, but she survived that horrible day in November, the day of mass killing. Her name is Paula. Several months ago, we had been on holiday together and we were at the Tel Aviv airport, and we heard the name of the Nazi hunter, Simon Wiesenthal, over the paging system. We met him at the concierge desk and when he had finished his business, we asked to talk to him. Thankfully, he had some time, so we went to a café, and we told him about the Stomping Mare. Paula had witnessed the Stomping Mare's cruelty to children. How she separated them from their mothers and threw them on a truck headed for the gas chambers. Mr. Wiesenthal said he would research this for us. At the beginning of this month, he told us that she was living in Queens, New York with an American husband. Mr. Wiesenthal said*

CHAPTER SEVENTEEN: HANNAH FALL 1964

he told a reporter about it as well as referring the matter to American immigration authorities.

It made my blood run cold to realize that she was living near you, David, and your children. I don't know if there is anything you and David can do. I plan to contact the American authorities and tell them what I know.

Please write back and let me know if you are aware of these developments and any insights you might have.

I know this is an ugly chapter to re-open, but the Stomping Mare should not be allowed to live a peaceful life in America after all she has done.

I miss you, my friend.
Sincerely,
Miriam

Hannah looked up at the clock. She quickly folded the letter and put it in her make-up drawer in her vanity. She covered it with a couple of bottles of nail polish. She didn't want David to find the letter. She picked up her glass of wine and started to steam the vegetables when David walked in the door.

David leaned in and kissed her cheek. She took another sip of wine. "I thought we would have meatloaf and some steamed vegetables for dinner. I have to start packing for The Pines after dinner." She smiled at him as she started setting the table.

The weeks they spent at The Pines were a welcome reprieve. Hannah spent extra time at the pool, and she managed to act as if nothing was wrong when David came to the resort for the weekends. They played cards in the evenings and spent their days by the pool. David would occasionally go in for a swim, but typically, he read in a lounge chair. Hannah found herself watching him. He was handsome, with his salt and pepper hair, blue eyes, and the sharp cleft in his chin, which people remarked reminded them of the actor Kirk Douglas. Hannah noticed that David could sense when people were looking at the concentration camp tattoo on his forearm. He would reflexively cover it with his hand. It occurred to Hannah she didn't even know which camp he had been at and she didn't know any of his camp story, his cattle car ride, his horrific years, or what he did to survive. Maybe he truly could not talk about it.

Back at home, the kids were back in school. Max was now in eighth grade, and Rebecca in sixth grade. They had started to resist Hannah's fussing over them and were irritated when she asked what they wanted in their lunches. The house was quiet now, and Hannah and the cat, Siggi Two, curled up on the couch together to watch the *CBS Morning News with Mike Wallace*. The phone rang, and it was Weston Bradley.

He cleared his throat. "Is this an okay time for you to talk? I thought if I called later in the morning, it might be a time when you could talk about the case against the camp guard, Mrs. O'Neal."

Hannah lit another cigarette, "Yes, I can talk now. Is there some news?"

"Yes, I was able to get in touch with a friend at the State Department, and he put me in touch with a guy named Vince DeMarco in the Justice Department with the Immigration and Naturalization Service. He is working this case on the information provided by Mr. Wiesenthal. I spoke with him on the phone, and he is interested in talking with you. Are you willing to talk with him?"

"Yes, I'm willing to speak with him. How should I prepare?"

"Well, I'm willing to be your pro bono legal counsel, and we would need to go to his offices in Washington, D.C. Is that something you can do? I've tentatively set an appointment for about two weeks from now."

"Yes, I can make that happen." Hannah's mind was racing. How could she make it happen, and what would David say? She thanked Weston and hung up the phone. She went downstairs to the basement and opened her tea tin box with her emergency cash. She believed she had enough to take a train to Washington D.C. and back and to stay a few days. Though it made her nervous to drain her emergency savings, she thought it was worth it. She decided to wait until the very last minute to tell David. She packed a suitcase on a Thursday night after dinner. David came into the bedroom and looked perplexed. "Hannah, what are you doing?"

"I'm going to be gone for a few days. I'm going to Washington, D.C., early

CHAPTER SEVENTEEN: HANNAH FALL 1964

tomorrow morning to talk to the Immigration and Naturalization Service about my former concentration camp guard. I'm going to help them, and I will be back on Sunday."

David froze and stared at her. Hannah closed her suitcase. "Hannah, I thought I was clear when I told you that you are not to be involved in this. You are not going to Washington, and you are not talking to anyone."

"David, I'm not asking for your permission. I'm telling you I'm going. I understand you don't want to be involved; you don't ever want to talk about that time in your life, and that's fine. I'm going, and I'm doing what I can to get that woman out of our country, and hopefully, she will face justice."

David came over and put his hands on her shoulders. "Don't you know what you do affects me and the children? I'm telling you not to go because it is not a good thing for you to be involved in—dredging up the past like this. Even though this is not Austria or Germany, there is still prejudice against us, and there are people who hate Jews here. I'm telling you this for your safety. I'm telling you this because you made a promise to me that we wouldn't bring up that part of our past, and I take that seriously."

Hannah sat on the bed. "I always thought I was the only frightened one, but you are too. I have to do this for my sister. I promise I won't involve you or the children. I'm leaving tomorrow."

David left the room and did not say another word to Hannah. He was asleep when she left early the next morning. She took a cab to the train station, and when she arrived, Weston Bradley was waiting for her. He had a briefcase and looked very determined.

He smiled at her, and it seemed a bit forced. "I will have a cab waiting for us when we arrive in Washington. I took the liberty of booking a hotel, separate rooms, of course, and later this morning, we will have a couple of hours with Mr. DeMarco, and then we can explore the city and see a few monuments."

Hannah nodded. She had never been to Washington D.C., and although she was nervous about her appointment at the Justice Department, she realized this was the first time she had ever traveled by herself. She had selected one of her favorite suits, a knock-off Chanel-style suit in a light beige. She wore dress shields because she was afraid of having sweat stains on her suit. She selected simple gold jewelry. She wanted to look credible. When she rehearsed in her mind what she would share about the camps and the Stomping Mare, it sounded like a crazy fever dream, and she wondered if this Mr. DeMarco would believe her.

Weston put his hand on the small of Hannah's back as they walked up the steps of the Justice Department entrance on Pennsylvania Avenue. They were shown to Mr. DeMarco's office. Hannah was relieved to see Mr. DeMarco with his tie loose and his shirt sleeves rolled up. He had dark wavy hair and what Hannah came to know as a "New York" accent. She asked if he was from New York. He smiled, "Yes, ma'am. I'm from Brooklyn."

Hannah smiled, "Good. I'm glad. Do you mind if I smoke?" He pushed the ashtray to the corner of the desk and nodded. Weston took out a notebook.

Mr. DeMarco opened the file folder in front of him. "Mrs. Schneider, it is my understanding that you have information about a Mrs. Helma Braun O'Neal, also known as the 'Stomping Mare' who is suspected of crimes against humanity as a guard at both Majdanek and Ravensbruck concentration camps, is that correct?"

Hannah's throat temporarily constricted as if the words had lodged like a bone in her throat. She cleared her throat and managed to start speaking.

"Yes, at Majdanek. I saw her kill people. She killed my sister. We called her the Stomping Mare because the camp guards didn't wear name tags, so we came up with names for them. We called her the Stomping Mare because she got people on the ground and stomped on them, sometimes to injure them, and sometimes she killed them this way." The words again lodged in her throat, and she willed herself to suppress the stinging tears pooling in her eyes. "This is how she killed my sister, Rebecca Goldberg. It was at roll call. She, she got my sister on the ground, and I saw it. She stomped on her head. She killed her."

Hannah was startled as Weston made a sort of choking sound, Hannah noticed how tightly he was gripping the chair, and he turned to Mr. DeMarco. "I think I need a cigarette, too." Mr. DeMarco tossed him a lighter.

CHAPTER SEVENTEEN: HANNAH FALL 1964

"Mrs. Schneider, how do you know that Mrs. O'Neal is the Stomping Mare, the guard you knew at the camp?"

"I saw the newspaper story and picture. I knew immediately it was her. I also drove to her house and followed her while she was doing her marketing, and I'm completely sure."

Weston turned toward her, and his face was flushed. "You shouldn't have done that. Don't ever do anything like that again."

Mr. DeMarco leaned back in his chair. "You should follow that advice from your legal counsel, Mrs. Schneider. This will be difficult. Just so you know, I was in the army during the war, part of the force that liberated Dachau. So, I have a little bit of an idea of how it was there, and I wanted to share that with you because I know it pretty much defies the confines of language to try and describe it. I understand a little of what you may have endured, and I want you to know I'm committed to bringing this woman to justice."

Hannah relaxed. The tension drained from her shoulders, and the tightness in her throat subsided. She felt she could trust Mr. DeMarco. Finally, someone else who understood. For close to an hour, she recounted arriving at the camp and the Stomping Mare killing the old woman during selection on that first day. How life was in the camp, and for the first time ever, recounting how Rebecca died. She was proud of herself for getting through it without breaking down or crying. Mr. DeMarco nodded and took down notes as she spoke.

"Thank you, Mrs. Schneider. I know this could not have been easy," he said as he stood up and shook her hand and then Weston's hand. He let them know that he would be in touch, and it was still early in the process.

Once the elevator door closed, Weston slung his arm around Hannah's shoulders and exclaimed, "Good God, Hannah! I'm speechless, and that's pretty rare for me. Let's get drinks, sound like a good idea?"

He had a big smile on his face as he pulled her closer and kissed her forehead. Hannah laughed and agreed that drinks during lunch were in order.

They got a table at the Old Ebbitt Grill. The mahogany and brass bar and elegant tables were full of men in suits with cigarettes, cigars, and martinis. Hannah asked Weston if they were all politicians making deals.

"Yes, politicians and crooks, although there isn't much of a difference, and of course, slick lawyers like me."

Over lunch and a few drinks, Weston asked about her childhood, her sisters and parents, and life in Vienna. She told him about her grandmother in France and the kindly farmers who tried to hide them. "I think my sister Rebecca should have been the one who survived. She was smart, strong, and she was a talented musician. I'm just this housewife, and I'm not educated or skilled or very interesting."

Weston put his drink down. "Whoa, just stop right there. So, you speak three languages, you are raising two bright kids, you survived a concentration camp, immigrated to America, and built a successful life with your husband, and you think you're just a mousy nobody? I think not! Oh, and I'm leaving out the fact that you are a total knockout on par with Elizabeth Taylor, so why don't you try that identity on for size? Or how about the fact that you are taking on some crazy psychopath camp guard by helping the government build a case against her? But, yeah, tell me about how you're not interesting."

Hannah laughed. "Well, since you put it that way! But now tell me about you."

"This *is* very boring. I'm the only son of an old New York family that had sunk into genteel poverty when my father lost a ton of money in the stock market in 1929. My mother is an uptight woman who loves the Daughters of the American Revolution luncheons and cruelly judging people. I went to an Ivy League college and law school. I learned to fly planes when I was a teenager, and that is something I love. I was stationed in England during the war, and I flew forty bombing missions over Germany. After the war, I married the girl I was supposed to marry, who came from a family like my own family. That's what you were supposed to do, so I did it. I joined a law firm, became a partner, and I work with a lot of rich, boring people. I'm a hopeless cad, and I love to chase women. It's not my wife's fault. She is the way she is because she was brought up that way. We're unhappy, but people

CHAPTER SEVENTEEN: HANNAH FALL 1964

like us don't divorce, so we live separate lives. I give her money, and she gives me freedom."

Hannah was stunned. "Wow. I wasn't expecting the unvarnished truth. It doesn't sound boring at all. So, you try this on for size—you are handsome, funny, and smart. That's what I see."

Weston took Hannah's hand. "It's late afternoon, almost the golden hour. Do you want to go for a walk and look at the monuments?"

"Yes. I would like to see the statue of Lincoln."

"Well, it's a bit of a walk, but let's go."

Hannah and Weston walked to the Lincoln Memorial hand in hand. Weston read the lines etched behind Lincoln. He told her a lot about Lincoln and the Civil War as they walked back to the hotel. They had dinner in the hotel restaurant, and then he walked Hannah to her room. They stood at the door, and he gave her a long, deep kiss, and then pulled away. "I think I'd better leave you here. I don't trust myself right now." He kissed her again. "Good night, Hannah."

Hannah fell into a deep sleep. The next morning, she called home and spoke to the kids and then David. "Hi, David. I gave my statement to the Justice Department, and now they are following up on it. The man I talked to said it is early in the process, so I don't think much of anything will be happening for a while. I'm spending the day today just looking around and being a tourist. I know you don't approve, but I'm glad I did it. I feel relieved. I'm just taking this weekend as a break. I will be back mid-afternoon tomorrow."

David sighed. "I'm disappointed you've taken this step, Hannah. Hopefully, it won't have negative repercussions for you and for us. I don't know what's going through your mind, but we can talk tomorrow." He sounded more sad than angry, Hannah thought.

Hannah and Weston spent the day looking at tourist spots in Washington. Hannah liked listening to Weston hold forth and tell her all about some aspect of American history. That evening, they had dinner and talked for hours. Weston walked Hannah to her room again.

Hannah took his hand. "You should come in with me."

"Hannah, I don't think I should."

"I want you to. I don't care that you don't trust yourself. Let's make love. I want to. I thought you were a hopeless woman chaser. Well, here I am."

Weston laughed. "Well, I am, but you have foiled me. This whole process takes a little cynicism on each side. I chase beautiful women, get to know them superficially, we go to bed together a few times, and that's it. Usually, she's bored, and I'm bored, and it is, in the grand scheme of things, pretty meaningless. In this case, I think I might fall in love with you. I hate to say it, but I think your husband is a pretty stand-up guy, and you're angry with him now, but later, you will come to deeply regret straying from him. Then you will be stuck and eventually realize I'm not what you need or want."

Hannah reached up and touched his cheek. "But I want to be with you."

Weston pulled away and smiled. "You are killing me with this! Good night, Hannah."

The next morning, they stood together at the train station, and Weston pulled Hannah close. "I did want to make love to you, and now I'm wondering if I will regret my decision. You're so beautiful." He kissed her and held her tightly for a long time.

Hannah pulled away from him and rested her hand on his chest. "Thank you for helping me. I couldn't have done it without you. It means so much to me to do this not only for myself, but for my sister and family. Thank you for making it possible. Thank you for my weekend away and for making me feel special."

Chapter Eighteen: Helma Fall and Winter 1964

In the months following the publication of the newspaper article, Helma was feeling only slightly more comfortable. She and Charles had returned to church, and Helma was gratified to learn that most of her neighbors and those who attended church with the O'Neals didn't believe the charges against her. They believed that Wiesenthal had made a mistake.

Even though the attention generated by the *New York Times* article had died down, Helma could not shake the feeling of a dark cloud hanging over her. They had learned from their lawyer, Mr. Perry, that there was an active effort at the Department of Justice to pursue the case. She had learned that there was an Immigration and Naturalization official, a Mr. DeMarco, who was very passionately pursuing it. Helma had learned that Mr. DeMarco was interviewing these "so-called survivors," as Helma referred to them. Apparently, there were refugees in the United States who had survived Majdanek.

Helma tried to keep herself busy with knitting projects. She was knitting quite a pile of blankets and baby clothes for the church Christmas Bazaar, which was months away. Even while knitting, she couldn't keep her thoughts about the impending legal actions out of her mind. She reproached herself for thinking she could live among Jews in America. She understood that she and Charles would be living in Queens, where there were many Jews. Now she wished she would have insisted on a new start in another part of the country where there were fewer Jews, or negroes, even. Maybe somewhere in the west, like Montana or Idaho.

Now, when she went out, she saw the Jews at the markets or when she was at the fabric store to find more yarn, she couldn't help but think they might be these "so-called survivors" making up some story about how the war was especially hard for them. It was so frustrating, as she put so much effort into putting the past behind her, and now, twenty years later, it was being thrown back in her face.

She was so thankful for Charles. He was patient and supportive, even of Helma's bad moods. She confessed to him how uncomfortable she felt going to the market and fabric store because they had so many Jewish neighbors, and she couldn't help but feel vulnerable.

"Darling, this is just in your mind. You think people are looking at you or that they are against you, but they're not. They are just going about their business. Yes, there are a few that are refugees who came after the war, but most of those Jews went to Israel. A lot of the Jews here have been here a long time, and they are okay. You mustn't allow yourself to get paranoid."

Helma called Mr. Perry and asked if there was anything she could do to help with her case. He suggested finding some documentation regarding her imprisonment and the amnesty granted her by the Austrian government.

Helma decided to ask Greta for help. Over the years, she had kept in touch via letters, postcards, and gifts to Greta.

> *Dearest Greta,*
>
> *I hope you are doing well. Your Uncle Charles and I had hoped to make another trip to Austria next year, but sadly, it doesn't look like we can make that happen. I do miss you and your mother. I hope she is doing better. I have kept her in my prayers since you have shared with me your worries about her declining health.*
>
> *The reason that Charles and I won't be able to come over to visit is that a most maddening thing has occurred. I have been wrongly accused of crimes relating to my wartime service. I don't know if you've heard of an Austrian man named Simon Wiesenthal. He made quite a name for himself a few years back pursuing Eichmann, one of the*

CHAPTER EIGHTEEN: HELMA FALL AND WINTER 1964

leaders of the Nazi movement. This made quite a splash with the Jews in Israel and stoked their desire to gin up a lot of nonsense about supposed crimes committed against them so long ago during the war years. Well, apparently, this Wiesenthal character has trained his sights on people like me, people who were just doing their jobs. Now I have some legal troubles in the United States. I guess this is a way Wiesenthal can continue to get money from his wealthy Jewish benefactors, by coming up with ever more outrageous stories about regular people like me to cause more hysteria about a war that happened so long ago.

This is most troubling, as it might lead to some legal issues down the road. We have retained a lawyer, and we are saving our money for any future legal expenses we might have relating to this case.

I am hoping that you can help me. Since you are in Austria, it would be so helpful if you could see about assisting us with finding the court records relating to the amnesty I was granted by the Austrian government after my imprisonment by the Allied tribunal after the war. You were very little, but maybe you remember my time away after the war. Your mother was such a loyal friend to me at that time. Perhaps she can be of assistance as well. Anything you both can obtain in Austria and send to me would be so wonderful.

It's a difficult time, but I couldn't be more blessed to have Charles by my side! He has been and continues to be such a wonderful support to me, and he has arranged the lawyer and everything.

Both Uncle Charles and I are so proud of you for earning your teaching degree! You will be the first in our family to graduate from college. Your father would be so proud. He was incredibly bright as well, and you clearly take after him.

With Love,

Aunt Helma

Helma was angry that this whole situation had seemingly overtaken their lives. She and Charles couldn't travel to Austria for Greta's graduation from college. Helma was so proud of her for earning her teaching degree and paying her way through school by working. Her poor niece didn't have her father, just her weak and sickly mother. It would have been nice to be able to give Greta a little support, but because of the web Helma was caught up in, she had to focus all of her energy on defending herself.

Charles tried to cheer her up, even planning a short getaway to the northeast during fall to see the changing leaves. They took long drives and stayed at a charming Inn in New Hampshire. At least the long drives provided Helma a little bit of a reprieve from her trouble.

After her trip, she was delighted to find a letter from Greta in the mailbox.

> *Dear Aunty,*
>
> *I'm so sorry to hear that you and Uncle Charles will not be able to travel to Austria to see us. I'm also very sorry to hear that you are caught up in some sort of legal troubles. Mr. Wiesenthal is known here in Austria as his headquarters are in Vienna. I suppose a person understands why he might have taken on such a task, but I don't know why he would pursue you. I do remember right after the war when you went away. Mother said it was a miscarriage of justice because you were guarding legitimate prisoners and not involved in any horrible activities that Mr. Wiesenthal would concern himself with. I will do my best to track down any documentation I can find here in Austria and send it your way.*
>
> *Thank you so much for your congratulations and it makes me so glad to know that my father would have been proud of me. Mother often says he was very smart and a very dedicated soldier.*
>
> *Give my best to Uncle Charles.*
> *Love,*
> *Greta*

Helma was so grateful for her niece. Maybe when all this ridiculous legal trouble is over, Helma could find a way for Greta to come to America. Maybe she would consider moving here. It would be nice to have her here when Helma and Charles were in their elder years, and that way, they would have

CHAPTER EIGHTEEN: HELMA FALL AND WINTER 1964

a caring family member lend them a hand. Greta had Klara's gentle nature, but she was smart like her father. Helma would get angry when she thought how Wiesenthal and other Jews wanted to make her pay for their suffering, but no one was to blame for her family's suffering. After Hans had been lost during the war, and her niece had been left without a father, there was poor Klaus. The communists took him prisoner during the war and then kept him as slave labor in some Siberian mines for ten years. That was real suffering!

Charles had convinced her to take an active part in the church's Christmas Bazaar and bring all the knitted blankets and baby clothes to sell herself. The weekend of the Christmas Bazaar, Helma was pleased with all the compliments she received for her knitting. It was clear that many of their neighbors and church friends thought the charges against her were false, and Helma couldn't possibly be the sadistic camp guard as alleged.

As the Christmas Bazaar was wrapping up, Charles cajoled Helma to come to the kitchen in the church basement, where they were serving hot chocolate and Christmas cookies. Charles put his arm around Helma's waist as they enjoyed the children singing Christmas carols. Helma allowed herself to relax a little and enjoy the festivities. Maybe the legal issues would get ensnarled in red tape, or hopefully, people would tire of that Jew Wiesenthal's grandstanding, and the case against her would go away. Helma made that her Christmas wish.

Chapter Nineteen: Hannah Fall–Winter 1964

After Hannah came back from Washington, David acted as if she had never left. They settled into an uncomfortable truce, automatically going through all of the motions of the life they had established over the past sixteen years. Hannah picked up her household duties, making meals, packing lunches, sewing costumes for Rebecca's play, and helping Max get everything he needed for his science fair display.

Hannah and Sylvie continued their routine of weekly visits to the Beauty Bar and swapping recipes. Sylvie used to come by Hannah's house after the kids were off to school, and David was off to work. Sometimes, they would exercise in front of the T.V. during the "Jack LaLane" program and end up lying on the floor laughing. Other times, they would have coffee and cigarettes and talk. Hannah could sense that Sylvie knew something was amiss but would only gently probe for information and would eventually back off and change the subject when she sensed Hannah was tensing up. Hannah was grateful for Sylvie and the fact that Sylvie helped Hannah relax and feel a little bit normal.

The daily mail became a lifeline for Hannah. She had resumed her correspondence with Miriam. It took her a while to collect herself and write to Miriam about all that had transpired since the *New York Times* article.

Dear Miriam,

CHAPTER NINETEEN: HANNAH FALL–WINTER 1964

Thank you for giving me the background information about how the Stomping Mare had been discovered and that Mr. Wiesenthal set the ball in motion to uncover her whereabouts. It's a shocking twist of fate that she is, as you said, my neighbor here in Queens. She lives only a few miles from our house. This probably wasn't a good idea, but I did go to her house and watch to make sure it was her. It is her. She is like any other American housewife. She lives in a small house with a very average-looking American husband. She has two dogs, and from a subsequent news story, I understand she is viewed as a "nice lady" by her neighbors and knits things for church sales!

In September, I went to Washington, D.C., and spoke to a young man in the Justice Department who was investigating her. He seems very sharp, and I trust him. He was in the Army and helped liberate Dachau. He did tell me that this would be a slow process.

The other part I'm struggling with is David—he does not want me to be involved at all or to ever talk about anything that happened in the past. I am completely defiant, and we are in a very hard spot. I don't know if our marriage can survive this. I'm so afraid I will lose him, but then I know I must do my part to bring the Stomping Mare to justice.

I wish we lived closer to each other—I desperately need a friend who understands.

All My Love,
Hannah

Several weeks after their return from Washington, she received a call from Weston Bradley. He invited her to the same café where they had met before. She had butterflies in her stomach while she tried on different outfits and alternated between coral pink and bright red lipstick.

Weston stood up when she entered the café and kissed her cheek. It had been over a month since they kissed as they departed from the train station. Hannah nervously fumbled for a cigarette as Weston ordered them both coffee. Weston reached over and took Hannah's hand.

"Hannah, I'm afraid I have some bad news. Our friend Mr. DeMarco called, and he is not getting a lot of traction on investigating Mrs. O'Neal. I guess there is a lot of pressure on him to put this on the back burner, and they aren't devoting a lot of resources to this, so you shouldn't expect much to happen."

Hannah stamped out her cigarette; she felt herself starting to tense up.

"Why? What does that mean? I don't understand when they know they have a Nazi criminal living here, why would they not pursue this?"

"I'm not really sure, and I'm not sure even Mr. DeMarco knows. He is sort of a low man on the totem pole. I still have some friends at the State Department and in the military, and they aren't really interested in pursuing the Nazis anymore. It's about the communists now, and they are willing to overlook the past in making new alliances against the communists. It's also about the space race. The United States picked up a few crackerjack scientists who served Hitler, and it seems they are willing to overlook and gloss over the Nazi pasts of some of these guys."

Hannah sighed and lit another cigarette, "How disappointing. I thought this country was about standing up for what is right. It must be nice to have so little at stake that you can gloss over the murder of millions."

Weston just looked down into his coffee cup. After they had lunch, Weston asked her if she wanted to go for a walk. He helped her with her coat, and they walked hand in hand down the street. It was a sunny and crisp fall day.

"I'm so sorry, Hannah. I wish I had better news."

Hannah squeezed his hand. "It's not your fault. Thank you for all of your help." Weston stopped her and rested his hands on her shoulders, "Don't give up so easily. I don't think DeMarco is going to give up. He's like a dog with a bone. Stay strong. You may have to wait a while, but something could happen."

Hannah smiled. "Thank you. I won't give up. I have a friend in Israel who is also like the dog with a bone, as you said Mr. DeMarco is. I'm sad that it will take a long time and that awful woman is free to live in her house and live a happy life."

Weston leaned in and kissed her. "Hannah, I think about you a lot." Hannah pulled away from him. "I think about you too. It's a very

CHAPTER NINETEEN: HANNAH FALL–WINTER 1964

complicated feeling. I thought maybe we could have a fling, but maybe it would be more consequential than that, and I have to really think that through."

Weston looked a little defeated as Hannah tightened her coat closer to her body and looked down at the ground. A wave of guilt overcame Hannah when she thought of David. "I need to go home. My children will be home from school."

Weston suddenly looked older and sad as he kissed her cheek and said goodbye.

On the drive home, Hannah couldn't shake the sinking feeling of disappointment and despair. It was impossible to believe that the officials in the United States would allow the Stomping Mare to continue to live freely in Queens, walk her dogs, and knit baby blankets for her church sales. Did it even matter that she murdered possibly thousands of people?

Hannah resumed her nightly ritual of a drink and one or more pills to help her sleep. She couldn't help but feel David watching her as she went about her daily routine and when they sat in the living room together in the evenings. For the first time in several months, she was taking more pills and wondering if the day would come when she would feel so much despair that she would take the whole bottle at once.

The week after Thanksgiving, as they were lying in bed together, Hannah felt David take her hand. It was the first time he touched her in months.

"Hannah, it is so hard to see you this sad. I know our trip to Florida last year was ruined at the very end, so I made reservations to go to the resort again in a week. We can fly down there and relax. It's not good for us to be so distant from each other."

Hannah felt herself choke back tears. "Thank you. I do need to get away. I think it would be good for us. I've been feeling so low lately."

The days passed quickly. Hannah looked out the window of the plane as they departed for Florida. She hoped that the trip would help lift her out of the pit she had been in ever since Weston let her know that the case against the Stomping Mare would not be pursued very aggressively. In addition to that disappointment, Hannah was feeling guilty about her feelings for

Weston.

On the first day at the resort, Hannah swam for hours in the pool. She found herself sinking to the bottom and looking up at the waves of the blue water and the sun hoping that she could feel something different when she broke the surface of the water.

That evening, she and David dressed up. It didn't have the same sense of excitement that it did last year, but it was still beautiful. When they got up to their room, Hannah put her nightgown on and sat at the edge of the bed. David sat next to her and exhaled heavily.

"Hannah, I know you are determined to pursue this case against the camp guard. I guess I can't stop you, but I need to try to stop this from tearing us apart and perhaps affecting the children. Don't you see that by your pursuing things of the past, things that can't be changed, you could endanger all that we have now?"

Hannah just stared straight ahead and didn't look at David. "Do you love me?"

David crossed his arms and leaned forward toward Hannah. "What? What are you talking about?"

Hannah stood up and looked at him directly. "I'm talking about love. I want to know if you love me. If you ever loved me, or if you just felt pity and obligation and married me."

"How can you say this to me? What on earth are you talking about?"

Hannah felt herself getting angry; she noticed she was balling up her fists. "I heard you tell Sam on the first night we were in America that you felt sorry for me and married me out of pity. All I could do was try to become a wife to you and a mother to our children, but the minute I wanted something for myself when I wanted to do something about that horrible, horrible woman who killed Rebecca, you abandoned me."

Hannah noticed that David was pale. All the color drained from his face. He sat on the edge of the bed and buried his face in his hands. He was silent for a long time. Hannah sat next to him. She gently touched his arm. When he looked up, his eyes were red.

"The day I found you in the DP camp, that was the most joyful day of my

CHAPTER NINETEEN: HANNAH FALL–WINTER 1964

life. I knew then that I had a purpose in life, and that purpose was you. I looked forward to seeing you every day. I prayed for your health and your progress every day. You grew brighter and more beautiful—and so strong. So much like your father and so much like Rebecca. It wasn't pity that I felt, or obligation, just gratitude. All I ever wanted to do was protect you. After we married, I saw you struggle to be a wife and to be a mother and how you love our children. You attend to every detail of caring for them, every meal, every time you stood over Max and ruffled his hair when he did his homework or when you ironed Becky's Camp Fire girl uniform. When I work, I think about the evening when we sit in the living room together, and you read a magazine or pet that silly cat, and I can just look at you and marvel at how beautiful you are and how lucky we are to have found each other. What are the odds that we would find each other? It's only God's work. Do I love you? I love you, but love is too small a word. You are my reason for being."

Hannah felt the tears streaming down her face. "Oh, David, I was so wrong. I couldn't see this about you and about us. Why are you so against me testifying against this Nazi who killed Rebecca? I don't understand."

David took Hannah's hand. "I don't want us to be caught up in the past. I don't think it's a good idea. I'm concerned that you will get tangled up in things that get out of control and threaten all we built here. I'm not like you, Hannah; I can't talk about the camps. I can't do it, and I won't do it."

They both lay on the bed together. Hannah rested her head on David's shoulder. After a while, she mustered the courage to ask what they were going to do. David was quiet for a few more minutes.

"Well, as I said, I know that you can't give up. I just want to shield the children from any knowledge of this. While I understand it is something you need to do, it's not something I want to be involved in. Is that enough for you, Hannah?"

"Yes, it's enough. Sadly, I don't think the government is going to actively pursue her. It might be a while, and I'm worried it might never be."

"I'm sorry, Hannah. I really am."

When they returned home, Hannah knew that she needed to get in touch with Weston. They met downtown at their usual café. Weston leaned in and lit Hannah's cigarette. He stared at her for a moment and exhaled heavily before leaning back in his chair, and he straightened his tie. "I've been in this situation enough times to sense what is going on here. I think you're going to tell me that you can't see me anymore or even use a word like 'mistake.' I hope that's not the case, but I have that sinking feeling."

Hannah took a deep drag on her cigarette. "Wow, I didn't know your skills included mind reading. I can't see you anymore. It's just too hard and confusing. I love my husband, and I realize that my husband and I have something together that I can't risk losing. I'm sorry."

Weston was quiet and looked out the window. Large, fluffy snowflakes were coming down. He asked Hannah if she wanted to go for a walk. They walked in silence for several blocks and occasionally stopped to admire the Christmas displays in the windows. Weston put his arm around Hannah, and she saw their reflection in the window. Weston was tall and distinguished looking with a camel coat and a red scarf, and he was wearing a fedora, which many men had stopped wearing as men's styles had become so casual. Hannah looked at herself and her fitted emerald-green coat and paisley scarf. Even with her bouffant hair, she only came to Weston's shoulder. As she stared at their reflection in the window, she imagined her life if she was with Weston. He looked down at her and said, "It's getting cold," and walked her back to the car. He leaned over and kissed her, and she embraced him and felt the warmth from his body even through his coat.

"Goodbye, Hannah. I'm going to miss you. Even though we aren't able to be friends, or whatever we were, because it was more than friends, I will still keep tabs on the case against that camp guard monster. Don't worry, I will keep it professional, and I promise never to make you uncomfortable."

"Thank you, Weston. That is very kind of you."

"It is kind of me. Uncharacteristically so. I'm afraid I'm turning into a nice guy, which sounds pretty boring. Promise me one thing, though—you won't give up. Keep fighting, and don't give up on it."

"I promise I won't give up. Thank you for all you have done for me. You changed my life."

Chapter Twenty: Helma 1971

The campfire had started to dim, so Helma grabbed a few more logs from the firewood that Charles had split that morning. Helma leaned back into her camp chair and continued to knit. She knew it would be a few hours before Charles came back from fishing at the lake. She wasn't looking forward to cleaning the fish but would enjoy the dinner of fresh fish cooked over an open fire.

It was dusk, and Helma poured herself a glass of iced tea. She made sure there were a couple of frosty bottles of beer in the cooler for her husband. Helma rarely drank alcohol and she never smoked, she considered regular consumption of alcohol and smoking a sign of weak character. Thankfully, Charles didn't smoke and only had a beer on occasion. Often, he indulged while they were camping after a successful day of fishing.

Helma stood up when she saw Charles coming up from the lake, three fish in hand. She stood up to take the fish.

"No, darling, you relax and keep up with your knitting, I will clean these fish and start cooking them up!"

"All right then," she said with a smile. Helma stood up and got a bottle of beer for Charles. She settled back down in her camp chair and kept knitting. Charles came out and put the fish on the fire.

"Thank you, Charles. This is so lovely. I wish we didn't have to leave. It would be wonderful to stay here forever and leave the modern world behind."

"Yes. We could be like the pioneers. I think we would be good at it. We could build a log cabin together. I know you are already good at gardening, and we could have a vegetable patch and fresh fish or game every night."

Helma sighed. How she wished she was able to turn this fantasy into reality. She patted Charles' arm and whispered in his ear, "Oh, how I wish we could make it so." The next day, they drove back home.

They had purchased the truck and the camper five years ago. Helma had loved travel so much, and it was difficult for her to have that taken away because of the legal troubles dangling over their heads. It was harder and harder for Helma to contain her anger over this unfair case against her. She knew she could be irrational, swinging between rage and then paranoia about the Jews in their neighborhood and all the Jews who had something to gain by keeping this case alive.

That Jew, Wiesenthal, was trying to make himself some sort of celebrity by chasing after people who were just doing their jobs during the war. She felt he had trapped her. She tried not to think about it, and usually, she could go months at a time without giving it a thought, but then Mr. Perry would call with one of his occasional updates. These updates usually infuriated Helma. It was always vague and always annoying. He would talk about this "Mr. DeMarco," who was still pursuing the case when it didn't seem that the rest of the U.S. government was interested in it at all.

The other heartbreak in Helma's life was the loss of her dogs. Both had to be put down within several months of each other as they both developed hip dysplasia. Helma couldn't bear to see both dogs suffer from lameness. She and Charles adopted another dog, and this time as much for protection as companionship. Helma adopted a German Shepherd, a dog like the dogs she handled at the camps. Charles named the dog Rex. Helma thought the dog would scare off any people who might harass them. Charles thought she was overreacting, as the news about Helma's past had died down in the media, and no reporters or protesters had been around since 1964.

Both Helma and Charles became increasingly dismayed year after year as they felt the country had sunk further and further into degradation. The opposition to the war in Vietnam, the Civil Rights movement, women's rights, and even the way young people were dressing in sloppy clothes and unkempt hair. Sometimes, Helma would hop up and turn off the evening

CHAPTER TWENTY: HELMA 1971

news in disgust.

Helma was happy that at least Mr. Nixon had been elected and his "law and order" message would hopefully be followed up on with all the hippies, communists, and militant negroes. In addition, Helma was disgusted by the young people's lack of patriotism during the Vietnam conflict. It made sense to her, though, as a natural outcome of all of America's "tolerance" and lack of any racial or patriotic unity. She could only shake her head when she thought of such things and only wonder if people really understood how threatening certain people and communism are. She was happy that she and Charles were of one mind on this, although Helma felt Charles had a naïve hope he maintained about his homeland.

These pressures made the camping escapes that much more valuable for Helma and Charles. It was a long drive, and they made it home late in the evening. Charles picked up the Sunday New York Times from the front porch. Helma heard him sigh heavily and saw him shake his head as he read the paper spread out on the dining table.

Helma came over and looked over his shoulder. She quickly read about a massive leak from the Pentagon, the so-called "Pentagon Papers." Someone had taken secret information and given it to the newspaper.

"This is horrible! It is treason. Say what you will about the Reich, but we were disciplined. No one would have even considered such a betrayal, and no ethical journalist would have been involved in such a betrayal of their own government. Does anyone even care that this country is being destroyed by disloyal rabble?"

Charles could tell that Helma was on the edge of one of her angry tirades. Over the past several years, he noticed she could be set off by any number of things, especially the case against her, but also what she viewed as the degradation of America in the last few years. Charles rested his hand on her shoulder.

"Helma, darling, these things are out of our control. We may not like things as they are right now, but they come and go in cycles. Things will get better. We had a long drive back, so why don't you draw yourself a nice warm bath and relax? We don't have to unload everything tonight. You need your rest."

Helma took a deep breath. She knew she had to continue to try to control her anger. Charles was so kind and patient. She didn't want to upset him or to be a burden. She tried to relax in the bath and to remind herself how fortunate she was to have someone like Charles to support her.

The next morning, Helma was scrubbing out the cooler. She liked to make sure the camper was spotless and in good order any time they came back from a trip. She was just finishing up the cooler when the phone rang. It was their attorney, Mr. Perry.

"Hello, Mrs. O'Neal. I'm afraid I will need to see you and Mr. O'Neal in my office tomorrow. There have been some significant developments in your case."

"Is a meeting really necessary? My husband works, and I'm not sure he could take time off on such short notice. This has been dragging on for what? Seven years? What could possibly be happening that you couldn't just update me by phone." She could hear the tension in her voice and tried to moderate it. "I mean, really."

"Mrs. O'Neal, I promise you this is serious. Your extradition hearing date will be set. It's not only the U.S. government that's involved. I have some information about the pursuit of Majdanek trials in both West Germany and Poland, and they are pursuing charges against camp guards."

Helma sat down slowly. She suddenly felt very cold.

"Mrs. O'Neal, are you still there?"

"Yes, Mr. Perry. Did you say West Germany and Poland were pursuing Majdanek cases? Do you think this has anything to do with me?"

"I do. That's why I need you and Mr. O'Neal to meet me at my office at 11:00 a.m. tomorrow. I will give you a detailed account of what has been happening."

The next morning, Helma was scrambling eggs and frying bacon while Charles was reading the paper. Helma noticed that her hand was shaking. She decided to have an extra cup of coffee.

Mr. Perry wore a mushroom-colored suit and burnt orange wide tie. Helma wavered between disgust and amusement about Mr. Perry's bad

CHAPTER TWENTY: HELMA 1971

suits and greasy combover. She was glad Charles was here. For the first time in many years, she was nervous.

Mr. Perry gestured for them to sit down. "Mr. and Mrs. O'Neal, I wish I had better news. As the years went on with nothing happening in this case, I had expected it to drop into obscurity. That would have been the best outcome. However, that is not what has ultimately happened. Mr. DeMarco has successfully pushed on through over the years. The date of your extradition trial will be set soon. Mr. DeMarco has been collecting survivor testimonies over the years, both here in the States and in Israel. No doubt, he is cooperating with both the West German and Polish authorities. It looks like survivor testimony will be a part of this, which makes this an exceptionally challenging case, not only from a legal perspective, but also from a public relations perspective. We need to prepare ourselves and develop a couple of different strategies."

Helma balled up her fists and felt the rage bubbling up inside of her. "Who are these so-called survivors? Why would Jews from Israel be relevant? Are these Jews just making things up and getting paid by that Jew Wiesenthal to gin up sympathy for their plight so they can exercise more control and get more money? Survivor! I'm the survivor; my family died fighting the communists and other sub-human garbage!"

Charles grabbed Helma's arm, and Mr. Perry stood up.

"Mrs. O'Neal, you need to control yourself! You must stop these tirades. This type of attitude will not help at all. We need to come up with a plan, and you flying off the handle is not going to help."

Charles stood up. "Thank you, Mr. Perry. We trust you to guide us in the right way. I will work with my wife to make sure we can all work together for the best outcome."

Helma walked ahead of Charles to the car. She was still seething with anger. She took deep breaths as she walked through the rain-soaked parking lot. She smoothed the front of her dress and smiled sweetly as Charles opened the passenger side door of the car for her.

Chapter Twenty-One: Hannah 1971

Hannah concentrated on the finishing touches on the cherry angel food cake. She dropped the cherries carefully on top and put the glass dome over the cake on the cake pedestal. She wanted everything to be perfect for this last celebratory dinner before Rebecca left for college in California. Max had been attending Columbia University and had lived at home for a year before finding an apartment near campus with a couple of friends but was coming for dinner. Hannah had ironed the tablecloth and brought out the china. Even though Hannah and Rebecca had been at odds for much of Rebecca's teenage years, with arguments, door slams, and tears, it seemed like Rebecca was softening toward Hannah a little bit. Rebecca picked out a pattern and fabric, and Hannah made a couple of cute sundresses for Rebecca. David complained that they were too short, but Hannah was happy with how pleased Rebecca was and that she had chosen to wear one of the dresses for the special dinner tonight. Just as Hannah was setting the table, Max came in and kissed her cheek.

David patted Max on the back. Hannah knew that David missed having Max around the house and that David would be heartbroken tomorrow when it was time to put Rebecca on the plane to California. Rebecca was the apple of David's eye.

Hannah watched David and her suddenly grown-up children talking over dinner. It seemed so strange that things had flown by so quickly, the day-to-day of getting them to school, to activities, lazy summer vacation days at The Pines, and finally, here they were, ready to go out into the world on their own, leaving her and David alone together at home.

CHAPTER TWENTY-ONE: HANNAH 1971

Max was just finishing his plate when he asked the question that David and Hannah had learned not to ask. "So, Sis, what are you going to study in California? Did you choose your major yet?"

Rebecca looked angry, and she frowned. "I haven't decided yet. I just know I want to get out of here, go someplace new. I've figured out what I don't want to be."

Max smiled. "Okay, tell me what you don't want to be."

"I don't want to be a housewife. I don't want to just take care of a couple of kids and get my hair done every week and keep my house super clean and clip recipes from magazines and spend my evening smoking and drinking and watching 'Hawaii Five-O' before popping a couple of Valiums to sleep at night. I care about what's happening in Vietnam and people's rights. I'm not going to be useless."

Hannah felt her cheeks burn, and she gripped the napkin on her lap. Her throat was dry.

Suddenly, David's hand slammed violently on the table. Both Max and Rebecca jumped in their seats, and their eyes became as wide as saucers.

David was yelling. He never yelled. "You do not disrespect your mother in this home! Not ever. She has devoted her life to your care. You have no clue what your mother endured at your age. We've both protected you from that. Stop for a moment and think about all that she has done for you. Look at that dress on your back, which was hand-sewn for you by your mother. Your mother and I came here with nothing, and we worked to give you everything!"

Rebecca was staring down at her plate. "I'm sorry, papa."

"Don't apologize to me. Apologize to your mother!"

Rebecca cleared her throat and looked up at Hannah. "Sorry, mother."

Hannah struggled to regain her composure. It was a pretty big shock to see herself through Rebecca's eyes.

"It's okay, Rebecca. I think it's a good thing that you care about Vietnam and civil rights. I care about those things, too. I'm glad things are changing so that young women can pursue careers, and I'm glad you have this opportunity to go to college. This is why your father and I came to America, to give you and your brother these kinds of opportunities. You are very young. You don't know what life will have in store for you yet."

Hannah took a deep breath and put the napkin on the table. "I made a dessert. Maybe the cherry angel food cake can cheer things up."

She stood up to walk to the kitchen. David brushed her arm as she walked by. She was slicing the cake when Max came into the kitchen.

"I'm sorry, Mom. She didn't mean it. I always thought you were a cool mom. You're also one of the prettiest moms, so don't stop getting those weekly hairdos."

Hannah turned and smiled at Max. She brushed his long hair from his forehead. "You should come to the Beauty Bar with me and Aunt Sylvie. Cut some of that hair so we can see your handsome face."

Max laughed and helped Hannah bring the cake into the dining room. The next morning, the three of them saw Rebecca off at the airport. Hannah was comforted by the extra-long hug she received from Rebecca, and she thought, maybe this is just another rocky patch.

When they got in the car to drive home, David turned down the radio. "Are you feeling okay, Hannah?"

"Yes, actually I am. I think we have two wonderful children, and now they are grown. It seems so strange. The house is going to be so quiet."

David laughed and said, "I'm actually looking forward to that."

Hannah re-painted Max's room and made it into her sewing and crafts room. She had started volunteering with Sylvie at a YWCA program for children in need. She sewed clothes and toys for the kids and taught sewing at the free daycare a couple of days a week. She also volunteered with Sylvie to take meals to elderly shut-ins, and sometimes, she would stay and visit and read the newspaper or listen to them play the piano. With some of the Austrian immigrants, they would reminisce about Austria before the war. A few of them were survivors, but they never talked about that.

Hannah and David had made their trip to Boca Raton an annual ritual. They would spend the two weeks after Thanksgiving, just the two of them, enjoying the resort. Now that the kids were grown, they were making more travel plans. David wanted to see all-American landmarks, like Yellowstone

CHAPTER TWENTY-ONE: HANNAH 1971

and Mt. Rushmore, and he wanted to go to Texas in hopes of seeing real cowboys at a rodeo.

Hannah was just unlocking the door from her grocery shopping trip when she heard the phone ringing. She put down her bags and breathlessly answered the phone.

"Hello, may I speak to Mrs. Schneider?"

"This is she. Who may I ask is calling?" Hannah was hoping she wouldn't end up trapped on the phone with some vinyl siding salesman.

"This is Mr. DeMarco from the Department of Justice."

"Wow. It's good to hear from you. It's been a while."

"Yes, I think I called you back in '68 to let you know the case was still alive and I was making some progress. In the last three years, I've made a lot of progress. We're getting ready to set Mrs. O'Neal's extradition hearing, and we are gathering survivor testimony. We will need your help."

Hannah collapsed into the kitchen chair, and her keys dropped to the floor.

"Are you there, Mrs. Schneider?"

"Yes, I'm here."

"Tell you what, I'm home in Brooklyn visiting with family. I know a really nice bakery in Queens where we could meet. I could give you the full update in person, and you can ask any questions you would like. Is tomorrow afternoon okay?"

"Yes, sure, Mr. DeMarco."

Hannah was in a trance as she wrote down the address of the coffee shop. She was having a glass of the expensive scotch when David came home. Hannah turned on the TV.

"You know, ever since that blow-up with Rebecca, I feel guilty about watching *Hawaii Five-O* and it makes me mad. I love that show, and I have a crush on Jack Lord."

David laughed. "Are you thinking about that fight? Is that the reason for the scotch? You shouldn't let it bother you. I have some good news on the subject of Hawaii. I think we could swing a trip out there this fall. It would be a change from the Florida routine. Maybe you will run into Jack Lord."

Hannah laughed. She decided not to tell David anything until after she met with Mr. DeMarco. It was hard to believe anything was going to happen after all this time.

Hannah arrived a little early at the coffee shop. She brought a notepad with her to take down some notes about the case. She wanted to make sure she correctly captured all the details.

Mr. DeMarco looked the same as he did in 1964. The only difference was his hair was a little longer and had strands of silver. Hannah wondered if he would recognize her. He smiled broadly and walked right up to her. "Hello, Mrs. Schneider, you are looking well."

He gestured for her to sit down. They ordered coffee and pastries.

"Thank you for meeting me, Mrs. Schneider. I know this case has been dragging on for years, but now things are really moving. Mrs. O'Neal's extradition hearing will be set probably in nine months or so. It's been really tough going. The department isn't behind this, and I had to raise private funds to travel to Israel to collect survivor testimony. Thank God for your former counsel, Mr. Bradley. We couldn't have done it without his help."

"I'm sorry; what did Mr. Bradley do?"

"He donated a lot of the money for the Israel trip, and his firm provided some pro-bono legal assistance. He knows some of the higher-ups at the State Department, and he applied some pressure over the years on this case. He was a big help. The other major thing is that both the West German and Polish governments are pursuing Majdanek cases. The West German one has involved extensive research, and Mrs. O'Neal would be only one defendant among many if they go ahead with the trial, which would be the first time Germans would be trying a holocaust case like this. But we need your help. I'm looking for a number of survivors to testify to Mrs. O'Neal's actions in the camp. Is that something you're still willing to do?"

"Yes, of course. I do feel a little concerned that this will be a dead end. Why did it take so many years to finally get a hearing?"

"There was no support in the Justice Department for this case. No resources, no money. Sometimes, files would mysteriously go missing. I ended up being a one-man band, with help from survivors, Mr. Wiesenthal,

CHAPTER TWENTY-ONE: HANNAH 1971

and people like Mr. Bradley, willing to use their influence to keep the case alive. My wife helped me translate documents from German and talk to survivors. She's been a big help. It's been a hard road, but worth it."

"I had no idea. Your wife speaks German?"

"Yes. I met her in Germany after the war. She was a war bride. My family was a little unhappy at first. They expected me to marry a nice Italian girl or even an Irish girl as long as the girl was Catholic. My wife is Lutheran to boot."

Hannah smiled. "Do they like her now? How is the family visit going?"

"Oh yeah, they love her now. She's the reason I'm so addicted to pastries; she's a great baker. We had a big family celebration. My cousin's gangster novel is being made into a movie."

"Ah, yes! I read *The Godfather*. Very fascinating, I'm excited to see how they bring the Corleone family to the big screen."

"It was a bestseller. Maybe I should have been a writer instead, like my cousin."

"No, Mr. DeMarco, you have done an amazing thing to try to bring the Stomping Mare to justice. I remember you told me you were part of the American force that liberated Dachau. You know what it was like." Hannah's voice trailed off.

"Mrs. Schneider, I probably don't know exactly what it was like, but I've talked to enough survivors to know I couldn't give up. I won't give up. I promise."

Chapter Twenty-Two: Helma 1972

Both Helma and Charles were startled out of bed suddenly by a crashing sound at the front of their house and by their dog, Rex, barking loudly in the living room. Charles leapt out of bed first, and Helma grabbed her robe and followed him down the hall. Rex was barking and jumping at the front door. Helma saw the growing flames through the front window, consuming the rhododendron by the front door. Charles ran to the kitchen to get the fire extinguisher from under the kitchen sink. He turned to her as he opened the front door and yelled, "Call the fire department!"

Helma scrambled to the phone, grabbed the phone book, and turned to the emergency numbers on the inside flap. For a quick second, she couldn't remember her address, but she quickly recovered and gave them the address and took control of Rex as Charles battled the flame, licking the front of their house with the small kitchen fire extinguisher. One of their neighbors ran over and turned on the garden hose, and helped douse the flames.

Helma could hear the sirens from the fire engines and the police cars. She saw the lights come on in all of her neighbors' homes, their faces peeping out of closed curtains or cautiously opening their front doors. She knelt down to calm Rex. How she hated to have everyone looking at them. Since the extradition trial started, they had been back in the news. Charles kept a gun by the bed. They had received threatening phone calls and some radical Jewish group had targeted them. The fire crew extinguished the remaining fire. The rhododendron was destroyed and there were burn marks on the front siding of the house. The police were looking around. One of them

CHAPTER TWENTY-TWO: HELMA 1972

found some broken glass and said it looked like someone threw a Molotov cocktail at the house.

The next day, as they had made their way to the courtroom for the extradition hearing, there were a number of reporters waiting for them, asking about the bomb thrown at their home. Charles broke the rule that Mr. Perry had imposed by speaking to them. Helma could tell that he was angry.

"Some radical Jewish group, probably linked with communists, threw a Molotov cocktail at our home. I sleep with a gun by our bed. My wife is being treated unfairly for things that happened so long ago. International Jewry has an agenda, and I think we're the victims of it."

Mr. Perry came scrambling down the hall and shut down the talks with reporters. It was another day of procedural hearings. Mr. Perry had persuaded Helma and Charles to surrender her citizenship to placate the Justice Department and Immigration and Naturalization Service.

Helma didn't agree with the decision. Especially since her niece had done so much work compiling the paperwork demonstrating that she was granted amnesty by the Austrian government, and she had served a couple of years for her role as camp guard. She thought the time served, and the amnesty might solve her problem, but she had only been held accountable for her time at Ravensbruck, not Majdanek. In addition, Helma didn't disclose this in her immigration paperwork as she had served the mandated time and had received amnesty. In light of this, Mr. Perry believed that it was the best course of action to surrender her citizenship. Helma fought this idea, but Charles had a lot of trust in Mr. Perry's legal advice. Now, she was trapped in this extradition hearing, where they were trying to force her out of America by declaring her an "undesirable alien."

Mr. Perry waved off the reporters and hurried Helma and Charles into a small room near the main courtroom. He exhaled heavily and reminded them about his orders not to speak to the press. Charles looked agitated, and his face was red. "I remember your caution about not talking to reporters, but this is getting ridiculous! Some radical group have gone from making harassing calls to throwing bombs at our home! My wife is being maligned in the press as if she is some sort of Nazi mastermind, not just a guard who was simply doing her duty."

Helma rested her hand on Charles' forearm. "Darling, I realize you are defending me, but the press is not going to be fair to us. The 'lying press' is what we called them back in Germany until Hitler brought them to heel. America has the same problem: liars, controlled by Jewish interests, and let's face it, they're radicals bent on destroying this country. Mr. Perry is right. We shouldn't waste our breath talking to them."

Mr. Perry was at the table opening his briefcase and reviewing the case so far. He had a small bottle of Pepto-Bismol, took a big swig of the pink milky liquid, and cleared his throat.

"Now, I have some not-so-great news. Mr. DeMarco has arranged for the testimony of several concentration camp survivors from Majdanek. A few from here in the States, and one woman from Poland. He also is submitting testimony from other survivors that are unable to testify in person."

Helma shifted in her seat and folded her arms. "These people were prisoners, not 'survivors.' I wasn't the one who decided who came to the camp. I was merely guarding them and maintaining order. That was my job. I'm so sick of these so-called 'survivors' complaining, making themselves martyrs and victims. It's ridiculous."

Mr. Perry shuffled his papers. "Well, our challenge becomes how to minimize their impact. My strategy will involve emphasizing the decades that have elapsed since the alleged crimes. It has been three decades since these events transpired, and as you said, Mrs. O'Neal, your role was limited in scope. However, it will be difficult to handle the descriptions of the, um, brutalities carried out upon women and children. So, Mrs. O'Neal, I need to know from you what types of activities you might have participated in keeping order with the women and if these reports are accurate, children, in your charge."

"I supervised the women who worked at the camp. The children were sent elsewhere. I managed the prisoners in the camp and made sure they worked, and yes, meted out punishment to those who did not work and were disobedient and disruptive."

CHAPTER TWENTY-TWO: HELMA 1972

Mr. Perry looked down at his papers and looked pale. He took another swig out of his Pepto-Bismol bottle, and he spoke very slowly. "About the children going 'elsewhere,' as you say. There are allegations that you participated in selections and sent children, sometimes very young children, babies, and toddlers, to be gassed in the gas chambers at Majdanek. This will be brought up in the testimony, so we will need to prepare a response."

Helma tightened her jaw and tried to suppress her rage. She swallowed hard and willed herself to try to sound reasonable. "Mr. Perry, as I said, I didn't make the decisions about who came to the camp, and I didn't make the decision about how the camp was structured. I supervised people who were capable of work. If a person or child were incapable of work, they were sent elsewhere. What was done to the people incapable of working was no concern of mine. I was there to supervise the women and keep order. That's all I did because that was my job."

Helma stood up, smoothed her tailored jacket, and adjusted the scarf around her neck. "Mr. Perry, I've said all I'm going to say on this matter. I also request that you stop calling them 'survivors.' It's absurd. It was wartime, and they were prisoners. You know, my brothers are dead. One brother was in a communist slave labor camp for ten years! You don't see me prattling on about being some sad survivor. It is your responsibility to clear this up for me. I surrendered my citizenship on your advice. You should make sure to come up with an ample defense against these people."

Helma had started to open the door when she heard Mr. Perry mumble under his breath, "Good God, I can't wait until this is over."

Chapter Twenty-Three: Hannah 1972

Hannah was sewing new curtains for one of the elderly shut-ins that she and Sylvie visited on a weekly basis when the phone rang. It was Mr. DeMarco. "Hello, Mrs. Schneider; I have some news regarding Mrs. O'Neal. She has surrendered her U.S. citizenship. I think it's a bid to try to get the Justice Department to go easy on her in the extradition hearing. I'm lining up witnesses from Majdanek to testify this summer. Are you still willing to testify?"

"Yes, I am. Is this really happening? Do you think anything will come of it?"

"Most definitely. I'm working with a very high-powered attorney, Mr. Scavino. We are lining up witnesses and will be pressing for Mrs. O'Neal's extradition. The West Germans are working on a Majdanek case. Your friend from Israel, Miriam Kalinski, is working with the West Germans on their case. I know it's been a long road, but I will be in touch with a date for you to testify; the hearing is set to start in a couple of weeks."

"Okay. Let me know the dates that I need to be available. Thank you, Mr. DeMarco."

Hannah stared at the floral fabric lying on the sewing machine. She felt paralyzed. She couldn't resume sewing the curtains. She stared out the window at the tree in the backyard, wondering what it would be like to see the Stomping Mare again. The last time she saw her was at the butcher shop the day she followed her through her neighborhood on that summer day in 1964. In the years since she had lost hope that anything would happen, and now she was faced with testifying in court. She would have to confront the

CHAPTER TWENTY-THREE: HANNAH 1972

Stomping Mare.

Even though it was after 9:00 p.m. in Israel, Hannah called Miriam. "Hello, Miriam?"

"Hello, Hannah! I thought I might be hearing from you. I understand that the Stomping Mare surrendered her U.S. citizenship. That's good news."

"Yes, the investigator, Mr. DeMarco, just let me know, and I'm going to testify against her in the case. I guess there are several survivors here, in Canada, and even in Europe, who are planning to testify here in New York."

"That's good, Hannah. It's happening. There might be some justice, after all. The Germans are working on their case as well. They are compiling a case against those monsters—Bloody Bridget, the Angel of Death, and now the Stomping Mare."

"They are making a case against Bridget and the Angel of Death, too? I can't believe it."

"It is really happening at last, Hannah. You keep me posted on the case in New York, and I will keep you posted on what I hear about the case in West Germany. Take care of yourself, my friend."

"You take care too, Miriam."

Hannah put her chicken and lentil casserole in the oven, poured herself a glass of wine, and rehearsed in her mind how she would break the news to David. He was loosening his tie as he walked in the door. Hannah helped him take off his jacket and poured him a glass of scotch. He looked at her and arched his eyebrow. "So, did you and Becky have another blow-out over the phone?"

"No, it's not that. Let's sit down to eat."

Hannah dished a plate for herself and David and sat down.

"I had a call from Mr. DeMarco. The extradition for the Stomping Mare is happening. I will be testifying soon, probably in a few months. She's surrendered her citizenship. There is also a case in West Germany against her and the other camp guards at Majdanek. I talked to Miriam about it today."

David sighed. "I know that this is important to you, Hannah, but I can't revisit that time in our lives. I really wish we could have left that all in the past and that we just enjoy the life that we built here. I don't think I can be a part of it, and I hope you are going to keep to our agreement to keep our children out of this whole situation."

"Yes, I have no intention of bringing the children into this. I don't want them to be exposed to what happened with that horrible woman. I understand why you think the way you do, but I can't just let this go. I need to testify."

David nodded and ate in silence. He went to bed early. Hannah slipped into bed beside him and drifted off to sleep. Suddenly, she was jarred awake as David sat up in bed screaming. Hannah was shaking him, and he was soaked with sweat. Hannah flipped on the lights, and he was looking at her with a crazed look in his eyes. He covered his face suddenly and started weeping. This was the first time Hannah had ever seen him cry like this. She was confused and scared. She grabbed the glass of water next to the bed and encouraged him to drink. She rubbed his back; his pajamas were soaked through with sweat, and he was clammy.

Finally, he wiped his face with the sleeve of his pajamas and seemed to regain some composure. "I had a nightmare about the camp. The work I was involved with was to help the camp doctors with what they called 'medical experiments,' but really, it was torture and butchery. They performed sterilization experiments. They castrated men and filled the wombs of the women with corrosive substances. These prisoners were awake and given no anesthesia or pain medication. They died in excruciating pain. I was helpless to do anything for them. I didn't have any access to anything that could help. When they mercifully died, I had to prepare their bodies for autopsy. Tonight, I dreamed of their agonized faces and the piles of bodies."

Hannah wrapped her arms around him. "I never knew this. I'm so sorry. I've never seen you have a nightmare like this."

"I've had them in the past. They come and go. I've tried to train my mind to focus on good things as I drift off to sleep or think about baseball statistics. That has been the way that I've tried to control it."

Hannah sighed. "I'm so sorry, David. I know this legal case of mine is causing you distress."

CHAPTER TWENTY-THREE: HANNAH 1972

David's eyes were red and very sad. "It's not your fault, Hannah. I know why you want to do it, even though I wish you didn't. My nightmares have come and gone over the years, but maybe with time, I'm becoming less successful at suppressing them."

"You don't have to suppress anything with me. You know I would understand if you wanted to talk about it."

"What would that do? I don't want to talk about it. I don't want it to be in my mind or part of my life. I want you, the children, and our lives here and now to be the focus of my thoughts and energy. I'm going to take a shower now and put on some fresh pajamas." There was an edge of anger in his voice.

Hannah turned out the lights and lay in bed feeling guilty that perhaps the renewed case against the Stomping Mare was causing David to have night terrors. As he lay in bed beside her, Hannah rested her head on his chest and said quietly, "I love you so much."

David held her tightly. "You are everything to me. We will survive this. We have already survived so much."

The hearing had begun. The case focused on procedural matters for several weeks. Hannah received weekly phone calls from Mr. DeMarco regarding the progress of the case. The case was garnering some coverage in the media. The Stomping Mare's home had been attacked by protesters who threw a Molotov cocktail into their yard. The Stomping Mare's husband gave an interview complaining that they feared for their lives and that now he kept a gun near their bed. Mr. DeMarco let her know the survivors would be testifying at the end of the summer.

Mr. Scavino reached out to Hannah to meet with her and help her prepare for her testimony. He let her know that the Stomping Mare's attorney would try to trip her up and minimize survivor testimony by accusing them of seeking some sort of irrational revenge by reviving things that happened decades ago. Hannah was becoming increasingly nervous.

Finally, the day had arrived. Hannah made her way to lower Manhattan to the Immigration Building, where the hearing was being held. The first survivor testimony would be today, and Hannah's testimony and others would be the following Monday. Mr. DeMarco let her know it might be a good idea to attend and hear the testimony. He said there were other survivors from Queens who would be there as well. Hannah got out of the cab and walked into the building. The corridors were crowded with people, including some members of the press. Mr. DeMarco spotted her and waved to her to come over to join the small cluster of people surrounding him near a bench. As she got closer, she saw Weston Bradley in the crowd. She drew in her stomach and wished she had chosen a less matronly dress to wear. Mr. DeMarco greeted her.

"Mrs. Schneider, I believe you know Mr. Bradley." Hannah nodded and smiled at Weston.

Mr. DeMarco gestured to a petite blond woman. "This is Mrs. Weiss; she is from Kew Gardens as well."

"Please call me Sonja. I believe I know you. Our children attended the same elementary school. Your son's name is Max, is that correct?"

"Yes, it is. I don't recall meeting, though."

"Max used to come to our place to play stickball with my son. Very nice boy, your son. I understand he is at Columbia now?"

"Yes. I'm so sorry we haven't had the opportunity to meet until now."

Hannah then realized Mr. DeMarco was waiting to introduce her to an elderly gentleman in the group. She nodded at Mrs. Weiss and turned to the older man. "This is Mr. Korman. He will be testifying today." Mr. Korman made a slight bow, "Pleasure to meet you, ladies."

"Ladies, Mr. Bradley and I need to chat with Mr. Korman about his testimony."

Sonja took Hannah's arm. "Mrs. Schneider and I will go get some coffee."

They walked to a less crowded corridor to a coffee and pastry cart. "So, Mrs. Schneider, you were in Majdanek?"

"Yes, I was, for a little over a year. Then I was transferred to a camp in Germany."

"That's a long time to survive in Majdanek. You're not Polish, either. Everyone I knew in Majdanek was from Poland, like me."

"I was from Austria originally. I came to Majdanek from Drancy in France.

CHAPTER TWENTY-THREE: HANNAH 1972

I was in the sorting warehouse, which I think helped me survive there for so long."

Sonja nodded. "I got there in the fall of 1943. I worked on sewing uniforms. I came with my family. My mother was gassed on arrival, but my father, sister, and I were put to work. I was able to find the section my father was in. He didn't look good at all. I had some extra bread, and I threw it over the fence to him, but the Stomping Mare caught me. I was lashed somewhere between twenty-five and fifty times. My back was stripped raw and bloody by her. Somehow, I made it back to the barracks, and they managed to find some salve for my back, and I kept dipping in and out of consciousness. My sister said she would take my place for roll call that next morning, and then the Stomping Mare sent my sister to the gas chamber that morning."

Sonja stared at the coffee in the paper cup. Hannah could tell she wouldn't be able to share more of the story. Hannah reached out and touched Sonja's shoulder. "I'm so sorry. It's brave of you to come to testify. How did you hear about the Stomping Mare living here in America?"

"I saw the news article back in 1964. I couldn't believe that bitch was living here in Queens! There are lots of Polish survivors in Kew Gardens and in Queens."

Hannah nodded. "I saw the article, too. I was so angry, and it's been so frustrating waiting all this time to get her out of America."

Sonja nodded, and they continued chatting as they walked back to the main corridor. Sonja turned off for the restroom, and Hannah saw Weston waiting for her by the courtroom door.

"It's very wonderful to see you, Hannah. Your son is at Columbia, huh? Congratulations."

"Thank you. My daughter is at Cal Berkeley. They are both off at college now."

"Congratulations again."

"My daughter hates me." Weston laughed. "I think all young people hate people our age now, so that sounds pretty normal. I don't have any kids of my own, but I understand mothers and daughters are very often at odds."

Hannah nodded and smiled. Weston was dressed in a nice suit. His only compromise to the new casual look was his lack of a tie. His hair was short and thinner and more white than dark blond, and the lines had deepened around his eyes, but he was still very fit and handsome. He put his hand on the small of her back and guided her into the courtroom. They sat down together. Hannah strained to try to get a look at the Stomping Mare. She could only see the back of her head. The Stomping Mare's attorney, Mr. Perry, was very portly and had a combover.

Mr. Korman looked frail and scared as he sat down and prepared to give his testimony. He shared how he was "a horse," camp parlance for the men who hauled heavy wagons.

In heavily accented English, Mr. Korman shared one of his encounters with the Stomping Mare. "I was hauling coal to the kitchen in the women's section of the camp. There were two women, Polish women that I knew before Majdanek. A mother and her daughter. I saw her, the guard; we called her 'Kobyla,' which is Polish for mare, but now she is known as Mrs. O'Neal. She was beating these two women unceasingly with a whip. Her whip had a piece of metal at the end. She had a fearsome dog with her, too. She beat and beat them both with this whip, and they lay bleeding on the ground. She whipped them to death."

Mr. Perry folded his arms, "So, did you do anything to help these two women? Or did you just watch these alleged murders take place?"

"This was the camp. I was a prisoner, and she was a guard. It was certain death to intervene with a guard. I would have been shot on the spot."

"So, Mr. Korman, you just watched these alleged murders and went about your business, and now you're here to point the finger at Mrs. O'Neal for things that happened decades ago. Things that you just stood by and watched?"

"No, this is not the case. The Nazis set up these death camps, they were killing innocent people."

Mr. Korman was clearly struggling for the right words when Mr. Perry raised his voice and spoke over him. "Isn't it true that you're here for revenge? To punish a simple housewife for things that happened over thirty years ago?"

CHAPTER TWENTY-THREE: HANNAH 1972

Mr. Korman looked flushed and was struggling. "No, not for revenge, but for justice. Many innocent people were killed for no reason."

Mr. Perry spoke over him again. "Isn't it true in wartime, many innocent people are killed? Cities are bombed, civilians get caught in the crossfire, and other tragic occurrences, and yet, Mr. Korman, you are singling out a low-level camp guard, who is now a powerless housewife, for special punishment. It sure seems like revenge."

Mr. Scavino stood up and objected. Hannah couldn't believe what she was hearing. The lawyer was trying to make Mr. Korman the criminal. Hannah clutched her purse to her abdomen tightly; it was the only way she could stop her body from shaking. The judge sustained the objection. The badgering from Mr. Perry continued. Mr. Korman was trying to explain witnessing the hanging of a young woman. He couldn't manage the correct English terminology. Now, Mr. Korman was visibly shaking and sweating. Mr. Perry raised his voice again. "Do we need a Polish translator, or are you not really sure about this alleged hanging?"

Mr. Korman looked to be on the verge of collapse as he weakly said, "I know what I saw." The judge at least had enough compassion to call for a recess. Hannah jumped up and hurriedly left the courtroom, shaking and disoriented, she scrambled to find a quiet corner to have a cigarette and calm her nerves. She heard Weston call out her name behind her. "Hannah! Slow down."

She stopped in a side corridor, and Weston came up to her as she was fumbling in her purse for her cigarette case. Hannah dropped her purse and started hyperventilating. Weston crouched down and stopped her from hitting the ground. He picked up her purse and helped her to sit down on a bench. Hannah managed to find her cigarette case, but she was too shaky to get a cigarette out of the case. Weston took a cigarette out and put it in his mouth, lit it, and handed it to Hannah.

Weston was rubbing her shoulder as Hannah took a deep drag on the cigarette. "Hannah, that was the first drag on a cigarette I had since we first met DeMarco in 1964. I had a cigar on V-J Day, and then I quit smoking cold turkey. It was tough to quit, so don't tempt me into starting back up again."

Hannah sat up straight and tried to steady herself. "I don't know if I can go through with this. I never thought that the witnesses against her would be treated the way Mr. Korman was treated, as if somehow we're looking for revenge or worse, that we were in some way complicit with the horrible things that went on there."

"You can do it. That's the attorney's strategy. He wants to drain the confidence of the witnesses and minimize things with that 'just a low-level guard following orders' bullshit. The more people testify to her atrocities, the better the charges will stick. You can't let Perry rattle you. I was there when you shared your story with DeMarco. You can do this. I promise you that you are strong enough to do it."

Hannah took a drag on her cigarette again and stared ahead while people filed back into the courtroom. Weston put his arm around her as they walked back into the courtroom and took seats closer to the front. As the proceedings resumed, Hannah got a good look at the Stomping Mare. She had straightened her hair into an unflattering haircut, but her white suit was perfectly tailored. She had a look of contempt on her face as she stared at Mr. Korman while Mr. Scavino gently questioned the frail older man.

The questioning of Mr. Korman concluded, and he was finally excused from the stand. Mr. Perry stood up and then grabbed his stomach, and he crumpled to the floor in pain. The courtroom was abuzz as the court officers helped Mr. Perry out of the room. The judge banged his gavel to bring order and to summon Mr. Scavino to the bench. Police officers were coming in and out of the courtroom, and Hannah looked back to see the commotion in the corridor just outside. After about a half hour, the judge announced that Mr. Perry had been taken to the hospital and that there were protesters outside, and on this basis, he adjourned the proceedings for three weeks.

People were jostling and shoving to get out of the courtroom. Hannah and Weston were separated. Once Hannah managed to get out into the corridor, she saw poor Mr. Korman backed up against a wall by a scrum of reporters with bright klieg lights and their cameras. They persisted in their

CHAPTER TWENTY-THREE: HANNAH 1972

questioning, even as he held his hand protectively in front of his face and said he had nothing to say. Thankfully, she saw Mr. DeMarco intervene and help Mr. Korman leave. As she looked down the corridor to the main doors, she saw protesters shouting and tangling with police officers; some of the protesters had signs with "Nazis Get Out" on them.

Hannah was pressed to the wall by the crowds as she saw the Stomping Mare, escorted by her husband, emerge from the courtroom. She held a copy of the day's newspaper over her face as the hive of reporters, and their bright lights encircled her as she tried to make her way to the door. Hannah felt someone grab her arm. It was Sonja Weiss. She helped Hannah get outside the building, but Hannah lost sight of Sonja in a swirl of protesters. She saw a man pushing through the crowd. It was David. He shouted her name, and she ran through the crowd and collapsed in his arms, and she wept.

Chapter Twenty-Four: Hannah
September 1972

Hannah and David jumped in a cab after pushing through the protesters and police. David was catching his breath as he loosened his tie. "My God, what a madhouse, Hannah! I'm glad you're alright. I kept thinking of you all day alone in the courtroom, and I knew I had to come pick you up at the end of the day."

She looked at David, and a flood of memories came back to her. When she was a little girl in the train station in Vienna, when he came and visited every day while she was recovering in the DP camp, how he reassured her when they first came to America, and that night in a Florida resort when he laid bare his deepest feelings for her. All this time, she had been thinking that David did not support her pursuit of justice, but when it really mattered, he was there.

Hannah exhaled and could hardly believe what had happened that day. She was thankful that the judge had called the recess for three weeks, as it would give her time to mentally prepare as she now knew what she would be facing.

The next night, Sam and Sylvie came over for dinner and a game of cards. They had finished the take-out Chinese and were one hand into their bridge game when the phone rang. Hannah answered it.

An angry male voice growled, "You better not testify, you Jew bitch."

Hannah's mind raced. How did this person get her phone number? Did they know where she lived? She steadied herself and replied. "Who is this?

CHAPTER TWENTY-FOUR: HANNAH SEPTEMBER 1972

How did you get this number?"

"Don't think it's too late to get shoved in an oven if you don't keep your mouth shut!"

Hannah was shaking as David grabbed the phone. David said hello a few times and turned to Hannah. "They hung up, what did they say?"

Hannah tried to stop herself from shaking, but her whole body was trembling. Sam and Sylvie were as still as statues at the table with their mouths agape. David grabbed Hannah's arms and shook her. "Was it about the trial? Did they threaten you?" Hannah could only manage to whisper, "Yes," before she broke down sobbing. Sylvie leapt up from her chair and came to comfort Hannah. Sam stood up and put his hands on David's arm. "Let her go, you're hurting her! What's this all about, David? What is going on?"

Hannah was sobbing in Sylvie's arms, and David's face was red with anger. "I knew you never should have gotten involved in this, Hannah. I was afraid of this happening! This is why we need to leave the past in the past! Our lives were perfect here. Now this!"

Sam's voice was rising in anger, too. "David, will you tell me what in the hell is going on? What are you talking about?"

David closed his eyes, drew in a deep breath, and put his hand gently on Hannah's shoulder. "I'm sorry, I shouldn't have grabbed you and yelled like that. Don't worry; I will make sure we are safe. It might not escalate beyond threatening calls, but regardless, I will make sure you're okay."

David told Sam and Sylvie about the trial and Hannah's upcoming testimony. Sam and Sylvie were both stunned. It took a moment before Sam was even able to speak.

"So, there is a Nazi guard who killed Hannah's sister living in Queens?! That's insane. You both should pack your bags and stay at our house."

David objected, but Sylvie intervened. "Just for tonight. Tomorrow, you can set up some sort of security for your house, but now you don't know if this caller has your address, and you don't have any extra security now."

That night David and Hannah were in the same twin beds at Sam and Sylvie's they had slept in when they first came to America twenty-four years ago. Hannah stared at the ceiling and wondered if David had been right all along, that maybe it would have been better just to be quiet. The next day, David put locks on all the windows and installed an extra light over the garage. He contacted the police and requested extra patrols in their neighborhood based on the threat. Hannah called Mr. DeMarco, and he said that Mr. Korman had received similar threatening calls, and he was working with the police and F.B.I. to try to figure out who was making the calls and the true nature of the threat.

"We just don't know yet where these threats are coming from, Mrs. Schneider. We're working on it. The calls to Mr. Korman haven't gone beyond threatening and nuisance calls, so we're hopeful that's all it is. Mrs. O'Neal's case is on the radar of some Neo-Nazi group associated with the Klan called the 'Patriots' or some such name. They believe in the big Jewish conspiracy agenda that Mr. O'Neal believes in and has talked publicly about in news reports. The F.B.I. is looking into it."

Hannah thanked Mr. DeMarco and hung up the phone. She tried to distract herself with a new sewing project and tried to pretend everything was normal. The phone rang. David was at work, so Hannah answered it with trembling hands and a tense "Hello."

"Hello, Mom, are you alright? You sound strange."

Hannah exhaled, sat at the dining room table, and grabbed her cigarette case. "Thank goodness it's you. Max, I'm fine. We've just had a few rude prank callers in the past few days, that's all."

"Okay. That's weird. I called because I ran into Jerry Weiss downtown, and he said his mom, and you are testifying in a case against a Nazi concentration camp guard? That you and Mrs. Weiss were in the same concentration camp during the war and that you met up because you're both testifying against this woman that they are trying to kick out of the country? How is it I know nothing about this?"

Hannah opened her cigarette case and took a few drags off the cigarette before answering. "Yes, I met Mrs. Weiss for the first time a week ago. The case is postponed, but both Mrs. Weiss and I will share what we know about this woman because she's a criminal and doesn't belong in this country. I

CHAPTER TWENTY-FOUR: HANNAH SEPTEMBER 1972

didn't tell you because you shouldn't concern yourself with these types of things. It happened long before you were born. I also do not want you sharing this information with your sister."

"What is it with you and Dad? I literally know nothing about your lives during the war."

"Why would we burden you with that knowledge? What good would it do you? The whole reason we built the life we have is so that you and your sister can have happy, productive lives. Why would we bring up these horrible things? You should concentrate on your studies."

Max was quiet for a few seconds. "Okay, cool. I guess the guy I used to play stickball with in grammar school knows more about my mom's life than I do. That seems fair? Do you want me to come to the hearing? Can I help you in any way?"

"No. I don't want you at the hearing. As I said, this is something your father and I don't want you or your sister to be involved with at all. Is everything okay with you? Do you need any money?"

"No, I don't need money. I'm fine. I can tell by the tone of your voice I'm not going to get anywhere with this, so I will let you go."

"Your father and I are only doing this to protect you and your sister."

Max exhaled and was quiet for a few seconds. "Okay. I won't say anything to Becks. I love you, mom."

Hannah felt tears sting her eyes. "I love you too, darling."

Hannah stood in front of the mirror in a purple dress with gold buttons. Purple was Rebecca's favorite color. Hannah remembered a purple scarf Rebecca used to wear with a grey raincoat. Hannah remembered looking out of the window as a little girl in their home in Vienna, and watching for that purple scarf on rainy days. The night she lay in bed at Sam and Sylvie's house, she was filled with anxiety and doubts, but just now the anxiety eased as she remembered Rebecca. She had been so vibrant. How brave her sister was during the war and in the camp. How she didn't back down from the Stomping Mare. She remembered how loving her sister was and how many days when Hannah was very little that her sister took care of her, bought her treats when they were exploring Vienna, and finally, how in the camp, during the most horrific time of their lives, her sister found her extra food and at night how Rebecca stroked Hannah's shaved head and hummed songs to her until she fell asleep. Hannah felt stronger just thinking about Rebecca. She knew she would have loved Hannah's purple dress.

David decided to come with her. Even though he still wished that Hannah had not been involved in the case at all, now he was invested in her safety. They drove to lower Manhattan. This time the Immigration and Naturalization building was a little quieter. No protesters clamored outside the building. There were fewer reporters lingering in the corridor.

Hannah spotted Mr. DeMarco and Weston. Hannah introduced Mr. DeMarco. "David, this is Mr. DeMarco, he works for the Immigration and Naturalization Service and has been helping me with my testimony these past few months." David shook Mr. DeMarco's hand. David turned to Weston, and Hannah's stomach flipped, and she stumbled over her words. "This is Weston, I mean, Mr. Bradley. You've met him before at a hospital fundraiser, um, a few years ago."

Weston interrupted and shook David's hand. "My firm did some work for the hospital's foundation in 1964 and now I'm providing pro bono legal services in this case." David shook his hand and nodded politely. Mr. DeMarco narrowed his eyes, trying to discern the awkward subtext of this exchange. Hannah could tell he knew there was more to the story. Hannah searched David's face to see if on some level he knew about her and Weston. The four of them fell into a sudden silence as the Stomping Mare, her husband, and her attorney whisked by them on their way to the hearing room. David was staring at them and spoke in a low voice. "So, that's her. I could kill her with my bare hands."

Weston murmured, "I would gladly help you."

There was a low buzz as the hearing was called to order. Hannah noticed that the Stomping Mare's attorney looked sickly and pale, like the stuffing had been knocked out of him. She heard that he had been hospitalized for a bleeding ulcer. It was not surprising that working with the Stomping Mare burned a hole in his gut, thought Hannah.

The first witness was a woman from Poland. She was a dentist. Hannah

CHAPTER TWENTY-FOUR: HANNAH SEPTEMBER 1972

was in awe of how confident she seemed. She was tall and so dignified. What had worked in breaking down Korman had no chance of working on this witness.

Head held high the woman recounted what she had seen in the camp. "Kobyla, who is the woman here," she gestured to the Stomping Mare, "I saw her separate children from their mothers. Sometimes she told the mothers there was a special place in the camp where the children would have milk twice a day. Of course, that was a lie. The children were sent to be gassed. Sometimes, she didn't bother with the lie. She grabbed the children and threw them, like sacks of flour, in the back of the truck and off those children went to the gas chambers. She beat, whipped, kicked, set dogs on those desperate and weeping mothers. I wrote it all down after the war. I remember her and her cruelty so well because I kept track of the truckloads of children that were sent off to be murdered."

The entire courtroom was enveloped in a momentary stunned silence. The lawyer made several weak attempts to cast doubt upon her testimony, but to no avail.

Hannah was called next to the witness stand. David squeezed her hand as she stood and made her way to the stand. Hannah stared straight ahead as she passed the Stomping Mare at the table to her left. She sat and smoothed her purple dress and folded her hands on her lap. She stared directly at the Stomping Mare who had a frozen frown on her face. She had a bright multicolored scarf and was wearing a neatly tailored tan suit. Her eyes narrowed as she stared at Hannah as if trying to place her.

The Stomping Mare's gray and sickly lawyer approached her and asked her name and how she knew "Mrs. O'Neal."

Hannah cleared her throat and looked beyond the Stomping Mare to David. He was leaning forward in his seat. A row back from David, Mr. DeMarco and Weston sat together. Hannah's throat still felt dry as she began to speak.

"I first met Mrs. O'Neal, who was known to me as the 'Stomping Mare' when I arrived at Majdanek in 1943. She was separating the women into two lines. One to the gas chamber, and one to the camp to be put to work. An elderly woman tried to stay with her daughters instead of going in the other line. The Stomping Mare, or Mrs. O'Neal, struck the woman and began kicking her when she fell to the ground. She kicked her in her abdomen several times, and then brought a boot blow down on her head. The old woman's body was shaking. The Stomping Mare brought her boot down again and cracked open the woman's skull, killing her."

Mr. Perry, the attorney, rubbed his chin, and asked, "How did you know that this woman was dead?"

"We were all made to walk past her as we entered the camp. She lay there motionless in a pool of blood as we all passed her."

"How do you know that it was Mrs. O'Neal, this 'Stomping Mare' that you speak of?"

"When we were brought into a building to surrender our clothing and items and to be shaved and to be deloused, I was crying. The Stomping Mare came very close to me and struck me across the face. The Stomping Mare was at our roll calls almost every morning. She often struck, whipped, or set dogs on women during roll calls. I did my best to steer clear of her as she had a reputation of being cruel and sadistic."

Hannah looked at the Stomping Mare as she said this. The Stomping Mare had an angry scowl on her face and Hannah noticed she was crumpling a newspaper in her lap under the table.

Mr. Perry asked, "I was not asking for gossip or an opinion. You say you saw another alleged murder."

Hannah took a deep breath and paused. She reached for the glass of water and took a sip as her throat was unnaturally dry. "Yes. It was at roll call at the beginning of November of 1943. As I said, the Stomping Mare was at roll call in the morning practically every day. She singled out my sister to be killed. I shouted and lunged at the Stomping Mare, and she punched me, and I fell in the mud. I tried to get up."

Mr. Perry interrupted her. "So, you confess to assaulting Mrs. O'Neal in this confrontation?"

Hannah paused. "Well, I was a malnourished 15-year-old girl performing slave labor in a concentration camp with wooden shoes and a burlap

CHAPTER TWENTY-FOUR: HANNAH SEPTEMBER 1972

dress, and she was an all-powerful camp guard with a whip and steel toed boots threatening the last family member I had alive. The rest of my family was gassed at that camp. To say that I 'assaulted' her is a gross mischaracterization of that situation. The Stomping Mare fought with my sister. She got my sister down on the ground and began kicking her and stomping on her. I was trying to crawl toward her." Hannah had to stop and catch her breath and steel herself to go on.

"I was crawling, but I couldn't get to her. The Stomping Mare stomped on her head. I kept crawling closer. The boot came down hard, so hard, and cracked her skull open and blood spattered on me and spattered everywhere. That was how my sister was killed."

The hearing room was eerily quiet for a few seconds. Hannah saw that David had buried his face in his hands.

Mr. Perry made a choking sound and cleared his throat. "You allege that your sister was murdered, and she was possibly an unruly camp inmate, and you cannot definitively confirm that the old woman and your sister were, in fact, murdered by Mrs. O'Neal. You testify to conflicts that involved disobedience by inmates, and it was Mrs. O'Neal's job to maintain order in a camp where she was greatly outnumbered. This occurred three decades ago, so are you actually sure that these conflicts you allege actually unfolded as you claim?"

Hannah felt anger rising in her. "If you're asking me if I clearly remember being sent to a camp where my mother, sister and father were gassed and where my other sister and I were starved and abused. Yes, despite the passage of time I clearly remember that. If you're asking me if I remember seeing my sister's skull crushed and being spattered with her blood as I crawled through the mud, yes, even though 29 years have elapsed, I remember it clearly."

Hannah's face was burning. Mr. Scavino asked a few questions and Hannah was excused. Hannah glared at the Stomping Mare as she walked past the table. Hannah took a few deep breaths to try to get her anger under control. She looked toward David as he stood up and the hearing was adjourned for a lunch break. It seemed to take forever for Hannah to reach

David. He held out his hand, and only when she grasped it did Hannah feel her body start to relax.

Mr. DeMarco came up to them and put his hand on her shoulder. "Thank you, Mrs. Schneider, for your powerful testimony. I know it's been a long road and a difficult one."

Weston was standing next to Mr. DeMarco. "Yes, very powerful and strong testimony. You should be very proud."

Hannah thanked them both. People were milling out of the hearing room. David took Hannah to a side door so they could avoid the reporters. They left through a service door and made their way to a café a couple of blocks away.

David ordered coffee and sandwiches. He gently grasped Hannah's hands across the table and was quiet and seemed to be composing himself before he could speak. "Hannah, I'm so sorry that happened to you and to Rebecca. I loved your sister, maybe less of a romantic love and more of a brotherly love, but she was so brilliant, fun, and kind. There was no one like her. I'm not happy that you are wrapped up in this case with that horrible guard, but that doesn't change the fact that what you have done is very brave, and it honors Rebecca's memory."

Hannah squeezed David's hands. "Thank you so much. I know it was hard to hear and the longer this goes on, I think sometimes you were right that it may have been more difficult than I anticipated, but for Rebecca, I feel like it was the right thing to do."

David went to work the following day, but Hannah went back to the hearing to listen to the testimony defending the Stomping Mare. Hannah stopped by the coffee and pastry cart before heading into the hearing room. She saw Weston.

"Amazing testimony, Hannah. You're a tough lady, and you handled it perfectly."

"I was scared, but you, Mr. DeMarco and Mr. Scavino helped so much with preparation, and it was nice to have my husband at the hearing too."

"Yes, I was surprised to see him. I'm glad he's supporting your effort. A real handsome bastard, that guy. I was kind of hoping he had become

CHAPTER TWENTY-FOUR: HANNAH SEPTEMBER 1972

fat, bald and kind of gnome-like in the past years so I would look more handsome by comparison because I still carry a torch for you Hannah."

Hannah laughed. "You have no idea how flattering that is for a middle-aged housewife to hear. I'm sure the torch dimmed a bit after seeing me after all these years." Hannah patted her stomach. She was a little heavier and had more wrinkles than when they first met, but she still turned a few heads when she went swimming at the resort in Hawaii on a recent trip.

Weston winked at her. "It's burning brighter than ever. I love a gal who can verbally eviscerate an evil Nazi concentration camp guard."

Hannah sat with Sonja Weiss and Weston as the testimony resumed. A teenage neighbor nervously took a seat on the witness stand and recalled how he had accidentally broken a window with a baseball and how kind the Stomping Mare had been in forgiving him and paying for the repair herself, he also remembered her making pancakes for him and his brother. Yet another neighbor remarked on what a wonderful gardener and dog owner the Stomping Mare was and how she must not be the same woman who was this sadistic camp guard.

Then the neighbor said something that shook Hannah at her core. Mr. Perry asked, even if she had been a camp guard all those years ago, would it change your opinion of her? And the neighbor paused before finally saying, "No. It all happened so long ago that we should just move on."

Hannah slumped in her seat. Because her sister and so many others had been brutally murdered nearly thirty years ago, it didn't matter? Because someone kept their yard nice and took care of their dogs, they were no longer accountable for past wrongs?

The next witness was the Stomping Mare's husband. He had dirty blond hair with too much Brylcreem in it, and he looked sweaty and nervous.

"My wife is a wonderful lady, and she was just doing her job as a guard. She wasn't a bigwig making decisions," he said. Hannah thought he looked irritated just having to answer questions.

Mr. Scavino asked what he knew about her role as a camp guard. "She did tell me about it before we were married. It was looked into in Austria, and she did serve a couple of years and she did receive amnesty. No one has made note of that here, but she did pay her debt to society, and she should be allowed to move on with her life."

Mr. Scavino asked for specifics about what Mr. O'Neal knew.

"She was a guard for women prisoners. These prisoners were sometimes resistance workers, murdering soldiers, or malingerers, perverts, or other undesirables. My understanding is that Ravensbruck was a re-education camp."

Sonja Weiss scoffed so loudly at this that the judge banged his gavel and called the proceedings to order. Mr. Scavino asked what Mr. O'Neal knew about Majdanek.

"I know she was there for a short time, doing her guard work and then she was very sick for many months at the end of the war. After the war, like I said, she paid her debt, and the Austrian government gave her a full amnesty. She took care of her brother's widow and his little girl. The good in her life outweighs any bad she might have been associated with, and this is a big witch hunt for someone who was a simple camp guard and you're all making out like she is Eichmann or Hitler himself."

Hannah just shook her head. She remembered what her grandmother Hortense used to say, "There is a lid for every pot." There was even someone for the Stomping Mare.

Finally, the day arrived when the Stomping Mare herself was called to the stand. She wore a nicely tailored white linen dress with a wide collar. Her hair was a grayish blond which she had straightened into a limp pageboy style. She seemed so slim and ladylike now, compared to the broad shouldered and aggressive woman that struck such fear in the hearts of the women in Majdanek.

Her attorney gently questioned her about her life now. The Stomping Mare went on about being a homemaker, her knitting for church sales, and her dogs. She skimmed over her service as a camp guard, dismissing it as "just a job" and saying it was like any prison guard today. Her attorney questioned her in detail about her time served in Austria and the amnesty she received.

Mr. Scavino asked her about the allegations of beatings and murders.

CHAPTER TWENTY-FOUR: HANNAH SEPTEMBER 1972

The Stomping Mare's face transformed into something familiar to Hannah. The mouth clenched into a thin line, the brows furrowed, and the already deep-set eyes narrowed. The Stomping Mare's rage was barely contained.

"I was one guard among many prisoners. Some of them were violent. I maintained order to the best of my ability. This 'Stomping Mare' business is just a rude nickname dreamed up by prisoners. I didn't choose who came to the camp. I just maintained order in a very difficult environment."

Mr. Scavino folded his arms, "You say you 'maintained order.' The testimony here is that you beat, whipped, and stomped people to death. The testimony we have heard is that you sent women and children to the gas chamber."

The Stomping Mare's face grew red, and her voice grew angry. "I chose women who were fit for work, what happened to the others was not my concern. Not part of my job."

Mr. Scavino asked again. The Stomping Mare was struggling to maintain her composure. "I may have struck an unruly prisoner, that's possible. As I said, I just maintained order as instructed. It was my job. I wasn't doing anything illegal."

Mr. Scavino pressed her on the children in the camp. She continued to struggle to maintain control of her anger. Hannah saw that she paused for a breath. "I suppose there were children that came to the camp. I don't recall seeing many children under the age of nine. As I said, my job was to guard the women who were fit for work. I supervised them and followed my orders as assigned. There were many people who came to the camp. That was none of my concern."

Hannah drew in her breath. The audacity of the lies and the utter lack of any responsibility was shocking. To his credit, Mr. Scavino continued to try to get the Stomping Mare to respond to the allegations laid out in court. Her exasperated replies amounted to some variation on "just doing my job," and how she was not responsible for decisions at the camp. She even tried to make herself into a victim, posing as someone who, as a simple and lowly guard, had been unfairly targeted.

Hannah watched as the Stomping Mare left the witness stand and saw that her husband, who was seated behind her, gave the Stomping Mare an encouraging squeeze on the shoulder. As court was adjourned, Hannah made her way to the door of the hearing room feeling numb. She couldn't conceive of the version of what happened by the testimony she just heard.

She gathered in a group with Mr. DeMarco, Weston, and Sonja Weiss. All were quiet. Finally, Mr. DeMarco broke the silence. "We expected something like this from her and her attorney. It's not surprising." He shrugged his shoulders as he said, "Now we wait."

Chapter Twenty-Five: Helma 1973

It was Good Friday. Helma had returned from the store with fresh fish she was planning to make for dinner. She was in the bedroom considering two different floral print dresses she might wear to Easter Sunday services when she heard a knock on the door. She hung the dresses up and answered the door. Two men in trench coats were at the door.

Helma put her hands on her hips. "How can I help you?"

The taller of the two men spoke. "Mrs. O'Neal, we are here to take you into custody. The government of the United States will be extraditing you to the Federal Republic of Germany."

Helma tightened her jaw. She felt her face growing hot. Thoughts began racing through her mind. She knew Perry had told her that her appeal had been denied, and they even appealed to the highest court in the land, the Supreme Court, which also denied her appeal three weeks ago. She hadn't considered the charges pending in Germany. She had grown so used to the endless years of legal red tape she mentally prepared herself to continue to be in limbo for years to come.

The other man jarred her out of her thoughts. "Ma'am, we don't want to make this difficult."

Helma waved him off as if swatting a fly. "Yes, yes. Do you have paperwork? Can I call my attorney?"

Helma was walking to the phone before the man could even answer. They were pulling the documents out of their coats as she dialed Perry's office. Helma crossed her arms as Perry talked in more legal jargon, while all she wanted to know was if he was going to make sure she didn't have to stay in jail. She finally got Perry to promise to get word to Charles. She then turned to the two startled officers as she grabbed her purse and coat.

"I won't give you any trouble." She shooed them out of the door with her purse and walked alongside them to their car. As they pulled away from her house, she took a last look at the yard and wondered if Charles would be able to maintain the yard in the event that she had to be away for a while.

Helma was shocked and furious when she discovered that she was being booked into Rikers Island prison. She found the booking process humiliating. As the prison wardresses walked her through each step, she thought, I'm no different from them! I just did my job, and look at this mess!

Her horror magnified when she saw her cellmates. She called over one of the guards. She lowered her voice as she spoke to the guard, whom she felt certain would understand that Helma did not belong there. "Excuse me. I haven't been convicted of anything, and I'm not facing charges here; my charges are pending in Germany, and I believe I will be cleared of wrongdoing there. Considering that, I do not want to share a cell with negro prostitutes."

The prison guard folded her arms. "Sorry, lady, you don't get to pick your cellmates. Everybody has a story, and if you're so innocent you wouldn't be here. I don't know what you did in Germany, but I bet it wasn't good if they want you back there. My husband served over there, and he still has nightmares about that war and the things the Germans did, so if you want sympathy, you're barking up the wrong tree."

Helma drew back as if the woman had slapped her. She was shocked; she thought this white woman who was about her age would understand. Maybe she was a Jew?

Helma sat back down. She kept her distance and didn't engage with the other women in the cell. After a few hours, a new guard was on duty. A younger woman. Helma beckoned her to the cell. "Excuse me, do you think I could get some writing paper and a pen? I just want to write a letter to my niece. It would be a great comfort to be able to do that." Helma smiled and used the most meek and polite tone of voice she could muster.

The young woman sighed. "I guess that would be alright." She brought a

CHAPTER TWENTY-FIVE: HELMA 1973

few sheets of paper, a pen, and an envelope over to Helma.

Helma nodded. "You are most kind."

Helma sat down. It was actually a relief to be able to concentrate on composing a letter to Greta. Now that she was likely to be headed to Germany, she would be able to see Greta again, and perhaps Greta could be of assistance in helping her navigate the legal situation there. At least this was one bright spot she could focus on until Perry was able to arrange bail for her.

Dearest Greta,

You will be shocked and upset to learn where I am now. Unfortunately, I have been arrested. I'm in an American prison, and it's not a pretty sight. I was arrested on Good Friday, and now I'm spending the early morning hours of Holy Saturday among the worst and most vile kind of people.

You would not believe the dirty dealing which has gone on in my case. Of course, there has been tremendous pressure and all the financial means of the 'chosen people.' America is full of Jews who wield enormous influence in the legal system. Their influence can be seen in the decline of this country and the lack of values evident in the younger generation here.

My arrest is the result of a pending extradition to Germany. Apparently, I'm going to be held to account for decisions the German government made over 30 years ago. Uncle Charles doesn't know why they are going after me, a guard, for simply doing my job!

We will be in Germany someday, I suppose, if the wheels of the legal system continue in motion. Oh, how I will miss my house and lovely garden, my loyal pup and most of all my beloved, your Uncle Charles. What a tremendous support he has been to me during these trying times.

I'm mindful that Easter is a season of hope! So, I put my trust in God. I hope you had a blessed Easter, my dear niece. Keep me in your prayers.

Your Loving Aunt,

Helma

Helma didn't get much sleep, so she was in a little bit of a fog as she was escorted to a visiting room, and to her relief, she saw Charles and Mr. Perry. Charles looked very worried, and Mr. Perry looked drained. Mr. Perry talked about the effort underway to get her out on bail. Helma folded her arms and glared at Mr. Perry. She had been losing confidence in him ever since he collapsed in the courtroom last year. He didn't seem to fight as hard after that. She explained the horrible conditions and that she was sharing a cell with common prostitutes. She didn't think this appeal to Mr. Perry was working.

She knew a few feminine tears would spur her tender-hearted Charles to get her out of there. Her voice trembled slightly, and she started to cry quietly as she explained her situation. "I hardly slept at all last night. I'm sharing a cell with streetwalkers who could be violent and so dirty I don't know what types of disease I may be exposed to by being in such close proximity. And, who knows what type of drugs they may have taken? They could be out of control at any moment."

Charles looked alarmed. He knew it was rare for Helma to express any fear or to cry at all. He promised to pull out all the stops to get her out of the situation.

Helma spent a couple of nearly sleepless nights in her cell. She felt a sense of relief when she was brought to the visitor's room and saw Charles and Mr. Perry. She was feeling confident she was heading home. Mr. Perry smiled as they sat down. "Good news. We have arranged for a transfer from Rikers Island to Nassau County jail, your own cell, and a much better environment."

Helma frowned. "How is this good news? I thought I would be going home?"

Mr. Perry folded his hands. "I'm very sorry, Mrs. O'Neal, but the German government considers you a flight risk, so no bail was granted in your case."

As Helma was escorted out of the prison, the middle-aged guard who had blown off Helma's request for different cellmates was sitting at the desk.

CHAPTER TWENTY-FIVE: HELMA 1973

She smiled at Helma as she held up a newspaper with the headline "Nazi Housewife Nabbed" and said, "I didn't know you were a celebrity Nazi! No wonder you wanted special treatment, master race and all."

While the county jail was a slightly better accommodation, it was still very difficult to be around common criminals, and she was not allowed to knit in her cell. She was allowed to write letters, and Charles came to visit her on every possible visiting day.

Her extradition was in a holding pattern. Helma had time to think back on the hearing last year. She scoffed at how dramatic the prisoners' testimony had been and how each of them more or less admitted to being involved in some wrongdoing when they received some sort of punishment. Many of those who testified, she couldn't place. So many thousands of prisoners cycled through in such a short time it was hard to remember any particular prisoners. They were always doing something, like stealing food, lying, and slacking off at work, and it was so hard to keep order with them all. Nobody talked about how hard she worked to keep order and to serve her country.

She also thought about how ineffective her attorney was, especially after he had been hospitalized for his ulcer. There was some little Jewess in a purple dress who was sharp with him, and he couldn't even stand up to her! Helma thought she remembered her as one of Letty's pet prisoners she kept in the sorting area.

Finally, in early August, she was informed she would be boarding a flight for Germany. When she arrived at JFK airport, there was a reporter from *The New York Times*, the investigator in her case, Mr. DeMarco, and fortunately, Charles was there with her luggage and, most thoughtfully, her knitting kit.

She overheard Mr. DeMarco complaining about how difficult her case was to prosecute due to missing files and lack of support from the Justice Department. Helma rolled her eyes at this, considering how full of Jew money his coffers must be! It was clear that they had pulled out all the stops just to come after a "small fry" like her.

The reporter talked to Charles, and Helma's heart was warmed by his comment. "I'm standing by my wife. I love her and I will be by her side in Germany or anywhere I need to be. You won't find a finer lady than my wife, and this is just some crazy witch hunt by some influential Jews and communists who want to dredge up the past."

The reporter asked for her thoughts on her extradition to Germany. Helma wasn't going to answer, but she gestured over to the German officers who would be escorting her on the plane, and she said, "I haven't spoken German in so long. It sounds strange to me now. I guess I will have to get used to it. I hope these airline people don't lose or damage my knitting kit. I have knitting projects I would like to work on."

The reporter looked perplexed as Helma was escorted away. She boarded the plane headed for Germany.

Chapter Twenty-Six: Hannah 1975

Hannah loved traveling to San Francisco. Something about the beauty of the city appealed to her. She and David had spent time here visiting Rebecca at college over the past four years. Rebecca had grown more distant and, like many young people her age, more critical of Hannah and David's suburban lifestyle. Hannah didn't really understand how to break through to her or why Rebecca judged her so harshly. Now, they were in California for Rebecca's graduation. Max was flying out from medical school in Minnesota.

On the morning of the graduation, Hannah wanted to look her best. She booked an appointment in the hotel's salon to have her hair styled in an elaborate updo and have a professional manicure. She had purchased a new white dress with a yellow floral design. Hannah always had a little nagging insecurity at these events. Often, the parents of Rebecca and Max's peers were well-educated. When they talked about where they went to college, Hannah would just stay quiet or say she was "educated at home while growing up in Europe." That sounded kind of sophisticated and so much better than the truth.

David kissed her cheek when she walked out of the salon. "You look so beautiful, Hannah. That color suits you."

They met Max in the lobby of the hotel. He had just flown in from Minnesota and dropped his bags off at the front desk, and they were off to the graduation. Hannah grabbed an extra graduation program for her scrapbook. Now, both of her children were grown, and both college graduates. David beamed with pride throughout the whole ceremony.

Hannah knew how important it was to him that the children received a quality education.

After the ceremony, they all went to a vegetarian restaurant that Rebecca had chosen. The restaurant had lots of plants in macramé hangers and Eastern-inspired linen tablecloths. When they sat down, Hannah reached into her purse for her cigarette case.

Rebecca frowned. "Mom, there is no smoking in here."

Hannah picked up a small green glass dish. "Oh, I thought this was an ashtray?"

Rebecca just rolled her eyes, and Hannah put her cigarette case back in her purse. The menus came, and Hannah wasn't sure what to order. Rebecca had a few recommendations. While they were waiting for their meals, Hannah mustered the courage to ask Rebecca a few questions about her plans.

"So, you are now a college graduate. Do you and your boyfriend have any plans, or are you considering when you might marry?"

Rebecca's face grew red. "There is a reason I've never introduced you to him, and that question is one of them. We're happy as things are. I know it shocks you that people consider a life not being a wife who lives in the suburbs, gets her hair shellacked into crazy bouffant styles, bakes casseroles, and waits for her husband to get home. I'm not into it. Why don't you ever ask Max when he's getting married?"

Max threw up his hands. "Hey, don't bring me into this! And for your information, any time I call home mom always asks about 'any nice girls' I might be dating. I'm too busy. Medical school is crazy. We all get it Becks, you're more enlightened and you'll never have mom and dad's 1950s lifestyle, but that's no reason to shit all over it."

David frowned. "Max! Your language! Becky, I know you consider us hopelessly old fashioned but we are concerned for your happiness. We would like to see you settled into a stable life, with a wonderful husband and it is common now for wives to have careers and work. It would be nice to hear about your career direction now that you have finished school."

Max smiled. "Yes, are you still going to work at that weird bead shop and continue to be a Hindu?"

CHAPTER TWENTY-SIX: HANNAH 1975

Rebecca turned to Max. "You can be a real jackass, you know! Yes, I'm still working at the shop. We sell crystals and a lot of other things, and you know I'm a practicing Buddhist; you just say 'Hindu' to be a jerk." Rebecca smacked Max with the napkin.

Hannah held up her hands. "Okay, you two. Even though it's oddly reassuring to find you both fighting like you have since you were little, it's just not appropriate at a restaurant. Let's act like we raised you to have some manners. Now, we can enjoy this lovely garbanzo bean paste." Hannah noticed David stifling a laugh.

When they flew back home a few days later, Hannah was a little sad that the "children" were truly grown-ups living their lives in other parts of the country and that all four of them being together would be rare.

In late September, Hannah noticed that David was coughing more and losing weight. He insisted he was fine, but Hannah wasn't so sure. By mid-October, David was really sick. Hannah finally insisted he stay home from work, and she made some chicken soup. He still insisted he was fine and wanted to go back to work. Hannah called Sam.

"Sam, he's having trouble breathing, and he won't listen to me." Sam came over and coaxed David into a doctor's appointment.

Hannah's hand was shaking as she smoked a cigarette quickly before stamping it out at the door of the hospital. She raced to the information desk to find out David's room number. Sam met her at the door of David's room.

"Hannah, he's okay. He will be fine. He has pneumonia. That's why he had so much trouble breathing. They are taking good care of him."

David made an effort to sit up in bed when he saw Hannah. "Hello, my darling. Sorry about this. I guess it was a bit more than a cold."

Hannah held his hand and waited with him until he fell asleep. In their nearly 30 years of marriage, she had never seen David ill. He was always healthy and energetic. He regularly put in ten- or twelve-hour days at work and always seemed fine. It was shocking to see him wheezing for breath and struggling to sleep.

He was discharged a week later. As they were checking out and receiving the at home recovery instructions, the doctor mentioned something about a follow up with a heart specialist. David confidently nodded, patted the doctor on the back, and went on about how well he felt.

David insisted on driving them home. "Don't be so worried, Hannah. I feel fine. Actually, very excited to have shed a little weight."

"What did the doctor say about a follow-up about your heart?"

"Oh, that's all very routine. You know I'm sixty now, so it is time to be paying a bit of attention to my heart health, but not a problem."

Hannah drew in her breath. She couldn't shake a nagging feeling that David was minimizing things to try to protect her.

"Do you think we should have the children come home for Thanksgiving? Perhaps you should take a leave of absence from work."

"Nonsense. I will be back at work next week. I feel perfectly fine. While I adore our children, I think I would rather have Thanksgiving without Becky condemning us for eating a turkey and Max goading her into arguments. You want me to rest, that Thanksgiving scenario sounds anything but restful. I think Max is too consumed with studies, and I think Becky made it clear she wants 'her space' as people of her generation say." David chuckled and patted Hannah's leg.

David went back to work, and Hannah was testing out new recipes from a heart-healthy cookbook, when the phone rang. It was Miriam.

"Hello, Hannah. I have news. The trial in West Germany, in Dusseldorf, is starting at the end of November. I've been in touch with the prosecuting attorneys, and they will have an opportunity for survivor testimony, probably early next spring. I'm planning to go, along with my friend Paula. I think you should talk to the survivors who testified in New York and see about coming. I can get you in touch with the attorneys in Germany."

Hannah paused. It was hard enough to testify in New York. She couldn't imagine traveling back to Germany and facing the Stomping Mare once again. But it would be amazing to see Miriam again and to have her support to face another trial. Despite all the heartache that might be involved, her sister Rebecca's face filled her mind's eye, and for a moment, she couldn't breathe. Yes, she decided she would go. She had to.

CHAPTER TWENTY-SIX: HANNAH 1975

"Yes, I will check in with Mr. DeMarco and the others I met to see what we can do. Hopefully, David will be feeling better and both of us can make the trip next spring. It will be wonderful to see you and have you by my side when I face the Stomping Mare again."

"It's not just her. Bloody Bridget, the Angel of Death, the last camp commandant, and a few other guards will be on trial as well. They will all be together. I guess the Germans started investigating Majdanek in the '60s, and they have been compiling names and evidence, so it's more than the Stomping Mare, although she is arguably the most evil one of the whole group," Miriam scoffed as she said this.

Hannah's mind swirled. It was hard enough to have faced down just one of them, she couldn't imagine seeing them all again in a courtroom, but with Miriam and David with her, she felt she could make it through testifying again.

Miriam interrupted Hannah's thoughts, "So, what's wrong with David?"

"He had a short stint in the hospital with pneumonia a couple of weeks back and the doctor said something about his heart, although David just brushed that off and won't share anything about it with me."

"David is very strong and so madly in love with you, that his heart is probably stronger than the doctors give him credit for."

Hannah smiled, "That is a sweet thing to say, Miriam. Better be careful; people will say you're getting soft in your old age."

Miriam laughed. "Oh no, I'm still that little bundle of aggression! You can ask Benny and Daniel; I'm bringing them with me to Germany, too."

It brought some comfort to Hannah that both Miriam and Benny would be there with her when the time came to go to Germany.

That evening, Hannah hesitated to share the conversation she had with Miriam, not because she was worried about how he might react to the information about the upcoming trial in Germany, but because he looked very tired. He also was not pleased with the new heart-healthy meals Hannah was cooking.

"I can't add just a bit of salt, Hannah?"

"No, you can't. You must eat well and get healthy. You still look unwell and still too thin."

"I'm going to stay too thin if I can't have a little flavor, and there hasn't been dessert in so long."

Hannah thought he reminded her of the kids when they were little. She smiled, "I will come up with some heart-healthy desserts for you. I have some important news to share. Miriam called me today. The Stomping Mare's trial in West Germany starts at the end of November. It's not just her; it is a few camp guards and others on trial. The survivors will be called to testify next spring. Miriam, her friend Paula, who was also in Majdanek, and she's bringing Benny and their son Daniel with her to the trial."

David looked serious. "Well, I would not bring our children and expose them to that, but we can't leave the job half done. We will go and do what we can to make sure that woman and any others are brought to justice. It's a privilege; so many other survivors never see any justice for what was done. We haven't seen Benny and Miriam since they left the DP camp for Palestine all those years ago. That will be a wonderful reunion."

Hannah felt herself start to relax. She was so grateful that David would be at her side, supporting her.

A few weeks later, they enjoyed Thanksgiving at Sam and Sylvie's house. Hannah noticed that David didn't eat very much, even though Sylvie's meal was not part of the "heart-healthy" diet. His face looked tight as if he were concealing pain. Any time Hannah asked he would smile and just deny feeling unwell at all.

At breakfast the next morning, Hannah noticed a short story about the trial in the paper. They noted that "Mrs. O'Neal," as they referred to the Stomping Mare, was a *former* Queens housewife.

Two weeks later, Hannah had dinner and even a dessert ready for David. He was typically very prompt, but Hannah found herself putting his dinner plate on the stove to keep it warm. She sat at the table and read an article about First Lady Betty Ford's trip to Hawaii. David was more than an hour late. Then, there was a knock at the door. Hannah opened the door, and Sam stood in front of her with his hat in his hand.

"Hannah, David's back in the hospital. He asked me to bring you to him."

CHAPTER TWENTY-SIX: HANNAH 1975

Hannah nervously smoked as Sam drove her to the hospital. When she got to his room, Sylvie was sitting next to the bed, her eyes were swollen and red rimmed as she stood and embraced Hannah. David had oxygen tubes in his nose and an IV. His eyes flickered open when Hannah leaned in close, and he spoke in a whisper. "I'm so sorry, darling. I'm not feeling well at all." He paused and closed his eyes again. Hannah felt terror rip through her as he was clearly struggling to speak as he said, "Maybe it is time to call the children and ask them to come home."

Hannah stood up and her body suddenly felt frozen to the core. She didn't know how she would find the words to tell the children what was happening. Sam came to her side and put his arm around her and guided her out of the room. They stood in front of the pay phone together, and Sam said, "Hannah, do you want me to make the phone calls?"

Hannah cleared her throat, "No, I need to do it. Thanks, Sam."

Hannah called Max first. That would be the easiest call to make. He was silent for quite a while before he said, "I will get the next flight I can. I will see you soon."

The next call with Rebecca was tough. Hannah couldn't seem to make her understand, or Rebecca just couldn't receive the information. Finally, Hannah said, "Papa is very, very sick. He wants to see you because he wants the chance to say goodbye." Rebecca was crying so hard she couldn't say anything more. Hannah hung up the phone and rested her forehead against the hard metal of the pay phone, trying to muster the energy to leave the phone booth and go back to David's room.

Hannah slept in David's room that night. The next morning, Sylvie brought her fresh clothes. Hannah nervously looked for things to do, rearranging the chairs in the room, and anxiously checking on David and making sure he was comfortable. After lunch, Max came into David's room. He stopped in his tracks when he saw David lying in bed. Hannah walked over to him, put her hand on his arm, and guided him to the bed. David grabbed Max's hand and squeezed it. Hannah felt the tears burning her eyes. She walked over to the window and stared out. The window looked over the parking garage and the HVAC unit. The HVAC unit was blowing the snowflakes upwards, so it looked like the snowflakes were shooting up to the sky rather than falling down. Hannah felt the tears streaming down her cheeks as she listened to David.

"Max, I was dreaming last night about your grandfather and the time he asked me to be his assistant at the university in Vienna. I admired him so much. He was kind and intelligent. I felt so lucky that he invited me to his home for dinner. That is when I met your Aunt Rebecca, your Aunt Esther, your grandmother Anna, and, of course, your mother. There was such a commotion. Your mother was a little girl, about eight, and she was a daredevil. She had crawled out her bedroom window and was climbing on the roof with a pillowcase that she flapped around like wings. Everyone was frantic, but your grandfather leaned out the window and called to her, and she came straight away, and he hugged her so tightly. Your Aunt Rebecca called her 'monkey girl.' Your grandfather laughed and laughed, but your grandmother Anna didn't think it was so funny. Your grandfather decided to get your mother involved in competitive swimming to channel some of that energy. Now, I need to tell you something that I never wanted to tell you. I have to tell you about the camps."

Hannah felt her throat tightening and the tears continuing to stream down her face as she saw the reflection of Max and David in the window. Max softly urged his father to go on.

"Despite your grandfather doing everything in his power to protect his family, they were sent to a camp called Majdanek. He, your grandmother, and your Aunt Esther were gassed on arrival at the camp. Your mother and Aunt Rebecca were forced laborers in that camp. A very cruel camp guard murdered your Aunt Rebecca. By the grace of God, your mother survived. This guard lived in America, and your mother testified to what she saw, and now the guard is on trial in Germany. I can't go with your mother to help her, so I'm asking you to go."

Hannah heard Max answer through a strangled sob. "Of course, I will do anything you ask."

David continued. "After the war, I found your mother. Another miracle. She was so ill and so thin, but that gleam was in her eye that was there just as

CHAPTER TWENTY-SIX: HANNAH 1975

it was when she was a little girl. She became stronger every day. I thanked God that I found her, and God gave me my purpose in life. To love this beautiful woman and build a life with her in this wonderful country. I never wanted you and Becky to know the pain and sadness of our lives before America. I wanted to erase it all. That was a foolish thought, but it was done out of love. Please look after your mother and sister for me."

Hannah turned from the window to see Max crumpled to the floor on his knees, his face on David's hand as he sobbed. David had turned his head to the opposite wall so his son could not see his tears.

The next day, Sam and Sylvie brought Rebecca from the airport. Like Max, the sight of her father froze her mid-stride when she walked into the room. Sam put his arm around her. David shifted and tried to sit up a bit, but he couldn't. He managed a feeble smile. "It's my beautiful daughter. Will you come give me a kiss?"

Rebecca crossed the room and kissed his cheek. She started weeping and collapsed into Sylvie's arms. Hannah stood up helplessly. Sam suggested they go out into the lounge, and he would sit with David.

The lounge had gaudy plastic orange chairs which clashed with the Christmas tree in the corner. Sylvie was comforting Rebecca, and Max walked over and touched her shoulder. "I'm so sorry, Becks."

Rebecca looked up red-faced and screamed at Hannah. "How could you let him get so sick?! Why did you wait so long to tell us!"

Hannah stepped back. "I didn't know he would get so sick so quickly. I'm sorry."

Rebecca still looked angry. "You probably weren't paying attention."

Max sat down next to her. "Becks, that's really not fair. I mean, it's horrible that Dad is so sick, but it's not mom's fault. We need to be supporting mom now."

Rebecca folded her arms. Max motioned for Hannah to sit down. Sylvie quietly left the lounge. Max took a deep breath. "Dad told me some difficult things yesterday. Mom is going to need to go to Germany to testify against a concentration camp guard."

Rebecca looked incredulous. "What? I knew Dad was in a concentration camp because of the tattoo on his arm. He never allowed us to ask about it. Mom doesn't have a tattoo."

Hannah was looking down at the floor. "Not all of us were tattooed. We had metal tags with our numbers at the camp I was at."

Rebecca exhaled heavily. "So, is that why when we were little, you used to hoard canned food in the basement? Why did you lie to us? Why did you act like everything was normal? Why were you so distant? You just cooked, cleaned, read magazines, popped Valium and got your hair done every week for years. You had this big secret, but you never told us."

"Becks, for such a supposedly enlightened person, you can be pretty fucking cruel. Dad and Mom kept it from us because it was dark and horrible, and they wanted us to be happy. That's all. They did everything they could for us to have a nice life. You know that. Do you think you could be supportive if you came to Germany?"

Rebecca folded her arms and narrowed her eyes. "No. I don't think I will be coming to Germany. I've dealt with this bad energy and superficiality from Mom long enough. I don't think I should go."

Hannah couldn't bring herself to speak. She was exhausted and beaten down. She wished she knew what this deep, unspoken need Rebecca had that she could never fulfill. Max reached over and took Hannah's hand. He looked up at Rebecca. "Well, we should probably go back and see how Dad is doing."

Max and Rebecca stayed with Sam and Sylvie over the next couple of days. They would all visit during the day, but Hannah never left the hospital. In the evenings, David would ask her to read from a John le Carré novel, Tinker Tailor Soldier Spy. Hannah loved these quiet evenings. She adjusted his pillow and made sure he was comfortable. Just before she was settling down to read, he grabbed her hand and asked her to lean in close. Hannah was surprised to see how bright his eyes looked and how he looked at her with longing and desire. She leaned in and kissed him deeply. He smiled. "Oh, how I hope I get out of this place, and we can go somewhere romantic for a vacation."

Hannah laughed. "Will Mr. le Carré be joining us?"

CHAPTER TWENTY-SIX: HANNAH 1975

"Of course, I wish I had known how soothing it was to have you read to me earlier! I would have asked you to read aloud more often."

Hannah was fumbling to find the folded page where they had left off, and she felt David's hand touch her forearm. He smiled at her. "You know I love you very much."

Hannah smiled. "Now you're just flirting with me to get me to read some extra chapters tonight."

David winked at her. "Guilty as charged."

Hannah read for what seemed like over an hour. She glanced over at David, and his eyes were still open, so she willed herself to keep reading. Her eyelids grew heavy, and the words started to blur on the page. She rested the open book on her chest and thought she would pick it back up after a short rest, but she plunged into a deep sleep.

"Mrs. Schneider," came a soft voice leaning over her. She looked to the side of the chair, and the book had dropped to the floor, and a little daylight was breaking through the gray haze. "Mrs. Schneider," the nurse said again. Hannah turned and looked at her. "Mrs. Schneider, he's gone."

Chapter Twenty-Seven: Helma 1975

At least the jail in Germany was nicer than the Nassau County jail. Helma had her own cell and was allowed to arrange the cell as she wished. Most importantly, she was able to knit, and that was a great comfort to her. She was also encouraged by her new defense attorneys, who had been appointed to her by the court. She thought that they seemed sharp, and unlike Mr. Perry, they didn't seem to buy into the victim mentality of the Majdanek prisoners.

At first it was strange to Helma to be back in Germany. She felt so thoroughly American in her own mind after all these years, and she had to work a bit to get back to understanding and speaking German. However, it did come back to her, and she was able to easily converse with her attorneys in German.

A few months after Helma arrived in Germany, she received her first visit from Greta. Helma was led to the visitors' room and saw Greta nervously sitting at the table. Helma could sense that Greta was agitated. Greta was wearing a light blue jacket with embellishments on the collar and wide-leg jeans. Her shoulder-length straw-blond hair was wavy, and Helma thought at least she was still attractive and might still be able to find a husband in her thirties.

Greta tried to be cheerful when she greeted Helma. "Auntie! It is so good to see you, and you are looking good despite the circumstances."

"Thank you. It is so wonderful to see you. I appreciate you coming here; I know it is an uncomfortable place to visit. You were so helpful during my trial in the United States; I'm hoping you can help me here. I don't know

CHAPTER TWENTY-SEVEN: HELMA 1975

the court system here, but I'm hopeful that it is free from that corrosive Jewish influence that has overwhelmed the courts in America. You would not believe the dirty dealing and unfairness! I am encouraged by my legal representation here. My attorney in America was weak. He completely buckled under pressure. I hope you have kept the copies of the documents you found in Austria. If the Americans wouldn't pay attention to them, maybe the Germans will."

Greta smiled nervously. "Yes, Auntie, I have them all. I will make sure to provide them to your attorneys." Greta took a breath before continuing. "I do have a question though, Mama said that you were not a guard at a concentration camp, but at a regular prison camp. A camp that had legitimate prisoners and that you weren't involved in the gassing of people. But when I read the news clippings from the court in America and the testimony of some of the people, it was that kind of camp. Majdanek was a concentration camp."

Greta was nervously biting her lip and looking down at her hands. Helma was trying to contain her rage and was calculating the best way to respond.

"Oh Greta, darling, this is what I mean when I say dirty dealing and unfairness. I was a guard of the prisoners sent to me. You know the guards don't say who the prisoners are; they just faithfully do their jobs, and that's what I did. There was so much propaganda after the war, and sadly, there was no one telling your generation the truth. You had to believe that we are all bad and you should be ashamed of our country. In wartime, tragic things happen. The Allies and the Jews decided to capitalize on this, and they had a very, very powerful propaganda machine in place, and that is what your generation grew up on. It's not your fault that you are susceptible to these sorts of stories. You know me. Remember, I taught you to read, to knit and helped take care of you and your dearly departed mama?"

Greta thought for a moment and then held up her head. "I want to trust in what you are saying, Auntie, because you did take care of me and sent me nice things from America, and Uncle Charles is so kind. I want to try to understand, so I will be paying attention to the trial here in Germany. You are my only living close relative now that Mama is gone."

Helma nodded. "Thank you, sweet Greta. It's not your fault that you misunderstand these things. Like I said, after the war, the Allies and the Jews, and don't even get me started on the communists, had a story they needed to spin, and they were able to do that with very powerful propaganda and fake stories. Now, some things in wartime get violent, but that happened on all sides. But only the Germans are held to account. It's like after the first war, the Great War, only the Germans were blamed, and so many false atrocity stories were made up. Now that things from the Second World War are dying down after so many decades, the Jews and others who can benefit have to stir things up again. They come after simple people, lowly guards like me, and make a show trial. It's disgusting."

Greta nodded and promised to bring Helma more materials for her knitting and promised to write faithfully.

Helma had a long wait in jail until the trial started. During that time, Charles split his time between America and Germany. He was semi-retired, so he worked a part-time schedule, but the cost of attorneys and travel was straining their finances. In discussions with their new German defense attorneys, it became clear that they should be prepared for a long trial, possibly as long as a couple of years. They were warned that they should also be preparing themselves for the potential outcome of a guilty verdict and additional years in jail. Helma and Charles were now fifty-six years old, and a twenty-year sentence or more for Helma would amount to a lifetime sentence. On one of Charles' visits, Helma could tell that all of this was weighing heavily on his mind.

He initially tried to be cheerful and pulled out some pictures of the dog in their yard to demonstrate that he was keeping up with the yard work and tending to the plants and the garden and that Rex was healthy and happy.

"Sweetheart, I'm following your instructions with the garden to the letter, and I have to say everything looks great. Your instructions were so detailed that it made it easy for me to keep everything up. You're so good at gardening that you should write a gardening book while you're here to keep your mind occupied. I would write the endorsement because if a knucklehead like me can maintain a garden on these instructions, then anyone can."

CHAPTER TWENTY-SEVEN: HELMA 1975

Helma smiled sweetly, but she guessed that all the flattery about the garden was cover for some more unpleasant news.

"Charles, you look tired and strained. Is something bothering you?"

"Frankly, I'm very tired. I think it's time we face some hard facts. I don't think I can keep travelling back and forth, and with the trial starting, I want to be here supporting you full-time. I can't keep up the house in America and be here all the time. It just doesn't make sense. If we sell the house, we can live pretty comfortably, if frugally, in Germany for years. I can pick up the odd job here and there to keep us afloat."

Helma usually had to gin up tears to get Charles to do what she wanted, but now the tears were coming quite naturally when she thought of losing the tidy little house in Queens, the one that she had so lovingly cared for and where all her happy memories were made. She choked back sobs and tried to talk to Charles. "It's just too awful to think about, losing our home. We have so many happy memories there, that it breaks my heart in a million pieces. It is just torture being dragged through trial after trial. It is so unfair."

Charles nodded sympathetically. "I know. It is hard for me to see such a kind and lovely lady, who just wants to take care of her home, go through what you're going through. Don't worry, we will figure something out, and I will be by your side every step of the way."

Finally, the first day of the trial arrived. The courtroom in Dusseldorf was very stately, but very modern inside, with marble floors and very large corridors outside the courtroom. The courtroom itself had wood paneling and very elaborate chandelier light fixtures hanging from the high ceiling. The trial drew a lot of media attention.

Helma had brought the latest copy of *The New York Times* with her and held it up to her face so they couldn't get a good picture. She had chosen a white tailored suit, black belt and shoes, patterned scarf, and a white hat which she had knit herself. She wanted to look good because she knew she would be seeing Bridget, Werner, and the last camp commandant, Hackman. She hadn't known him well as he was only there a few months, but she remembered admiring him for how well and how boldly he led them in carrying out their mass extermination day in November of 1943.

There would be other guards there, but Helma didn't remember their names or have any recollection of them. They were all seated together, with their attorneys interspersed between them. As she settled in her chair at the end of the table, she looked over and saw a thick, portly man with ruddy red skin. It was the dark black hair that gave him away. It was very thick, and there was not even one strand of gray. He had grown out his sideburns in an Elvis Presley style, thick and wide. He was wearing a suit, but Helma could tell it was cheap. Helma leaned across her attorney and whispered, "Werner, is that you?"

Werner's eyes were still bright blue, although now his face was puffy and lined. He startled back as if he had been hit with a jolt of electricity. "Helma! I can't believe it. You look wonderful; life in America has agreed with you." He chuckled and said, "Yes, indeed, it is me, Werner!"

The court was called to order. The judges and jurists were seated in front beneath a large, white enamel cross. The presiding judge, Judge Bogen, had thick and wavy white hair and a sonorous and deep voice. He seemed slow and deliberate, letting out a low and almost imperceptible sigh as the attorneys droned on with various points of legal procedure.

Helma looked over at the prosecuting attorneys. They were young, mostly in their early thirties. They had longer hair and beards. She could tell they were cut from the same cloth as the long-haired radicals in America. What a disgusting shame that generation had become! So thoroughly taken in by Jew and communist propaganda. They were very useful tools for the Jews and communists, who made them so ashamed of their country and of what their fathers and mothers did during the war; so ashamed here they were persecuting people who had committed supposed "crimes" which happened three decades ago. They had no understanding of what it was like back then or how much had been lost.

Finally, there was a recess. Helma made her way to the corridor with Werner. As they walked, they were catching up on each other's lives. Werner stood next to a standing ashtray and lit a cigarette. "Nobody bothered me after the war. I went back to Hamburg and started working at my father's auto repair shop, got married, had a few kids, and just lived life, you know.

CHAPTER TWENTY-SEVEN: HELMA 1975

And then, about ten years ago, someone came snooping around asking about what I was doing during the war and if I was a guard at Majdanek. I said yes, I mean those military records are still around, and I said to them, 'so what?' Well, then it was going to be this big trial of 1,500 people from Majdanek, and then they did more investigating, and the pool of people who would get prosecuted finally boiled down to fifteen, so here we are. It's like winning the lottery, but instead of money, you get punished at a phony show trial."

Helma laughed. She was relieved to see that Werner was unchanged. He still had a dry humor and nonchalance. She was so grateful he wasn't one of those sad sacks moaning about what they did during the war and groveling for atonement. Helma noticed Werner looking at an extremely obese older woman struggling to walk across the wide marble hall toward them. Helma noticed Werner put up his hand to wave her over. "Helma, it's Bridget, she will love to hear about your life in America."

Helma was completely stunned. As the woman drew closer, Helma could see she had bandages on ulcerated sores on her legs. Her dress was a cheap double-knit polyester that was too tight across her chest, and as she came even closer, Helma noticed oily food stains above Bridget's left breast. Bridget was breathing heavily as she came up to Werner, who re-introduced her to Helma. It was all Helma could do to restrain herself from physically recoiling in disgust.

Bridget's eyes brightened as she turned to Helma. She started talking in pleasantries, but Helma's mind drifted back to the Bridget she knew at Majdanek. A great beauty with ultimate confidence. An excellent horsewoman and a disciplined camp guard. It was hard to believe the woman now standing before her complaining about her myriad health problems was the same woman from thirty years ago.

Helma was lost in her own thoughts of how low Bridget had sunk in life and how Werner, while in slightly better shape, seemed almost as sad and slovenly as Bridget. They must have lost the pride and discipline they all had when they were young and serving the cause of the Fatherland. Finally, Werner tapped her on the arm.

"Time to stop daydreaming, Helma. It's back to the courtroom we go."

Chapter Twenty-Eight: Hannah 1976

In the days after David's passing, Hannah walked around in a fog. She was thankful for Sam and Sylvie, who greeted the rounds of guests that came to the house. Sylvie took command of the kitchen, efficiently serving and organizing meals, wrapping up leftovers, and filling the dishwasher at regular intervals. Sylvie was also a comfort to Rebecca, who seemed to lean on Sylvie in her grief while keeping a respectful distance from Hannah. Max seemed to easily slip into the role of man of the house, along with Sam, during the time of shiva. A large floral arrangement arrived. The card said, "With sincere condolences, Vince and Frieda DeMarco." It took Hannah a moment to register that Vince DeMarco was "Mr. DeMarco" from the New York trial.

About four days after David's death, Hannah felt the energy drain out of her. She went to the bedroom to rest. She ran her hand over David's side of the bed, trying to absorb the fact that he would never be there again. She curled up in a ball, bringing her knees up to her chest, protectively knotting herself together and closing her eyes. She tried to picture the days when the mourning was past, and the children returned to their lives, and she would be in the house by herself, without her familiar evening routine with David. She felt herself drifting to sleep and then there was a gentle tap at the door.

It was Sylvie. She gingerly shook Hannah's shoulder. "I hate to wake you, but it's a long-distance call from Israel. Your friend Miriam."

Hannah stretched and rolled over to David's side of the bed to pick up the phone on his bedside table.

"Hello, Hannah, your son called us yesterday to tell us the news. We are

CHAPTER TWENTY-EIGHT: HANNAH 1976

heartbroken. Benny and I just can't believe it."

"Thank you for calling. I can hardly believe it myself. He tried to protect me from how very sick he really was, and so it was a bit of a shock at how quickly it all went."

"Such a good man. It's so terrible to lose him. I remember meeting him at the DP camp all those years ago. He was such a gentleman and so intelligent. He loved you so much, Hannah."

"I know. I wish I would have realized how much he loved me earlier in our marriage, maybe I would have appreciated him more." Hannah sat up on the side of the bed; she shook the bottle of sleeping pills, mentally calculating how many were left.

"Hannah, stop that. David knew you loved him. Remember your birthday thirty years ago?"

"Huh. I completely forgot that today is my birthday."

"I can tell you that David traded everything he had of value to get you that big chocolate bar for your birthday, and he made sure it was a wonderful birthday for you. He organized it. I knew how much you meant to him. You must be strong, Hannah. David would not want you to let this break you."

"I know Miriam. I don't know where I will find the strength to keep going."

"You need to meet us in Germany in a few months. We will be there to support you. I will never give up on you, Hannah."

Hannah started to cry. She remembered Miriam dragging her out of the infirmary, getting her to the DP camp, and insisting that she was going to make it.

"Listen to me, Hannah. You're strong enough. David believed it, and I do too. So, will I see you in Germany?"

Hannah reached over to the bedside table, grabbed a tissue, and took a deep breath.

"Yes, you will see me there."

"Good! It's your forty-seventh birthday. You have a lot of life ahead of you, Hannah. You can't give up."

Hannah found herself chuckling. "I need you around to remember my birthdays and tell me how old I am. I keep forgetting."

"Oh, don't worry. I will be very vigilant about picking on you for being an old lady."

Somehow, the conversation with Miriam helped Hannah recoup her strength and make it through that horrible week. Finally, the time came when the children were ready to head back out, and Hannah was on her own. Sam came over and helped her review her finances. David had taken care of everything, and Hannah realized that she had never balanced a checkbook or filled out checks for the mortgage and utilities. Fortunately, David had left her in a good financial position, and the house was nearly paid off. That night, Hannah made dinner for Sam and Sylvie, and they played cards after dinner as they had done hundreds of times before, but this time, the fourth chair at the card table was empty. It didn't seem possible that David was gone. Hannah never imagined her life without David. Some days, she thought he might just walk through the front door as if nothing had happened, and Hannah would make him dinner, and they would spend a quiet evening or have a night like tonight, playing cards and laughing with Sam and Sylvie as they had done hundreds of times over the past decades.

About a week later, the phone rang. "Hello, Hannah, I'm sorry I didn't call sooner. I heard about David. I'm so sorry, my deepest sympathies."

"Oh, thank you, Weston. It's okay. I mean, I'm okay."

"I don't know why, but I felt strange about calling, but I am sorry. I just got to know David a little bit years ago, but I could tell he was a good man. You and I haven't spoken in a few years, so I guess I didn't know what to do." He cleared his throat and continued, "Which is unusual for me, because, as you know, I'm incredibly suave and sophisticated, almost at a James Bond level of sophistication."

Hannah laughed. "And you are also so humble."

"It's nice to hear you laugh, Hannah."

"Honestly, it's nice to laugh after the couple of months I've had. It would be great to hear about you. How are you doing?"

"Well, I'm wrapping up my law practice and retiring. Susan and I are going to travel. I'm very late to the game, but I'm going to try to be the husband I

CHAPTER TWENTY-EIGHT: HANNAH 1976

should have been for all these years. It's hard to have regrets about some of the things I've done, but maybe it's not too late."

"It's not too late. Good for you. I wish you well."

"I also wanted to call because Vince DeMarco let me know you're headed to Germany soon to testify again, and I really admire you for going. I know that it can't be easy to go back to Germany, but I hear Germany is much nicer now that Hitler is dead. In fact, I think that is true of almost everything. Everything is better without Hitler."

Hannah found herself almost doubled over in laughter. "Oh, Weston, thank you so much. It's been so long since I laughed this hard."

"I'm glad I could be of service. Take care of yourself, Hannah."

In March, Max came home to help Hannah get ready for their trip to Germany. Hannah packed and re-packed her suitcase many times. She decided to pack the purple dress again, thinking that would be good luck. Max had taken care of all the arrangements, the flight, and the hotel accommodation. For Hannah, hearing German on the plane was more disconcerting than she realized it would be. She found herself tensing up when she heard the flight attendants speaking German. It was even worse when they arrived at the hotel, and she was back for the first time since leaving the DP camp. Max tried to communicate, but he didn't speak German very well.

Hannah found herself agitated and frustrated as she spoke German to the hotel clerk. She and Max chose to have dinner in their room, as Max could tell how on edge Hannah was feeling. The next morning, Hannah woke up early and tried several different dresses. She finally settled on the white and yellow floral dress she had worn to Rebecca's graduation. Before heading to the courthouse, Max and Hannah had coffee and pastries in the hotel café. Hannah fidgeted and only took a few bites before they took a taxi to the courthouse.

As they entered the courthouse with its high ceilings and large marble-floored corridors, Hannah was searching the crowds for Miriam. The last time she had seen her in person was shortly after she and David were married at the DP camp and then Miriam and Benny had left for Israel. They were both teenagers back then.

Hannah saw a cluster of three people by a bench. A young man in an Israeli military uniform, an older man with frizzy gray hair, and a petite woman with short brown hair with her hands on her hips. It was Miriam. Before Hannah even knew what she was doing she found herself running across the marble floor. Miriam turned and stretched out her arms and yelled, "Hannah!"

They held each other in a tight hug and cried. The moment was finally broken by Benny, who tapped Hannah on the shoulder. "Hey, Hannah, remember me? I would like a hug, too." Hannah laughed and embraced Benny. He looked the same, very compact and muscular. Hannah turned to see a young man who was a carbon copy of Benny. He was wearing a crisp Israeli military uniform. Miriam, beaming with pride, introduced Hannah to their son Daniel. Hannah drew Max into the group to introduce him. Max blushed as Miriam kissed his cheek and then went on about how good-looking and handsome Max was and how he must have so many girls after him.

Benny and Miriam updated them on the progress of the trial as they walked to the main entrance to the courtroom. Down the corridor, Hannah noticed a cluster of men with briefcases, and then she saw her, the Stomping Mare. She was wearing a dark red dress and had a copy of *The New York Times* under her arm. She was talking to a stocky man with black hair and outsized sideburns. A large woman, who seemed to struggle to walk, was following closely behind them. Miriam pointed to the large woman. "That's Bloody Bridget and the Angel of Death with the Stomping Mare."

Hannah held her breath as they drew closer. She felt Max's hand on her shoulder. Miriam's son, Daniel, was red-faced. He shouted as they passed, "They should all hang like Eichmann!"

Then, all heads turned to Daniel, and a police officer quickly came over from the door of the courtroom. Max intervened and settled the situation in his broken German. Hannah realized that Daniel might look like Benny, but inside, he was one hundred percent Miriam.

Finally, it was time to file into the courtroom. The large courtroom had

CHAPTER TWENTY-EIGHT: HANNAH 1976

high ceilings, rich wood paneling, and modern chandeliers. Behind the judges and jurors was a white enamel cross. The presiding judge had a deep voice. Hannah was finally adjusting to hearing everything in German, but it still gave her a pain in her stomach, and she had to keep reminding herself that this wasn't Majdanek and that she was going to be okay.

There was a map of Majdanek at the front of the courtroom. Paula, Miriam's friend, was set to testify soon. Hannah felt nervous for Paula, remembering what it was like to walk to the front of the courtroom and have the Stomping Mare sitting there. Now, it was even worse, with all fifteen of the defendants, including the camp commandant.

Paula took a deep breath, and the prosecuting attorneys, all younger men, asked her about a hanging at the camp.

"In our block, we had a young girl among us. She was thirteen, maybe fourteen. Her whole family had been gassed on arrival. Somehow, even though she was so small and so young, she had been selected for work. The other women, Polish women, Jewish women, we were all protective of her. She was like the daughters some women had lost or like a little sister. She was someone to love and protect in that horrible place. We thought if she were Christian, not Jewish, that it would increase her chances of survival. The Polish Catholic women coached her so she could pass as a Christian. I don't know how, but the Stomping Mare found out about her lying about being a Christian and decided to make an example of her. We were all gathered for morning roll call and there were gallows set up in the yard. And she was shaking and standing on a stool with a noose around her neck. She was so small, just a child. She was shaking, and the Stomping Mare was yelling at us about lying. The Stomping Mare turned to her and asked her if she had anything to say."

Paula stopped for a moment; her voice was cracking, and tears started to spill down her cheeks. "In her childlike voice, she looked to us with pleading eyes, and said, 'remember me.' And then the Stomping Mare kicked the stool out from under her. She left her hanging in the yard all day, so for evening roll call, we had to see her lifeless body just hanging there."

Hannah felt the tears coming. Max reached over and held her hand. Paula continued to answer questions as the prosecutors asked a dozen different ways for her to confirm that it was indeed the Stomping Mare, now in this courtroom, who had done this horrible thing.

The defense attorney badgered Paula about every detail. They kept asking her if the rope was hung from a hook or a ring. Finally, Paula, overwrought and angry, admitted she didn't know. Somehow, the defense managed to use this detail to discredit her. Hannah slumped in her seat. It was a repeat of how Mr. Korman was treated in New York.

The trial was exhausting. In the evening, Miriam and Hannah walked arm-in-arm down the street. This was one compensation, Hannah thought, to be able to be with Miriam again. At the pub, Miriam, Hannah, and Benny sat together at a table, and Max and Daniel sat at the bar. They seemed to be fast friends.

The next day, Hannah and Miriam went to court early while Benny, Daniel, and Max were getting breakfast. Hannah and Miriam were meeting Sonja Weiss, who had arrived to take part in the hearing. Hannah introduced Sonja to Miriam and the three of them were chatting when Miriam suddenly stopped talking. Hannah turned to see a bird-like woman scurrying toward them. Her dark hair was pulled back in a severe bun, and she was wearing a white turtleneck and blue smock-like dress. Miriam squinted and said, "My God, I can't believe it. That's Letty."

Sonja turned to Miriam with a puzzled look. "Who's Letty?"

"She was one of our guards," Hannah interjected. "She was our supervisor in the sorting warehouse."

As soon as Hannah finished talking, Letty walked quickly toward them with a smile on her face. Hannah felt like her feet were bolted to the floor, and the terror was rising inside of her, and she reminded herself again that she wasn't in the sorting warehouse and Letty had no power over her anymore. Letty walked up to Hannah with her hand outstretched. Hannah just stared down at Letty's hand as Letty said in a sing-song voice, "Hannah, it must be you. Even after all these years, you look the same. Those large hazel eyes! It is good to see you again."

Hannah struggled to put together a coherent sentence. "I'm sorry, are you

CHAPTER TWENTY-EIGHT: HANNAH 1976

a defendant? I didn't see you at the trial yesterday."

"Oh no, I'm not a defendant. I was summoned by the court to testify. Such a dark time and such a hard time for everyone. I let the court know that, to the best of my ability, I tried to protect the unfortunate souls at Majdanek. Protect my 'little chicks,' as I used to say about the women who worked for me."

Hannah stared at Letty with her mouth agape as Letty rummaged around in her purse and pulled out a handkerchief. "I even brought this handkerchief that the women so lovingly embroidered for me. To thank me."

Hannah shook her head. "Your story isn't true. You didn't help us. You were a part of it. Don't speak to me to try to get me to endorse this false story of yours."

Miriam stepped forward. "What Hannah is trying to say in a polite way is fuck off!"

Letty drew back, and Miriam continued. "Oh, you don't remember me? It's Miriam. Fuck off with your story, you fucking Nazi."

Letty straightened her back. "I remember you. A dirty guttersnipe." Letty turned and quickly scurried away.

Sonja turned to them. "Ladies, I think we need to take a smoke break before the hearing begins today."

Hannah was astonished as Letty shared her story in the courtroom, still portraying herself as someone who was deeply sympathetic to the women working in the sorting warehouse as well as the women prisoners who sewed uniforms, which she also occasionally supervised. She talked about how nicely she treated the Polish woman who cleaned her room, and she even brought out that handkerchief. Hannah strained to get a look at the Stomping Mare during Letty's testimony; she could see the anger almost rising off her like steam.

Later that day, Sonja shared the story she told Hannah in New York and testified to in the Stomping Mare's extradition hearing. Hannah reached over and took Max's hand. She could see the color draining from his face as he listened to the brutal story. It occurred to Hannah that for Max, Sonja was his friend's mom, a housewife who gave them snacks after a game of stickball back in Queens. How disconcerting it must be to hear this testimony. It made her wish that she had come alone, just to spare Max from having to hear her story in this courtroom.

Finally, the day of testimony had come to an end. Hannah sat down on a bench in the corridor. Down the hallway, she could see the Stomping Mare with her attorney and a blond woman in her thirties. Miriam had told her that it was the Stomping Mare's niece. The young woman had an armload of papers and files. While Hannah was watching them, she felt Max sit down beside her. She watched the young woman who seemed to be arguing with the Stomping Mare. The Stomping Mare's stupid American husband seemed to be arguing with the young woman, too. The young woman turned and was briskly walking away, and suddenly, she twisted her ankle and tumbled to the ground. Max jumped up and raced over to her. Hannah followed him. Max gently checked her ankle. She smiled kindly, "Thank you. I think I'm fine. Just too clumsy."

Max helped her stand up as Hannah gathered the young woman's papers for her. Max held her hand as she took a few steps. "I think you might want to reconsider the shoes. Those platform heels make for nasty falls." He smiled at her as she took the papers from Hannah and left.

Hannah and Max walked to a café for dinner. Hannah felt as if she had passed through the looking glass, with Letty rewriting history, and how strange it was that all these decades later, Max was taking care of the niece of the Stomping Mare.

Chapter Twenty-Nine: Helma 1976

The first few months of the trial were exhausting exchanges about procedure. Helma was pleased that her defense team was tougher than Mr. Perry. One of the first challenges was to dismiss a historian as an expert witness. This historian was to provide history and context to the trial, but the defense team fought against him as much of his training was with Jewish academics. The papers decried this as a throwback to the antisemitism of the Nazi era, but Helma felt that it showed some backbone on the part of the defense team, and at least they were trying to have a fair trial. Helma applauded any effort to minimize the Jewish influence, which was so insidious during her trial in America.

Helma found herself spending most of the time at the trial with Werner and Bridget. They slipped back into a comfortable friendship just like they had back in Lublin when they would go horseback riding or to their favorite café. Werner had a wry sense of humor about what he called the "show trial" and how they were like animals at the zoo. Helma found it especially galling that groups of schoolchildren were brought in to witness the trial. She felt this was just another point of indoctrination to fill their young minds with propaganda.

After all these years, Helma still felt intimidated by the commandant. While all the other guards seemed common and slovenly, the commandant was a fit and elegant man even though he had to be in his mid-seventies. Early in the trial, the commandant was describing the origin and structure of Majdanek. As he was explaining the various groups of prisoners at the camp, Helma noted that he called them 'Untermenschen' it loosely translated to

English to mean 'sub-humans', but it was the correct phrase for the people at Majdanek from the time of the Reich. Helma knew that the commandant was still faithful to the Fatherland. Helma found herself fortified by his calm demeanor and his clear belief in the values of the Reich.

Helma felt grateful for the continual devotion of her husband, Charles. Heartbreakingly, it became obvious that they would have to sell their home in Queens. Charles gave their dog to the Gleasons, the family that had come to vouch for Helma at the trial in New York. Helma was angry that not only was she dragged through this show trial, but she also lost her beautiful little home in New York when all she had wanted to do was to live out her years in peace with her dear Charles. At least he was able to visit her regularly and bring her knitting supplies and books as well as copies of *The New York Times*. She liked to read the paper from New York during breaks in the trial and used the paper as a shield when pesky photographers and cameramen would descend on her at the trial, shoving their lights and their cameras in her face.

Greta occasionally came to the trial. Helma could feel Greta drifting away. It was so maddening that Greta was falling for the propaganda. Helma enlisted Charles to talk to her. Helma knew that Greta looked up to Charles and he had such an easy way about him that Helma felt that Charles could bring Greta back into the fold.

A few months into the trial, the attorneys let them know that the court would be hearing "survivor" testimony. Helma knew that this would sway the judge and jurors. It was frustrating to have to listen to their stories again after New York. On the first day of what Helma called the "prisoner" testimony, a very emotional woman spun a tale about some young girl who was hanged. She skimmed over the fact that the prisoner was lying. It frustrated Helma that the emphasis was on how young the prisoner was because Helma had said time and time again that she didn't pick who was a prisoner a Majdanek, she just kept order among the prisoners. As they were taking a break in the hallway, there was a cluster of these so-called survivors who had come to testify. Werner was smoking a cigarette and staring at the clusters of people, apparently former prisoners of Majdanek. Werner

CHAPTER TWENTY-NINE: HELMA 1976

seemed to be staring at one man in particular, a short man with brown hair.

"That little guy. We used to mess with him. We would make him carry heavy stones from one side of the field to the other for no reason. We always marveled at his endurance. We would take bets on the time it would take him to collapse. We used to bring him to the yard when we were drunk and play Russian roulette and watch him flinch with each click of the gun." Werner shook his head and laughed.

Bridget took the cigarette from Werner and took a drag. "This was before your time, Helma, but we used to have a little fun with the ladies, too. We used to get high heels and complicated dresses that were way too large or small on the prisoners and make them dance or run in these crazy get-ups. It was free entertainment."

Werner snapped his fingers. "Andre! That was his name. I should probably go over and greet him, right?" Werner smiled as he started to walk over to the man. Werner raised his arms. "Andre! Andre, my friend. It's me, Werner."

The man's eyes grew wide, and he started backing away from Werner with a terrified look on his face. He stumbled as he walked backward. "Andre, why so shy? I'm just coming over to invite you to visit me in Hamburg. Now that you're in Germany again, why don't you come visit me?"

The terrified man couldn't respond, but just stumbled away as Werner put out his cigarette and laughed. Bridget was laughing, too. Helma didn't find it all that funny, but in a way, it was reassuring that these so-called "survivors" were still petrified of them and still as pathetic as they were thirty years ago.

The next day of testimony, Helma was pleased that both Charles and Greta were at court, and she would be able to see them during the breaks. She repositioned the newspaper in her lap so she could surreptitiously read the paper during the lengthy hours of testimony. She was reading as the next witness began speaking. Helma froze. She looked up, and it was Letty! She was talking about just trying to do her job and her efforts to protect women prisoners who worked for her. She was re-casting herself as sympathetic to the prisoners but powerless to help them. She then prattled on about how a group of prisoners were so grateful to her that they embroidered a special handkerchief for her, which she promptly pulled out of her pocket.

Helma's astonishment turned to rage. How dare she help in this disgraceful circus of a show trial? It was one thing to keep your mouth shut, but quite another to come testify against your former colleagues and pretend that you were oh-so-concerned about these Jews, traitors, and other undesirables. Helma folded her arms tightly across her chest. She could feel her face burning, and she took deep breaths. Finally, Letty was excused. Helma glared as she made her way across the courtroom.

The next testimony came from a woman who had testified in New York. Helma rolled her eyes. They were recycling old testimony from her last trial. This woman talked about a beating with a whip and then her sister being sent to the gas chamber. Helma glanced back. It seemed to be making a deep impact on the court spectators, even on Greta, who had a worn and saddened look on her face.

The court adjourned for the day. Helma was making her way out of the courtroom, hoping to snatch a little time with Charles and Greta. Out of the corner of her eye, she saw Bridget with Letty. She was shaking her fist in Letty's face. Helma approached and heard Bridget dressing her down. "You act so saintly now. Such a friend of the Jews now! You used to take the gold from their teeth! You took so many nice things from the warehouse; now you act innocent!"

Helma grabbed Letty's arm. "You snake! You are a traitor. You forget that we all knew you. You'd better be careful."

Letty yanked her arm away. "Helma, I'm not going to jail. I'm doing what it takes to survive. Don't act like you all didn't treat me like some little fool, and now you talk about loyalty? Who is the fool now?" Letty marched away through the crowd.

Helma turned away and searched for Greta and Charles. She saw Greta holding some papers and file folders. Helma knew she had to calm herself and approach her niece in the right way.

"Greta, darling, what an exhausting day. Thank you so much for coming and giving your support. What are all these papers?"

CHAPTER TWENTY-NINE: HELMA 1976

Greta looked down. She couldn't look up at her aunt. "I'm so sorry, Aunt Helma, I can't do this anymore. These are all your papers, I wanted to give these to you because I won't be seeing you anymore. I can't in good conscience continue to support you because of what you were a part of during the war."

Helma exhaled. This was so tiring. It was so hard to keep Greta on track as she was falling for all the propaganda of the trial.

"Greta, I've told you this before. What you're seeing and hearing here are all exaggerated stories by Jews and communists who are out for revenge. They are coming after us to keep their lies alive, to distract from their schemes."

"Aunt Helma, I don't believe you. I'm sorry. You and Uncle Charles have been so kind, but I can't support you."

Thankfully, Charles came over. "Charles, can you talk sense to Greta? She is confused and is falling for all this dramatic testimony."

Charles nodded and leaned over to talk to Greta. "Listen, sweetheart, you know I fought for the United States in the army during the war, right? And some of the stuff that was done was extreme, but it was wartime. Everyone had to serve their country. Your aunt served Germany just as a prison guard. She wasn't a decision-maker. She was just doing her best. You know she was devoted to you, and she's a good woman. She's being dragged through the mud and needs your help."

Greta looked up. "I'm sorry, Uncle Charles. I'm not going to be a part of it. Here are the files."

Charles patted her hand. "No, Greta, you keep them. We are all tired and overwhelmed. Think and pray on this and remember how your aunt took care of you and you will reconsider."

Greta looked at Charles. "No. I'm not going to reconsider."

Helma leaned in and glared at Greta. "You are a disappointment. My only blood relative. My brother Hans, your father, would be disgusted at such a betrayal. You're weak like your mother!"

Greta turned and started to run away. Charles grabbed Helma's arms and turned her toward him. "Helma! Stop it. She's overwhelmed. You are driving her away and making it worse."

Helma struggled to regain her composure. She had forgotten what a soft spot Charles had developed for Greta over all these years. She had to think quickly to bring Charles' focus back to her. She relaxed her body. "Oh Charles, I feel a bit faint. Could you help me to that bench?"

Charles walked her over to the bench. "I don't know how much more I can take, my darling. The woman who testified, who was a guard, was one of my dearest friends. We were roommates when we worked at the airplane factory in Berlin. She told us she was lying to save her skin. To top things off, now Greta has been led astray. I'm overwrought."

Charles patted her hand. "I'm going to keep working to see if I can get you out on bail. I'm going to set up my life here in Germany to support you. I know things are hard, but you need to be strong."

Chapter Thirty: Hannah Spring and Summer 1976

Hannah, Miriam, and Sonja were having breakfast together before the day's testimony was set to begin. Over the weeks that they had been at the trial, it had become clear, that the survivor testimony had to be detailed and specific. The prosecuting attorneys realized that the survivors may not have precise details about incidents of killings and what role specific guards had played. It was frustrating to try to share the story of the camps for each survivor as they testified.

Miriam was going to testify in the coming weeks. She was quizzing Sonja over breakfast on what she thought the best way would be to present her story. As Sonja spread preserves on some toast, she sighed. "Miriam, I think the best thing to do is to speak very specifically about things that you saw and try to remember the camp and all the details as best you can."

Miriam looked down at her coffee cup. "I agree, but we all know what went on there. It wasn't just what we saw. It went on all the time, non-stop killing and torture. It's maddening how the Germans are pursuing this in the courts. So many of them wiggling off the hook and getting these short sentences, like in the Auschwitz trials in Frankfurt about ten years ago. So many were released, and the others served four years or so. Ridiculous."

Sonja just shrugged her shoulders. "Not much we can do. That's the law. I think the best strategy is to be as detailed as possible. I understand the judges, jurors, and all the attorneys, both the prosecutors and defense attorneys, are going to Majdanek, and they will tour the camp. They will make the visit in the next month or so. That's how detailed they are in collecting the precise story; they are actually going to go see it for themselves."

Hannah furrowed her brow. Strangely, she never really thought about the camp being intact and people actually visiting there. She had worked so hard at pushing everything out of her mind she felt as if the camp only existed now in memory, not as a physical place. "Wait a minute. Majdanek is still as it was? They allow people to go into the camp and see it?"

Sonja lit a cigarette. "Yes, it's pretty much intact. Some things have changed, but they have a director there who provides information to visitors, sort of like a living history tour. After the trial in New York, I went to the camp, to Majdanek, in 1974. I felt like I wanted some way to close the chapter, and I felt so strongly after the trial that I wanted to say goodbye to my sister. I went with some friends who weren't in the camp, and they thought I was crazy to want to go back. The director was very nice and helpful. It was very strange to walk around and see it, pretty much as it was. I guess the Germans didn't have time to destroy it because the Soviet army got there faster than anticipated. The crematorium was one place I hadn't been to, and I wanted to see it. I had a little packet with me, and I leaned into the crematorium where they put the bodies in, scraped away a small amount of ash, and put it in the packet, so I could have it to remember my sister and family. I wanted to have something that felt like a reclaimed chance to honor their deaths."

Hannah stared at Sonja in stunned silence. Miriam touched Hannah's arm. "We should go to Majdanek. We should visit as free women and walk through there, so we remember exactly for our testimony. We can say goodbye to your family, too."

Hannah turned to Miriam. "I don't know. I can't imagine going there and walking around that place."

Hannah could tell Miriam's mind was made up. She was already planning to get Benny to arrange the train tickets and the rest of the transportation. Hannah didn't know if she could manage a trip back there. It was hard enough to be back in Germany, to say nothing of going to Eastern Poland and back to Majdanek. Hannah hoped that red tape or some other issue

CHAPTER THIRTY: HANNAH SPRING AND SUMMER 1976

would make it impossible for them to go, but Miriam was determined, and at the end of the week, they were preparing for their trip.

In the hotel room, Hannah reluctantly packed her bag for the trip. She looked up and noticed Max shyly entering the room. "Mom, I don't understand why you don't want me to go. I want to help you, and I want to see it."

Hannah felt anger rising in her. "I do not want you to go to that place! Your father and I came to America and protected you from all of the horrible things that happened during the war. I didn't even want you to come to this trial in Germany. This trial is bad enough, I don't want you to carry the memory, of the place your grandparents and aunts were murdered. You are absolutely not coming."

Max sat on the bed, looking a little wounded. Hannah sat down beside him. "Your father and I love you children so much. We wanted you to be happy and free of all the pain and sadness that we experienced. If this trial had not come up, we would never have spoken of these things to you or your sister. I didn't ever want to come back here or talk about those terrible days, but I had to." Hannah squeezed Max's hand and leaned in to kiss his cheek. Max exhaled and slumped on the bed, nodded his agreement, and then left the room.

One of the prosecuting attorneys, a young man with a bushy dark brown beard and wearing an oversized blue sweater and a white shirt with a wide collar, was explaining the plans for the trip to Majdanek for the judges, jurors, and attorneys in a few months. He was assisting them as they traveled into Poland and finally to Majdanek. When they arrived, he said he would wait for them. It was cold and windy, as Hannah remembered it. The buildings were as Hannah remembered them, but it was so empty and silent now. The director chatted away as he welcomed them and offered all sorts of information about the camp. The communist government of Poland used Majdanek to illustrate the evils of fascism. Benny engaged the director in conversation as Hannah and Miriam walked arm in arm to the old sorting warehouse. It was wide and like an empty barn. A mountain of shoes was restrained in a wire cage in one corner of the warehouse. Shoes of men, women, and children jumbled together with a faint wisp of the smell of their long-dead owners. Hannah closed her eyes and remembered the long hours of sorting clothes and valuables or Letty yelling at them or striking their hands for sorting things too slowly.

They made their way to Field Five, where the women's barracks were. They were empty now and only had a few bunks. Hannah and Miriam walked through the barracks silently as Benny and the Majdanek director waited outside. Miriam walked over to a corner and loosened a piece of wood. "I remember when I first came here, and this was your hiding place for the extra food, and you gave me your sister's portion." Miriam walked back over to Hannah and placed her hand on her shoulder. "I always remembered that. You had just met me and gave me extra food, which was like gold here, and you were still sweet and kind even in spite of this horrible place. You still are, Hannah."

Hannah smiled. "I can't believe we are here. It's all so strange. I remember you being so strong, and you're still so strong!" They both laughed and started to walk out of the barracks.

The wind made Hannah's face numb, and she wrapped her jacket around her even more closely and wandered alone through an empty field. She tried to remember all the mornings and evenings of roll call and searched for the exact place where it happened, where the Stomping Mare grabbed Rebecca and where the Stomping Mare punched her. Even harder to visualize was when Rebecca was on the ground, and Hannah was crawling toward her. Hannah paced around the ground and looked back at the barracks, trying to remember. She felt this was the spot and knelt in the clumped dirt. Her face was so numb she didn't feel the tears streaming down her face. She reached for her necklace and felt for the amethyst pendant David had given her. Purple was Rebecca's favorite color. Hannah's numb fingers fumbled at the clasp of the necklace pulled off the amethyst pendant, and frantically dug at the earth and buried the pendant. A stone of remembrance for Rebecca. Hannah crumpled on the ground and wept.

Hannah felt Benny's hands on her shoulders. He spoke softly. "Let me help you up, Hannah. We should go now." Hannah wiped her cheeks, looked up,

CHAPTER THIRTY: HANNAH SPRING AND SUMMER 1976

and took Benny's hand. They walked toward Miriam and the camp director and started the long walk out past barrack after barrack. The director gestured over to a low-slung building. "There is the gas chamber." Hannah stared at them as they walked by and whispered, "Goodbye." She pictured her parents and her sister Esther, not as they were when they were shoved off the train, but rather how they were in Grandmother Hortense's sunny garden in the days before they had to hide in a cold barn and before this horrible, unimaginable place. As Hannah dipped in and out of sleep on the train back to Dusseldorf, she had flashes in her dreams of her grandmother's garden and of her father rolling up his sleeves, her grandmother's parasol, her mother drinking tea, Esther with a sketchbook, and Rebecca's bell-like laughter. The dream glimpses of them felt so real.

Hannah and Miriam were going to testify on the same day. Hannah ironed the purple dress that she had worn for the trial in New York. She pulled her hair up in a French twist and clipped on gold earrings that matched the oversized gold buttons on the dress. She wanted to look good, competent, and credible. Max tapped on the bathroom door. "Are you ready, mom?"

Hannah stepped out of the bathroom, and Max was adjusting his sports coat, looking a little nervous. Hannah smoothed the lapels of his coat. "It will be a hard day. You will hear about how your aunt was killed, but I have to do this. I have to tell the whole story in detail if there is any hope for justice."

Max nodded. "Let's go, mom."

As Hannah and Max walked into the courtroom, Hannah saw Vince DeMarco. He introduced his wife, Frieda. "We came to witness some of the trial and to hear you, Hannah. I'm retired now, so it was also a trip to see Frieda's family here in Germany." Hannah was grateful to have another supporter in the courtroom; as they walked in, Mr. DeMarco patted her back. "You will do a great job, Hannah. You were one of the strongest witnesses in New York."

Hannah testified first. The walk to the witness stand seemed to last an eternity. She kept her eyes focused on the white enamel cross, and then she turned and sat and faced the guards. She focused her attention on the

Stomping Mare. She had a sour look on her face. The Angel of Death looked bored with his hands folded over his stomach. Bloody Bridget looked pained. Hannah knew that Bloody Bridget was playing up her health issues, which was a common strategy of older accused Nazis.

Hannah took a sip of water. She recounted her story the same way in which she had in New York, but in German. She was careful to be precise about the details and was calm. She tried not to look at Max because it would upset her. The defense lawyers tried to make her stumble on the details, but she kept her answers succinct. The prosecuting attorneys framed Hannah's testimony as part of a larger action by the Nazis. Operation "Harvest Festival" was a killing day in retribution for the escapes and rebellions that had taken place in other camps and other parts of Poland. Hannah testified that the day Rebecca was killed was the day of mass killing. She told them about the mass zigzag trenches, the blaring band music designed to cover the constant gunfire. After the questions about the "Harvest Festival" day, Hannah was excused. She decided not to look at the Stomping Mare as she passed by her. As she sat next to Max, he squeezed her hand and whispered, "You did a good job, Mom."

It was Miriam's turn to testify. Hannah was hoping that Miriam could control her emotions. Unlike Hannah, who had the benefit of testifying earlier in New York, this would be Miriam's first time testifying in front of the Stomping Mare and the others. Hannah felt her chest tightening as Miriam's anger was barely contained as she recalled her experiences at the camp, and about what she saw during "Harvest Festival." Then, the questioning turned to her interactions with the Stomping Mare.

Miriam straightened her back. "What I remember about her, the woman called Mrs. O'Neal now, but we called the Stomping Mare, is her cruelty and murder of small children." There was a buzz in the court. Hannah looked over, and the Stomping Mare was whispering furiously to her attorney. The judge called for order and allowed Miriam to continue. "I remember, as a translator, I translated her instructions to newly arrived mothers with small children. Very small, some babies and toddlers. The Stomping Mare would yell and separate these children from their mothers, who were screaming

CHAPTER THIRTY: HANNAH SPRING AND SUMMER 1976

and crying. The Stomping Mare tore the terrified children from their mothers and threw them violently into trucks headed for the gas chamber. She grabbed children by their hair and threw them in. She whipped and beat the mothers. One woman was crying and clinging to her child. Her child looked like a toddler who was weeping and clinging to her mother. The Stomping Mare struck this mother with a whip, and the terrified child started to run away. The Stomping Mare pulled out her sidearm and shot that toddler."

The courtroom erupted in horrified gasps. The Stomping Mare was telling her attorney that this was a lie. Hannah looked around. Everyone looked shocked. The Stomping Mare looked angry and animated. The judge called for a lunch recess, and the court would reconvene in two hours.

Hannah felt herself perspiring and feeling nauseous. Many people were gathered around Miriam as they exited the courtroom. They met by the exit. Benny was leaving to get a table for them at a café, and Miriam would wait for Hannah as Hannah went to the restroom. Hannah splashed her face with water and dampened a paper towel to hold on her neck and hoped that would ease her headache. She opened the restroom door and, in the distance, saw the Stomping Mare. Her shoulders were squared, and she was walking with the intensity she had at the camp, and she was headed for Miriam. Hannah quickened her pace. In Hannah's mind, images of the day the Stomping Mare grabbed Rebecca flashed before her and she felt terror well inside of her. She found herself running to Miriam as the Stomping Mare grabbed Miriam's arm and started shouting, "You are a liar!" She shook Miriam and screamed at her while commanding her to retract her testimony. Hannah saw Vince DeMarco running to them with a police officer. The police officer pulled The Stomping Mare away, and Vince DeMarco was shouting, and his wife was furiously translating. Hannah grabbed Miriam's shoulders. They were both breathing heavily.

Hannah walked Miriam over to a bench by the door. "Are you alright? I can't believe she grabbed you like that!"

Miriam regained her composure. "I can believe it. She is completely unchanged. She's a monster."

Hannah looked up and saw Max headed toward her, walking quickly, and he was winded. "Your friend, Mr. DeMarco, is in the courtroom and he is explaining what happened to the judge. He is pretty upset. What happened out here?"

Miriam waved her hand. "The monster was acting like a monster. What's new? I'm hungry. Let's all get some lunch."

Hannah was taken aback by how easily Miriam was waving this confrontation off. Hannah's throat was still constricted with fear. She couldn't tell if it was fear from today or the fear she felt as the scenes of the Stomping Mare grabbing Rebecca and eventually getting her thrust to the ground and finally killing her ran vividly through her mind. Maybe it was the visit to Majdanek or giving the testimony again, this time in German, that made those moments seem so immediate and real.

After lunch, the trial resumed. The presiding judge called the proceedings to order and asked the Stomping Mare to stand. In his deep voice, which seemed to vibrate with barely contained anger, the judge reprimanded her for her conduct and, in a moment that clearly enraged the Stomping Mare, said, "You are not a guard in a concentration camp anymore. You're in my courtroom."

Hannah had planned to stay to listen to more witness testimony for a few more weeks with Miriam, but one morning, Hannah found herself unable to move out of bed. Her stomach was sour and aching, and her head was ringing. If Max weren't with her, she imagined herself going into the bathroom and swallowing all of her sleeping pills. She curled into a ball on the side of the bed, looking at the clock. Max would be tapping on her door soon, ready to take her to breakfast and escort her to the courtroom for another grueling day of testimony and a day of looking at the back of the Stomping Mare's head and wondering why she had been free for so long.

Max tapped lightly on the door. Hannah asked him to come in. She could tell by the look on his face that the hollowness she was feeling was apparent to him. "Max, I'm not going today. You should go. Please sit with Miriam and Benny and give them my apologies. I know we had planned to stay a few more weeks, but could you call and see if we can get on a flight home

CHAPTER THIRTY: HANNAH SPRING AND SUMMER 1976

tomorrow? I can't stay here anymore. I need to go home."

Hannah tried to stop herself, because she hated to cry in front of her son, afraid of how this whole scene might worry him, but her strangled sobs couldn't be stopped. "I need to go home. I miss our house. I miss your father. This place is crushing me."

A look of terror passed over Max's face. "I'm not leaving you mom."

Hannah sat up, grabbed a tissue, and composed herself. "No, darling, please go to the courthouse and sit with Miriam and Benny. Let them know we plan to leave early. I need to rest and get ready. I promise you; I will be fine."

Max reluctantly left. Hannah tried to get a few more fitful hours of sleep. She took a bath and packed her things. These small tasks left her exhausted. She curled herself on the bed again and stared at the wall. She had the same feeling of dread and emptiness that she had at the camp. She remembered lying on the upper bunk in Majdanek, staring at the wall and hoping to die, to be released from suffocating pain.

Max tapped on the door. He brought in a tray with tea and some crackers. Hannah tried to look okay, but it wasn't working. She could see concern and fear pass over his face. "Mom, I made the travel arrangements; we are headed back to New York tomorrow night. Aunt Miriam is here, and she wants to talk to you. Is that okay?"

Hannah smiled, realizing that Miriam insisting Max call her "aunt" had taken hold. Miriam was an irresistible force. Hannah nodded. "Yes, I will see Aunt Miriam."

Miriam came into the room. Hannah could tell she was a little shocked to see Hannah in such a state. Miriam sat on the bed next to Hannah and took her hand. "Look at me, Hannah." Hannah turned to look into Miriam's dark, intense eyes. "I know this has been very hard for you. I know how much you loved your sister. You did the right thing, facing the Stomping Mare, not once, but twice. You honored your sister's memory. You should be proud. But I'm worried for you, Hannah. I've known a lot of survivors in Israel. They let the past gnaw away at their insides, and their pain has engulfed them. They may have escaped death at the camps for a few years, or even decades, but the camps kill them from the inside. You have to be stronger than the pain. Don't let it take you down. Will you promise me?"

Hannah nodded. She thought about her children and what David would expect of her. "Yes, Miriam, I will hang on."

Miriam held Hannah in a tight hug and then did something that caused Hannah's tears to flow again. Miriam stroked Hannah's hair and started humming. As Hannah wept, Miriam rocked her in her arms and continued to hum a song. It was so much like the times Rebecca would sing to her when they were falling asleep. Hannah felt if there was a God. He was giving her this supernatural comfort.

The next afternoon, Max and Hannah met Miriam and Benny in the hotel lobby to say goodbye. Miriam made a huge fuss over Max, how handsome he was and what a good son he was. Hannah had to laugh at Max's red face and his embarrassment. Benny gave Hannah a kiss on the cheek. "You're still so sweet and beautiful, Hannah. I'm so glad we spent some time together." Miriam jokingly elbowed Benny. "Hey now, no flirting!"

Max and Hannah headed to the airport in a taxi. Hannah pretended to read magazines on the flight home, but she couldn't concentrate. She kept flipping through the pages and forgetting words as soon as she read them. Max was reading a book but would shoot a concerned glance her way every once in a while. Finally, they arrived in New York. As they were walking, Hannah saw Sam and Sylvie. Funny, she thought, how many things circle back around. The last time she came to New York from Germany, almost thirty years ago, Sam and Sylvie were waiting for her and David. It was the first time they met, and Hannah was a nervous teenager.

Sylvie gave an enthusiastic wave. Hannah kept scanning the crowd to see her daughter's long dark hair and bohemian outfit in the crowd. As they got closer, Max gave them both a hug. "Hey, where's that crazy sister of mine?"

Sylvie looked nervous and fussed with her purse for a moment. "She really planned on being here, and when we spoke, she always wanted updates on how everything was going in Germany. She's just so busy in California right now that she couldn't make it."

Max looked angry. "Busy with what? Eating tofu and selling those stupid

CHAPTER THIRTY: HANNAH SPRING AND SUMMER 1976

beads? What the hell?! She was supposed to be here for Mom."

Hannah sighed. "It's okay. It's fine. I just want to go home."

It took Hannah several weeks to convince Max to go back to Minnesota and pick up his medical school studies. Hannah had the peace she had been craving. She went through David's record collection and listened to albums from when the kids were little, back in the '50s. She listened to Frank Sinatra's "Songs for Young Lovers" almost nightly, remembering how she and David would dance in the living room. She went back to volunteering to deliver meals to the elderly, and she taught herself how to make quilts. After the chaos of the trip to Germany and the trial, this was what she needed. She still kept tabs on the progress of the trial with updates from Miriam and Vince DeMarco.

On the fourth of July, she made an American flag cake with blueberries and strawberries for the big barbeque Sam and Sylvie were hosting. It was America's 200th birthday. Hannah sat in a lawn chair on Sam and Sylvie's patio and listened to the boom of the fireworks and the excited reactions of her friends. She was so happy to be home.

Chapter Thirty-One: Helma 1976–1977

Helma found herself struggling to control both her anger and her boredom as the months of prisoner or so-called "survivor" testimony dragged on. She thought that their stories were played up for dramatic effect to stir the sympathies of the judges, jurors, and spectators. It appalled her that young German students were brought in to hear these lurid tales and were shamed even more into thinking the Reich was especially bad and evil when everyone knew these types of things happened in warfare. Although no one spoke these ideas aloud, the harsh truth was that some people were like vermin, and the sensible thing to do is to eradicate vermin or at least keep it contained, not let it run rampant. That wasn't something people would admit to anymore, Helma thought, although it was true nonetheless, and a person only needs to look at the degradation of this current generation to see it.

Helma was sad about the argument with Greta. Unfortunately, Charles wasn't skilled enough on his own to persuade Greta back into the fold. Helma thought this was something she would have to handle herself, and she would let the trial move on from these in-person "survivor" testimonies before she would make another approach to Greta in the hopes of patching things up. It was so disappointing to see how susceptible Greta was to these stories and how weak-willed she could be. Helma thought it all went back to breeding. Hans should have picked someone stronger than Klara, someone who shared his passion for upholding the ideals of the Fatherland, not some silly girl like Klara. The weak strain also came from their mother, Helma thought, so maybe Greta had inherited these defeatist traits from both her

CHAPTER THIRTY-ONE: HELMA 1976–1977

mother and grandmother.

One day, the "survivor" testimony included two prisoners Helma remembered. These two were Letty's "pets" that she protected in the sorting warehouse. One of them had testified against Helma in New York and recounted the same story here as well as talking about a day of special operations called "Harvest Festival," which, of course, the prosecution had cast as some nefarious and evil thing, but it was war, and they had their mission. Helma had even earned her War Merit Cross during that operation. It wasn't surprising to hear from this prisoner from New York. What was outrageous was the next of Letty's special prisoners, a low-class Jew now living in Israel. This prisoner made up an outrageous lie accusing Helma of shooting a child! The courtroom erupted in shocked murmurs, and Helma turned to her attorney and whispered angrily. "I didn't even carry a sidearm around prisoners! Maybe a whip or a truncheon to keep order. This is a lie! I never shot anyone!"

The judge called for a two-hour recess, and Helma angrily yelled at her attorney, who was brushing her off. Charles tried to calm Helma, but she pushed past him to the corridor of the courtroom, chasing after that lying prisoner. Helma grabbed her arm and demanded that she retract her testimony immediately. Before long, the other prisoner, the one from New York, came running over, and then a police officer from the courtroom was pulling her away. Helma could not believe it, but there was that meddling investigator, DeMarco, from the United States Justice Department. He was shouting at the officer and insisting that they speak to the judge. The American investigator was telling the judge that Helma had threatened a witness. Helma turned to her attorney. "How can this American investigator speak to the judge?!" Her attorney insisted she stop speaking.

After the court recess, the presiding judge asked Helma to stand. He reprimanded her in front of everyone in court. Helma felt humiliated. How could he single her out and baselessly accuse her of acting like the distorted version of this vicious camp guard that these "survivors" had been providing false testimony about? Later that day, Helma was again reprimanded by her attorney for interacting with the witnesses.

The months wore on, and finally, the court was coming to the end of survivor testimony in Germany. The judges, jurors and attorneys were now journeying to Poland to personally look at Majdanek. It provided Helma with a little reprieve from the daily trial. Charles came and visited often. He brought her a flyer that he had collected from outside the courtroom from a group called "Silent Help." Helma read the flyer with interest. At least there was something to counteract all the negative propaganda and was telling the truth about how overblown the publicity around the camps and that the real threat was from the communists and the Jews, who had outsized financial and governmental power and influence. Charles brought in a few more flyers. Apparently, the group was handing them out weekly during the trial.

"Helma, I met the lady handing these flyers out. She was very nice. She brought doughnuts and coffee for all of us who were supporting the defendants. I guess this group provides help for ex-servicemen and women having to deal with all of these accusations and court cases, and she said they have been around since right after the war."

The trial resumed. Helma had become bored of the company of Werner and Bridget. Helma found Werner common and boring, and his vulgar jokes were wearing on her. Helma understood that it was part of Bridget's strategy to use her poor health to try to get out of the hearing, but Bridget's constant moaning about her myriad of health issues and the way in which she so easily shared the ulcers on her legs to pathetically vie for sympathy was embarrassing. Helma was glad that she maintained her pride and dignity. She felt more of an affinity for the commandant. He seemed to be taking the trial in stride. He always conducted himself with unapologetic confidence and he was clearly a man of intelligence. Helma decided to ask him if he knew anything about this "Silent Help" group.

"Ah, yes, a wonderful organization. They have been around since the late 1940s. They are a group dedicated to aiding loyal members of the Reich. They helped a number of associates of mine make it to South America to start new lives. This is my second trial, and Silent Help provided assistance to me in the earlier case. You and your husband should see about what

CHAPTER THIRTY-ONE: HELMA 1976–1977

assistance they might provide for you."

The trial continued to drag on for months. It was the start of 1977. The lawyers for the defendants were working on securing bail, as it looked like the end of the trial was nowhere in sight. Helma was hopeful, as the publicity and coverage from the prisoner testimony was dying down, and interest in the case was waning. Besides, she thought, she had been in jail since 1973 while not having been convicted of a crime.

Charles was making inroads with the Silent Help organization. On one of his visits, he was accompanied by a petite, blond, middle-aged woman. She was very nicely dressed. She extended her hand to Helma as Charles excitedly said, "Sweetheart, this is Mrs. Burwitz with the Silent Help group."

The woman smiled as she greeted Helma. "I'm Gudrun Himmler Burwitz, and I work with Silent Help."

When Helma heard the name Himmler, she was a bit taken aback. Mrs. Burwitz smiled. "Yes, Heinrich Himmler was my father. I was just a girl during the war, but now I'm doing my part to restore his reputation by helping his former associates and those who remain loyal to the Fatherland. The commandant told me of your plight and all that you have gone through in America. You were just trying to start your new life, and you became a target."

Helma exhaled with relief. She couldn't believe her good fortune to meet such an esteemed person whose father was a leader of the Reich. "I'm very flattered that you have taken an interest in my cause and are willing to help us. As you can imagine, this has been a tremendously difficult time for me and my husband."

Mrs. Burwitz smiled. "I realize that. We at Silent Help have been watching this case with great interest. We have been working with some of our more friendly connections to try to get you out on bail. We call our group Silent Help, because those who share our beliefs need to be quiet, but they still have positions of influence and have funds."

Charles chimed in, "Helma, they have been so kind to me, and I even have a lead on a job and a new apartment."

Mrs. Burwitz continued, "We were happy to assist your husband in finding work, and we have associates who are connected in all sorts of industries."

Helma and Charles visited with Mrs. Burwitz for a while. Helma noticed a beautiful silver brooch that Mrs. Burwitz wore on her scarf. The brooch was made of several horse figures, and upon closer inspection, Helma could see that the horse figures were shaped into a swastika.

"I see you noticed my brooch. It was a gift from my father. One of the few things which I was able to save during those chaotic days after the war. I like to wear it in my work for Silent Help. I consider it a lucky talisman."

A few weeks later, Helma was thrilled to learn that she would soon be out of jail on bail. Her bail was paid by Silent Help. Charles picked her up and drove her to their apartment outside Dusseldorf. It was small but cozy.

"I tried to make it nice, but I know you will make it so much better. I'm so glad to have you home." Charles had a small gift and fresh flowers on the table. He was working as an electrician now on a regular basis. He had purchased Helma a beautiful silk scarf as a gift. "I know how you like to wear scarves with your outfits at court."

***

The next morning, Helma made some scrambled eggs and toast and packed a lunch for Charles. It reminded her of the happy days they had back in Queens. After breakfast, Helma took the streetcar to the Dusseldorf courthouse as her trial continued.

Chapter Thirty-Two: Helma 1977–1999

Life for Helma and Charles in their tidy apartment outside Dusseldorf took on a routine not unlike the routine that they had maintained back in Queens. Helma did the housework and cooked the meals, and every morning, she packed a lunch for Charles for his work as an electrician. Helma was impressed at how quickly Charles had picked up some basic German and she assisted him in learning from German workbooks on the electrician's trade in Germany. He didn't have regular work, just occasional jobs that he received through the network of Silent Help. Money was tight. They had some funds from the sale of their home in Queens, and that broke Helma's heart. She loved that little house, as well as the beautiful yard and their pet dogs. Their tiny apartment didn't have any outdoor space, not even a patio for potted plants, and a dog in this tiny space was out of the question. Helma reminded herself to be grateful. It wasn't a jail cell, and she and Charles were together.

Most mornings, Helma boarded a streetcar to make it to the courthouse for the trial. The trial seemed to drag on without end. Now, many of the defendants were out on bail, and some made excuses not to attend the trial or showed up late or for only part of the day on trial dates. Helma prided herself on always being on time and never missing a day.

On weekends, Helma did the marketing and would occasionally treat herself to a trip to the fabric and notions store. She would buy new skeins of yarn and maybe a few buttons to knit herself a new sweater, and she would work on a colorful knit blanket for the worn and drab sofa that came with the apartment. Helma loved those shopping days. She felt like any other

German housewife ticking her grocery list and walking back home with her little pull cart of groceries trailing behind her.

It was 1978, the third year of the trial. Interest in the trial had plummeted. Helma felt that she again had some anonymity. She had confidence in her German defense attorneys as well as the work of Silent Help. Helma was thrilled to have been contacted again by Gudrun Himmler Burwitz. Mrs. Burwitz inquired if she might be able to visit the O'Neals to give them an update on some exciting developments that they could take part in for the benefit of Silent Help.

Charles chuckled at Helma's maniacal cleaning of the small apartment. Everything was deep cleaned. Helma borrowed a rug steamer from a neighbor and sent Charles off to a local pub for the day while the apartment aired out. Helma baked strudel and had both coffee and tea on hand for Mrs. Burwitz's visit.

Mrs. Burwitz arrived alone and looked very elegant in a cream-colored sweater and gold jewelry. As soon as they had settled down with their tea, Mrs. Burwitz explained the purpose of her visit.

"All of us involved with Silent Help have been watching the trial with great interest. It appears the West German government does intend to persist and continues to invest quite a bit of money in the trial. We believe it might be one of the last of these large-scale holocaust trials. We believe things are changing. More people are starting to question the Jewish version of these events. We have our own academics and scholars who are successfully challenging the version of events pushed by the Jews and their powerful allies. While Silent Help does maintain a low profile, we do have gatherings. We have a gathering, a special dinner of some of the remaining loyalists of the Fatherland and of those younger people who are waking up to the truth. This will take place in your hometown of Vienna. We would like you and Mr. O'Neal to be our special guests so that we may shed a little light on your plight."

Helma was thrilled that her case had risen to the forefront of the agenda of Silent Help and was excited to learn that those loyal to the Fatherland still gathered. "I'm most flattered by the invitation. Because of the trial,

CHAPTER THIRTY-TWO: HELMA 1977–1999

and because the constraints the court has placed on me, I'm not allowed to travel out of the country, as much as I would long for a visit to Vienna. My husband may be able to attend."

Mrs. Burwitz looked at Helma and raised an eyebrow. "I wouldn't be so sure, Mrs. O'Neal. We have many connections within the legal system here. We couldn't offer you a long visit to Vienna, just a quick jaunt to attend our dinner. We would make sure there was no trouble for you."

Helma glanced over to Charles, who simply shrugged. "Well, Mrs. Burwitz, if you say you can make it happen. I trust you after all you have done for me and for Helma. I would be happy to help with the dinner, but I think it really should be Helma's story. She's the one who has suffered the most."

After Mrs. Burwitz departed, Helma and Charles discussed the possibility of the trip to Vienna. Helma asked Charles if he would reach out to their niece, Greta, to see if she would be willing to come. Charles was eating the last few bites of his second piece of strudel. "I would be happy to go to Vienna to see Greta. I miss her. Maybe since some time has passed, she might be a bit more understanding."

Charles went to Vienna to see Greta. He took the train and stayed for a couple of days since it also provided an opportunity to connect with some old Air Force buddies who happened to be traveling through Vienna at the same time. When Charles arrived home, Helma was standing next to the stove with her hands on her hips. "Well? What happened? How is Greta? Is she well?"

Charles smiled sheepishly. "Oh, she looked fine. We didn't visit very long. She asked me to bring this letter to you, and she didn't really talk very much with me."

Helma worked hard to conceal her disappointment. She should have known that Charles lacked persistence and skills in these sorts of interpersonal matters. He didn't have the ability to press through to get the desired result. Helma arched her eyebrow. "We don't have secrets. Why don't you open it and read it to me?"

"Are you sure?"

"Yes. I'm sure. You spoke with her. Maybe you can add a little more context to the letter. You said she looked well but didn't share anything else. Is she still in the family home? Has she married?"

"She's still in the family home. She's fixed it up very nicely, and no, her name was the same, and she didn't say anything about a fella. She was pretty frosty with me, so I just want you to be prepared that this letter probably doesn't contain any opportunity for reconciliation, okay?"

Helma sat at the table with a cup of tea and nodded, and Charles opened the letter. Charles glanced at her with a worried look as he started reading.

Dear Aunt Helma,

It was wonderful to see Uncle Charles, and while I appreciate the spirit behind trying to reconcile, I'm sorry, but that's just not possible. Before I outline my reasons for this decision, I want to make sure that you know that I'm grateful for all that you did for me in the years after the war, and for all the gifts and attention you and Uncle Charles lavished on me as a young girl and teenager. I was the envy of many of my friends when I would receive packages all the way from America.

All of these kindnesses blinded me for a long time. The evidence was clear and right there, but I steadfastly refused to see it until it was undeniable at the trial in Dusseldorf. It is a source of shame that my family were ardent Nazis with an irrational hatred of Jews and an affinity for violence. That all ends with me. I won't be a party to promoting a lie, about what you did during the war, and I don't want contact with you.

I'm sorry for Uncle Charles, as he seems to be drawn into your hatreds and lies. I wish things were different, but they aren't, and it was long past time for me to face the truth.

Sincerely,
Greta

Helma again felt the white-hot rage burning inside of her. She flung her teacup against the wall, and it shattered into tiny white shards. Charles stood

CHAPTER THIRTY-TWO: HELMA 1977–1999

up in shock. He paused and put his hand on her shoulder. "I understand you're hurt and disappointed. Greta's generation doesn't understand the war. As you've said, that generation grew up on Jewish propaganda. It's sad, but you must control yourself, Helma. These outbursts are unacceptable."

Helma forced herself to calm down. She knew it was important for Charles that she restrain some of these more negative emotions. "Of course, you're right, Charles. I will clean up this mess."

A few months later, Mrs. Burwitz made contact and confirmed that she had made arrangements for Helma to slip out of Germany to Vienna for the Silent Help banquet. Helma was nervous, but she and Charles travelled by train to Vienna. They would head back to Germany immediately after the banquet, but Helma was giddy with anticipation. The trial was boring, and their tiny apartment remained drab despite her best efforts to develop it into a home. Helma had a new outfit for the occasion. A red suit with new black patent leather heels. She hadn't felt so glamorous since she took the train to Berlin in her new suit in 1941. The feeling was much the same, as she and Charles were escorted to a private banquet room in a hotel.

There were some handsome young men at the door, but as they were speaking to Charles and Helma, Mrs. Burwitz came through the double doors of the banquet room.

"Mr. and Mrs. O'Neal! So lovely to see you. Come this way. We must have security at these events, as you can imagine, there are elements who would wish to disrupt us. We have our wonderful young people of the *Junge Nationalisten* here to learn and serve."

Helma looked back appreciatively at the young men, who must have been born years after the war and looked at Mrs. Burwitz with amazement. These young people had the bearing of the Hitler Youth. It was obvious that the same traditions were maintained by Mrs. Burwitz, Silent Help, and others. Mrs. Burwitz continued, "Yes. We are a strong organization. Silent Help is but only one element. So many people are involved in government. For instance, I worked in West German intelligence before I married my husband, who is also politically active. We must keep fighting to stop the plague of international Jewry and communism."

THE NAZI HOUSEWIFE OF QUEENS, NEW YORK

The ballroom was packed, and Mrs. Burwitz was definitely a celebrity. The room had red bunting, and some of the older men were wearing their SS pins and insignia. It was a subtle display compared to what was seen in the '30s and '40s, but the feeling was the same. A wave of excitement and nostalgia washed over Helma. She was so happy to learn the Fatherland survived in some form. It gave her hope.

The speeches of the evening were rousing. Many were about contemporary politics and the efforts to take a strong stand against communism. Then Mrs. Burwitz spoke. She talked about the trial in Dusseldorf and asked Helma to stand. Those around her applauded. Mrs. Burwitz talked about keeping faith with those who had been loyal to the Fatherland and not abandoning them when the Jewish press and prosecutors with communist sympathies were out to make an example of them. She then talked of her father and the glory days of the Reich. As she stepped away from the podium, she received a standing ovation. With wine glasses and beer steins aloft, the crowd began singing the Horst Wessel song, the anthem of the Nazi Party, which had been banned since the end of the war. Tears welled in Helma's eyes. It had been so long since she felt this wonderful sense of belonging.

She caught a glimpse of Charles seated with arms folded at the table. As the song ended. Helma put her hand on Charles' shoulder. "What's the matter, darling?"

"You know, I agree with getting rid of the communists, and I know that the Jews have way too much power, but I'm not in favor of a Nazi revival. You know, Hitler and all that, in some ways, they went too far. That's why we had the war. We needed to rein him in, and I just don't agree with bringing all that back."

Helma struggled to make sure her contempt didn't show on her face. How did he think we were going to get rid of communists and Jews?

She had to remind herself that he was an American. It was important for them to look good, and they were just too weak to do the dirty work that needed to be done. Now, America is in decline. Negroes and Jews were too powerful, and their young people were grungy communists who lost Vietnam. When she remembered this, her contempt turned to pity for

CHAPTER THIRTY-TWO: HELMA 1977–1999

Charles.

Helma became an ardent supporter of Silent Help. She made sure to collect their flyers and newsletters which were handed out at the trial. Prosecutors, judges, and jurors traveled abroad to gather testimony of camp inmates and other witnesses. They even gathered more evidence when they interviewed Bridget from her hospital bed as her health rapidly declined. In 1980, Helma realized that this trial had now lasted nearly as long as the war. Finally, her attorney said the trial was drawing to a close. He tried to prepare Helma for the potential of her receiving a harsher sentence than the other defendants. Helma didn't believe it. After all, she was just a lowly guard, and the commandant, who was in charge of the camp, would receive a harsher sentence than her. The lawyer tried to explain that with German law, it was the evidence of people being directly involved in the killing that would result in the longer sentences, and there had been compelling testimony that Helma had been directly involved.

Helma balled up her hands in anger. She expected this sort of incompetence from her weak American attorney, but she had more faith in the German attorneys. They had done well in countering the prosecutors and the so-called "survivors."

She banged her fists on the table in the small conference room. "Why should I have a longer sentence? The 'killing,' as you have called it, was done under orders. It was not illegal. I was a camp guard, like any other guard who must maintain order, and if the prisoners were put to death, there was a good reason for it!"

As the day of the verdict and sentencing drew closer, Helma comforted herself with fantasies of Silent Help somehow wielding their influence to get her off the hook. She refused to accept that she might face a harsh sentence and return to prison.

Finally, in June of 1981, nearly six years since the trial had begun, the verdict and sentences would be handed down. Presiding Judge Bogan intoned each with his commanding voice each sentence. The commandant received twelve years, Bridget received twelve years, and Werner only received six years, others on trial received only four years. Helma held her breath as she waited for her sentence. She heard Judge Bogan's deep voice intone a life sentence for her. *A life sentence!*

She vaguely heard people yelling in the gallery. Some were angry about the short sentences for the other defendants. She could hear Charles shouting about the sentence being unfair and that this is not what he fought the war for, to see this miscarriage of justice. The officers of the court were moving to take her into custody. As she turned around the courtroom was complete pandemonium. People were yelling, reporters and photographers were jostling to get Helma's photo. A bright light and camera were shoved in her face. She shielded her face with her hands and wished the officers were moving her a little faster through the courtroom.

Helma felt numb as she was booked into prison. A tiny comfort was that she would not be sharing a cell. Her cell at least had a little window. The prison matron let her know she could decorate her cell and have some personal things. She asked Charles to bring some books and photos of their camping trips in America.

Helma kept to herself in prison. She didn't socialize with the other prisoners. Charles came and visited her weekly and brought her books and yarn for her knitting. She had also taken up crochet and made crochet doilies that she gave to Charles for church charity sales. Helma held out hope that Silent Help may provide some assistance. Mrs. Burwitz stayed in touch with sympathetic letters in the early days of Helma's prison time, but the letters waned, and Mrs. Burwitz and Silent Help were assisting another high-profile Nazi, Klaus Barbie, the "Butcher of Lyon." In the mid-80s, Helma followed the case closely, and Charles brought her newspaper clippings and magazine articles about Barbie and the trials. There were other cases as well. John Demjemjuk, the autoworker from Ohio, who was accused of being "Ivan the Terrible." Helma's notoriety had faded. No one ever spoke of the "Stomping Mare," the dog-loving housewife from Queens.

Every once in a while, Helma wished she was free. Especially when she gathered with other inmates and guards to watch on the small black and white television as the Berlin Wall was torn down and West and East Germany were reunited. Helma wondered what it was like to be out in this

CHAPTER THIRTY-TWO: HELMA 1977–1999

new world where communism was fading away and everything was rapidly changing.

Helma knew she was aging, but it was more alarming to see Charles age, and loneliness was taking a toll on him. He was too old now to continue to work. He was able to collect his Social Security payments, but it wasn't enough to hold on to even their tiny apartment. He had to move into an even smaller studio apartment. He made the best of it, he said it was easier to clean and it was near a nice park.

Despite her efforts to try to keep fit, Helma had gained weight. The prison doctor diagnosed her with diabetes. It was the terrible prison food, thought Helma.

Helma noticed that a cut on her foot wasn't healing. She kept it clean and changed her bandage on a regular basis, but her foot remained red and puffy. After a time, it became uncomfortable to walk on, but Helma thought it would eventually heal on its own. She ignored the pain and kept changing out the bandage on her own. She finally demanded to see the doctor when part of her foot was turning black and oozing.

The doctor examined her foot and came back with a diagnosis that shocked Helma. He put his hand on her shoulder reassuringly. "I'm very sorry, Mrs. O'Neal, but we will need to remove your foot. That's the only solution at this point."

As she was put under the anesthetic, her mind drifted back to January 1945 and Letty's wedding to the shell-shocked one-legged soldier. Helma remembered thinking what a pathetic specimen he was, and now she, too, was going to be a pathetic cripple.

The only good part of the whole ordeal was that Helma was going to be released from prison due to her medical condition and, of course, her age. She was nearly eighty years old and in terrible health. She was transferred from prison to a nursing home.

Helma almost wished to be back in her prison cell. The nursing home smelled of urine and the caregiver assigned to her was a Turkish immigrant. Helma did not like to be handled by this woman and complained several times to the nursing home administrator.

Charles came to see her frequently. Now that she was feeling better, he came by with her knitting kit. She fumed that her request to change her caregiver had been ignored. "Charles, you wouldn't believe it. Some dirty Turk, who is probably a Muslim, too, is my caregiver. I understand Germany is full of these Turks, like a flea infestation. How is Germany making these kinds of mistakes again? After all, we did during the war to make it a pure country."

Charles shook his head. "Now Helma, I'm sure she is doing a perfectly fine job. There are some Turkish families in my building, and they seem nice enough."

Helma was determined to get rid of this caregiver and complained frequently and loudly. But the administrator did not reassign her. One morning, Helma had enough. The Turkish caregiver came in, and Helma threw her hot mug of coffee at the woman.

A few hours later, Charles came to the nursing home with a suitcase. "Helma, you have been kicked out of here. What were you thinking? You could have severely injured that woman. You're lucky you are not headed back to prison."

"I don't care." Helma hobbled over to the wheelchair as Charles packed her things.

Helma was shocked at the tiny studio apartment. They didn't have a stove, just a hotplate and a tiny refrigerator. The queen-sized bed took up most of the room, and that is where Helma now spent her days, knitting or watching T.V. shows with Charles.

When the weather was nice, Charles would insist on taking her to the local park. Helma worried about Charles having to carry her in a wheelchair down the steps of the stoop. He tried to cheer her up by offering to buy flowers or buying her a pastry at the café. Sometimes, Helma would think she saw her accusers from the trial. On one day in particular, when Helma was wearing a pink sweater, one she had spent weeks knitting, they were out at the park, and Helma was admiring the dogs that people would walk through the park, and she thought she saw a woman staring at her. A woman with large hazel eyes. Helma felt she had seen her before, maybe at one of the trials, but then she shook it off. After years of trials and reporters seeking her out, she was now an anonymous old woman. No one knew who she was anymore, and no one cared.

Chapter Thirty-Three: Hannah
1978–1994

In 1989, Hannah had finally sold the house in Queens and moved out to San Francisco to live with Max and his family. He had purchased a house with a mother-in-law suite. It was separated from the main house by a set of double doors. It had a small kitchenette, sitting room, large bedroom and bathroom and sliding door to the wooden deck. Max had done all that he could to ensure her comfort.

The decision to move was made after Sylvie died. She had become ill just a few months after Sam passed away. Sylvie developed lung cancer. Hannah drove her to her radiation appointments, and after the appointments, they would sit at Hannah's dining room table and have coffee and, if Sylvie could manage it, a few bites of something Hannah had freshly baked for her. They reminisced about their vacations to The Pines with the children, the weekly card games, and Sam and David's obsession with baseball and how their minds were filled with baseball statistics that they would argue about. Hannah would badger Sylvie to eat a little more, but every day, Sylvie was fading. Hannah struggled to stay strong for Sylvie's sake, but the sadness pulled on her heart when she thought about losing Sylvie. Hannah couldn't imagine life without Sylvie, who was a patient and caring mother figure, an encouraging and jolly friend, and the foundation of Hannah's life in America.

After Sylvie's passing, Max had become increasingly worried about his mother. He was especially alarmed that Sylvie's lung cancer did not at all

CHAPTER THIRTY-THREE: HANNAH 1978–1994

deter Hannah from her one-pack-per-day smoking habit. Max didn't like the idea of her alone in the house or of her driving herself around in the old green 1977 Chrysler Cordoba. She had refused his many offers of buying her a new car.

"I like this car. It was the first car I bought on my own after your father died. Green was the color of the first car we bought in America. I just loved those ads with Ricardo Montalban. He says the cars have 'Corinthian leather.' I don't know what that is, but it sure is nice leather."

Max just shook his head. He paid a local mechanic to call his mother and make her bring the car in for regular maintenance.

Hannah appreciated how Max made an effort to look after her, even if, at times, it felt a little patronizing. He was dutiful and so much like his father. She spent years resisting his offer to move. She didn't want to be a burden, and she didn't want to be constantly pestered by her doctor son to quit smoking. The other consideration was her daughter-in-law, Sandra. Hannah remembered flying from Queens to Minnesota a few days before their wedding in the summer of 1979 and attending a picnic that Sandra called a "potluck." Sandra's many plump aunts set up a long table filled with trays of yellow-colored casseroles and a salad made of shaved carrots and raisins. Sylvie and Hannah walked through the buffet line of casseroles in the church basement. Sylvie leaned over and whispered to Hannah, "I think these are all potato and cheese!"

Sylvie and Hannah sat together at a scuffed Formica table in the brightly lit and spotless church basement. A couple of the aunts joined them at the table. Like Sandra, they seemed to think Hannah's accent indicated she didn't understand things. They spoke very slowly and nodded vigorously when Hannah was speaking. One of the aunts asked about Sylvie. "So, Hannah, is Sylvie your older sister? Max calls her Aunt Sylvie."

"No, Sylvie is my cousin. She and her husband Sam helped us come to America after the war. Sam is my late husband's first cousin. My husband and I were in a displaced persons camp, and they helped get us out."

Sandra's aunt gasped, leaned over, placed her hand on Hannah's arm, and whispered, "We watched that mini-series on the holocaust. Was it really that bad?"

Hannah had heard about a mini-series airing on T.V. about the holocaust and realized this T.V. show had ignited interest and speculation about the camps and was certainly a sanitized version of events. She straightened up in her chair and cleared her throat. "I did not watch it, but I can assure you it was much worse than what is permitted to be shown on television. My entire family was killed, as was my late husband's. Our families were gassed in a crowded gas chamber, and their bodies were incinerated in an oven. That is why we are so few in number here at the wedding. Max's aunts were murdered."

Sandra's gossipy aunt's face dropped as she withdrew her hand. Hannah realized what she had done and tried to recover the situation. "I'm sorry, this isn't what we should be talking about on such a happy occasion. I'm quite a collector of recipes, but I haven't seen a recipe that includes carrots and raisins. It seems like a wonderful summer salad. Might you have the recipe?"

The now ashen woman mumbled, "I will go find out who made that dish." And with that she quickly jumped from the table and scrambled away.

Hannah slumped in her chair. She immediately felt bad for how she spoke to Sandra's aunt. She knew it was anger born of sadness. She felt so alone without David. She imagined him at this church basement potluck. All of Sandra's aunts would be smiling slyly at this handsome man with the strong jaw and exotic European accent. David would have loved it. Hannah remembered how much David loved anything authentically American. He would have enjoyed these earnestly kind Minnesotans.

The wedding was held in a Lutheran church. It was packed with Sandra's family, but Max only had Hannah, his sister, her current boyfriend, and, of course, Sylvie.

Sandra was always friendly, but Hannah suspected it was forced. Her smile when she saw Hannah seemed artificially bright, and she spoke to Hannah as if she were a slightly deaf and developmentally delayed person.

Max and Sandra had their daughter, Jenna, in 1981. Hannah flew to California for the birth of her first grandchild. She felt a literal pang in her

CHAPTER THIRTY-THREE: HANNAH 1978–1994

chest that David wasn't alive to experience this.

Hannah waited anxiously at the hospital and absent-mindedly flipped through fashion magazines while she watched the corridor for Max. It was a relief when Rebecca showed up. Surprisingly, Rebecca offered to bring Hannah coffee from the cafeteria. Rebecca and Hannah were speculating about name choices when Max walked toward them with an enormous smile on his face. "It's a girl. A beautiful girl. They are both fine."

Rebecca threw her arms around her brother and let out a whoop of excitement. Hannah felt a wave of emotion overtake her body. She put her hand over her heart and closed her eyes to absorb the moment and regain composure. She allowed herself a moment of pure joy as she watched her children embrace. Rebecca and Hannah were sitting in the room with Sandra, who looked tired but happy and a perfect baby girl, resting quietly. As they all were chatting, a page came over the hospital P.A. system for Max. He looked a little annoyed, but he was still a doctor and assumed there was a patient issue.

A few minutes later, Max reappeared with a concerned look on his face. "Mom, there is an important phone call from Aunt Miriam in Israel for you."

Hannah struggled to grasp what Max was saying. He took her arm and led her out into the corridor. "Aunt Miriam says it's about the trial in Germany, and she has urgent news to share with you." He walked slowly with her to the phone. Hannah suddenly felt like everything was in slow motion. She was nervous about what she might hear and a little angry that the ugliness of the trial was intruding on her happy moment. When she picked up the receiver, Miriam sounded jubilant. "Congratulations on your granddaughter! I have more good news for you. The Stomping Mare has been sentenced to life in prison. Life. In. Prison. The others received ridiculously mild sentences in comparison, but at least that evil bitch is going away forever."

Hannah couldn't bring herself to feel anything about the Stomping Mare. She was so tired of the trial and the many years of having to revisit the brutal experiences of Majdanek. "Thanks for letting me know, Miriam. I know it sounds strange, but I don't feel happy or excited. I guess there is a sense of satisfaction that there is a little justice, and I'm glad this chapter is finally closing."

"I understand, my friend. I'm happy that there is a little justice in this world, and maybe more of those monsters will be held accountable. You should be proud of all that you did, and I know it was a struggle. Now, you have a new chapter. Enjoy that beautiful grandchild."

After Miriam got the complete update about the baby, Hannah hung up the phone. It was a jumble of emotions, but one that stood out clearly and which would have given David the most satisfaction was that all she wanted to do was forget all of the hardship of revisiting her time in the camp and even thinking about the Stomping Mare ever again.

Hannah experienced with Jenna what she had heard about so many mothers experiencing when their child was born. She held the tiny baby in her arms and felt a flood of emotion. Surprising herself, she softly sang a little song in French that she remembered her grandmother singing around her house in France. A song she hadn't even thought of since she was a little girl. Hannah enjoyed watching Jenna grow from baby to toddler to young child. She talked on the phone with her weekly and visited a few times per year. Max and Sandra celebrated Christmas, and Hannah came to their celebration with beautifully wrapped presents for Jenna.

Hannah's relationship with her own daughter, Rebecca, was still not close, but had become less strained. After several years of random boyfriends, Rebecca had a long-term relationship with Terry, who pulled his thinning grey hair back in a straggly ponytail and listened to a lot of Grateful Dead. With her inheritance from her father, Rebecca and Terry bought a yoga studio in San Francisco. Rebecca continued to wear long flowing dresses and skirts and had a side business reading people's chakra and selling crystals and stones that Rebecca believed promoted healing. Max found all of that ridiculous. However, he was a loyal older brother and invited her and Terry to family dinners when Hannah visited.

When Hannah finally made the move to Max's house, it took Sandra and Max a few days to unpack and set up Hannah's little apartment. Max was surprised at how little Hannah wanted to bring from the house in Queens. Hannah had narrowed it down to a few items and, of course, her latest cat,

CHAPTER THIRTY-THREE: HANNAH 1978–1994

Siggi, number six.

On the third day, Rebecca arrived wearing a multi-tiered purple skirt, a jingly ankle bracelet, and sandals.

After she greeted everyone, she turned to Max, "I thought I would come over and see if I could help settle mom in."

Max looked resigned, "That would have been a helpful offer about three days ago. She's all set now."

Sandra offered Rebecca some coffee, but she refused and asked if they had herbal tea instead. This set Sandra off into digging into a cupboard and coming up with a box of Earl Grey tea, which Rebecca impolitely refused as well. Rebecca spent about thirty minutes or so looking at Hannah's new quarters and then kissed Hannah on the cheek and left.

Jenna came into Hannah's sitting room and flopped on the couch. "Dad says Aunt Becky's an idiot."

Hannah laughed, "Well, she does things her own way. But it's not very bright to not wear a bra at her age. Good foundation garments are the basis for a nice figure. You know, I used to make clothes for your aunt. Would you like me to make you a dress? We can pick out the fabric together."

Jenna enthusiastically agreed to the idea.

Over the years, Jenna became Hannah's focus. Spending the days sewing outfits for her and going to her school events is what Hannah looked forward to the most. After school, Jenna would flop herself on Hannah's loveseat and talk about her day. Sometimes, she would lie on the chair with her Sony Walkman on her ears and bopping her head while Hannah prepared a snack for her in her little kitchenette.

* * *

One night at dinner, after Jenna had left the table, Max turned to Hannah and looked very serious, "Mom, there is a new movie out about the holocaust, called 'Schindler's List' and we are going to see it and take Jenna to see it too."

Hannah shrugged, "Well, there have been plenty of movies about the holocaust. If you feel Jenna is ready to see such a movie, you're her parents."

Max looked uncomfortable and leaned in, "Mom, I think it's time to tell Jenna about what the holocaust meant to our family. What happened to you, and the brave thing you did in testifying against that woman."

Hannah looked down at her plate and shuffled a few heads of broccoli around with her fork. "I wish I didn't have to tell Jenna anything. She could just have a normal grandma." Hannah wanted to finally leave the pain and darkness of that time behind her, and now, in some way, it would be infused into yet another generation. She wanted her beloved Jenna to be a carefree American girl without this dark legacy hanging over her.

Max took her hand, "Mom, people need to know what happened. There are people denying it happened. Jenna will at least be able to share your story in the future when people forget."

After Jenna had seen the movie, she sheepishly came into Hannah's room. Hannah patted the loveseat. "Why so shy? Come on in."

"Grandma, I saw the movie, and Dad said you lived through that. He said I should talk to you about it."

Hannah took in a breath. "I wish I hadn't lived through that. I wish you didn't have to hear this story. I wish you had a normal American family. But wishing doesn't make it so. I was a little girl when we left Austria and lived in France. I lived with my grandmother, too. Her name was Hortense. After the Nazis invaded France, we hid on a farm. But we were discovered, and the family that helped us was shot right in front of us. Then we were on a train, packed in with no room. When we arrived at the camp, my mother, father, and sister Esther were sent to the gas chamber. My sister, Rebecca. That is who your aunt is named for, and I went to work in the camp. It was a horrible place, and I can't find the words to describe it. The camp had a very mean guard who killed my sister. That guard came to America, and I ended up testifying against her. I went to Germany and testified against her again, and your father came and helped me. She's in jail. I guess that's a little bit of justice."

Tears were streaming down Jenna's face. Hannah pulled her close. "Don't cry. We're safe now. We're okay now."

Chapter Thirty-Four: Hannah
1996–1999

Hannah got a call from Miriam. "It is our fiftieth wedding anniversary, and Benny, Daniel, his crazy wife, my granddaughters, we are all coming to California! We are coming to visit you and then do California tourist things, like the big park with the carnival rides and rodent mascot." Miriam stopped to catch her breath. Hannah could almost see her tiny, now gray-haired friend gesturing wildly to illustrate what she was saying.

Hannah laughed. "Rodent mascot? You mean Disneyland? Well, it will be very exciting to see you all. I can't wait."

Max and Hannah met Benny, Miriam, Daniel, his wife Rivka, and their twin daughters, Ava and Shoshanna, at the airport. Hannah felt her heart race with excitement as she rushed to give Miriam a hug. It was the first time they had seen each other in person since the trial in Germany. Hannah glanced over and saw Max and Daniel in a tight embrace. It occurred to Hannah what a bond they must have built during those dark days of the trial in Germany.

Max had a big barbeque on the deck. During quiet moments, Sandra nervously rearranged the salad bowls and bags of chips on the table, while Daniel's wife Rivka seemed to have a little too much to drink as the night went on.

Max's daughter, Jenna, was fifteen now and a tall, lanky girl who would clearly develop into a beauty, thought Hannah. She was very sweet to the twin girls, who were eight. She was teaching them cartwheels on the lawn when Hannah found a moment to speak with Miriam alone.

Hannah turned to Miriam. "So, tell me everything. How are you?"

Miriam gave her a sly smile. "Give me a cigarette, and I will give you the update." Hannah gave Miriam a cigarette and lit one for herself. She felt as if she and Miriam were teenagers sneaking a smoke, especially when she saw Max's disapproving look.

Miriam caught the look, smiled, and looked at the cigarette. "I'm not allowed these anymore, but it's a special occasion. The update. Benny is the same. He always has so many interests and schemes. I'm glad I'm in charge of the retirement money. Daniel is calming down, and he is a good father to the girls. Rivka, well, she's crazy. The problem is we all live together. Rivka gets hysterical about the slightest things. It's maddening. This younger generation. They're so fragile! We spoiled them. What about you? I see your son is still the golden boy. So handsome, taking care of you and giving you that beautiful granddaughter. What is happening with that ungrateful daughter of yours?"

Hannah chuckled. "Things are better with me and Rebecca, but still not good. Maybe you're right. We spoiled them, and nothing we did was good enough. I just don't know." Hannah smiled when she saw Miriam roll her eyes. "I think Rebecca is doing okay. She has a steady boyfriend who suits her and her lifestyle, and they come to family dinners here sometimes and she is sweet to Jenna." Hannah shrugged, she didn't know how to explain to Miriam that while she was sad about her relationship with Rebecca sometimes, it was just time to accept it for what it was.

The next morning, they were having breakfast on the patio. Miriam had two curled and faded pictures. One was Benny and Miriam on their wedding day. The other was Hannah and David. Jenna was holding the picture of her grandparents. "Grandma, you look so young!"

"I was so young. Only a few years older than you are now. I was seventeen when I married your grandpa."

Jenna looked down at the photos again. "It looks like you and Aunt Miriam are wearing the same dress?"

CHAPTER THIRTY-FOUR: HANNAH 1996–1999

Hannah smiled. "Yes, it was hard to find pretty dresses, so Aunt Miriam gave me her dress. I wore it at a special dinner on my first day in America. It was cream colored and silk, such a pretty dress."

Miriam playfully elbowed Jenna. "You see, your grandma was a great beauty! She still is, even now. Look at your grandpa, though. You never met him, but he was a wonderful man. So kind and such a gentleman."

Jenna held the photograph and nodded. Hannah felt a lump growing in her throat. How sad it was that David never met Jenna. Hannah started clearing the coffee cups and plates. "Well, we better get moving if we want the full San Francisco tourist experience."

The whole group walked around San Francisco, going to Fisherman's Wharf and other spots. Miriam and Hannah walked arm in arm through the crowds. It made Hannah chuckle to see Miriam crane her neck at all the different people and make smart comments under her breath. Hannah caught a glimpse of them in the window. Two grandmas. Older ladies approaching their seventies. Hannah thought about how, as scared fifteen-year-old girls fighting for survival in the camps, they could have never imagined themselves as grandmothers enjoying a sunny day in San Francisco with their families. She looked at Jenna walking ahead with Daniel and Rivka's twin girls and realized she and Miriam were Jenna's age in the camps.

Miriam, Benny, Daniel, Rivka, and the twin girls headed to Disneyland after several days in San Francisco. Max and Hannah brought Benny, Miriam, and Daniel's family to the car rental place. Hannah couldn't help but laugh at all the arguing about who was driving which car. When it was finally sorted out, Miriam pulled Hannah aside and gave her a long hug.

"Hannah, this is the last time you will see me."

"Oh, I don't know. We might come visit you. We will see each other again."

"No, I'm sick. I will be dead within six months. I have late-stage cancer. I wanted to see you one more time. Don't worry about me. I'm ready to die. We are the fortunate ones. We got to really live."

Hannah felt her throat constrict, and her eyes welled as Miriam embraced her tightly again. "Don't you dare cry. It is not sad. I'm glad I'm here to tell you I love you and thank you for being my sister."

Hannah wanted to speak, but the moment was too unbearable. Miriam just touched her cheek and said, "I already know." The noise and bustle of the car rental place faded. Hannah was frozen in place as Miriam smiled and shuffled her granddaughters into the car. Hannah felt a wave of coldness come over her, and she clutched her sweater closer. She wasn't even aware that Max was standing next to her. "Hey, mom, are you okay?"

Hannah didn't answer and she didn't know how she was going to force herself to move to the parking lot and Max's car. Max put his arm around her. "Don't be sad mom. It was a great visit. We will see Aunt Miriam again."

Hannah could only manage to nod her head as Max walked with her to the car, and they drove home.

A year later, Miriam was gone. Miriam didn't want to talk to anyone in the late stages of her illness. She sent Hannah a short note with a packet of pictures from their visit to California, and she added the faded wedding picture of Hannah and David from their wedding day at the Displaced Persons camp, into the collection of new photos. Hannah got a frame for her wedding photo and a photo of her and Miriam laughing together on the deck during her visit. It was very hard to believe Miriam was gone and now there was no one left from her old life in Europe, who remembered the time in the camp.

It was the spring of 1999. Hannah was sitting at her small dining table with a cigarette, trying to figure out what to get Jenna for her graduation gift, when Sandra knocked on her door.

"So sorry to bug you, but I have this elderly man on our phone line asking for your direct number. He says he's an old friend from New York. His name is Weston Bradley. Does that name mean anything to you?"

Hannah stared at Sandra in disbelief for a moment. "Yes. Give him my number. I know him."

Sandra nodded, and Hannah listened as Sandra said, "Yes, Mr. Bradley, she remembers you."

Almost immediately, Hannah's phone rang. She stared at it for a moment before picking it up.

CHAPTER THIRTY-FOUR: HANNAH 1996–1999

"Hello?"

"Hi Hannah, sorry to bother you after more than twenty years. I suppose you're surprised I'm still alive. Well, it still surprises the hell out of me too."

Hannah laughed, "It is a surprise, but a nice one, and it sounds as if you haven't changed much."

"Oh, I have. I'm in a God-forsaken *active senior living community* in Florida. I don't get around too well on my own, and I'm a widower now. Susan died several years ago. I have some friends who talked me into moving here. All of these old fools are driving golf carts around. We all spend our time watching *Wheel of Fortune* and wearing nylon tracksuits. Remember when we would dress up? Remember when we met at that benefit gala? We knew how to dress."

Hannah laughed. "I don't think I will ever forget that night. I like that Wheel of Fortune game show! I don't wear a nylon tracksuit, though. I live with my son, his wife, and my granddaughter. But you knew that you tracked me down."

"Yes, I wanted to check on you. Thankfully, I can still get *The New York Times* delivered to this ridiculous place. There was an article today that I wondered if you saw or if you knew about this—Helma O'Neal was released from prison in Germany."

The words hung in the air for a moment. Hannah shook her head as if she could rattle the news out of her mind.

"Hey, are you still there? I guess you hadn't heard. I double-checked the news with Vince DeMarco, and he confirmed it. A medical discharge. She has diabetes and had her foot amputated. She's living with her husband, that bastard is still alive too. They are in Dusseldorf. I thought you should know. It's a small notice in the paper; it's buried, but I immediately thought of you."

It was as if she was coming out of a trance. "Thanks, Weston. I hadn't heard. I didn't know. It's funny; there were no medical discharges in the camps." She surprised herself when she let out a bitter laugh. "They just let us die. How nice for her that she is out and spending time with her husband."

"Hey, I know it's rough news. She won't be around much longer. I'm not much of a churchgoer, but where she's headed next could be the final consequence she deserves."

Hannah felt herself getting angry, "I thought she was getting a consequence here! I thought she would die in prison. That is the least that could happen!"

"Hey, I'm on your side! It's crazy, but that's how it is."

Hannah put her hands in her carefully coiffed hair in frustration, and she paced around her room. "I'm sorry, thanks for calling me. It is great to hear your voice. I'm just upset."

"Understood. I will give you a callback and check in on you. I know this isn't the news you wanted to hear."

Hannah looked at herself in the mirror to reassure herself that she didn't look too crazed. She touched up her lipstick, threw on her sweater, and headed to the door. She told Sandra she was walking to the coffee shop. She heard Sandra's voice trailing after her to offer her a ride.

She bought a coffee and a copy of *The New York Times*. Weston was right, it was buried and no picture. A small article that stated, "Helma Braun O'Neal, former Queens housewife and concentration camp guard released from prison in Germany." Hannah folded the paper up in frustration. She didn't finish her coffee. She couldn't believe that this was happening. She felt herself walking quickly and sweating as she made her way home.

Hannah skipped dinner, and she didn't sleep well. She turned things over in her mind. All she could manage to feel was anger. There was no justice, and now she felt she had to do something. Something that would make it right. How would she get a gun in Germany? Was she really prepared to murder Helma and go to jail? She confirmed the thought in her mind. *Yes.* David was gone, Jenna was grown and off to college. It would be a hardship to be in prison, but worth it. In her rage, Hannah couldn't imagine any other solution.

The next morning, she was in touch with the travel agency. She would leave the week after Jenna's graduation. She planned to visit France and Austria before going to Germany. She wanted to see the places her family had lived and close that chapter to prepare herself for life in confinement

CHAPTER THIRTY-FOUR: HANNAH 1996–1999

she pictured after murdering Helma.

Max was confused. "Why the rush? When things slow down at work, Sandra and I can go with you. I thought you never wanted to go back. You hated it when we went to Dusseldorf."

"Yes, it was that horrible trial. That was a long time ago. I want to see a few things before I'm too old to travel."

"I understand that, but why can't it wait a few months so we can go with you?"

"I don't want you and Sandra along. This is something I need to do on my own."

Max sensed that, like the smoking, Hannah would not be moved. He drove her to the airport. As she got ready to board the plane, tears welled in her eyes. She thanked him for being such a caring son.

After landing in Paris, Hannah rented a car to take her to rural France to see if her grandmother's house outside of LeMans was still standing. She stopped at a coffee shop that was still there from the 1930s. She looked through phone books to see if by any chance Caroline Dufour was still alive. It seemed unlikely, as she would be in her nineties or even older. She scanned the phone book and found Annette Dufour first, but figuring she had nothing to lose, called the number.

Hannah's French-speaking skills easily returned to her once she was back in France. Annette Dufour sounded friendly when she answered the phone.

"So sorry to bother you, but do you know Caroline Dufour?"

"Yes, she was my aunt. Unfortunately, I have to inform you that she died several years ago. Were you a friend of hers?"

"In a way. I knew her a long time ago. I was just a child, and I was living with my grandmother. Your aunt worked for her. My grandmother's name was Hortense Blauer. Does that name mean anything to you?"

There was a long silence on the phone. Annette finally said, "I know that name very well. I think we should meet in person, Mrs. Schneider. Can you meet for brunch tomorrow?"

Annette Dufour was a plain, middle-aged lady with red hair. Hannah figured she was in her late fifties. She greeted Hannah warmly.

"It's so wonderful to meet you. My aunt often spoke of you and your family and prayed many days for your family. I took care of her toward the end of her life. She was my father's sister. She worked for Madame Blauer for many years, starting when she was a young woman in the 1920s."

Hannah was so excited that she had made this connection, she asked Annette to tell her more.

"I'm so glad you contacted me. My aunt and my father were in the French resistance during the war. My father was one of the men who drove your family to our relatives out in the countryside to hide. My father and aunt were so devastated by the discovery of your family and that the Nazis had murdered our elderly relatives. Pierre Dufour was my great-uncle. I'm certain that Pierre and Henrietta did not regret their decision. Our entire family was committed to the resistance. Your grandmother and your father helped to fund some of their work. Madame Blauer was a hero to the resistance. I'm sure you know your grandmother was killed in 1944. The Nazis left her alone for a time because she was an old woman, and they figured she was not a threat. What they didn't know, for at least a while, was that she had been using her beautiful jewels and some of the jewels your father had smuggled from Austria to fund the French resistance. Madam Blauer's home was a meeting place for French resistance fighters, including my father."

Hannah's memory drifted back to the pre-dawn day and the two men who drove them to the Dufour's farm. She remembered her father and grandmother in hushed meetings with the men in her basement, and now she knew her grandmother was an active member of the resistance. Hannah knew that she had been shot, not deported to the camps, but didn't know this tantalizing and inspiring bit of history about her grandmother.

Annette continued, "My aunt said that your grandmother was going to be sent to the camps but refused to leave her home. She said to the Germans, 'You can shoot me in my garden. It will save some space in your camp and accomplish the same result.' The legend was Madame Blauer refused a blindfold and stood unshaken before her firing squad."

Hannah thought this story must certainly be true, as it sounded very much

CHAPTER THIRTY-FOUR: HANNAH 1996–1999

like her grandmother.

Annette dug around in her large bag, produced a picture in a frame, and handed it to Hannah.

The framed photo was one Hannah had seen many times. The handsome faces with their dark mustaches stared back at her. Her two uncles in uniform had died for France during the First World War. When she was a little girl, after her lessons, she would sometimes go into the sitting room and stare at the photo of her uncles.

"My aunt said this was Madame Blauer's most treasured possession. She snuck it out of the house before the Germans completely ransacked the place. She held on to it. I put it in a trunk of my aunt's things to save. I didn't know why, but I just couldn't let the photo of these handsome soldiers go, and when you called, I dug it out. I knew they were your uncles."

"Thank you so much, Annette, you have been so kind." Hannah held on to the photograph and smoothed the faces she had seen when she was a girl. "I wanted to know if the house is still there?"

Annette shared that the house stood abandoned after the war and was eventually torn down to make way for a new road and some tract homes.

Annette drove Hannah to the new road and the tract homes that were now where the house and the gardens once stood. Back at the hotel, Hannah embraced Annette and thanked her.

"It was a pleasure to meet you, Madame Schneider, and to be able to return the photo to its rightful owner. Your grandmother was a great lady and a hero to the resistance."

After France, the next stop was Vienna. The last time Hannah had been there was February 1938, when David had taken her and Rebecca to the train station on that rainy grey day. She was only nine years old at the time.

The city was as beautiful as she remembered it, but very disorienting. It took her some time to figure out how to get to her old neighborhood, and home, if indeed it was still there. She distracted herself from the emotionally fraught task of going back to her childhood home by seeking out some art galleries. She looked at many paintings and works of art. She inquired about a relatively unknown painter, Sophie Goldberg. She didn't get any information until hitting upon one gallery, specializing in early 20th century art, shared that Sophie's works were considered 'degenerate art' and were destroyed during the Nazi occupation. Hannah felt herself angrily walking through the streets, looking for a café to sit down and have a cup of coffee and calm herself. She had held out a little hope that the artwork of Rebecca's mother had somehow survived. How Hannah wanted to make their concentration camp fantasy of reclaiming Sophie's paintings come to life. The beautiful art could be displayed in Max and Sandy's light-filled home in San Francisco, and it could be an heirloom for Jenna.

She had to force herself to stop being a tourist in her former hometown to finally give the address to the cab driver and head back to Döbling, the 19th district, in Vienna.

When Hannah got out of the cab, she just stood in amazement that the house was still there. The street had been widened, and an ugly carport was placed in the front of the house, along with an incongruous blue gate. The house itself maintained its stately appearance. It was tan with brickwork details and the original windows. She stood outside for a time, appraising all the new construction and the much wider street before walking through the blue gate and ringing the doorbell.

A young woman in her early 30s answered the door, "Can I help you?"

"Um, yes, this is a very odd request, but I was wondering if I could look around inside the house. I lived here when I was a little girl."

"I'm very sorry, but you must be mistaken. This house has been in my family for generations. I don't think this is the house you grew up in."

"It is the house I grew up in. I lived here in the 1930s. My parents bought it in the 1920s."

The young woman paused and said, "I don't think so. It was my grandparents' home. I believe they inherited it. But, please, do come in. I will show you a picture of my grandparents; perhaps you were neighbors."

As she walked through the house, Hannah's heart raced. It was her childhood home. The decor had changed, but as she followed the young woman, she noted that the grand mahogany staircase and woodwork in the dining area were unchanged. Hannah drew in her breath as she walked

CHAPTER THIRTY-FOUR: HANNAH 1996–1999

through the French doors into her father's old study. It was his large wood desk in the middle of the room. The books were gone and replaced by ugly tourist knickknacks.

The young woman turned around with a picture frame in her hand. Hannah looked down at the picture and exclaimed, "Ernst and Marta!"

The young woman smiled. "Yes, Ernst and Marta were my grandparents. This was their home; perhaps you lived in a nearby home? They were your neighbors?"

Hannah worked to contain her anger.

"This was my family's home. Your grandparents didn't inherit this home. They didn't buy this home. This home was a reward for them. For their loyal service to the Nazi regime. For sharing information about a Jewish family who fled to France, and whatever other services your grandfather may have rendered to them. He was an early adopter. A member of the Nazi party before the Anschluss."

The young woman stood mute and pale before she managed again, "I think you must be mistaken."

"Don't worry. I'm leaving, and I won't trouble you. This all happened well before you were born. There are people your age all over Europe with lovely homes, furnishings, jewelry, and works of art that they 'inherited.' But it is all a lie. Their grandparents sold out their Jewish neighbors and picked through their possessions. And they got away with it!"

The young woman stood frozen in the study as Hannah raced to the front door, through the blue gate in back to the street. As she sobbed and walked to a pay phone to get a cab, she wondered why she thought it was a good idea to see her old home.

The next morning, she was on a train to Dusseldorf. She had already obtained a small revolver with Annette's help when she was in France. She didn't tell Annette the reason for the gun, other than saying she was fearful being an older woman traveling alone. Annette laughed and said, "This is Europe, it is not violent like America."

Hannah had also managed to get the address for Charles and Helma. That was pretty easy, there weren't very many "O'Neals" in Dusseldorf.

THE NAZI HOUSEWIFE OF QUEENS, NEW YORK

***

The next day, Hannah found a cafe across the street from the O'Neal's apartment building. She thought she would observe them and decide where and how she would kill the Stomping Mare. She felt surprisingly calm as she had her coffee and pastry and watched the front door of the building. She bought a German paper and struggled to read German. The sun was bright, so she took a seat at one of the outside tables. It had been a couple of hours, so Hannah walked up and down the block, and then it happened.

An elderly man in a loose cardigan backed out of the front door of the apartment building and gently eased a wheelchair down three steps. As he turned, Hannah saw her. She was crumpled in the chair. Her right foot had been amputated mid-calf. Even though she had a blanket on her lap, Hannah could see the stump dangling below. She had a knitted hat on her head, no doubt she had knitted it herself, and a light pink sweater.

Hannah crossed the street and followed at a distance. After a short time, they came upon a small shop selling flowers. Charles tried to buy the Stomping Mare flowers, but she refused each bunch he presented to her. Eventually, he gave up and they proceeded to the park ahead. There was a broad walkway with benches on either side. After a while, they stopped. Charles sat on a bench with the wheelchair-bound Stomping Mare next to him. Hannah sat on a bench across the walkway.

Many people were walking and biking through the park. A couple walked through with a wiry terrier dog. The Stomping Mare was smiling, and the young couple brought the dog over to her and let her pet it. Hannah found herself amazed at how delighted the Stomping Mare seemed to be while interacting with the tiny dog.

Hannah had spent time thinking about her choices. She knew the choice to get the gun was driven by the rage inside of her for all that she had lost. The visit to her home in Vienna fueled it even further. It made her think of the tens of thousands of items she sorted in a warehouse that were given to Nazi collaborators and their families, and those items were now just regarded as "family heirlooms" from Grandpa and Grandma, with their

CHAPTER THIRTY-FOUR: HANNAH 1996–1999

sinister history completely papered over. There was another voice in her head. David's soothing voice, with his insistence on letting go of the past. As she aged, she knew there was so much wisdom in his thinking. She heard Weston's voice. His sense of humor and how she imagined him telling her there was no way it was worth it for her to go to prison. She thought of the collateral damage, like her daughter Rebecca, and how fragile she was underneath her selfishness and bravado. Then, what caused her the most conflict was Jenna. Her beautiful granddaughter headed to college with so much in front of her. It would be painful and embarrassing to have her grandmother hauled off to prison for murder. She thought of the anguish of her son Max, who would go to all sorts of trouble and expense to help her.

Hannah put her hand in her purse and stroked the revolver. She knew that this was the time and place. There was no point in letting this drag out. She wondered if she would shoot Helma in the chest or face? It had been such a long time since she had seen people murdered. It was back in the camps with Helma where she saw people get shot, beaten, or electrocuted when they threw themselves on the fence as a form of suicide. She saw people die slow deaths by starvation or illness. She pictured the Stomping Mare's death. There would be blood all over the pink sweater, she thought. As Hannah imagined this, she looked up again. A young couple with a baby stopped to talk to Charles and Helma. When they left, Charles took Helma's hand in his. He appeared to be comforting her.

Hannah's hand lifted from the gun. She looked at them again for a very long time. People passed by and didn't notice the three elderly people sitting in the park. None of them could have imagined the tangled history they had shared over the past six decades. Nobody could look at the old woman with the amputated foot in her wheelchair and pink sweater and imagine what a monster she had been. How she tortured and beat people to death, how she threw little children into a truck that was headed for a gas chamber. A monster, but it was a monster that Hannah chased to this pretty park in Germany, far from her home in America and the life she had built there.

Hannah thought somehow it was fate that she had been chained to this monster her entire life. The monster who had cruelly murdered her sister in the camps, and then all those years of building a new life in America and thinking she was safe, but she wasn't. The monster lived near her, and Hannah then had to face the monster again in courtrooms with the support of Weston, David, Vince DeMarco, Miriam, and Max. Now, the monster was loose again. Hannah felt the outline of the gun as she gripped the fabric of her purse. She looked at the Stomping Mare again. She was slumped in her wheelchair, and her husband was stroking her hand. She wasn't the Stomping Mare anymore, and she wasn't a monster, just a sick and twisted old woman. Hannah realized that the chains weren't real either. She wasn't chained to the Stomping Mare for life.

Hannah felt her resolve beginning to weaken. She no longer had a burning rage inside her. She thought rationally for a moment about what would be accomplished by killing a sickly old woman in this beautiful park. All the beautiful things she had accomplished in her life flashed through her mind again – David, Max, Rebecca. All her loved ones were there with her, too. The Stomping Mare could not take them away.

Hannah felt the tightness in her chest subside. She stood up and walked out of the park; she walked to a secluded area next to the duck pond and threw the gun in the pond as the ducks nearby squawked at the splash of the gun hitting the water. She felt the pain and anger drain from her body, and for the first time, she finally felt free.

About the Author

Stacy Kean is a first-time author of the historical fiction novel, *The Nazi Housewife of Queens, New York*, based in part on the true story of the first Nazi war criminal who lost her U.S. citizenship and was extradited to Germany in one of the longest war crime trials in German history in the 1970s.

Her debut novel is a fictionalized account of the Nazi concentration camp guard and a concentration camp survivor who courageously testifies against the sadistic camp guard after she discovers that not only is the guard alive but lives in America only a few miles away. The novel is a sweeping look at sixty years of history as lived by two women who find themselves striving to achieve the goal of the idealized mid-century American housewife.

Stacy Kean is a native Oregonian and earned a Bachelor of Arts degree in History from the University of Oregon. An award-winning communicator, she has built a career in nonprofit communications and marketing. She is a member of the Public Relations Society of America, The Historical Novel Society, and The Oregon Historical Society. The mother of an adult daughter, Stacy and her husband live in Portland, Oregon, with a three-legged cat. In her free time, she enjoys traveling around Oregon and baking.

SOCIAL MEDIA HANDLES:
 Instagram https://www.instagram.com/skeanwrites/
 Facebook: https://www.facebook.com/profile.php?id=61553663750697

Twitter/X https://twitter.com/smoekean
Tik Tok @smk1671

AUTHOR WEBSITE:
stacykeanwrites.com